The Academy

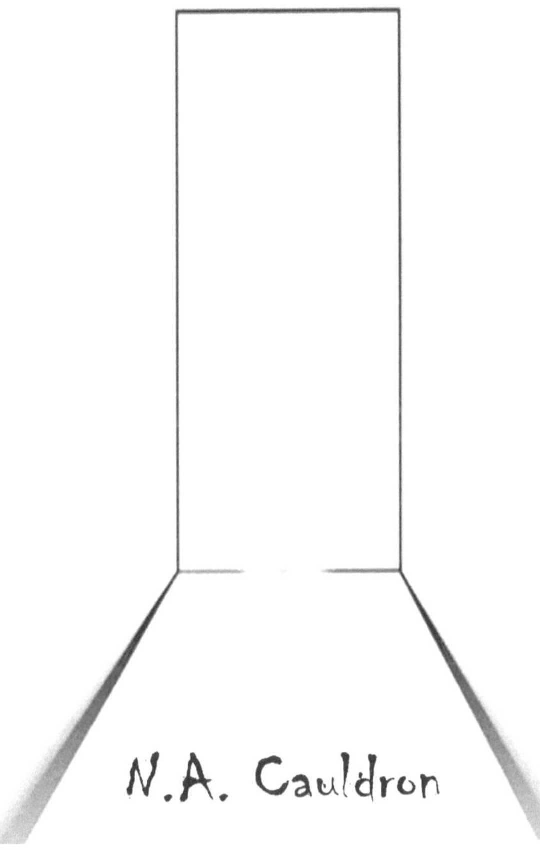

N.A. Cauldron

Cover illustration and design by Debby Styles copyright © 2020
Wiggling Pen Publishing, 222 Hwy 95, Walker Lake, NV 89415
All rights reserved, including the right of reproduction in whole or in part in any form.

Printed in the USA
ISBN paperback: 979-8-9867839-0-1
ISBN ebook: 979-8-9867839-1-8

https://nippi1.wixsite.com/nacauldron/

Also by N.A. Cauldron

THE CUPOLIAN SERIES

Anya and the Secrets of Cupola

Anya and the Power Crystal

Anya and the Cavern of Trials

ALSO BY N.A. CAULDRON

Fishing for Turkey

Inhabitants

What Does Spider Poop Look Like?

DEATH

The first day of my Death will be ingrained in my mind forever, but that's the usual around here. Contrary to the first day of Life, the day we enter Death is easily remembered, and often our most vivid memory.

I appeared with the wall of the Maze before me and the Curtain behind me. I can never forget that wall, no matter how hard I try. Smooth and black, it lacked any clues as to what it was made of. I still don't know, but that doesn't matter. That wall was never ending, and the hallway it formed wasn't about to give away any clues either, no obvious doorways or turns to escape my personal hell.

I turned and watched the Curtain behind me whorl with shades of brown. Mahogany and maple dancing together like cake batter refusing to mix. Although it radiated some kind of light, it did not penetrate far enough into the hallway to reach the wall. But mine did. That was the first time I noticed it. My glow. More about my glow later, but suffice it to say, when you look down at your feet and notice you can see the floor beneath them, you know, through them, and that they're radiating light, you're gonna freak out a little. And that's just what I did. I started running.

My body provided my light as I ran, a dim bulb in the darkest of caves. The wall beside me refused to reflect any of my illumination as though it had a personal grudge against me. And, even though I never tired physically of running, I did tire mentally after a while. My journey became mind numbing, fruitless. I stopped running and waited motionless in the dark stillness of the hallway. Maybe the hallway was waiting for me to stop trying before it showcased its secrets.

Nothing happened.

The endless structure of the Maze's wall intimidated me when I first arrived. But now, after running next to it for I can only imagine how long, it felt like a companion. An entity stuck in the same boat as I, a boat full of nowhere to go and nothing to do but stand and wait.

My fingers ran along its flat face. The smoothness was indescribable, almost as though it wasn't there. It was cold, but not so cold as to make it uncomfortable to touch. I pushed against it. The solid, firm wall stood with so much arrogance it didn't even feel the need to prove itself by pushing back. I reached as high as my arms would let me and tried to feel how far up it went. It was no use. There was no ceiling, no top of the wall to climb over. It was no longer my companion.

I turned to face the Curtain, hoping it might be different. Its spinning eddies frightened me more than the still black of the wall, but I was out of ideas.

My breath caught in my throat, and my feet refused to cooperate as I urged them forward towards the Curtain. A blazing heat radiated from it, warming my face. My eyes squinted, and my body recoiled in reaction. I forced my hand out and pressed against it.

"Ouch!" The hallway swallowed my voice. The expected echo never came.

I looked around, half expecting someone to respond to my scream, but nobody did, something I would later be grateful for. I was caught between fire and ice. Trapped more like it. Out of options, I sat cross-legged in the floor and stared down the torturous tunnel of doom I had earlier called the hallway.

It might have been minutes; it might have been years. I had no way of measuring how long I sat there. I was never hungry. I did not sleep. But there came a point when I decided to try again. What if I just needed to go a little further? Sitting here wasn't getting me anywhere.

I dragged my fingers along the eternal wall next to me and began my walk. I became a zombie of sorts, a mindless body just going through the motions without realizing my actions.

It took several seconds to register what I had felt. And when I did, I stopped to wonder. Had my fingers really deviated? Was I starting to imagine my mind's desires? I returned to the location in question and ran my fingers across the wall again. There it was. A crack. A perfectly square, three-sided ditch that ran all the way from the floor to the unseen top of the wall. Its angles were so sharp they almost cut me when I ran my fingers across them.

I pressed my fingertips into it and pulled against the sides, first one way and then the other. After a moment I thought I felt it give to the left. I pulled again, and this time it opened the slightest of millimeters. I continued until I thought I could squeeze through. First my head, then my hips. When the last of my slight body grazed the edge of the doorway I had made, I laughed with relief. I was out!

As my eyes focused on the darkness ahead of me, my joy waned. Another hallway. Only this hallway didn't have the brown light of the Curtain to keep me company. As I took my first steps into isolating blackness, I had to remind myself, "I had asked for this." I turned back to reassure myself I could always return to the hallway if I wanted, only, there was no more hallway. The giant door I had opened had shut, or never existed, I'm not sure. Either way, a dead end now stood where the door had once been.

I ran up to it and placed my palms against it. The corners between the newly formed dead end and the two walls which now confined me were seamless. Panic found me.

My breath came in great heaves as giant tears fell from my cheeks and chin, and my face contorted into a painful shape. My fingers grasped uselessly against the barren wall behind me as my glowing, transparent body slid to the floor that lay beneath my feet. I couldn't take anymore.

Again, the amount of time that passed is unknown, but I did eventually resume my search for a way out. Maybe it was a distant sound that triggered my motivation. Maybe I felt something. Whatever happened, it caused me to push myself up from my twisted ball of self-pity and continue. With the dead end at my back, I gazed ahead. Emptiness. More and more emptiness.

My feet carried me without my instruction, away from the dead end and into the dark. I was crying so hard, it made running straight impossible. So I used the walls for support to keep from falling. This didn't help much when one wall disappeared, and I fell sideways onto the cold, hard floor that was as black and lifeless as those cursed walls.

The fall hurt. I know. Weird. It's obvious by now I'm a ghost, so nothing should hurt anymore. But that's not quite how it works. You'll see.

The shock from the fall interrupted my fear. I pushed myself up and hurried back to the hallway I had fallen from. Did it close behind me too? Was I being herded by a chain of cattle gates to a destination I dare not think about?

The hallway had not disappeared. It remained exactly as I had left it. I fell against the wall and sighed in relief. Tiny tears of happiness fell from my eyes. I wiped them away. I now had a choice. Do I continue straight, or do I take this turn and see where it leads me?

So far my journey had been nothing but straight. Straight, straight, straight. From one never-ending hallway to the next. I tried the new path.

The new path soon became several. First right. Then left. Then a four-way intersection. The appeal of having choices wore off quickly. I almost longed for straight again.

I sighed a spiritless sigh and fell with my back against the wall. My body eased slowly to the floor; my eyes stared straight ahead, as lifeless as the walls around me. I had run out of tears. Past panicking, past scared, I had reached the point of giving up. For good this time.

I stared unblinkingly into the blackness. Motionless. I didn't utter a single sound. I held my breath to make it easier to hear. Maybe I was missing something. Maybe there was a broken intercom speaker announcing directions, and if I stayed quiet enough, I would catch them.

After a while, I realized I was still holding my breath. The urge to inhale never came. The act of breathing was enjoyable. It felt nice to fill my chest with whatever surrounded me and let it out again, but it wasn't necessary. So I didn't. And that's when I heard it.

VOICES

"This way," said a distant man's voice.

My ears perked.

"I don't hear it no more," a second male voice said.

"Well, find it then!" the first voice snapped. "I'm not getting wisped because you're too stupid to catch a fawn!"

Their words made no sense to me, but their tone sounded dangerous. My body took over. My eyes shut, my fingers, my toes, my chest, my legs, everything turned to stone. I waited, and concentrated on listening for more.

"I need more, man. I can't, I can't concentrate. Why don't Ronnie send the wraith instead of us? Isn't this their natural habi— habi—, isn't this where they live?" They sounded closer.

I turned my face toward their voices and opened my eyes. A faint light came from around the corner.

The first voice sounded like it was coming through gritted teeth. "Because the wraith *eat* more of 'em 'en they bring back."

A dull thud sounded, followed by a huff of air and a groan.

"Geez, Freddy. I was just asking." the second voice said.

"Well, stop asking."

The glow around the corner brightened ever so slightly. I remained silent stone.

"If Ronnie finds out you lost us another one… Keep your mouth *shut* next time!" Another dull thud sounded.

I waited. The voices never spoke again. The glow grew brighter, stopped, then grew further and further away until it disappeared completely. I was once again alone in the dark.

I exhaled. I liked the dark now. The dark was safe. Boring, but safe.

I ran in the opposite direction. I wanted to get as far away from the voices as possible. Right, left, right, straight, left. I couldn't keep up with where I was going. I wasn't trying to keep up. When I thought I had enough distance between us, I slowed to a walk. I tried to maintain one direction now. When I had to turn, I corrected myself as soon as possible.

Another sound came. Somewhere, nearby, a person was humming. A young person. A female person. It came closer.

Three corridors branched from the four-way behind me. Which one held the person with the hum? The path to my left started to glow. A slight illumination.

I backed away instinctively, like the prey who smelled the predator. I turned and ran, hiding behind the first branch I came to.

The humming grew louder, and the light got brighter. Then it stopped. No more humming. The light stood still. I dared to ease more of my face out from behind the corner and peek. My eyes widened as a little girl stepped out from her own corridor and into the four-way.

She looked very young, not more than eight years old. She carried a lantern, like the ones you see in an old railroad museum. She gave no indication of recognizing my presence as she stared straight ahead, sniffed once, then lesser so a second time, then entered the next corridor.

Her light vanished. I crept from my hiding place and stood at the edge of the hallway she just entered, terrified to look down it. I listened for any clue she might still be there. I took an unnecessary breath. Then two. Then three. And peeked around the corner. There was nothing there. It was as black as the rest of the empty Maze.

I took a step in, allowing my fingers to trace the wall next to me as I went. Blackness as far as I could see.

A light turned on a mere inch from my face. It was the girl's lantern. She stood, her glow fully restored, her face motionless and expressionless behind the lantern.

"Hello," she said.

I screamed and sprinted in the other direction.

She followed. I turned my head around to check my progress. Floating about a foot off the floor, her ghostly figure glided smoothly in my direction. And much faster than I was running.

I concentrated on speed then, resisting the urge to look back. I stretched my legs as far as they would go and pumped my arms until I'm sure I looked ridiculous, but I didn't care. The fear inside me exceeded any other thought or feeling. I tried turning the corners to make it harder for her to follow, but that only resulted in me banging into the opposite wall and slowing my progress instead.

I was sprinting down a particularly long piece of corridor when the sensation of being constricted halted my path. It was almost as if time itself stopped while my body hovered in the air, oblivious to gravity and its previous forward motion. I couldn't breathe. I couldn't move. I soon knew why. Coming through my chest was the girl's lantern, followed by her. As she exited my body, the squeezing sensation ended, and I fell to the floor shaking. She stood before me, that same blank face, full of innocence yet filling my soul with indescribable terror.

I pulled myself up, my hands groping the walls for support, my feet backing away from her. We stared at each other. The lion and the gazelle assessing each other's next move. I spun and sprinted away.

I thought I heard a sigh, then the squeezing sensation came again. I watched the lantern float out of my chest, dragging her body behind it. This time I didn't run away when she exited. I realized the futility of it all.

"Stop doing that!" I yelled, my voice quivering from the convulsive shaking of my body.

"Stop running from me." Her head tilted to one side as though almost amused.

Although by now I understood the senselessness in running, I couldn't stop myself from spider crawling away from her. She stood her ground.

"What do you want?" I demanded.

"Follow me," she said, and then walked away as though I didn't have a mind of my own and would do what she said when she said.

I thought about what to do. This girl came from somewhere, potentially the same somewhere as those two men, so this Maze had at least one end or area where other people originated from. I could walk away from her and try to find that area. Which, I realized, might have other people like those two men, or even those men themselves.

Then again, she didn't act like those men did. Not that this girl wasn't the world's number one example of freak-me-out creepy, she hadn't tried to hurt me … yet. And she acted better skilled than they had, like she could protect me from them if she needed to. If she wanted to.

As her light disappeared around a corner up ahead, that ever present fear I told you about took over and made my decision for me. *Go.*

I ran to where I last saw her light, letting the fingers of my left hand brush against the wall to find the corridor she had vanished into. A faint glow emanated from the depths of one hallway. I entered and ran to catch up before she took another corner. She made no indication she knew I had fallen behind nor that I had caught up with her. I kept close.

We walked together for a good while, turning here or there. My courage waned on several occasions, but I managed to keep it under control enough to stay by her. During all this time, however, she never said a word, not one mention of who she was, where we were going, what we were doing. The silence eventually became too much for me.

"What is your name?" I asked.

She sighed, already bored with our "conversation," even though it had only been four words. "Lydia," she answered. She said nothing after that. She acted like she was trying to build up enough energy to ask the next question, like she didn't want to but knew she had to. I tried to wait patiently. "What is yours?" she finally asked.

I stopped. It didn't matter that she was still walking and I was now trailing possibly too far behind to ever catch up. I was too stunned to move. "I don't know," I barely whispered. And I didn't. I hadn't thought about it before, but up until I was unceremoniously dropped between the Maze and the Curtain, I had no memories at all.

That whisper caused her to stop. She turned around to gaze at me with the first emotion I saw from her, surprised confusion. "What do you mean, 'you don't know'?"

I stammered in my response. How was I to explain what I didn't understand myself? "I mean… I…" My eyes wandered in a vain search for the answer. "I don't know who I am. I don't know where I am or why I'm here—"

She interrupted me, "You're dead."

It took a moment before I could talk again. "I—I'm what? What do you mean, I'm dead?"

Her arm raised the lantern above her head as she approached me until I could feel its warm glow against my cheek. "You're a ghost. You're dead." She turned and walked away.

I stood there. Frozen. Unable to sit and cry or run to catch up, not that I knew which one was the correct choice. I couldn't even think past the knowledge I was dead. I'm assuming she stopped walking and came back for me, because I remember her being there for the next part.

With her lantern by her side this time, she said, "Let me know when you're finished."

She stared at me, unmoving. I backed away a couple of steps out of impulse. When my wits made their selves known again, I asked, "Finished with what?"

Only her lips moved when she spoke. "Coming to terms with your Death."

I blinked. Several times. I wasn't sure what to do. Check that. I had *no idea* what to do. How does one "come to terms" with their Death? I stared at her until I felt I had control over my limbs again. "I—I guess I'm done," I told her.

"Good." She turned and walked away.

I followed.

"Can you tell me more?" I asked.

She sighed. "Like what?" It was clear she didn't want to.

"Where we are?" I asked.

"We are in the Maze."

Well, that made sense. "Why are we in a maze?"

She shrugged. "No one knows."

That answer had two effects on me. It made me feel better I wasn't the only one who didn't understand something, but it also frightened me because *no one* understood it. She started humming again.

"What was the other place?" I asked. "The brown wall with swirls?"

"That's the Curtain. Don't touch it."

I had found that out already, but I wasn't going to admit it to her. "Why?"

"No one knows that either."

"No one has ever touched the Curtain?" I asked in disbelief. *I* had touched it. Surely other people had too. I mean it is right there when you first … die, or whatever it's called when you're plopped in the Hallway.

She swung around so abruptly I almost ran into her. "The Curtain divides the Land of the Living from the Land of the Dead. Crossing it has irreversible consequences. Don't touch the Curtain." She walked away again. Conversation over.

I had a million other questions, like what kind of irreversible consequences and when would we ever get out of here, but I held my tongue. For then.

We continued to weave through the Maze. Whenever Lydia turned a corner, I made sure to keep close. Too many turns too close together made it easy to lose sight of her glow.

As we made our way out of a particularly complex set of corners, I began to wonder how she found me so easily earlier when the others hadn't. "Lydia?"

She didn't answer, but she did stop humming, which I took as her reply.

"How did you see me?" I asked.

I almost ran into her again when she stopped to face me. I really wished she would quit doing that. My face filled with irritation she either never noticed or didn't care about.

Her normally blank expression held astonishment, with maybe even a little smile. A brief second later, and it was freshly composed. "I could see your glow from the edge of the Maze if I wanted to."

Her demeanor made me afraid to ask why, or how. I waited until we started down another corridor to ask my next question. "Where are you taking me?"

She kept walking this time. "The Academy." Her tone gave me the impression I should know what that meant.

"The Academy?"

So help me she rolled her eyes. "The Academy is a safe place for fawn to learn how to survive the Void." She sighed and then added, "Unless you don't *want* to attend."

Fawn. She just called me a fawn, the same word those men used. They didn't happen across my glow; they had been *hunting* for it. If I had stayed in the Maze, if I hadn't followed her when I had the choice…

And the Void. What was the Void? The Maze was bad enough, but she spoke like the Void was something I couldn't leave, something I had to "learn to survive" in.

I stood there with so many questions my mouth opened and closed like a fish gasping for air. She took my actions to mean, "Please continue walking," and resumed her leading. I gained control of myself and stayed at her heels.

Sometime later, when she quit humming again, I asked, "How long have you been dead?" I wasn't sure if that was a rude question or not. What were the social rules of the Dead? So I quickly added, "If that's OK to ask."

She frowned. "Over two hundred years."

I missed a step, causing my right foot to trip over my left. I tried not to notice it. Lydia returned to her humming, and this time she didn't stop. I spoke no more.

NEW BEGINNINGS

A steady glow filled the corner up ahead. I felt my body tense. My thoughts centered on escape again. I paused long enough to watch Lydia, my guide, for any signs of danger. She just continued to sigh a lot, showing no signs of apprehension. I decided to trust her actions. It wasn't easy, forcing my feet to comply, but I did.

When we turned the corner, the end of our short hallway opened into a blurred mass of light. A large structure resided inside it, but a milky haze blurred the details. Several blobs of light danced inside the haze. They were far smaller than the structure, like people. Some of them zoomed around the surrounding atmosphere of the structure, giving the appearance of moths near a flame.

Lydia peered up over her shoulder at me. "You must stay near me to cross the Veil."

I didn't want to "stay near her". I wanted to flee. What if two of those blobs belonged to the voices I heard earlier? What if she was with them, leading me to them?

She saw the fear on my face. "The Maze is not safe. The Academy is. You must follow me."

I glanced back at the Maze. The new light ahead made the darkness of the Maze seem darker, deeper. Turned it into the cavernous throat of a giant, ghost-eating monster that ended in a pit of acid. I turned back to her and weighed my options. Eternal darkness or hazy blob light? To anyone else, the choice might be obvious. To me, it was the choice of familiarity, albeit unpleasant familiarity, and scary new things. Although Lydia had seemed to not care for my safety at first, she did always stop if I got too far behind. Maybe she did care. Maybe the hazy blobs *were* safer, better than the lifeless, black Maze. I hugged the cold wall for support and inched towards her, my feet faltering with every step.

When I got close, she turned her back to me and floated into the frosted view ahead. The haze hugged her body, like a milky waterfall. Did it hurt? She didn't act like it caused her pain or discomfort. Would it wrap around me in the same way?

She grabbed my hand and pulled. I stumbled forward, my eyes squinted shut, my free hand over my head for protection. An odd sensation passed over my body, like feather-light water brushing against my outer surface. I opened my eyes and whipped my head around for Lydia. She was yards ahead of me with no signs of stopping. My escort was over.

I gazed at my surroundings, so much different than the Maze. A huge, colonial style building with white walls and long windows took up most of my view. Resembling an old town hall, it was complete with columns over the porch and square towers on all the corners. To my left, staring down at the Academy with unspoken authority, loomed a giant Clock. Its wide bottom spanning the distance of a house. Its wooden frame shining with the dark stain of varnished mahogany. It looked out of place, like a small old-fashioned mantelpiece house clock enlarged to ridiculous proportions. Its hands, had they been on a regular clock, would have been in the positions to read 9:25, but this Clock possessed no numbers. Instead, it bore tiny markers all around the outside. Coming down from the top, where the twelve should have been, was one long, heavy marker. The Clock stared down at me like a security guard, like a giant bouncer waiting to pounce should I commit the slightest infraction. And since I didn't know what any of those were yet, that wasn't the best thought to be having at the moment.

I turned my attention back to the main building. As I neared the front steps, several of the other ghosts stopped what they were doing and focused on my arrival. Most of them were children, like me, some younger, some older. Only one or two were old enough to label as adults.

I felt their stares boring into my back, and heard their murmurs and giggles which I knew had to be about me. I locked my eyes on the ground to keep from meeting any of their gazes. The floor here was comprised of the same obsidian nothingness of the Maze, only covered with a thick, swirling black fog that obscured my bare feet and fizzled out halfway up to my knees. It was then, as I waded through the ethereal clouds, I realized I was wearing nothing but a long nightshirt and panties. Great. It even had Snoopy on it. Their giggles sounded like they were being projected through megaphones now.

The stairs appeared to have grown out of the onyx ground. The fog only made it to the bottom of the third step. The porch, the railings, the windows, the doors, were all lustrously clean like a regular house that just needed a little weed eating around the corners, if you call ominous black clouds weeds. The top step opened into a porch that wrapped the whole of the school. Standing in front of me, with one arm holding one of the double doors open, was a tall woman with see-though fiery red hair and stern eyes. She wore a long, dull red skirt that reached to the floor and an ivory-colored jacket that cinched in hard at the waist with long sleeves and a frilly collar that poofed out from underneath. An odd pendant hung around her neck, some kind of disc held by a golden chain. The way she peered down her nose at me made my body pulse with a frigid, electrical charge, and somehow shrink in size more than it already had. The moment I was close enough, her other arm reached out, not in an inviting way, more in a "You will come with me" way. I did as she wordlessly instructed.

The inside of the Academy was much as you would expect from the outside. A large staircase went up the middle to the second floor landing where it split in two and wound its way around to the third. Pictures hung on the walls in thick, wooden frames, and a large rug lay centered in front of the stairs on the dark, hardwood floors. And of course, the walls, ceiling, and railings were all white.

I could see several doors from where I stood, a few to the left and the right with the rest along the back wall behind the staircase. My new escort led me through the first door on the left. And shut it behind us.

THE CLOSET

"Have a seat," she commanded, gesturing toward a stiff wooden chair in front of her desk.

I did as she said while she went behind her desk and sat down, in a chair just as uncomfortable looking as mine.

"My name is Mrs. Richards. I'm the Director here at the Academy."

I blinked, still too stunned to say anything.

"Lydia tells me you don't have a name."

"I... I..." My fingers wrung together without my control. I wanted to answer her, wanted to tell her, "I don't know my name," and her say, "Oh, it's Billie Jean Bobbie Sue III," and me go, "Oh, OK, thank you!" but I knew that wouldn't happen. I watched my hands twist themselves into knots. It took every ounce of effort not to cry.

She pursed her lips together in response and arranged some papers on her desk. "Well, no worry. Our genealogy team will figure something out." Her eyes met mine for a moment. "I wouldn't get my hopes up too much though. Their success rate isn't high."

For whatever reason, that one simple statement was enough to send the tears flooding out of my eyes again like blood from a deep wound. I didn't bother wiping them away as I sat there, my shoulders jerking from the sobs.

She kept talking like there wasn't a tormented dead girl losing it three feet in front of her. "I've arranged for one of our students to explain your schedule to you and show you to your room. She will be your roommate as well."

I was able to raise my head enough to look at her in response. I almost saw sympathy in her eyes. I wasn't sure if it was a delayed reaction to my crying or if my roommate was a terrible person or if my tears had obstructed my view to the point of hallucinating. Any of those options made my future look grim.

Another sob shook my body before a knock on the door caused me to quickly sniff, wipe my cheeks and nose clean, and twist my head around to see who it was.

"Come in," Mrs. Richards called out.

A nice-looking young girl poked her head through the door. Her hair must have once been a dirty blonde of sorts, but it was hard to tell with its present translucent state. She glowed warmly. "You wanted to see me, Mrs. Richards?" She had an odd accent.

I quickly double checked my face for leftover tears, threw my hair behind my ears, and switched my focus back to the Director with my hands tucked between my thighs.

"Yes, MaryAnn," Mrs. Richards answered the girl. "We have a new student."

MaryAnn came inside the office and shut the door behind her. I felt obligated to stare at her whether I wanted to or not. She wore a kind smile that almost made me break down again just because someone was hopefully, finally, going to be nice to me. My forced smile twitched a little as I blinked a few more times in rebellion against another wave of blubbering convulsions.

Mrs. Richards handed MaryAnn a slip of paper. "This is her schedule. Be sure to show her to each of her classes before she settles down in her room, number 22B."

MaryAnn's eyes lit up. "Oh! We're roomies then, ain't we, mate?"

I glanced at Mrs. Richards. From what she had said earlier, I guessed the answer was yes, but I didn't want to say anything. With the way I was feeling, the less I said, the better. But Mrs. Richards stared back at me like I should have already answered. "I guess so." My words were so weak they sounded like they came from a shy toddler.

Mrs. Richards nodded her head at us. "Dismissed."

MaryAnn held her hand out for me to take, but I wasn't comfortable doing that. Instead, I stood and tried to smile again in return. It was pathetic. She smiled weakly back and opened the door for me.

"Oh, and MaryAnn."

We both turned our heads to see what the Director wanted.

"Do find her some new clothes."

Instinctively I looked down. Glowing tears streaked the entirety of my gown. Poor Snoopy needed a lead umbrella.

I followed my new guide to the grand staircase where she stopped to study my schedule. "Hmmm... Looks like... Portals... Ethereal Dynamics... Invisible Arts... History — oh you'll like Mr. Prickett. He's amazing!"

I stood motionless, not having a clue what she was talking about.

MaryAnn's eyes rose from my schedule to meet mine. "Oh, sorry, mate! What was your name again?"

I took a deep breath and swallowed a fresh sob to prevent it from taking control. I still had to clear my throat before I could answer her. "I don't... I don't have a name."

Her face twisted in confusion. "You don't have a name? How is that possible?"

I shrugged. "I don't know. I mean, I guess I *could* have a name. I just don't know what it is."

Her gaze drifted down the front of my nightshirt. Distaste overtook her confusion, but she quickly removed the rude emotion from her face. When she glanced back up at me, she was smiling again. "Mrs. Richards was right. We better get you some clothes first." Aborting her previous course, she walked around the staircase to the back wall. "At least they're not burned. Or ripped. Or missing." A Cheshire grin stretched across her face as she opened one of the doors. Several nearby clocks chimed as she did. "Last new bloke that came through here had nothing but his hands to cover his doodle."

Behind the door lay a straight path that must have stretched on for miles. Globes lined up like railway cars hung from the ceiling. Eerie pale blue tufts swam within each one, giving off the only light in the long room.

"Let's see, you'll be a"—she glanced over my frame, making me very self-conscious in the process—"medium?"

Her eyes looked to mine for verification. I shook my head, not having the least idea what she was talking about.

"What size are you?" she asked, mistaking my head shake for a "no".

I shrugged—I was doing a lot of that lately. "I don't know."

I watched as the sympathy in her eyes morphed into annoyance, but she didn't act on it. She glanced over my entire body once again before taking off toward the other end of the tunnel of hanging clothes. "This is the Academy's closet. The Academy allows new students to get enough to start out with, but after that you'll have to wait for your rations."

I had to trot to keep up with her. "My what?"

"Your rations." She stopped to take a couple of shirts down from where they hung. "It's not like we have any stores around here."

"Oh." I said it, but it was so soft I doubt she heard me, not that it mattered. I'm sure by now she was pretty fed up with me. I would have been. New girl without any clothes or the slightest clue what was going on, not even her own name.

"Excuse me."

The voice made me jump. A man I hadn't noticed before was hovering next to me. He was very thin with short, dark hair on top. His gaze traveled all the way down his nose before reaching either of us.

"Hiya, Mr. Haught," MaryAnn greeted the man. "Mrs. Richards is having me bring this noobie in for some clothes."

She turned to face me. "This is Mr. Haught. He manages the closet."

Mr. Haught bowed. "Pleased to meet you, madam." He rose, directing his next statement at MaryAnn. "Please, only take the essentials."

"I've already told her about the rations, Mr. Haught."

He continued to glare down at us, as though waiting for one of us to start stuffing clothes into our pockets, of which I had none. I couldn't help but throw repeated glances over my shoulder at him from then on, something I'm sure made me even more suspicious in his eyes.

MaryAnn ignored him as she picked out shirt after shirt and held them up to me before deciding whether they would fit or not. When she finished, she hung the ones she didn't like back up then tossed the rest of them at me to catch. "See if those work."

I turned to Mr. Haught, who was still hovering almost directly over my shoulder, and stared at him questioningly.

He answered on cue, "This way, madam."

I glanced back at my soon-to-be roommate, but she was already searching for the next round of clothes.

He led me to a changing room between two sections of cloaks and shut me in. The light of the globes did not penetrate the room's walls. I wanted to open the door and let some of it in, but there was no way I was going to with Mr. Haught hovering right outside.

The mirror behind me echoed my glow, helping to keep the darkness at bay, but it still felt like the walls were closing in on me. The Maze had left its mark. My arms shaking with fright, I threw off my nightie and started trying on clothes.

The first shirt was tight but would work. The others fit too, but I didn't like the way any of them looked on me. I exited the changing room with most of MaryAnn's choices draped over my arm. She was nowhere near, so I hung the lacy this-is-something-my-grandmother-would-wear shirt and the ugly one with the peekaboo shoulders back up and grabbed a few of my own choosing: a mid-sleeve with the number "3" on the front and jersey stripes on the arms and a couple others that wouldn't stand out in a crowd. At least I hoped they wouldn't. I honestly had no way of knowing. After making sure those fit, I spent several more minutes finding the right pair of jeans. Then, wearing my new favorite outfit, I sought MaryAnn.

MaryAnn tutted at my choices but put her new collection back without argument. Before he would let us leave, Mr. Haught inspected my new outfit and bundle of clothes, tallying each item as he went. Still carrying my choices in clothing, he hovered over to a podium near the doorway and wrote something down in a thick book. I fidgeted nervously the whole time.

"This will suffice," he said, and handed the bundle back to me.

"Thank you, Sir," said MaryAnn, before leading me back out of the closet to the stairs.

THE ACADEMY

MaryAnn, my assigned roommate and mentor, took me to the second floor. Along the way, she told me a little about the school's history. "The Academy was built in 1802. You'll learn all about this in History class, but it won't hurt to hear it twice. It was originally…"

I tried to listen, I really did! But my thoughts were so fixated on my new surroundings and the apprehension of what might happen next that her words kept fading into the background.

When we reached the top of the landing, she opened one of the double doors in front of us and dropped her voice to a whisper. "Your dorm room is back that way." She jerked her head over her shoulder towards the left hallway and whispered, "I'll show you it later. This way is the classes." She gestured for me to go through the double doors ahead of her.

The hallway in front of us was wider than the others, almost as wide as the entryway in which the staircase stood. Shut doors neatly aligned themselves down either side of it which, much like the clothes did to the closet downstairs, caused it to look like an eternal tunnel that got smaller and smaller until only a pinhole existed in the distance. I can only imagine how many doors we passed when MaryAnn stopped and pointed at one labeled, "14H27".

"This is your Portals classroom." She held up my schedule and pointed to where the room number was listed next to the class name, "14H27". A few doors down, she pointed at a door on the opposite side labeled, "23N76".

"This is your History class where you'll learn all about the school and legends and the Void." Her voice trailed off. "And here," she pointed at a room about ten doors away labeled "5F3", "is your Invisible Arts classroom." She grinned. "Mr. Dinwiddie was a magician in Life, so his class can get *interesting*." She raised her eyebrows in meaning on the word "interesting".

"Wait," I said. "How am I supposed to find these rooms later? Why doesn't fourteen come after five or N after H or…?"

"Oh. That. The Director, Mrs. Richards, likes to change the school around a lot. She gets rid of old classrooms and makes new ones all the time. It's not that hard once you get used to it though." She pointed to the beginning of the hallway where we had first entered, and moved her finger all the way to the other end, indicating the entire right-hand side. "This side goes from A to M. And this side"—she did the same with the left-hand side only in the opposite direction— "goes from N to Z. I know most of the numbers are missing, but they're still in order."

I glanced at the doors nearest me. 123L47 came immediately before 1M13. After that was 2M26 and then 2M53. So, L comes before M, and 2 comes after 1, and 53 comes after 47. I smiled. I understood. "I get it," I said, a little louder than I should have.

"Shhh." But she was smiling. "See, I told ya. Easy."

She showed me all my other classes but the last one which she offered for me to find instead. We had to walk more slowly than before, but I found it without a hitch. With a beaming face, I followed her back to the entryway.

The double doors closed behind us. "Now for our room." She no longer whispered. "It'll be exciting to have a roomie again. It's been forever!"

I walked, she floated, down the narrow hallway with dark Wainscoting halfway up the walls and dark wooden doors the color of the Clock on either side. It felt nice, far more cozy than the one with all the classrooms. "What happened to your old roommate?"

"She graduated." She smiled. "People don't die on a school schedule, so we get fawns all the time. That means you get thrown into your classes midway. Sorry." She smiled apologetically.

I tried to remember what a school schedule was. Surely I went to school, but I don't remember doing it. As I tried to remember being a student, I suddenly found myself surrounded by bright windows with sunlight. Other children were there too. Sitting… Watching…

"We're here!"

Her announcement pulled me away from my memory with a harsh jerk. Is that what that was? A memory? I blinked several times and shook my head to bring myself to the present only to find MaryAnn licking her hand then using it to turn a doorknob. My mouth fell open.

She glanced my direction and, seeing my expression, shut the door back. "Oh. Sorry. Since ghosts can go through inanimate objects, it makes locks pretty useless around here. We go by ectoplasm instead. Your essence."

My eyebrows rose in confusion.

She explained further. "Spit, tears, stuff like that — they're all made of ectoplasm and make up your essence. That's what the doors are keyed to, our essences. They won't open for anyone else. You try it." She floated to the side so I could step in closer.

I shifted the clothes I was still carrying to one arm, grabbed the knob with my free hand, and gave it a twist. It wouldn't budge.

"Spit on it."

Ew. I wasn't sure I could do that.

"Just spit on your hand and turn the knob." She sounded irritated with my lack of desire to produce drool.

I gazed up at her, hesitant, and still not sure she wasn't messing with me. I licked the palm of my hand, keeping my eyes locked on hers, and twisted the knob. It worked.

I stepped inside my new room. Dark, decorative wood paneling covered all four walls. Against one end sat a single desk with two comfy looking chairs on either side of it. In the center lay a rectangular, decorative rug of reds and golds with two brown leather couches facing each other. I threw my clothes onto one of them. There was so much brown, I felt like someone had dropped me into a mudhole. A single globe containing the same blue tufts as what I saw in the closet was attached to the ceiling.

"Where's the bed?" I asked, which was odd considering I had no memories of my room when I was alive, yet somehow I knew there needed to be one.

Her eyes squinted as her brow dipped to one side. "How long have you been dead?"

I shrugged, suddenly more aware of how dependent I was on MaryAnn and all the others. I looked anywhere but at her and held my arms across my chest, rubbing my elbows with uncertain fingers as I did. "I don't know." It felt like I had wandered the Maze forever, but I still didn't feel tired.

She put one hand on each of my arms, stunning me into a statue. "Ghosts don't sleep."

"Oh," I said after a moment.

She continued to stare at me, as though expecting more of a reaction. Her statement didn't really affect me all that much. It's not like I remembered sleeping or anything. I just thought a bed was one of those standard things you put in a room, you know?

Her eyes narrowed suspiciously. "Aren't you upset about not being able to sleep anymore? About not being able to dream? Or excited about not having to?"

I shook my head. "No. I don't remember sleeping." I tried to keep eye contact with her after that but eventually started staring at the corner of the room again.

Her hands released their grasp on me. "Well, that's *one* good thing, I guess. I'll leave you here to get settled. I've got to get back to class. Don't worry. I'll be back with Twila to show you to dinner."

Dinner? If ghosts didn't sleep, I couldn't imagine why we would eat.

She must have understood my expression. "I'll explain later." She seemed in a hurry to leave. "You OK?"

I nodded, trying to act with the confidence I didn't have.

She turned on her heel, hollered, "See ya!" and left.

And I was alone. Again.

ALONE

I leaned my back against the door and faced my room. It appeared larger than it was now I was alone, intimidating. My eyes scanned its entirety, taking in everything I missed before. The wall to my left had a section of shelves built into it, and what books were on them appeared unappreciated. The couches and chairs were used but not to the point of making them look worn.

I walked to the shelves and slid out a book, *Confessions* by Jean-Jacques Rousseau. On the cover was a man wearing a silly white wig and a serious expression. I curled my lip up and tried the next one, *Mary Poppins* by P.L. Travers. That didn't sound as awful. I continued to pull out books one by one, seeing what all was available: *Repressing Your Inner Specter* by I.C. Clearly, *The Haunting of the Crystal Palace* by Ima Ghost, *The Complete Works of Benjamin Franklin*. I sighed. On the opposite end of the shelf was a stack of textbooks with notebook paper and pencils lying next to them. If MaryAnn had gone to class, why were her books here?

I took them and placed them on the table next to where she had left my schedule earlier. The pencils and paper were pristine. The books, however, were not. Their corners were torn, their pages bent and written in. Their titles correlated exactly with my schedule. I found that more than a coincidence. These must be *my* books: *Guidelines for Basic Portals, The Fundamentals of Ethereal Dynamics, Invisible Arts for Beginners, the History of the Academy and the Void*, and *Beginning Rules for Hopeful Haunts*. That last one sounded like the answer to my prayers.

I opened it up.

Welcome to the Academy!

If you're newly dead and deemed worthy enough to be recruited, then your delightful journey into Death has just begun! This book contains all the rules and regulations of the Academy (last updated 1956) and precautions one should take before journeying into the Living or the Void. We have rules for a reason, young ghost. Don't break them.

1956. 1956… I tried to think what that meant exactly. The year? If that were the case, what year was it now? When I tried to remember what a school schedule was, a partial memory surfaced. Maybe that would happen again, I thought.

I concentrated on what I knew. 1956. Year. Date. Time.

I gasped. Lit candles. Winnie-the-Pooh cake. The number eight.

The memory left me as abruptly as it came, but something about it lingered, a warm feeling of security, love. I wanted to go back to that memory, experience more of it, encounter those feelings fresh and strong.

I squeezed my eyes so tight it hurt and focused on the coveted images I watched fade with each passing second. I did not breathe. I refused to move. Everything but my mind and face went numb.

It never returned.

The memory was now just that, a memory. I could remember seeing what happened, could feel the shadows of those precious feelings, but I could not experience it as I once had. I wiped the corner of my eye before the tear of frustration could escape. I had cried enough for one day.

I continued reading.

> The Land of the Dead is a dangerous place, and it is for this very reason Emily Richards formed the Academy in 1801. Originally nothing more than a one-roomed schoolhouse, the Academy has grown to the recognized, secure institution it is today.

> You probably have a lot of questions, so let's get started.

Chapter 1
<u>Critical Rules</u>

> There are a lot of do's and don't's to learn about the Land of the Dead, but some are more important than others. This chapter explains the most important rules of all, the critical rules. Critical rules apply to the most

dangerous of circumstances and therefore carry the severest of consequences if broken.

Journeying outside the Academy is too risky to do alone or ill-prepared. The Void is filled with specters, demons, ghouls, phantoms, and various other evil spirits that prey on the innocent and ignorant. Which brings us to rule number one.

1. Don't leave the school grounds without permission.
2. Don't form a Portal without a license unless accompanied by a teacher.
3. Don't visit the Living without a license unless accompanied by a teacher.

Another dangerous place to wander alone is the Living. I know you have fond memories of your family and friends and think of the Living world as a safe place to be, but you're not alive anymore, and that world isn't for you anymore. You will learn the rules of the Living world in this and your Portals class. Listen carefully. They could save your soul.

As I read the words again, the thought of being dead finally sank in. It was real. I was once alive, but now I'm dead. I felt like I should be upset or something, but I wasn't. Even my inability to experience my memory from earlier had become nothing more than a slight hollow feeling, and that was fading quickly.

I lay across the couch to read more, but it didn't feel right, like I was in someone else's room. While I wasn't confused or scared like I was earlier, I still didn't feel comfortable … at home. I know I didn't know what home was, but this dorm room wasn't it. I sat back up and closed the book, laying it on the couch next to me, and explored the rest of the room.

A few posters of a rock band hung on one of the walls. Beneath them lie a guitar and tambourine. Rising from my couch, I picked up the guitar and strung its strings. The sound felt familiar. I strung them again, hoping to trigger more memories. None. I let my hand strum them up and down without stopping. I had no idea what I was doing, but the motion and sounds … I had done this before. Yes! A teacher. Clapping. Me sitting, strumming.

The memory left. It wasn't as strong as the earlier one, but I still wanted it to last. I strummed the guitar's strings in vain, again trying to inspire another memory, the same memory, I didn't care.

Nothing.

With a heavy sigh of defeat, I placed the guitar back where I found it. I left the music area and continued my detailed inspection of what was to be my residence here. On the wall opposite of the bookshelf hung a mirror. It was small and scratched, but it worked like any mirror should. I gazed into it. Faded, transparent brown hair hung straight and thin to the shoulders of a timid teenaged girl. Her cheeks were thick, chubby if you will, and tiny spots, brighter than the rest of her skin, sprinkled across the tops of her cheeks and the bridge of her round, upturned nose. I would later learn to call them freckles, but at that moment they looked more like someone had taken a highlighter and played a nasty prank on the poor girl while she slept.

So this was me, huh? I turned my head sideways to find my chin also turned up as if to match my nose. I liked it.

After memorizing my face, I looked deeper into the mirror. I saw me, but I also saw through me, all the way to the other side of the room. *My* room, I corrected myself. "My dorm room," I said with a sigh. It was time to accept it.

I walked back to the couch, fell into it, and stared at the door in wait. MaryAnn said she would take me to dinner. All I had to do was wait until she got back. But that was easier said than done. As time passed, I started to feel like I did in the Maze again, trapped and lost. Sweat formed on my palms, and I wiped the glowing liquid onto my jeans, leaving illuminated spots across my thighs. My legs started twitching, my knees bobbing up and down with impatience until I couldn't take it anymore and went to the door. I was just about to turn the knob and leave when two colossal booms rang out. The sound was enough to vibrate my feet through the floor. I froze with my hand still on the knob.

Then, a few seconds later, another noise caught my attention. Talking. It was just a murmur at first, down from the main entryway end of the hall, but it grew. Soon the noises of doors opening and closing, giggles, squeals, and boisterous chatter filled my ears until I could hear nothing else.

The other ghosts. It had to be. The massive amount of students I would be thrown into tomorrow. I started to hyperventilate. Questions sprang inside my mind like ants on a watermelon. What will they think of me? What will they say to me? What will they *do* to me? I didn't know how to act around one person, let alone hundreds, or however many I was about to become bombarded with.

I stared at the door, mentally begging it to stay closed. Permanently.

A familiar voice laughed outside it. A dusting of relief sprinkled upon my terror when I heard it. MaryAnn was laughing with what sounded like another girl. The knob turned. I jerked my hand away and stepped back.

"G'day, roomie. Tear anything up while I was out?"

The other girl next to her stared at me from behind a curtain of long, black hair. Her face was pale even for what I had gathered to be ghost standards, and the air around her screamed venomous.

MaryAnn threw her books in the floor and plopped onto the couch I had earlier labeled as hers. At least I got one thing right. The other girl joined her with a familiar air of confidence, as if she thought of this room as hers too. I tried to sit on my couch and join them, but my feet kept bumping into things, and my face still felt suspended in a perpetual expression of anxiety.

"This is my girlfriend, Twila." MaryAnn gestured to the black-haired girl.

Twila shook her hair out of her face and nodded ever so slightly in my direction.

"H-hi," I responded pitifully.

MaryAnn turned to her girlfriend and said, "This is my new roomie. I would introduce you, but she doesn't remember her name."

With that statement, Twila raised her face up to stare at me. However, unlike the pity or annoyance in everyone else's eyes, she showed warmth, like my not knowing my name somehow put me on her friendly list. I felt my anxiety weaken.

MaryAnn eyed the pile of books next to me on the couch. "I see you found your textbooks." Her face took on a bewildered expression. "You've already started reading them?"

"Um, yeah." I didn't have much else to do. "I just thought, you know…"

"Whadduya think of that, Twila? We got us a nerd for a roomie!" MaryAnn announced, making me feel even more uncomfortable.

I glanced over at Twila, hoping for some ridiculous reason she would explain what that meant or take up for me, because whatever it was, it felt like an insult. She just stared at me with that same expression she had earlier of curious appraisal.

When MaryAnn peeked over to see why neither one of us answered her and saw our fixed gazes on each other, her expression turned irritated. She jumped up from the couch and floated to the door, her glow slightly brighter than it was before. "Time to feed," she snapped.

THE FEED

Twila floated to MaryAnn and waited for me with an expectant almost smile. I glanced at MaryAnn. "You coming?" she asked, still sounding upset, but not as much.

I watched the throng of ghosts sweep past our doorway. Giddy chatting and laughter wafted into our room, urging me from my seat. I nodded.

As we entered the tide of students, most were too engrossed with their own conversations to notice the new girl, aka me, for which I was very grateful. A few stared at me, saw I was with Twila and MaryAnn, and then turned to whisper to whomever they were traveling with, at which point that person would turn to stare at me too. A couple of boys asked, "Hey, what's your name?" but since I had no idea, I pretended I didn't hear them and pushed myself closer to MaryAnn. Yeah, I know. Not the best way to make friends, but saying, "I don't know," repeatedly wasn't really helping either, so I didn't feel guilty taking the easier route. Besides, it's not like I remember a lot of experiences in talking to boys. None to be exact.

We traveled down the grand staircase and through two large doors at the end of a downstairs hallway, past the bench swings, down the porch steps, and onto the ebony floor I had almost forgotten. As my feet dipped into the black fog creeping its way up the bottom step, I remembered one of the rules I read from my textbook, "Never leave school grounds without permission." I wondered if this would be one of those times.

We walked close to half a mile, maybe more, about the same distance as halfway to the giant Clock, whose hands had not moved since I'd arrived. Our path lay between several sporting arenas: a baseball diamond, a volleyball net (but without the sand), even a bowling alley of sorts. There were so many I couldn't take them all in and keep up with MaryAnn and Twila, whom I somehow stayed with this whole time even though I tried to stay hidden from everyone else.

Several students flew overhead to the front of the crowd. I foolishly jumped, thinking maybe if I floated too it would be easier to keep up. My ridiculous action only resulted in drawing more attention to myself, the last thing I wanted to do. A group of girls chortled behind me, and MaryAnn gave me a sideways glance that screamed, "What is *wrong* with you?" I didn't have an answer for her, but I knew at this point my face had to be glowing radioactive style.

When I finally got the nerve to raise my face to its normal position again, I saw a faint whisper of white smoke rising in the distance against the black background. Everyone: students, teachers, Mrs. Richards, circled around it. As the smoke thickened, the other ghosts became more excited. Some sniffed the air, declaring their favorite meals.

"I smell cheesecake!"

"That's not cheesecake. That's vanilla pudding!"

"Hmmm, someone's having steak!"

"Move over! I haven't had fried chicken and beans in forever!"

None of it made sense. Were they just smelling the smoke? I glanced up at MaryAnn who now wore a smile. Had the smoke caused that too? "What's going on?" I asked.

She sank to the floor and walked, making it easier for me to keep up and hear what she had to say. "Dinnertime, mate! See, when the Living cook their food, the essence of it comes up here. The more they cook it, the more essence we get. Steak's one of our favorites, but we don't get much unless they burn it."

"So the only food we get is because of the Living?" I asked, terrified to know the answer and refusing to ask the other question blazing inside me, are the Dead dependent on the Living?

MaryAnn nodded and answered the one question I did ask. "Pretty much, yeah. But,"—she shrugged—"they're always cooking something, so we always have plenty to eat. We don't get everything we did when we were alive though, like raw fruit and veg, unless a real fire breaks out and a restaurant burns or something." She turned up her nose. "Burned salad's right nasty though, so I don't mind that. Hey, mate?" She turned to me and smiled, wanting me to agree with her.

I smiled back and tried to comply, but I couldn't relate to what she was talking about. I didn't remember eating.

Although I continued to get a few curious glances from the other students nearby, they were too eager for dinner to pay me anymore notice. The pillar of smoke thickened until it obscured the other side. Mrs. Richards announced, "There's plenty for everyone. Be sure to share. Remember, those of you with a hovering license need to rise to the top so the others have more room."

Everything happened at once.

About a quarter of the students, including MaryAnn, flew high above us, inhaling the smoke as they went with satisfied smiles on their faces. Everyone else rushed to the center of the pillar, trying to absorb all they could before it vanished. Barely a tuft escaped them.

The only ghosts not joined in the feeding frenzy were Mrs. Richards, those I presumed to be other school staff, me, and Lydia. Lydia stood off to the side by herself, her motionless body resonating ominously.

The swirl of ghosts around the thick billows formed an impenetrable wall. My hair fluttered behind me in the breeze they created. I didn't feel hungry, not that I had once since being Dead, so I didn't see the need to brave the crowd for a bit of smoke.

"I know it looks intimidating, but they won't hurt you."

The man's voice startled me, causing me to shoot several yards away without my control. Once I realized where I was, I twirled around like a drunken ballerina, wondering how I got there.

"I didn't mean to scare you." The man chuckled and walked over to me. He carried a friendly air, almost as if he were trying to put me at ease. "I'm Mr. Prickett. I teach History." He held out his hand. I shook it feebly. "You must be new. Will you be in my class tomorrow?"

The name Mr. Prickett sounded familiar. I mouthed it a few times before remembering what MaryAnn had told me earlier. "You'll love Mr. Prickett. He's amazing!"

"Y-yes," I answered, with about the same grace as my drunken ballerina twirl and pathetic handshake. "I believe so."

His smile was one of those reassuring smiles you couldn't help but feel relaxed around. He released my hand and placed his behind my back, directing me toward the pillar of smoke. "This is an Essence Vent." He waved at the smoke surrounded with what resembled sharks herding a school of fish before devouring them live, and he was talking about it like a peaceful picnic with grandchildren playing volleyball. "They appear all over the Void. It's one reason Mrs. Richards built the school here." He motioned back at the Academy. "That and the Maze, of course." He took in my confused expression. "You'll learn more about that in my class. Don't worry." He smiled.

There was so much to learn, how could I not worry?

We stood there, staring at the others consuming the essence from the Living which rose from the Vent. I glanced over at Lydia. She was watching something way above everyone else in the black sky overhead. I followed her gaze. Far into the distance, several pale, blurred glows swam and danced over our heads.

Mr. Prickett saw me and said, "Don't worry. The Veil protects us from them."

I remembered crossing the Veil with Lydia, but I still didn't understand what it was.

He saw my expression and smiled, immediately calming my angst. "It protects the students of the Academy from those who dwell in the Void."

Were they the same dangers who dwelled in the Maze? I wanted to ask him but didn't. Another question dominated my attention. If I had become the monster, the dead creature who sucked the burned life out of the Living, what was so much worse that *I* needed protecting from *it*? The idea made me shudder.

The pillar had waned by then, and most of the students were heading back for the Academy grounds. I searched the area for MaryAnn or Twila but couldn't find them anywhere.

"You better get some before it's gone," Mr. Prickett told me. "We only get this once a day."

I shook my head. "I'm not hungry."

"Oh, you wouldn't be. You're still a fawn. But if you don't do it now, you'll be ravenous by the time you get brave enough to."

My chest burned with apprehension from his warning. "What's a fawn?" I asked.

He smiled. "It's a member of the newly Dead. You. Don't worry. In a few weeks, you'll be just like everyone else. When you first die, you're stronger. Your glow, your power, everything. It's why it's so easy for Lydia to find you when she searches the Maze, and why you're not hungry."

I recalled my glow against the black of the Maze. "I could see your glow from the edge of the Maze," Lydia had said. It was an absolute miracle those two men didn't catch me.

"What about you?" I asked. "Don't the teachers get to eat?"

He smiled that soothing smile of his and took off for the top. I stepped closer to the smoky essence. Everyone else did it and survived. The school of fish wasn't fighting back, I told myself.

I allowed the front edge of my body to graze the tickling boarders of the essence and sniffed it. The smell was familiar. I couldn't place it, but I had smelled it before. I smiled. It almost brought back a memory. If I could just keep smelling it…

My body took over before I could think any further. My mouth opened, and my abdomen stiffened as I sucked the essence into my mouth. It flooded my whole being, first through my throat, coating it with a warming layer of goodness, then to my chest, my stomach. I drew in another portion. This one filled my legs, my arms. It reached to my fingers and toes, warming them with a relaxing ecstasy that now permeated my entire body. I felt like the monster I now knew I had become, sucking in the smoke like a wraith sucking a soul, but it felt so good, so filling, so … nourishing.

My body quit of its own accord. I tried to feed again, but I didn't need anymore. I felt full, like I couldn't hold a single additional vapor. But I wanted it.

I opened my mouth, sucked in the smoke, and waited for the tingling sensation to take over, to make my limbs feel like they were floating away from my body, to take my mind into euphoria. But this unnecessary meal wasn't satisfying like the last one. To say the last one had tasted good would be incorrect, for it wasn't the taste that I craved. It was the essence, and my essence was now full. I could hold no more.

I stopped sucking, stopped trying to feed. The knowledge I could do this again tomorrow was both uplifting and sad. I didn't want to wait that long, but I did get to do it again.

I stepped back, away from the fading pillar, and scanned the surrounding area. The only ghosts left were a few students and the teachers. The smoke had withered to practically nothing now, and I could see what I could only presume it had left behind: papers, wood, entire pieces of furniture, clothing, tin cans, a single-wide trailer. My jaw fell to my chest. What was happening here?

A few more ghosts, all dressed in denim overalls, began to pick the smaller items up and haul them back to the Academy. They were a variety of ages. Some appeared to be staff, others, students. They ignored everyone around them.

"Those are the Gatherers." Mr. Prickett startled me again. I jumped, but not as far.

"Gatherers?" I asked.

He nodded and walked toward the school, his hands in his khaki trouser pockets. I followed. "The Vents allow essences of everything to come through, not just food. These are items people have burned, whether on purpose or otherwise, and so their essence joins us up here."

"*Up* here." I said it as a statement, but it was more of a question.

He explained as we walked. "Yes, from what we can tell, we exist in a trans-dimensional … world of sorts surrounding Earth. As you can see,"—he gestured at the Academy—"this part is above part of the United States, over Maryland to be exact. So anyone who dies in that area usually arrives somewhere near here."

"Usually?" I asked, though I wasn't sure I understood *anything* he just said.

He nodded. "They arrive around this section of the Maze, but the Maze encompasses the entire Curtain. If they wander too far in the Maze—" He darted a glance at me through the corner of his eyes. "Anyway, most people who make it here died near the part we're over."

Before I could ask him to explain further, he patted my shoulder and said, "Well, enough of that. I'm sure you have loads of friends to make. Maybe even catch up with a few lost relatives?"

"But—" I started. He floated through the Academy doors far more quickly than I could have caught up with. "But I don't have any friends," I said, low enough no one could hear even if they had been listening.

I turned around. About a dozen or more ghosts hung around each sporting area, playing volleyball, throwing each other down the odd bowling lane. They were laughing and happy. There were so many of them and only one of me. I went back inside.

WISP

Students flittered in and out the Academy doors like bees near the entrance of their hive. And I was the imposer, the intruder, the new stranger to attack and gawk at. With my gaze kept low, I squeezed through the other ghosts and rushed up the staircase. "22B. 22B." By some miracle I remembered my room number. I repeated it under my breath as I scanned the door labels. The curious eyes of other students made it difficult to concentrate. Thankfully, these doors were labeled more logically than the classrooms, and I didn't have to think too hard. 20… 21… 22… Ah! 22B. I licked my palm and turned the knob, painfully aware of the still staring gazes and louder than polite comments of every other ghost in the hallway directed at my transparent back.

I shut the door, closed my eyes, and leaned back against it with a sigh of relief.

"So how was your first feed?"

My eyes flung open. I had been so happy to be somewhere I could shut everyone out that I didn't notice MaryAnn and Twila were already in there.

MaryAnn walked towards the set of drawers next to her guitar and tambourine. Twila turned her head around from where she was sitting on the couch, anticipating my response.

I glanced at her before answering, "It was … interesting." Terrifying, new, scary, and quite potentially dangerous.

MaryAnn chuckled. She pulled out the bottom drawer and began removing its contents, forming a pile of clothes in the floor next to it as she did. Then she reached far into the back to pull out an oddly shaped globe with several wiggly arms. I stepped back, wondering if it were a pet the Dead had or something. That bites. Anything was possible at this point.

Without putting the clothes away or closing the drawer, she sat the object on the table between the two couches. I could see it more clearly then. A multi-colored lantern type thing with tiny hoses coming out from all over. Live swirls swam inside the glass globe. They weren't as bright as the swirls in the bulbs which lit the rooms. Those glowed more than I did, illuminating entire areas. These floated around like ash above a fire, too exhausted to follow their own course.

She gave one hose to Twila and took one for herself as she sat down. They simultaneously sucked the ends of the hoses. As they did, the swirls inside the lantern pulsed and changed color from pale blue to brilliant orange. Instead of the gentle swimming they had done earlier, the swirls stayed motionless, growing in size and intensity with every pulse before returning to their original state. I couldn't help but notice a few of the swirls had disappeared when they did.

MaryAnn released her tube and exhaled slowly, methodically from her mouth. A bright orange mist escaped, curling and snaking its way like fire until it vanished into the atmosphere of the room. Twila soon did the same, except her puffs released in short bursts, forcing the vapors to form tight balls which spun in place until they also faded into the background.

"What are you doing?" I asked, too much in awe to care how stupid I sounded every time I opened my mouth and asked another question.

"Wisping," answered Twila, another helix of orange vapor winding its way into the room as she did, making her look more like a dragon than a ghost.

The colored shapes were beautiful to the point I wondered if they could be alive. "Wisping what?" I asked.

Twila and MaryAnn threw furtive glances at each other. Twila kept her eyes cast down while MaryAnn answered, "Wisp," her throat tight as she did. She coughed and then blew an oval resembling a mouth screaming in pain. My stomach tightened.

I had just sucked in my first meal, something I gathered my survival in Death required, so what they were doing shouldn't make me as uncomfortable as it did. Maybe it was the fact we were alone that made me so uneasy. Maybe it was that they kept the lamp hidden in a drawer.

I told myself I was overreacting and sat across from them, watching the display of their breaths. Twila leaned over and blew her smoke into my face. I sniffed it curiously. It smelled sweet. Sickeningly sweet. I began to cough uncontrollably. They both threw their heads back in laughter at my reaction.

I impulsively scrunched up my nose and waved the smoke away from it. The desire to consume it like I had the Vent essence did not exist. Far from it. In fact, just the idea of bringing that stuff into my body made me gag.

The room now reeked of sweet acid. My eyes watered. MaryAnn picked up a third tube from the lantern and offered it to me. "You want some, mate?"

I shook my head, my still teary eyes wide with a frantic fear of what it was. I'd had enough new experiences for one day. Besides, no matter what I told myself, I couldn't shake that uncomfortable feeling it was giving me.

Twila smiled at my reaction. "I think she's afraid."

With that she was right. I was terrified. Their attitudes and behavior had completely changed since before I watched them wisp. Their bodies, once erect with purposeful movements now wobbled lazily about as though not all their directions were getting through. Their eyes, still translucent and dull as any ghost, had somehow gotten duller, and could not hold their focus on any one spot. I didn't know what that stuff was doing to them or what would happen to me if I tried it like they wanted. And I feared their reaction if I didn't. They were the closest things I had to friends, and my roommates too, or at least one of them was. If I got on their bad side… Well, it's not like I could just walk out that door and—

"Ah, leave her alone," said MaryAnn before leaning her head back on the arm of the leather sofa and breathing out an intricate butterfly which flapped its wings before vanishing above her.

Twila snarled her lips at her girlfriend. Orange vapor in the shape of angry flames shot from her nostrils.

MaryAnn rose her head in response. "She's new, Twila. Hey,"—she sat the rest of the way up—"where's your schedule?" Her body made its way, confused and slow, over to the books next to me on the couch.

I quickly leafed through the pile before she could, pulled out my schedule, and handed it to her.

She gazed unfocused at it before flipping it over and handing it back to me. "Here's a map. Go find something to do."

"Maybe she could *read* in the *library*," Twila taunted. "You know. With the rest of the *nerds*."

MaryAnn and Twila both laughed at her insult, exhaling wisps of vapor into the air around them and falling over the cushions of the furniture as they did. That was it. Staying here would only get worse. If the library was where all the ghosts like me, all the "nerds" hung out, then maybe that's where I should be too.

LIBRARY

Afraid of what Twila and MaryAnn might do with them, I placed my books on the shelf before leaving the room with my schedule, and therefore map, in hand.

The halls remained just as crowded and intimidating as earlier. I crammed my map into my pocket, kept my head down, and hurried back to the entryway steps, where hopefully there were fewer ghosts to avoid. I was wrong. The entryway was filled with worse than a hallway full of girl ghosts staring at the new student and chatting about her. It was filled with girl *and boy* ghosts staring at the new student and chatting about her. They even talked about me right in front of my face!

"I wonder where she came from."

"She doesn't talk to anyone. Hey! What's your name?"

Please, not another "What's your name?" I winced with the thought of speaking. I don't know my name. Ha ha, yes it's so funny. Everyone laugh at the new girl.

"She must've been a suicide. They never talk."

I let my hair serve as curtains so the other ghosts couldn't see my face and pulled the map from my pocket. I didn't want to stop and study it, lest one of them try to start a conversation with me, or about me, so I peeked at the rooms on my map as briefly and inconspicuously as I could. It looked like I needed to go down the classroom hallway.

The moment the double doors shut behind me, blocking the noises of the others, I fell against the wall. Fresh tears burned the corners of my eyes and I banged the wall with my fist in frustration. Hello. My name is I don't know, and I will be your crying ghost for the evening. Thank you.

My eyes shot open with a gasp. Another memory. Sitting. Students mocked me. I was crying. I couldn't get up. I couldn't run away. Why couldn't I run away?

The memory ended. Panting, I stared down the classroom hallway before me. What was *that*? None of the other memories left me gasping for air I didn't need. No time to think about it now. I hurriedly wiped my face and continued my search for the library before anyone saw me in such a vulnerable position. A few ghosts lingered in rooms here and there, but they rarely, if at all, noticed me as I went past. Grateful for their lack of interest, I found a shadow in a dead spot, leaned up against the wall as flat and therefore inconspicuous as possible, and studied the map.

I was in the wrong hallway. The library took up nearly half the third floor, and I was still on the second. I retraced my steps back to the hallway entrance, folded my map, and shoved it in my back pocket to keep it safe. Six inches away from me were the double doors, the double doors which separated me from everyone else. A fresh batch of sobs threatened their way up my throat. I clinched my teeth against them and took a deep breath. I was *done* crying! I squeezed and opened my fists, bobbed on the balls of my feet. I could do this. A thought came to me. Maybe if I acted like everyone else, no one would notice how new and different I was. Can't hurt to try.

No more wet cheeks (I wiped away the two wet refugees still making a run for it). No fear on face (I attempted a smile which turned out to be more of a plastered grimace). No hair hiding face (I quickly tucked it behind my ears to make sure). Open. Doors.

No stares. Good. So far anyway. Without slowing, without glancing down or checking my map, I walked up the steps to the third floor and entered its classroom hallway. These rooms were quieter than the ones below. I walked past them slowly, resisting the urge to peek into every single one like the newcomer I was. A few dozen classrooms down, I met another set of double doors. Unlike the shiny white with brass handles I had seen until then, these were a deep mahogany, but featured the same brass handles. My hands shook, their glow reflecting off the glossy panels as I pushed on the cold metal bar to open the door.

Inside was the biggest library I had ever seen. Yeah, I know, I don't remember anything before now, including libraries, so that's not saying much, but providing I had actually seen a lot of libraries in my Life, this would have been bigger than all of those put together. Students had scattered themselves from one end to the other. Some floated up and down the shelves, browsing the massive collection of books. Some sat at perfectly aligned tables and studied. Behind the circular desk before me floated a stern-looking lady ghost with large glasses that kept sliding down her nose. In front of her sat a name placard which read, "Violetta Papenfuss, Librarian". She did not look up when I entered, and the last thing I wanted to do was introduce myself to yet another new ghost, so I made a beeline to the most secluded table I saw.

And there I sat, relishing in the quiet, the solitude, letting my mind wander. I didn't breathe. I didn't move. I finally got to where I didn't even hear. It reminded me being in the

Maze, alone, quiet, dark. Only now I was safe. As far as I knew, anyway. And I could leave anytime I wanted, providing that time would come.

As my mind journeyed freely through its thoughts and recollections, what few images I had from my Life memories flashed by in blurred segments. I remembered the comforting one. I tried to bring back that memory, the one with the cake and the candles. The one that made me feel loved. Wanted. Good. Happy. I closed my eyes. Maybe this time it would work. It didn't.

That memory was the only happy thought I had, and I wanted to relive it so badly it hurt. But I was tired of being upset all the time, so I pushed away the pain and allowed my thoughts to amble about again without guidance. They landed on a recent comment made by a girl in the entryway, "She must've been a suicide." Was I? Is that why I couldn't remember anything? Was amnesia my punishment for taking the easy way out?

"Excuse me."

I jumped out of my seat and hovered a split second before landing again. Ms. Papenfuss glared down at me through her glasses as though I had committed a terrible offense of some sort. "Can I be of assistance?" she asked.

Assistance to what? My staring at books? My accidental yet super cool hovering? "Um, n-no. Thank you."

Her eyes wandered over my empty table and then my bare person. It was then I noticed I was the sole student left.

"While I am obligated to stay within the library providing a student is still using it, and I am happy to do so," (Funny, she didn't *look* happy about it.) "I fail to see what part of the library you are actually using Miss…"

I could feel little ghostly essence bits floating up the back of my neck, like goosebumps. I didn't want to go anywhere else, nor did I want to admit to yet another ghost how I didn't know my own name. But sometimes we don't have choices. This was one of those times.

"I'm sorry." I stood and sidestepped my way around until she no longer stood between me and the door. "I'll … go back to my room. I guess." My feet moved me backward on their own accord. Her eyes continued to bore holes into me. "I'm sorry I bothered you," I said, then left before fear forced me to pivot on the spot and run out of the room.

Thankfully, she didn't follow, and even more thankfully, the classroom hallway was empty. I ran down it as fast as my ghostly legs would carry me and opened the doors to the third story landing. A few students still lingered about the staircase and dorm room halls, chatting with each other more quietly than before and playing cards while suspended in midair. No one seemed to notice me. I hurried back to my room and went inside.

FIRST DAY

The room was empty, which was somehow simultaneously both relieving and depressing. The contraption Twila and MaryAnn had been using sat depleted on the table. Tiny threads of mist struggled their way out the ends of the hoses. I turned my nose up at it and plopped onto my couch.

Time passes differently for the Dead than the Living. The Living have measurement devices to track time's movement: the sun, the moon, clocks, watches, phones, TV shows, hours of sleep, appointments. The Academy has the Clock, whose hands never move, and a sparse scattering of pendulum devices for announcing class changes, but these items are rare, priceless. Most of the Dead own no such devices. They have only the Vents to tell them a single day has passed between feedings. The other twenty-three and a half hours, we are without sunrise, sunset, the changing of the seasons, or electronics of any kind.

I know that electronics part sounds confusing. After all, the rooms of the Academy use "lights", but those aren't electrical lights. They can't "power" anything. They can't make a TV work or turn on a computer, which means no phones, aka time pieces or instant streaming to assess how many of our moments have passed or how many remain. We are the expedition party lost at the North Pole in winter, or the South in summer, living in the perpetual darkness of eternity.

So again, I had no method of measuring how much time passed. I only knew that it did as I sat staring at the wall and wondering what I was supposed to do next.

A loud bong of a Clock sounded, making me jerk from my seat. The last time it rang, classes ended for the day, and everyone went to eat. I stood at attention and listened, hoping to understand what this bell meant, all the while terrified I had somehow missed my entire first day of classes and it was already time to eat again. Doors opened and closed, and voices soon turned the dorm halls into a boisterous party zone. MaryAnn opened the door before I could poke my head through and investigate.

She was alone and acting more like the nice, bubbly girl who had first introduced herself to me. I smiled at her with relief.

"You ready, mate?" she asked as she shut the door behind her with a firm click.

"For what?" Please, for the love of the Dead, tell me what I'm supposed to be doing!

One of her eyebrows dipped. "For classes, mate." She grabbed a single strap of her patched backpack and slung it over her shoulder. Its dangling strings of beads clacked together as she did.

Before I could react, she was in the hallway. I threw my books together and ran out to meet her. Already halfway down the hall, her wavy blonde hair floated eerily behind her like a sheet in the wind.

"Wait up!" I called out and ran to catch up with her.

She turned around, surprised. "Oh sorry, mate. I forgot you can't hover."

Although her thoughtlessness made me irritated, I tried to hide it with a smile that probably turned out to be more of a pained poop face as I battled my way through the other students in the hallway to meet her. When I caught up, she hovered slowly next to me so I didn't get left behind again.

"Thanks," I said.

"Nah." She shrugged. "It was my fault."

Elbows and backpacks banged into me from my right side while I tried not to push MaryAnn into the door jams on my left. "Is it always like this?" I asked.

"Like what?"

Like *what?* You know, a sea of people floating their way through an unstoppable current. Laughter, shouting, and teasing so loud you have to yell to be heard by the person next to you. "This many people," I shouted … obviously.

I glanced over at her and saw a confused expression. "Didn't you go to school when you were alive?"

"I guess so." I didn't want to tell her about my memories. Not yet anyway.

"What do you mean, you guess so?"

We reached the grand staircase. Some students changed floors here, but most of them turned into the open double doors like we did. Three rivers merging into one. "I went to school. I just don't remember much about it."

She didn't answer, and I wasn't about to promote this conversation.

We walked in silence for several minutes. The open classes sucked in students like tiny caves pulling at our current. It didn't diminish the population much though.

MaryAnn slid into the next open classroom. "This is my first period."

I read the label above the doorway, "7F46".

"Can you find your way from here?"

I knew she would help me if I needed her to, but her face held the same feelings I had. She was hoping to be free of me. Even though I also desired to be alone, it still hurt to see she felt that way. I reached into my pocket for my schedule/map. Yup, still there. I stared down the hallway. So many students, so many classrooms. I wasn't ready for this. I could feel the fear rising, the bridge of my nose burning again. I kept my head down and focused on my schedule to hide my glowing face.

She rejoined me. "C'mon. I'll take you to your room." Her voice dripped with empathy.

"No," I croaked, then cleared my throat and forced a smile in battle against my true feelings. "I can do it."

Several emotions darted across her face as she watched for my reaction: confusion, hope, doubt, indecision.

"I'm fine." I promised her. I searched my schedule for the number of my first classroom. "14H27. Portals. On the left, right?"

"Right." She smiled, but it was clear she was still worried about me.

I put my schedule neatly between the pages of my topmost book and took off for my first class. It was clear MaryAnn meant well; she just wasn't very good at it.

The crowd had thinned enough I could trot now. As I did, I scanned the door labels for my Portals room. 3G13, 47G46, 2H1 … ah! 14H27! I went inside.

MY NAME

The classroom itself resembled your typical classroom, not that I remembered a typical classroom. A woman in a long dress hovered behind a sturdy wooden desk, her hair wound around her head in a lose bun like a halo with a knot in it. I searched the students' desks for an empty seat while desperately trying to ignore the curious eyes. When I found one, I weaved through the others and glanced at the teacher for approval. Her expression said nothing, but her eyes inspected me like I was a bug on display with a pin through my abdomen.

Her stare made me so nervous I bumped into one of the desks. A teenage girl with short, transparent black hair and an arrogant smirk snapped from behind it, "Who are *you*?"

"Uh oh," said a guy with glowing brown hair slicked into a flawless wave on the top of his amused head. "Fresh fish." His perfectly styled button shirt made him look more like a model than a real person.

Half a dozen students, all grouped around this one desk, this one girl ghost with the black hair, took me under their scrutiny. I was the intruder on their turf, and I was *not* welcome. I stood transfixed, a deer caught in their headlights. A fawn. This only fueled their enthusiasm for my torture.

The girl stood slowly, methodically from her seat. "I said"—she paused, her arms across her chest now—"what's your name?"

Actually, that's not what she said earlier. What she said was, "Who are you?" But I was not about to inform her of her inaccuracy.

"I-I don't know."

This caught them off guard. They were probably hoping I would say Charcee, Helga, or Schartzmugel, you know, some hideous name they could make fun of without even trying, but even though I didn't fulfill their fantasy, I had most certainly just made their day.

A grin spread across the girl's face. "You don't *know?*" She barked a "Ha!"

Her friends wore the same astonished and entertained expression she did.

I surveyed the rest of the room, hoping one of the other ghosts would jump in as my savior, or that the teacher would intervene. No such luck. A few students showed compassion, but were apparently too afraid to act on it. The rest were a mixture of stunned, amused, and apathetic. The teacher had her back to us now as she wrote on the board. The noise from the hallway was loud enough for her to pretend not to notice my conflict. At least that's the vibe I got.

"What are you looking for, no name? You think one of them can answer for you?" The girl jerked her head toward the other students.

The uninvolved students quickly busied themselves with other things. I turned my attention back to the hateful girl.

"You have no friends here, you stupid—"

The click of the classroom door shutting abruptly ended the conversation. The girl and her friends took their seats with innocent obedience, but not before she threw a scowl in my direction.

The empty desk I had been trying for was still two rows over. I tried to get to it as quickly as possible, hoping to avoid any more attention. Something hit my foot on the way, causing me to trip and drop my books. I knocked another desk over on my way down.

The room erupted in laughter. A few of her friends clapped and cheered at my performance.

"She can't even walk!" one of them shouted.

"Don't let her hover near you. She'll knock you out of the Void!" another teased.

I picked up my books, making sure my schedule was still tucked inside, and slumped over to the empty seat.

The teacher rapped the side of her desk with a ruler, immediately grabbing the students' attention.

"Please say, 'present' when I call your name. Brian."

A boy from the front row answered, "Present."

"Christy?"

A girl with frizzy red hair answered, "Present."

"Cisco?"

A boy whose skin had to be darker than mine when he was alive with hair so black it appeared dull compared to the rest of his glowing body answered, "Present."

"Darva?"

"Present." It was hateful girl. No wonder she wanted a name to make fun of. With a name like Darva, I would want someone to have a worse name too.

"Gregory?"

Suddenly I was in a different classroom. A memory. Names were being called out. People were answering, "Here."

And then it left. I was back to real Life, or real Death I suppose, awaiting my fate as the class dork.

"Yancy?"

"Present."

I didn't notice who answered that one. My recent memory was consuming all my attention because I think my name was about to be called in it. I was about to remember my name!

I gasped at the realization. The surrounding students stared at me. A few inched their desks away.

"And…" The teacher lifted her gaze from her list to stare directly at me. "I'm sorry, but they haven't given me your proper name, Miss…"

She expected an answer from me, but I had none for her. My face stung so much from the embarrassment I could see its radiant glow reflecting off the face of the ghost in front of me. The whole class already knew I didn't know my own stinking name, did I have to announce it again?

"Hello? Can you hear me?" The teacher wouldn't wait much longer before making this situation more horrifying than it already was.

"I … I don't know."

Darva and her gang burst out laughing. I let my hair fall to hide the tears I couldn't stop.

"Settle down," the teacher commanded. Though she lacked compassion, her sternness prevented further teasing. "Be sure you visit the genealogy department to get this straightened out as soon as possible."

Sure. I'll add that to my repertoire. I didn't dare look up. I didn't sniff. I didn't wipe away the tickling, glowing tears that ran down my cheeks. I refused to do anything that would reveal how weak and cowardly I really was. I felt the teacher's stare. She wouldn't let me get away without acknowledging her command. I nodded and hoped that was enough.

"My name is Mrs. Collins. Please turn to page 226 as we continue our lesson on Chapter 15, Finding and Avoiding Hidden Portals."

Class passed slowly. I didn't understand the lecture, so I kept my eyes on my book, not that it helped. I couldn't focus. I spent the whole class with my arms crossed tightly against my chest, my hair around my face, and my right foot bouncing up and down as I waited for it to end and Darva to do whatever she had in store for me when that happened.

The noise of the other students rising from their desks and talking again gave the only notification class ended. I wiped my now dry cheeks just in case and sniffed unnecessarily. Should I try to run ahead of Darva and beat her outside or stay behind? If I stayed behind, I would be trapped, the lone gazelle amidst the pride of lions. If I ran ahead, she could catch up, and I had a suspicion tripping wasn't her worst method of torture. I tried to blend into the middle of the non-Darva crowd.

Whether I bored her that quickly or my plan worked I neither knew nor cared, but it got me into the hallway and Darva far enough away I considered myself safe again. I stopped to check my schedule for what came next. Ethereal Dynamics, room 7S9. I shoved the paper back into my pocket and dove into the moving sea of students.

Room 7S9 was easy enough to find, and the class easy enough to sit through. I still had to endure stares and questions of my classmates, but *nothing* like last time. No roll call, no Darva. I'm not sure the teacher, Ms. Peach, even knew I was there.

Invisible Arts was another story. Like MaryAnn said, Mr. Dinwiddie used to be a magician, and the sight of a new student threw him into ecstasy with the idea of impressing me with his "magic". I wasn't impressed.

The lesson wasn't very helpful either, although his ridiculous antics were enough to keep the other students' attention off of me, for which I was very grateful. I could tell his class was going to be one of my favorites.

Then came History with Mr. Prickett. Several of the students' faces were familiar in this one, including Darva's. But when I saw Mr. Prickett, I smiled. He had been so nice to me earlier it put me at ease.

"Christina."

"Here."

"Darva."

"Here."

He hadn't announced roll call, brought the class to attention, or even shut the door, although he was on his way to do that now. As nearly late students hurried their way through the closing door, others took their seats and shuffled books and papers noisily around. Meanwhile, Mr. Prickett continued calling names despite the chaos.

"Gregory."

I gasp. A classroom. A boy sitting awkwardly in a chair near me. Another rocking back and forth in his desk. A teacher calling out names. "Gregory?"

The boy next to me said, "Here." It didn't sound right, not as clear as the students I sat with now.

"Hannah?" a voice in the memory called.

"Here."

That was my voice. It sounded different from what it did now, but I had felt the vibrations in my throat. That was my voice!

The memory vanished.

"Hannah!" I announced with a huge smile of relief.

Mr. Prickett stopped in the middle of "Matthew" and gaped at my outburst. Every other head turned my way, their curious eyes wondering what was wrong with me.

I hesitated a moment but then decided it was best to get it over with. "Hannah. My name is … H-Hannah."

Mr. Prickett flipped over the paper on his clipboard, presumably searching for my name. "I don't see you on here. Wait." He examined me more closely. "I remember you. Last night at the feeding."

I smiled and nodded.

He flipped through his papers again. "Ah yes. Here it is. 'New student, name unknown.' Well, I guess we know your name now, don't we?"

My smile grew.

"I'll let records know." He scribbled my first name down on his list of names. "I don't suppose you remember your last name, do you?"

I shook my head. I wasn't even sure what he meant by that, so no, I didn't remember it.

I scanned the faces of the room, my triumphant smile still on my face. None of the curious faces smiled back. When I got to Darva, she remarkably wore an even worse sneer than before.

ROBIN

Even if I hadn't made a fool of myself, history wasn't going to be my favorite class of the day. While Mr. Prickett did try to make it interesting, I didn't really care that a bunch of ghosts battled each other thousands of years ago, although I was curious as to how. What does a ghost use for weapons? He never answered that, and I wasn't about to raise my hand and ask. I had drawn enough attention to myself for one day.

When class ended, I rose from my seat, foggy-brained from the information dump. A bright glow caught my attention as I did.

"Only stupid people can't remember their name!"

Darva. I had forgotten about her.

"How can you be teacher's pet when you're so stupid?"

I stood there, shaking in fright, waiting for her to leave. She wasn't leaving. I may not have known what to do exactly, but one thing I had learned. Doing nothing wouldn't stop her from bullying me.

I stared her straight in the eye, refusing to break our gaze. "I — I don't know."

My answer only flared her anger. "You don't know anything, do you, you stupid dweeb!"

"Excuse me," Mr. Prickett said from behind Darva. He remained gentle but firm in his words. "What do you think you're doing Miss Bishop?"

I felt my body relax with his presence. Until Darva reached around me and grabbed my books. "Nothing. Just helping Hannah get to her next class."

My jaw fell and my stomach tightened. What was she up to?

"Come on, Hannah," she said with a gleaming smile that exuded friendly positivity.

Mr. Prickett took in my expression but said nothing as Darva grabbed my hand and lead me out the door. I threw a desperate look over my shoulder at Mr. Prickett at we left. He appeared irritated, but did nothing to stop her.

When we reached the hallway, Darva dropped my hand and flew ahead of me, cackling like an old witch. I watched as one by one she threw my papers and books into the air. I tried to catch them, but I was nowhere near fast enough to keep up with her.

"Here, I'll help you." A girl who looked about fourteen bent over to pick up my *Beginning Rules for Hopeful Haunts*.

I stood stunned, and afraid. Was this another trick? Another person pretending to be nice only to stab me in my already dead back when I turned around?

"It was Darva who did this to you, wasn't it?"

I eyed her cautiously. Was she a friend of Darva's? "Yes," I answered, but I refused to say anything more until I was sure of her intentions.

The girl smiled reassuringly at me. "I'm Robin."

She was a slight thing, nearly a foot shorter than me. I took my book from her. "Thank you. I'm … Hannah." Wow. I just introduced myself to someone for the first time. That was weird. Well, if she was a friend of Darva's, telling her my name wouldn't do any harm. Darva already knew that.

"Hi, Hannah. C'mon. We better get the rest before the other students do something with it."

She walked instead of hovered next to me. I couldn't help but like her for it.

"Why is she like that?" I asked before I could bite my lip. I still wasn't sure if she was one of Darva's spies or not, and this was some elaborate trap.

"She comes from old family," Robin explained.

Her body remained relaxed and sure next to mine. I didn't sense any hostility from her as she spoke. As a result, I felt more confident in talking to her. "Old family?"

"Her ancestors include famous ghosts like the original Salem witches, victims of the Titanic, the Brown Lady, and even Bloody Mary." She watched my face for a reaction.

"I'm sorry, but I don't know who any of those people are."

She blinked several times, stunned. "The Salem witches? Bloody Mary?"

I shook my head. Not a clue.

She bent over and picked up my disheveled history book from the corner. "Well, they're famous ghosts among the Living. They all died in horrible ways and now they take up the Void like royalty."

Oooohhhh. I nodded my head. "So she's mad because I didn't know that?"

She giggled. "Probably, but trust me, that doesn't matter. She just likes to be mean. And her family is so important, she gets away with a lot of stuff others wouldn't. I've heard they even give Mrs. Richards orders."

My eyes widened. That didn't sound good.

We continued to pick up my stuff until I had everything but my schedule. "There it is!" I pointed to a crumpled paper waving in the air up ahead.

"Hmmm…" Robin eyed the paper with skepticism. She quickly floated up and reached for it. It fluttered further down the hallway. "I figured as much," she said. "Someone's practicing their invisibility."

I jogged to where she stood and scrutinized the paper with slitted eyes. It was waving, but it was more like one end of it was controlling the rest of it. Like an invisible hand was holding it by the top and jiggling it. Taunting me with the bait. The question was, who was the fishing pole, and what were they going to do when they caught me?

"Can you turn invisible?" I asked Robin.

She shook her head. "Not that well. Not everyone can turn invisible in the Land of the Dead. Even fewer can do it as completely as that. What is that paper anyway? Is it important?"

I nodded. "Yes, very. It's my schedule and map."

Robin pursed her lips. "You *could* ask for a new one, but I wouldn't recommend it."

"Why not?" I readjusted the books on my hips and watched her face for an answer.

"Mrs. Richards doesn't like excuses, no matter how legitimate they are."

I pressed my lips together. Great. "Guess there's only one thing to do then."

"Yup." Robin held the straps of her backpack tight and flew at the paper. I wrapped my arms around my books and ran behind her. The paper jerked to the other side, behind us, in front of us.

"Oof!" Robin bumped into something. Some*one* more than likely.

The paper fell to the floor. I snatched it, crumpling it into my fist to keep it safe. We never saw who it was, but I could feel their presence get up and leave.

I walked over to Robin and reached my hand out for her to take.

"Thanks." She took my hand, but only to be nice. Her weightless body sprang into the air with no help from me.

"Hey," she said. "Me and my friends hang out in the craft room after school. Wanna come?"

"Um… I'll think about it." I could only imagine which feelings my face was expressing: fear, delight, skepticism. Fear. The truth was, I still wasn't ready to make friends. I still didn't know who *I* was.

"OK," she said, but her face fell when she did.

"I'm sorry. I-I don't think I'm ready to make friends yet."

"OK." She smiled. "We'll be waiting for you when you are."

OVERSEERS

By the time Robin muttered something about Poltergeist Studies and hovered to the opposite end of the hallway, the place was deserted. I quickly checked my schedule for which room to go to next. Beginning Rules for Hopeful Haunts, my last class for the day, and as far as I was concerned, the most important one. 24N16, next door to my History class. That was convenient.

I peeked through the long, skinny window. The teacher was already talking. Roll call was over. Technically, I could have opened the door, apologized for being late, told her my name, and taken my seat. But I'd had enough embarrassment for one day. Nope. I returned to my room. I needed some alone time. On my way, the thought of hanging out in the library for a while crossed my mind, but then I remembered Ms. Papenfuss and how much fun she was and wondered if she might realize I was ditching and get me in more trouble than I was assuredly already in for not attending my last class.

With my dorm room door shut behind me, I threw my books on my couch and plopped down next to them with a sigh. My body was still awake and energized, but my mind was exhausted. I stared at the walls and allowed my brain to process the day. When I got to the part where an undoubtedly invisible Darva played keep-away with my schedule, I took action to prevent such an episode from being an issue in the future. I closed my eyes, took two deep breaths, and set to memorizing my schedule and class locations. I was halfway through reciting it for the third time when the Clock sounded its two bongs. Classes were over. It was time to feed.

I rose from the couch, glad to know what to do for once. The other students were just now entering the dorm halls, and they would visit their rooms before joining me outside. That meant I would be first in line, and alone, I thought with a smile.

Avoiding the main crowd, I went out the front door and followed the porch to the back of the Academy. A half dozen bodies stood over the Vent area. They didn't glow, which I thought was odd, but seeing as how little I knew of this place, I didn't question it. I passed the volleyball net and a turf-covered area I hadn't noticed before with tiny wire arches protruding from it. Several colored balls hid in the fog amidst the arches.

A white light reverted my attention back to the area where the non-glowing people stood. My eyes widened, and I took an involuntary step back as several rays of yellow shot through the black bottom of the floor. The rays extended through the Veil like thin daggers into the Void. A bright white circle of fog emanated from the bottom of the rays and expanded outward, dissipating as it went until nothing but a thin wisp was left as it passed over my feet.

I felt nothing when the mist crossed my ankles. What was it made of? Was it made of nothing, as the black fog seemed to be? Or had I grown used to it, as one grows used to the air that surrounds them?

I heard the Academy doors open behind me, and the freed and hungry students' voices. My time for being alone had passed.

The beams of light disappeared by the time I shifted my focus back to them. There was no sign of the mist either. The few non-glowing bodies I had seen earlier continued to pace next to the Vent, closely monitoring its behavior. I approached the Vent with caution. Was I allowed here this early? Was it OK to see what I had just witnessed?

A bright white circle now lay where solid black floor once was. The Vent opening. Tiny strands of smoke puffed through from the Living. Their essence. Their offerings, whether intentional or not.

From here I could view the non-glowing bodies better, the Overseers. They wore goggles with darkened lenses, held onto their heads by an elastic band wrapped around it. Their white lab coats, all held tightly shut, hung below their knees. The parts of their bodies I could see, fingers, forearms, faces, had been charred black.

One of them noticed me and nodded to the others. Soon, all their goggled eyes were upon me. We studied each other from our separate positions. It was then I spotted the missing fingers, the lack of hair and ears. My hand flew to my mouth. They turned their backs to me and left without a word. I was by myself again, and fifteen feet from the Vent. I had been here yesterday and fed from it, but now, being this close to it, all alone, after what I had just witnessed, and with the Vent's opening gaping at me like a giant mouth waiting for its prey to just walk into it, I was afraid.

The other students were close. I could hear them. Essence rose full force from the Vent. I inhaled.

MR. CONSOLVER

I had finished and was walking back to the Academy when the rest of the students arrived. I took the long way around again to avoid most of the horde.

When I entered the quiet foyer, I couldn't help but stop and marvel at its grandness. I was too preoccupied before, following MaryAnn, trying to get to class, trying to avoid people. But now I could enjoy its beautiful architecture, the shiny mahogany railings, the carpeted stairs with little brass rods to push the carpet into place at the foot of each step, the paintings. I waited there, enjoying the views, embracing the work put into the decorating of this place, until the voices told me the others had returned from their feed.

I climbed the stairs to my dorm room. Halfway up, I paused. I was forgetting something. What was it? Was my schedule memorized? I recited it perfectly. No, that wasn't it. I took a few more steps. Was there anything I needed to do for tomorrow's classes, like homework or something? No, I had the rest of the evening free. Another step.

Wait. Genealogy. I had been told they would help me straighten out my name situation. Granted, that was no longer a problem, but I still felt it expected for me to show up.

Maybe they could help me learn other things, I told myself. Like anything.

I returned to my room and picked up my map. "Genealogy … genealogy…" I muttered to myself as I ran my finger across its surface, searching for the right location.

"Oh!" I squealed when I found it. It was across from Mrs. Richard's office. Figures. All the other offices seemed to be in that area. I should have searched while I was there.

I laid my map on the table and pressed it with one of my books, rubbing it back and forth to get the crinkles out. The map looked much older than it was. Maybe the genealogy counselor would get me a new one. I doubted it.

I neatly folded the map/schedule and placed it in my back pocket. Some students passed me in the hallway. I ignored them as I went downstairs.

At the bottom of the steps, across the foyer from Mrs. Richard's office, stood a door with a plaque overhead that read, "Simon Consolver, M.C. B.C.F.T." I had no idea what all those letters meant, but they weren't comforting.

The door was closed. I knocked on it slightly with my knuckles. After about a minute, I consented to my first knock's weakness and knocked again with three good raps. Scuffling from the other side told me someone was home. The knob turned, and I gritted my teeth, the reality of what I was doing finally hitting me.

A thin, young boy with short, dark hair answered, "Yes?" His voice cracked when he spoke. My mouth opened and shut several times as I contemplated whether I should continue to carry out my intentions or not.

"H—Hi." Better to get it over with. "I'm Hannah."

The boy's head jerked to the side. "And?"

"I, um, was told to see you?"

He dipped his brows in annoyance. "Not me you weren't." He was still blocking the halfway open door with his body. I was not welcome. "Do you have an appointment?" he demanded.

"Um … I don't know."

Rolling his eyes, he stepped aside to open the door. "I'll have to check the schedule," he sighed.

I forced my feet to take me inside.

He sat behind a small desk with several papers and open notebooks stacked neatly upon it. He grabbed a pencil from a cup filled with about twenty of them and twiddled it between his fingers as he flipped the pages of one notebook back and forth, searching for my name. "No. No Hannah." He stood. "Sorry," he said with a smile that radiated he was not sorry. "If you'd care to make an appointment, then we could—"

Before he could escort me out, I asked, "How do I do that?"

Irritation washed across his face as he sat back down. "How long have you been here?"

"Um…" I had to think. "About a day?" I shrugged.

"Then I'm sure Mrs. Richards has already made one for you."

"Then why isn't it in there?" I asked, pointing at the schedule book.

The weak reign on his irritation was waning. I thought I heard a low snarl.

"Maybe," I started, "maybe it's under a different name. I didn't remember my name until today."

"Well, *maybe* you should have said that in the first place." He sat back down at his desk and skimmed the entries of his notebook the briefest of seconds. "Mr. Consolver!" he shouted at a closed door nearby while ignoring my curiosity. "We've got a Jane Doe!"

A pale (even for a ghost) man with tiny eyes and fat jowls that wiggled when he moved opened the door. Without looking at me, he asked his secretary, the rude boy I had been dealing with so far, "Yes, Thomas?"

Thomas gestured in my direction. "Mrs. Richards set her appointment for last night. As Jane Doe."

Mr. Consolver gave me a quick once over before opening his door wider for me to enter. I complied.

"And next time, Miss Hannah," Thomas called just before I stepped into the other office. "Show up for your scheduled appointment."

My mouth fell open. What appointment? I wanted to shout. No one had mentioned an appointment. I mean, they told me I should come here, but they didn't say when or where or… I had to suppress a growl of frustration. It was clear arguing wouldn't improve my current situation. And who knew? Maybe Mr. Consolver could help me. I composed myself so as not to get on anyone's bad side.

Mr. Consolver's office was smaller than Thomas's, but more lavish. His dark, wooden desk and cabinets took up half the room. Papers burst through their cubbies and lay strewn across his working surface like he had thrown them into the air and let them land wherever they wished.

He shut the door and walked around to the other side of his desk. I supposed he expected me to sit in the corduroy padded chair with the metal frame, but when the door shut, I felt isolated, in danger. Not from Mr. Consolver, per se, just, new surroundings, new people. Again. I wondered if anything here would ever feel familiar to me.

"Please, have a seat." He gestured to the padded metal chair.

I still didn't want to, but I did.

"Mrs. Richards said you came yesterday, and that you don't remember your name. Is there anything else you can tell me?"

"Actually, I remembered my name today." I smiled with that fact. "It's Hannah."

"Hannaaahhh…?" He drew my name out expectantly.

"I don't understand," I said.

"Your last name?"

I shook my head infinitesimally. "Mr. Prickett asked me for that. But… I still don't understand what that means."

"Well," he said with a wave of his hand. "I'll see what I can do with what I have. How did you die?"

His question took me by surprise. I know it shouldn't have. We were all Dead here, but no one had yet to ask me that question. In fact, from what small time I had been here, I had already gathered it to be a rude question people didn't often ask. Some people were sensitive about their deaths. Let's face it, death isn't a pretty subject. A lot of bad things happen: murder, suicide, worse.

"Um… I don't know that either. Actually, I don't remember anything about my Life."

His face froze, like he was hiding his real emotions. "What's the first thing you *do* remember?"

"The Maze."

He nodded and turned to wipe his face with his hands.

"I do have memories!" I shouted with excitement. "Like, little glimpses of things here and there."

"Such as?" His leery to be hopeful eyes peeked out over his fingertips.

"Nothing really, just sitting in a classroom." Being made fun of. "That's how I remembered my name." I bit my lip. He was getting frustrated with me. "A memory," I added to fill the soon-to-be awkward silence.

Yet the silence continued anyway.

I avoided his gaze by looking at the floor, the ceiling, his desk, my own hands, anywhere but him. The other memory I had, the one with the cake, was too private to share. I wanted to relive it now. It made me feel safe. Familiar. Home.

"I see," he finally said, and then sat up to straighten his papers in a futile manner. "Well, Miss … uh … Hannah, I don't want to get your hopes up. Matters such as this are rarely solved. I'll look into things, but until you can remember something helpful, I'm afraid there's not much else I can do."

I sat there, waiting for more, for some kind of explanation as to why I was this way, why I couldn't remember what everyone else did. But he never responded.

My face fell and my eyes threatened to tear up. He couldn't help me. Well, *wouldn't* from the sounds of it. Something twisted inside my stomach. Anger. Fear. I had a dozen questions to ask him, to scream at his fat, pointless face, but I refused to break down in his office. I refused to become a blubbering, screaming idiot just because he was useless.

I gritted my teeth, shoving my emotions deep.

When I stood, he added, "If you *do* remember something useful, be sure to tell Thomas. He'll relay the information to me, and, if I find anything from it, we can set up another appointment."

That twist in my stomach got stronger. My teeth clinched harder.

He turned his chair away from me and returned to whatever it is he supposedly does, I couldn't tell. I opened the door for myself and went back into Thomas's office. Irritation still filled his eyes when I strolled past him, but I didn't care anymore. I walked out the door in a swift, hateful manner and slammed it behind me. I stood in the entryway, my back against the closed door that led to fruitlessness. As I did, that angry twist turned into pain. I mourned for the Life I didn't know, the memories I hadn't had. I couldn't stop the tears from falling this time.

RESEARCH

I could stand here and mope, accepting my doom to an everlasting amnesia, or I could do something about it. I wiped my face clean, ignoring the flippant rubbernecking of the passing students, and marched to the library.

As I stood in front of the library doors, I realized I wasn't as afraid as last time. Well, they say the first time is always the hardest. I glanced around inside before entering. A few students hovered by the shelves, others bent over books. Few if any noticed my arrival.

I rubbed my fingers across my face to make sure it didn't still show signs of my earlier crying and walked straight to Ms. Papenfuss's desk.

"May I help you?" she asked, far more cordially than I expected.

"Yes," I said. "I need to know what to do if you can't remember your Life."

She blinked once. "Have you met with Mr. Consolver?"

"Yes," I said, unable to keep the bitter tone out of my answer.

"I see," she said and swiveled her chair around before dismounting it, which considering she had been hovering instead of sitting was a strange thing to witness. She opened the little flap on the side that deterred students from entering her desk area and stepped down from her platform. "Follow me."

She took me to a large wooden structure with tiny little drawers, each with their own tiny little handle. She pulled one out. "This is a card catalog. It's just like the one you used as a Live One but on paper instead of a computer screen."

The way she twisted her nose and adjusted her glasses when she said "computer screen" made me think she didn't care all that much for them. Of course I had no idea what she was talking about at the time, so it didn't matter to me how she felt about them.

"You look for the title, author's name (last name first naturally), or subject you're interested in." She pulled out a drawer and flipped through its numerous cards. Bananas; Barrett, Monty; Basset Hound. The listings were endless. "Let's see…" She adjusted her glasses and licked her lips which resembled the paper of the oldest books here.

She floated to the top drawer, opened it, and flipped through its cards while muttering under her breath, "Acorns… Allen… Apples, oops, too far." A moment later she triumphantly pulled out a card. "Ah, here we are, amnesia." Her eyes squinted as she read it, "See Life: memory loss."

With pursed lips, she floated back to the floor next to me, perusing the drawer labels for the proper one.

"This should be it," she said, and pulled on the chosen drawer's handle. The drawer reached at least ten feet from the wall when fully extended. Its yellowed index cards were so tightly packed, I wondered how she managed to pull them apart enough to read even the topmost lettering.

Once again she jerked a card out. This time it was the one I needed. "Here." She handed it to me. "Don't forget to put it back." As she floated away, I realized, she's not really an old bat. She's rather helpful actually. It's just the lines etched in her face from whatever happened in her Life that made her look hateful. That and the way she peered over her glasses.

I spent most of the night pulling books from their shelves and skimming them to see if they would be useful to me or not. When I saw there were only a couple other students left, I piled my remaining collection onto one of the desks and rose to leave. Ms. Papenfuss offered for me to check them out, but I didn't want to be responsible for them outside of the library. Besides, I enjoyed having the excuse to escape everyone else, especially my roommate/s.

My dorm room hallway was nearly empty when I returned, and as I expected, MaryAnn and Twila were sitting on their couch, wisping. I lay on mine and stared at the ceiling, waiting for time to pass.

Twila puffed out a smoke necklace with a pendant.

"Oooo, nice one, Twila," said MaryAnn. "Watch this."

As she exhaled, she coughed to the point her eyes watered. I sat up, concerned. She rose from where she had been doubled over and glared over at me, her pained face turning into a sneer. "Aren't you going to change your clothes?"

"What?" I asked, confused.

"Change your clothes," she practically spat at me, and then continued on with her wisping.

I looked over at Twila, my mouth slightly ajar.

Her compassionate eyes stared into mine. "We still change our clothes here every day like we did when we were alive," she explained.

Not that I remembered changing when I was alive, but who knew? Or cared for that matter? I'm Dead! It's not like ghosts have body odor or anything. I hadn't seen any bathrooms: no toilets, no showers, not even a sink.

I didn't want to argue. "Oh. Thank you," I said.

She glanced over at MaryAnn before smiling reassuringly at me. "You're welcome." She scooted back into the couch and continued wisping, though she didn't seem to have the heart for it anymore.

I flashed my wary eyes at MaryAnn. She was lost to this world. I lay back down on my couch and continued my previous ceiling staring, but I couldn't help chancing periodic peeks at MaryAnn. Twila couldn't seem to either.

THE CLOCK

So that's how I spent the next two weeks. Go to class, eat, go to library, go to room. Oh yeah, and trying to remember to change my clothes everyday too, because apparently that mattered. I didn't experience any new memories during that time, which made me sad. I wanted more memories, especially like the cake one. Every night I concentrated on that one and the feelings of comfort and love it brought, hoping others would make their selves known to me. It became my place of refuge in this world of anguish. However, not only was I not successful, but what memories I did have began to fade.

By the end of those two weeks, that going to my room part became a problem. Twila's presence dwindled until I didn't see her at all the last three days, and MaryAnn became more and more of a danger.

I had learned that wisping was strictly against school rules, no doubt as to why. MaryAnn's alter personality was taking over her normal one, and it wasn't pretty. While I was new to this world, I was somehow smart enough to realize if her little machine was found in my room, it didn't matter if I used it or not, I would be punished with her for having it. I took to hiding it whenever she forgot to. She didn't seem to mind. I think she thought she had done it while she was high or something, and I wasn't about to correct her.

It wasn't that I was too cowardly to talk to MaryAnn about it, although I was, it was that she wouldn't listen. I know this because one day Twila called out to me after feeding.

"Hannah!"

I turned to see who it was, surprised to find Twila, her hair uncombed, and her face full of agony.

"How's she doing?"

It took me a minute to realize who she meant. "MaryAnn?"

She nodded. "I can't stop worrying about her. She wasn't like this before … the wisp." Her paranoid eyes darted to the sides before she whispered that last part.

I winced. I didn't want to hurt her, but I knew I was about to. "She just lies there most of the time, staring at the ceiling like she's not actually here. She doesn't respond when I try to talk to her, I'm not even sure she's attending class anymore."

Twila shook her head. Her eyes glistened with tears when she did. "She's not. She hasn't for days now."

I wasn't surprised. I twisted my head around, making sure no one could hear my next words. "I'm worried, Twila. Wisping is against school rules, and I don't want to get caught with it."

Twila's voice rose an octave when she next spoke. "Yourself? MaryAnn is dying, and all you care about is *yourself*?!"

Her words made no sense to me. "How can she die if she's already Dead?" I tried to be gentle about it, but some things won't go over well no matter how you do them.

"Just because you're Dead doesn't mean you can't die again!" she spat. "We don't live forever, Hannah!" And then she hovered away, her black hair flapping behind her.

What was *that* supposed to mean? We can die after we die?

I felt bad after that. Like maybe I should track down Twila and apologize, but I didn't know where she went. I didn't even know where her dorm room was. And let's face it, she probably didn't want to talk to me right now anyway.

I stood there, imagining the entire population of the Void staring at me, judging me for what they had just witnessed. I was the bad guy in their eyes. The selfish ghost who made their roommate's girlfriend scream at them for being too stupid to realize there was a second Death.

My initial reaction was to run hide in my room, but MaryAnn was the *last* person I wanted to see right now. So I went with my second reaction, run to the area with the least amount of students. I quickly scanned the grounds. The Clock, with its stoic authority staring down on all of us, was so far away from everyone else. Isolated. I had found my solace.

I could tell the Clock was big, but when I got close it felt more like being eaten than visiting a big building. Its monstrous hands now read 9:57. Interesting. A single locked door stood on the inside of one of its legs. I ran my hand along it, relishing the extreme smoothness of it, and wondered what it was for.

I was alone in my presence here. Not a single student floated near the Clock nor, therefore, me. I never found out why. It wasn't that it was off limits or anything. Maybe it was because it stood so close to the edge of the Veil. Maybe because most students considered it a lonely, boring place to be. Whatever the reason, I couldn't thank it enough. Being here, away from everyone else, completely alone, was relaxing to me. My heavy thoughts cleared. My anxiety waned. I smiled at the freedom.

I exited the underside of the Clock and walked several paces on. I wondered where the Veil started, how far it went, how far I could travel without consequence. Without danger. A muddy glow in my peripheral vision caused my head to spin in its direction. My feet carried me backwards as the glow walked slowly from my right to directly in front of me, where it stopped for a minute as if analyzing me. It had no features, no eyes, no mouth, just the blurry shape of a human body. When it finished, it moved on. No words, no indication of why it found me so interesting.

I found myself involuntarily following it. What was this creature? Was it dangerous? I gasped as I hit something sharp, something that tingled every part of me that touched it. The Veil. Not as painful as when I touched the Curtain, but enough to keep me from wanting to touch it again. As I rubbed my sore fingertips together, I realized. The ghostly figure on the other side of the Veil was just that, a ghost. I probably looked the same to it as it did to me, a weird, glowing, featureless blob.

I backed away. I was too close. I couldn't help but stare though. Out there, a mere ten feet from where I stood, was the Void. Critical Rule #1, "Don't leave the school grounds without permission." The rule warned of the Void being filled with all sorts of evil things I was just beginning to learn about in class. Nasty things. Deadly things. Twila had been right. You can die twice. Was that blur I saw one of those things? A demon? A specter? Or something even worse?

I stayed there, within the safety of the Veil, and watched other figures float in the distance. Some came as close as the first one, but most stayed far enough away to appear as glowing dust bunnies from where I stood, leaning against one of the Clock's legs.

As the night wore on, the ghosts thinned until I was eventually staring into blackness. I lost all track of time here. The Clock's chime gonged. Had I been alive, I'm sure it would have deafened me, but I wasn't alive, I was Dead, so it didn't work that way. Instead, it shook me. Imagine if you could see sound, if you could watch the waves travel through the air. Now imagine that air filled with smoke. That's what happened to me. My body waved. I'm sure if the sound had continued, it would have torn me apart, but it stopped. And I ran.

I didn't run because classes were now starting and I was about to be late for them. I ran because even though I didn't need to breathe, it felt like my lungs were being sucked out of my body. I *couldn't* breathe. As soon as I reached the Academy steps, I felt fine. I glared back at the Clock, my new friend turned traitor.

THE TEST

I didn't see Twila at all for the next two weeks. MaryAnn was wisping every day after school now, then lay motionless on her couch for the rest of the evening. I still worried about getting caught with her machine (I now knew to call it a hookah) in my dorm room and so avoided being there as much as possible.

What time I didn't spend in the library, either doing homework or researching my amnesia, I spent with the Clock, which now read 10:25. We had made up since the deafening incident of his inconsiderate bongs. I decided to forgive his lack of warning while he continued doing what he had since his creation without consulting me. It was too beautiful and comforting not to forgive him. That, and I figured out how to avoid being shaken to my second Death when he did bong.

A pattern occurred, one I didn't understand at the time. As the night passed, the number of ghosts on the other side diminished, until eventually, there were none. Then, as the next day came near, they would appear again. When the number of nearby ghosts increased to more than two or three, it was time to leave. The morning gong was soon to sound.

I also learned to turn invisible! Which I thought was super awesome cool. I wasn't very good at it of course. I was only at level one, which basically means I can walk around your living room and you not notice me, for a short while anyway. I still wasn't to where humans with special abilities couldn't see me (not that I wanted to be-more about that later), or touch stuff, but your basic walk-around-haunting-your-house skill I now had.

The library was a different story. Most of the books said to seek out already Dead family members and talk to them, which is a really stupid suggestion since if you remembered your family members, you would remember who you were to begin with and wouldn't be trying to figure that part out. Others were tedious, like *43,673 Ways to Make Sure You're Dead,* which actually suggested cutting your own head off. ... ... Ew. But every now and then I would find something useful. Like Mediums.

Mediums are these amazing humans with the ability to see and talk to the Dead, even if we're invisible. Well, basically invisible. Remember what I said earlier about different levels of invisibility? Anyway, one book said if I found a Medium, I might could use them to find my family, aka who I am. Of course, I had no idea how to do that yet.

Oh yeah, and I hadn't returned to Mr. Consolver either, and not just because I thought he was pointless. I still do, actually. It was because I hadn't experienced anymore memories. Nada. Nothing. Zilch.

My last class of the day, which I did finally make it to, thank you for asking, was Beginning Rules for Hopeful Haunts, or, Surviving the Void depending on your level of optimism. It teaches school rules (too boring to list here, though I will mention it covered hovering and invisibility limitations while within Academy grounds), Void rules (practically nonexistent), and rules when in the Land of the Living. The latter mainly consisted of—

-neither Living nor Dead can cross the Curtain under normal circumstances (not that I wanted to test that theory)

-the Living can exhibit great control over the Dead in the Land of the Living and are therefore very dangerous; and

-if you stay in the Living too long, your soul will deteriorate, aka, you'll die. That would be one of the many ways a soul can achieve their second Death, and no one knew what that was like, but everyone agreed to try and avoid it.

Not two days after learning invisibility, Mrs. Collins announced in Portal's class, "Mr. Dinwiddie tells me you have all learned the basics of Invisibility. Is this true?"

Let's say for a moment that it wasn't true, that somehow, Mr. Dinwiddie either missed someone or lied, would that missed student admit it? I sure wouldn't. So naturally, no one raised their hand, whether truthfully or not.

Mrs. Collins' piercing eyes roamed over all our heads, despite that a lack of response should have been obvious. "Good. Then I will hear no excuses for not taking today's test."

A cascade of groans washed over the entire classroom, including my own.

Mrs. Collins ignored us and seized the side of her desk with both hands. She pushed it out of the way, clearing a wide area from in front of the chalkboard. Not a single hair moved on her head as she did this. Then she grabbed her clipboard of names and called the first one. "Cisco."

Cisco rose from his desk, a confident smirk on his face. The boy behind him snickered. Mrs. Collins reached next to her chalkboard and flipped a switch I hadn't noticed before. It looked like a normal light switch, but instead of turning on any lights, the chalkboard started swirling, first one way and then the other. Cisco stared into it, almost as if he were bored. I glanced over at his friend's face. His eyes held wonder and apprehension.

Mrs. Collins announced, "The exam you are taking today will test your ability to enter the world of the Living via a general portal, come across at least one Living person, and then exit without incident. What is the number one rule, class?"

"You must not be seen," we all recited from memory. I saw Cisco's lips move to the words.

"Precisely. If you are unable to accomplish a single one of these tasks, you will fail the exam. Are there any questions?"

No one raised their hands.

"Good. And don't forget the second rule," Mrs. Collins added.

Once again we chimed, "School portals are not to be used by students without instructor supervision."

"Exactly," she responded, her long skirt stiffly bumping into her ankles like a bell as she approached Cisco whose gaze hadn't veered from the portal. "The portal will open to a random location each time. It will be your responsibility to determine the safety of said location. You will enter, find at least one Live One, stay within their vision *without being seen* for a minimum of one minute, and then return. Understand?"

Darva rolled her eyes and yawned. A handful of others shared her sentiment, but the rest of the class, even the ones who normally hovered with confidence, sat in their desks with a nervous stiffness.

Mrs. Collins turned her back on the class and nodded to Cisco. "Whenever you're ready."

It was only then I noticed what the portal had opened up to, a busy city street with red lights and pedestrians. Glad I wasn't him.

He shook his hands out by his side. Darva snorted and whispered to the girl between me and her. "Bet he can't even make it through." The other girl snorted too, only hers was from laughing instead of derision.

Cisco's fists clenched, and his body stiffened awkwardly for a moment before it faded, his once almost black hair now as translucent as mine. If done correctly, he was now invisible to Live Ones, though we could still see him. He turned to wink over his shoulder at the boy sitting behind his desk, placed one hand on either side of the portal's opening, stuck his head inside, and looked down.

"C-Coward!" Darva coughed unconvincingly. Her friends chortled.

While I wondered if Darva's "famous" family kept her safe from Mrs. Collins, and that was why she had yet to be disciplined for her actions, Cisco put one foot on the bottom of the portal's edge and jumped through.

I sat up in my seat and gasped. Mrs. Collins stepped in front of the portal and stuck her head through, swiveling it from side to side. Every now and then she would pull back and jot a few notes down on her clipboard. The rest of the class, even Darva and her gang, had their necks craned like mine, watching Cisco's performance.

Mrs. Collin's stepped away from the portal as Cisco jumped back into the classroom. He swaggered back to his chair with a smirk. His friend high-fived him then did a funny gripping thing with their hands when he sat down. Mrs. Collins reached over and flicked the switch off. The portal collapsed.

"Pass," she said with as much emotion as a potato.

Several other students went. Most reacted the opposite of Cisco, nervous and glad to have it over with. A couple of them acted like they knew what they were doing. When it was

Darva's turn. Her overly confident body gracefully strutted to the portal, smoothly turned invisible on the way, stepped inside it with the arched strides of a gazelle, and returned with a sneer on her smug face.

"Hannah?"

Um, what? No. No no no. I'm not ready yet.

The words never left my head, but they were there. Oh boy, were they there. Probably written all over my face. Like I said, I thought this test didn't apply to me. I opened my mouth to retort, but then saw Darva's mocking grin. If I cowered out of this, she would only behave worse towards me. The rest of the class was staring at me, waiting. Mrs. Collins began showing signs of impatience. It was now or never, I told myself, although never didn't sound like too bad an option, so maybe I should have told myself something different.

I forced myself to stand. Stinging, nervous currents sparkled throughout my body like land mines. Mrs. Collins flipped the switch. The chalkboard swirled clockwise. Counterclockwise. Clockwise again. Its outer edges reminded me of an eddy, ready to suck me into its black center, but this center held a family. They were sitting at a table, eating their evening meal. One mother, one father, one son.

I approached the opening; my legs trembled until I could barely stand. I wished I knew how to hover!

I took a breath and pressed on it, forcing it into the rest of my body while disallowing any to escape through my mouth or nose. A tingling sensation, like a milder version of the previous currents, washed over me, the feeling of turning invisible. I looked down at my hands, making sure everything looked at it should, and stepped inside.

I didn't breathe once. Not that I couldn't. Once invisible, you can let the air out and suck more in again. I was just too terrified to. The family continued eating as though a stranger had not just plopped into their home via an ethereal portal, and uninvited at that.

The son had his head down, poking at his food. He appeared to be about my age, skin the color of golden honey, hair black as the Void that hung in layers to his shoulders, and a single silver necklace draping around his neck. He seemed to be concentrating deeply on something.

I pulled my eyes from him to view his parents. They were staring at each other, but equally as silent. They had his features, his colors.

I gasped as my first memory in weeks hit me.

"Why is she a different color?" I heard the voice, but I couldn't place the face. Wait, a small boy with light brown hair and glasses too big for his face had asked someone behind me that question.

I glanced down. A dark brown hand lay on my right shoulder. Its contrast made my skin look even whiter than before. I tried to see who it belonged to, tried to turn the memory around in my head so I could identify who it was, but I couldn't. They were behind me, and my memories came solely from what my Living eyes saw at the time.

The memory left me as quick as it came. "Hannah," called Mrs. Collins, and I remembered the test.

I nodded in acknowledgement and walked around the table. The boy sat up when I passed behind him, but I didn't think anything of it at the time.

"Very nice. You're done." Mrs. Collins pulled her head out of the portal and turned her attention to the classroom.

I returned to the front of the table and made to join her at the Academy.

"Hey!"

I whipped my head around when I heard his voice.

"Who are you?" The boy's eyes were the softest, darkest of browns, and they were locked directly onto mine.

THE MEDIUM

If I had been alive, my breath would have caught in my throat. As it were, I stood there gaping at the Live boy at the table like a statue of an opera singer. Both parents glanced my way, but their eyes remained unfocused. They said something to him in a language I didn't understand. He blushed and looked away from me before answering them in the same language. They never glanced my way again, but he did.

"Hannah!" Mrs. Collins called from inside the classroom.

Quickly, before she found out and flunked me for being seen, I whipped back around and jumped through the portal. The last thing I saw were his eyes staring eagerly into mine, like he didn't want me to go.

When my feet hit the classroom floor, I struggled to keep my face from giving anything away. If Darva saw the way it looked a second ago, I was doomed.

I felt the portal close behind me. "Pass," announced Mrs. Collins.

I couldn't stop my eyes from flickering to Darva's desk on the way to mine. Yup, she was disappointed, angry even. Keep it calm, Hannah. Keep it calm.

I sat at my desk and folded my arms across my chest, pretending nothing special happened. Out of the corner of my eye, through the protective layer of hair I had strategically placed, I witnessed Darva staring at me, biting her lip and squinting her eyes in contemplation. She was way too smart for my liking.

I couldn't pay attention to the rest of my classmates' tests or my next two classes. All I could think about was what happened during *my* test. There were three Live Ones. And of those three, one saw me. Why?

As I sat through the first half of Invisible Arts, I remembered Mr. Dinwiddie telling us that basic invisibility only worked on 99% of Live Ones. The other 1% possessed special abilities, like Mediums. I gasped. (Thankfully it was in the middle of one of Mr. Dinwiddie's paltry magic tricks so no one noticed because they were too busy trying not to laugh.) I glanced around anyway then leaned back in my seat to think. That boy was a Medium. And that book I read said Mediums were able to help ghosts learn about their lives. I had to go back. I had to find that boy and ask him to help me remember. But how?

My leg shook up and down from the anxiety. I had a clue, my first real clue in finding out about my Life, in potentially accessing more memories. And I couldn't wait to act on it.

The rest of my classes passed in a painful, never-ending daze. I couldn't concentrate on any of my teachers, not even when Ms. Ohlson of my Beginning Rules class called on me three times to answer a question she had apparently asked that I never heard. Everyone's staring faces wondered what was wrong with me, but I didn't care what they thought. All I cared about was getting to the library.

When feeding was over, I practically ran to the library. I abandoned my original stack of books on amnesia and went straight to the card catalog. "Mediums, Mediums," I mumbled to myself while scanning the labels on the outside of the tiny drawers of cards. "Lo-Ly… Ma… Mc… Me!" It felt like my voice had echoed. I did a quick scan to make sure my excitement hadn't attracted too much attention. It hadn't.

The drawer pulled out easily enough. I flipped through the cards. "Medium" took up three on its own. I sighed but refused to get angry about it. This was a library in the Land of the Dead. What else did I expect? A brochure with answers to my every question and nothing else? Actually, that would be nice. Sadly unrealistic. But nice.

I took the first card with me and pulled every single book down on the subject. I had to ask for help on the ones overhead. Their piles filled my current desk, spilled over into another one, and filled it too. I put the card back. By then Ms. Papenfuss was ready to close, and from the glare she was giving me and my teetering stacks of books, I needed to leave sooner rather than later.

I returned to my previous routine. Every night after feeding, I studied my books in the library until it closed. Days passed, and I was no closer to visiting the Medium boy than when I had started. I decided to skip the library for tonight, take a break from all that research, and Ms. Papenfuss's dirty looks. I always put the books up when I finished with them, but I guess I didn't finish with them fast enough to suit her.

I didn't see MaryAnn at all during this time. She could've been with Twila or left the Academy completely. There was no way for me to tell. They might have kicked her out for wisping. Wisping was against the rules, after all. But if that were true, why was her hookah still where I hid it, under some clothes in a drawer? Wouldn't they have confiscated that in the process?

As I sat in my room pondering how to spend my time, I realized I didn't want to be alone tonight. Maybe I had finally gotten sick of my own company. Maybe somewhere deep down inside of me, my courage was trying to make an appearance. Whatever the reason, I decided to journey into the world of people.

About my third week here, I discovered a play area in addition to the sporting grounds. I was using my rations to purchase a much-needed backpack from the Academy closet when I saw someone enter the other door beneath the entryway staircase. Raucous laughter met my ears when the door opened, arousing my curiosity. When I peeked inside, I found countless tables surrounded by ghosts and topped with cards, board games, and various other pastimes. A couple of pool tables sat at one end, big plastic mats with colored circles at the other. A gramophone played upbeat music from the corner.

Someone bumped into me on their way in, I was still standing in the middle of the entrance. With my new backpack (an otherwise black bag covered with multicolored decorative skulls and a tiny coffin as the zipper) over my shoulder, I walked around the outside edge of the room. Everyone seemed engrossed with what they were doing. A table full of students heavily involved with their card playing reacted when someone yelled something about "super attack plus three". From what I sensed, it was a good thing. The groups by the pool tables were wiggling in beat to the music but otherwise quiet. And the group of students pretzeled over the dotted mats were laughing while someone shouted, "It's not fair if you can go through the others!"

I never felt the need to revisit that place, not even with tonight's desire for company. That place seemed too chaotic for me. I wanted to be *around* people, not *with* them. One allows you to appreciate the benefits of their presence without actually having to interact with them, while the other demands conversation. So, I strolled about the sporting areas instead.

Everyone there was with someone. Girl cliques, boy cliques, younger kids and older kids banded together in intimidating groups that spotted the campus like a pox. And I knew no one. Well, there was MaryAnn and Twila, but I didn't bother searching for either of them. Oh yeah. And Darva. I did search for her, for the sole reason of knowing where to avoid. She was on the sidelines of a football field, her focus fixed on the players and a silly grin on her face.

I turned the walk into a journey, observing everyone around me. If only I possessed the courage to walk up and say hi to someone. I could belong to a group. I could have friends. But the idea of introducing myself to a bunch of strangers frightened me more than being forever alone.

With a defeated sigh, I left the sporting area and visited my old friend the Clock. It was an odd thing, the Land of the Dead. The floor was a slick black with charcoal fog rising from it at least a foot. The ceiling, or whatever was above us, was also black. It had no end. There was no light source. Yet, somehow, we could see. The Clock's polished wood glistened as though somewhere a light shone upon it. I followed the reflection hoping, maybe, I could find its source. I never did.

I ran my hand along one of its thick legs. It felt smooth, like my fingers would mar its perfect beauty, but its polished image remained untouched. The archway formed by its two legs was wide enough for several students to pass under it at once. I let my fingers trail along the inside of one of its legs while I made my way to the other side. The side next to the Veil's edge.

The Veil protected us here. And thanks to the last few weeks of class, I now knew from what. The Void is what makes up the entire Land of the Dead. There are colonies here and there, usually consisting of ghosts who lived in the same era and wanted to carry their culture into Death.

These colonies are relatively safe, just a bunch of ghosts minding their own business. But then you get baddies: wraiths, demons, banshees, phantoms. Not all baddies are bad of course, just like not all colonists are good.

I stared out into the Void. There wasn't a ghost in sight. I hadn't been here much recently, not since I started spending all my free time in the library. As I stared, I wondered why the visible pattern in ghost population occurred. Why it went from several to none, then back up again moments before the new day bongs.

From what I had learned so far in my classes, most hauntings occurred at night. This made me wonder if the ghosts in the Void disappeared because they were haunting their families and then reappeared because morning was near in the Land of the Living. A twinge of jealousy hit me when I realized that possibility. Most of my classmates missed their still-alive family members. They got excited when they talked about the day they could freely haunt them. As long as my memories evaded me, I would never experience that joy.

Is that where they were now? Out haunting their loved ones? Jumping through portals to visit the Living? Wait. Portals. Argh! I hit my fists against the Clock's leg. How could I have been so stupid?

I ran back to the Academy, passing a couple of students along the way who watched me with curious eyes. Wondering why I was running I supposed. I had been researching Mediums all this time when I should have been researching portals.

I jerked open the Academy's front door, only to run into Lydia and Mrs. Richards. They were in the middle of what appeared to be a very serious conversation. Mrs. Richards looked worried.

"I'm sorry to have to ask this of you, but we must get them before— Hannah!" Mrs. Richards' face was livid. "We *walk* inside of buildings!"

"Yes, ma'am," I muttered. As I climbed the stairs, my hand running along its railing, I turned my head around. Mrs. Richards continued talking to Lydia, who stared up at me with that creepy gaze of hers.

"I'm visiting some people in the Void today," Mrs. Richards said.

Lydia shifted her attention back to the Director.

"I don't know why I bother," Mrs. Richards continued. "They're all a bunch of— May I help you, Miss Hannah!" It was not a question.

My face sparkled with embarrassment. I turned back around and climbed the stairs, slightly faster than Mrs. Richards would have liked, but I wanted to get out of there, and she seemed madder about my eavesdropping than my running.

The library was still open, nearly empty, but open. Keeping my head down and my gaze away from Ms. Papenfuss lest I get scolded again, I walked as quickly as I felt I could get away with to the catalog, jerked open its drawers and nearly ripped its cards apart in my search for operating portals. There were over a dozen books on the subject. I found what I needed in the second one:

> While a 'random' portal may indeed seem random, it is not. Due to the receptive nature of specific regions of the Living, much like their radio stations, the portal will cycle through the same coordinates until

the user will, eventually, run across
the same one twice.

Bingo.

I crammed the book back on its shelf, not really caring if it was the right place or not, and ran out the library doors. I heard Ms. Papenfuss scold in my direction before they slammed shut behind me.

My feet danced down the flight of stairs to the second level. I slowed my pace when I entered the classroom hallway. It wasn't easy. I kept having to force my legs to walk instead of run. I looked like a disabled, newborn gazelle. Thankfully no one was around to notice. When I reached the classroom, I quickly checked for anyone nearby. No one. I tugged on the door and went inside.

The chalkboard hung innocently on the wall, its switch which brought it to life next to it. I stood several feet to the side of the board, my throat burning from the excitement and fear. Could I find him again? What would happen when I did?

I flicked the switch. The portal opened. It flooded the room with a brilliant blue that swam with the fluidic motion of the portal's perimeter.

Giving it a wide berth, I stepped in front of the opening. It was night inside, but I could tell it was a park and not the house of my Medium. I flipped the switch off and back on again. A hallway filled with doors with a light by each of them appeared. Nope. Again. A museum. An old school. Someone else's house.

I continued my switch flipping until the Clock sounded. "Wraith dust!" I cursed, but only at a whisper. After making sure the switch was indeed in the off position, and that the room appeared innocent of my meddling, I walked to my room. It was more brisk than someone on an honest mission, and I let my hair dangle over my face, but no one stopped me. I had to hurry to make it back in time, ironic since the classroom I had just left was my first period.

TAO LIN

It took everything in me to survive that day. My leg shook up and down so hard in history class, the girl behind me kicked the back of my chair. I was so close to getting my answers I could taste it. I yearned for nothing more. Feeding time was but a chore in the way of my search for happiness.

I knew teachers often returned to their classrooms after feeding, where they worked on the next day's lessons and such. So even though the desire to return to the portal made me more nervous than MaryAnn craving wisp, I still didn't think it safe going until later that night. I paced in my room instead.

When I felt enough time had passed, I hurried to the classroom and went inside. This time I found an empty parking lot, a warehouse, a different family's living room (I inspected it to make sure), a swimming pool, a pond, an old barn, but not my Medium. The Clock sounded.

I hit the wall in frustration and returned for my books heavy hearted. How many more places would this wretched portal take me to? If I had to guess the number I visited today, I would easily say over a hundred.

With a heavy sigh, I grabbed my backpack and ran back to Portals, only to find the door shut. Dang it! I was late. I silently turned the knob and inched the door open, peeking inside as I did. No one was paying me any attention. I silently shut the door behind me and began creeping toward the back of the room.

"Miss Hannah!" It was even worse since she didn't know my last name, you know, because I still didn't.

I winced and turned to face her. "Sorry, Mrs. Collins. It won't happen again." I started for my desk again.

"Five hundred lines," she commanded before I took my first step.

My jaw fell. I knew exactly what she wanted, 500 lines of, "I will not be late." Due tomorrow.

She returned to writing on the board. As I slouched the rest of the way to my goal, I caught Darva grinning at me like a Cheshire who had just found her mouse.

With the prospects of 500 lines due tomorrow, and the yearning to continue searching the portal, despite its frustrations, the rest of my day passed slower than a drunk snail in tar. Not that I'd witnessed that.

When feeding time was over, I succumbed to writing my lines in my room, telling myself I had time to kill anyway while waiting for the teachers to clear. But the moment I thought it was safe to return, I couldn't help myself. Barely 100 lines in, I threw down my pencil and ran to my Portals classroom. Just twenty, I told myself. Just twenty. No more. Then I'll go back and finish my lines. No matter what.

I peered into the hallway for onlookers as the classroom door shut behind me. The chalkboard gazed at me with a blank stare. I smiled back, eager to begin. I flipped the switch. A forest, a cave, somewhere underwater (that was weird), a dark garage. More than twenty in, for I had not kept my promise, it happened. I came to a room with a table and chairs. Was this it? The room was pitch dark, but the shapes of the chairs mimicked those I remembered.

I leaned my head inside. No noise or movement tainted the shadowy calm. My feet treaded silently past the table and into the kitchen. 3:00 shone in green from a silver box with a small, dark window on the counter. As I stared into its neon glow, another memory stunned me motionless.

The same box, but black. Microwave. 6:27. The smell of hot dogs from a blue plate on the table in front of me.

"You have to cut them up smaller than that or she'll choke." A woman's voice. My mother's voice!

"Yes, dear. I know." Dad!

My fingers reached for a tiny piece of the meat. They looked odd to me, disfigured somehow.

Before I could learn any more, the memory left. I was standing once again in the Medium's kitchen. "No!" I screamed. My first memory in weeks, and it was exactly what I had been searching for. Never had I wanted a memory to continue so badly.

The sounds of my parents' voices lingered in my ears, and I tried to cage them, force them to never leave. The angry tears that promised to form abruptly turned cool. I had parents! Great tears of joy now blurred my vision, and I swayed where I stood. I reached out for the nearest chair to steady myself, but my hand drifted through it, and I fell to the floor.

Ghouls and banshees! I hadn't taken Poltergeist Studies yet. I wouldn't be able to touch anything here except for the floor. Somehow we ghosts, even without the ability to physically touch common objects of the Living, are able to walk on their floors and climb their stairs. Yeah, it never made sense to me either. Pushing myself up, I wiped the wetness from my face, sniffed loudly, and crept up the steps next to the portal.

I found my Medium in the second room on the right. He was in bed, asleep. I walked noiselessly inside. A red light shone from one of the two computers against the wall, their curved monitors illuminating the room with the shapes that moved upon them. A large bed filled the center. By its other side sat a weight bench surrounded with free weights. At its foot, a guitar.

I stood by his bed, my glow mixing with that of the monitors until his body was bathed in a bright disco of reds, whites, and blues. The boy who had called out to me during my test now lay sprawled in a tangle of sheets, which covered so little I could tell he was wearing nothing but a pair of white boxers. They contrasted perfectly with his beautiful skin, making it appear even darker than it normally would.

Before I could force myself to look away and find some way to wake him, his eyes flickered, and he groaned. "Wha's?" He pushed himself up, gazing with sleep-blind eyes in my general direction. "Whoa!"

Apparently that's when he saw me. And realized he was practically naked.

Grabbing what he could of his sheets and comforter, he scurried to cover the lower half of his body.

"Hi," I said, embarrassed but also unable to keep from smiling at his behavior.

"Can I help you?" he asked, annoyed.

"Sorry. I didn't mean to upset you." By this point, I had completely forgotten the reason for my visit.

He tucked his bedclothes underneath his thighs. "Just wake me next time instead of… Wait, you're that girl who popped in at dinner a while back, aren't you?"

I nodded. "And you're a Medium, aren't you?"

"Yeah." He sighed. "I'm a Medium." His eyes surveyed me where I stood, making me feel self-conscious about what I was wearing. I glanced down at my clothes. A grubby white T with a logo of something I didn't recognize and faded, torn jeans. Whew! No unicorns.

"Do you mind if I get dressed?" he asked.

"Oh! Of course not! I'm sorry," I said. And then stood there like the clueless idiot I am.

With a smirk and one cocked brow, he held one hand up and circled his finger, indicating I should turn around.

I mouthed an "O" and did as instructed. The street light shone in my eyes from outside. I stepped closer to the window, eager to witness more of the Living world. A paved driveway branched off the road labeled "Cecil Street". Every lawn was meticulously trim.

"You know, I've been hoping I'd see you again," he said.

I didn't understand why, but his words lit a hot fire in my chest that split into bolts of lightning. The bolts traveled down my arms and legs, and I found myself breathing faster. "You have?"

I heard him wrestle with his shirt as he spoke. "Yeah. Some weird stuff's been going on, and I was hoping someone could tell me what it was about." A zipper zipped. "You can turn back around now."

Slowly, as if asking permission as I did, I rotated back around to face him. He was busy making up his bed and didn't notice.

"What weird stuff?" My words flowed out without uncertainty. This was the first time I had spoken with a Live One, yet somehow, it was more comfortable than talking with ghosts.

He ran his hand through his hair, pausing to scratch the back of his head. Then he glanced my way as though just now seeing me. "I'm sorry! Would you like to sit down?"

He grabbed a chair by his computer and offered it to me.

I shook my head. "I can't."

His brow lowered in confusion.

"I haven't learned how yet."

Like a yo-yo, his brow rose until it disappeared behind his black hair. "You haven't learned *how* yet?"

"Yeah. Um, before we can touch stuff, we have to learn how. There's a class for it!" I announced, happy to know something someone else didn't for once. "Poltergeist Studies."

"Poltergeist Studies," he repeated, his face full of disbelief and wonder.

I lowered my gaze and saw my glow widen in my peripheral vision as I felt the blush. Did he have to put on trial?

"Is it OK if *I* sit down? I'm still half asleep." His voice sounded kind, putting me more at ease. He didn't wait for me to respond.

We remained silent for a moment, him in his chair, me standing like the awkward glowing elephant in the room.

"Um, what's your name?" I asked when I could take the silence no longer.

"Ugh, where are my manners tonight?" He stood and held out his hand for me to take. "I'm Tao. Well, Lin really. My parents are really traditional so I go by my surname first, but since you're American, you can call me Lin. Wait, you are American, right?"

I reached for his hand without thinking. My fingers went through his. When they did, I saw him shiver. Simultaneously, my hand felt like it had gone through fire. "Ow!"

"Sorry," He winced and sat back down. "I'm not thinking straight."

I inspected my fingers while rubbing them with my other hand. They looked unharmed.

He rubbed his palms on his thighs, not noticing. "So, back to what I wanted to ask you about. When people die, it usually just takes a few days for them to appear as ghosts, and then I can talk to them if I want. Well, not when *I* want. It's more when *they* want—"

I shook my head. "I don't understand."

He sighed and did that thing with his hair again. It wasn't an annoyed, impatient sigh, just a thoughtful "How do I explain this?" sigh. "In order for me to talk to a ghost, they have to want me to. If I know their name, I can call them, but I can't make them come."

"Oh," I said, and immediately thought of all the warnings we had learned about. "The Living will trick you. They will lie to you. They will tell you what you want to know, what you *need* to know to keep you there. Don't trust them." Was this what was happening now? Was he lying to me to get me to stay?

"Anyway," he said, "something happened here lately that's got me concerned." He paused, assessing my response. I put on a blank face and waited for him to continue. "I used to get visited two or three times a week. Sometimes by new ghosts, sometimes by familiar ones. But now, no ghosts visit me. At all. No new ones, no old ones, none."

I lifted my brow in wonder.

"I had one a few weeks ago. She acted so scared. She said something about a guy named Ronnie and being turned into wisp…"

I stiffened. Ronnie was the name the two voices in the Maze mentioned. And wisp…

"You're the only one I've seen since." He smiled. "That's why I was hoping to see you again."

I know it was stupid and naïve, but his words made all those warnings in my head vanish. There was no way I could believe Lin was dangerous.

"Do you know what's going on?" he asked, unaware of the party of thoughts in my brain.

I bit my lip. "Ronnie was the name I heard in the Maze."

"The Maze?"

I nodded. "And wisp is … a drug … I guess. My roommate smokes it to get high."

He sat silent a long moment before saying, "Maybe it would help if you told me your story."

"My story?" My gaze rose to meet his. His eyes were kind, curious. He kept his distance, even though I could tell he wanted to reach out and comfort me.

"Yeah," he said. "Most ghosts like to tell me how they died, who they were when they were alive, that sort of thing. Or at least they used to."

I turned to face the wall. That's when the oddest thing happened. My story spilled out. And that spill turned into a gush. It was like my words controlled themselves and were going to be heard no matter how much I protested. They told him about my amnesia, that I only knew my first name. About the Maze, the Veil, the Void, the Academy and my experiences there. My memories, and the reason I had sought him out. He smiled when I told him that part. He said a lot of ghosts came to him with questions, but none ever had amnesia before.

Every time I glanced at his face, his soft brown eyes urged me to go on until I had told him every single painful detail about my entire Death. Not once did he judge me.

When the last of my experiences was recounted, he waited until it was clear I was finished. "So, you can only eat what the Living burn," he confirmed.

"Yes," I said.

"What's your favorite food?" he asked with a grin that displayed his flawless row of white teeth.

It had taken me a while at first to distinguish between the different foods during my feedings, especially since I didn't have the memories from my Life to help me out. But by now I had gotten able to recognize meats, several vegetables, and chocolate. Yeah, chocolate was definitely in my "I know this" list. I glowed another blush. "Fudge brownies."

"Good to know." He grinned, and when he did, his dark eyes twinkled. And my stomach turned over.

Another round of awkward silence ensued. I couldn't help but notice him staring at me with such intensity I kept pushing my hair behind my ears even though it was already there. My cheeks burned with the glow of a thousand suns.

"Would you like to know who you were?" he finally asked.

A warm feeling of hope came over me, washing away my shyness. "You can do that?"

"I can try," he said. "Do you know when you died?"

I bit my lip. "I don't know." I shrugged. "A month? Maybe more?"

He nodded. "Anything else you can tell me?"

"Just my memories." I hadn't gone into detail about my memories earlier, just that I'd had them.

His expression urged me to continue.

"They're not very good." I relayed my memories to him, all of them. He grabbed a pad of paper from his desk and took notes. He acted methodical, not pausing or doing anything to shame me when my memories traveled down the awful path of being mistreated by classmates. Then he did something with one of his computers and started typing in some stuff.

Several minutes later, he turned back to me with an expression of optimism. "Tell ya what. You look into whatever's causing the ghosts to be too afraid to visit me anymore, and I'll try to find out who you were when you were alive. Deal?"

He held out his hand for me to shake. My stomach did another flip. "Deal," I said, and being the idiot that I am, went to grab his hand. Obviously, my hand went straight through his, and since I had already allotted the necessary force for contact, the unused momentum caused my body to fall forward, through him, and land on the floor. I'm sure my glow of embarrassment could now be seen in the next state.

He rolled his chair out of the way and moved his hands around awkwardly. "I'm so sorry! I would offer to help you up, but it would only make it worse."

Yes. It would only make it worse. My body was still burning in the places that had touched his.

"Oh crap!" He looked to the window.

I pushed myself up and followed his gaze. "What's wrong?"

"It's dawn. I have school soon, and I haven't gotten enough sleep." He grimaced. "I'm going to be tired all day."

Dawn. I gasped as the realization of what that meant hit me. "I have to get back!"

I sprinted to the stairs. The Clock would sound soon, if it hadn't already, and I would have to be in class. I skidded to a halt at the top of the steps. "Double crap!"

"What's wrong?" he asked, catching up to me.

Fear drained all the glow from my face. "If Mrs. Collins is already in her classroom…" I dared not finished the thought.

I ran down the stairs so quickly my heels never touched them. The portal was still open, a good sign.

"Thanks!" I hollered over my shoulder with a wave. I saw him wave back, a confused expression on his face. I jumped through the portal. Right into Mrs. Collins' angry face.

PUNISHMENT

"Miss Hannah!" The reflection of the portal's light swirled across Mrs. Collins' furious face. "I *am* surprised. I would have expected it from one of my more adventurous students, but *you*!"

Triple crap.

I could hear my approaching classmates in the hallway and knew this incident would not go unpunished. Mrs. Collins flipped off the portal, strolled over to the now normal chalkboard and wrote, "Continue working on the exercises on page 237."

She placed the piece of chalk in its precise place and said, "Follow me."

I complied silently.

If I thought my first walk along my dorm room hallway was embarrassing, it was nothing compared to the walk of shame I was now enduring.

"Ooo-oo-oooooo, someone's in trouuublllle," one student sang to the others who soon joined in with raucous laughter and snide remarks about my impending doom.

I knew Darva was nearby and had to be making fun of me with her friends. I peeked through my hair but didn't see her.

Mrs. Collins took me to Mrs. Richards' empty office. "You will wait here," she said.

"Yes, ma'am." Sitting felt inappropriate. The uncomfortableness of standing suggested my punishment had already begun. The relaxed world of sitting only added to my sins. I chose to stand.

The office seemed cold with no one in it but me. I didn't dare walk around, but my eyes wandered freely. I saw things I didn't the first time, all teary-eyed and fresh from the Maze.

In the back was a mock fireplace. Someone had stacked a few short logs on its grate. Tiny globes of light essence dangled over them.

On the far wall was a row of hooks, some empty, some with cloaks, hats, and other typical objects. Next to it was a doorway. I could just catch the edge of a quilt on a piece of furniture through its opening.

Mrs. Collins returned with the Director and shut the door. Mrs. Richards strode behind her desk with an air of livid authority. And sat.

She did not offer for me to sit, making me believe myself correct in my previous assumptions. I clasped my hands tightly in front of myself and faced my punishment with trembling terror.

"Mrs. Collins has informed me you don't have the proper respect for school rules," Mrs. Richards said.

"Oh no, ma'am. I—"

Her sharp glare cut me off. When it was clear I wouldn't speak again, she said, "Four days should do it."

Four days? Four days of what?! My eyes widened with desperate anticipation as my imagination went wild with all the horrible arrangements she could possibly have in store for me. Four days in the Void? Four days with no food? Four days in the Maze with the wraith and the demons I now knew lived there? I nearly fainted over that last thought.

"You can start today," she said.

My knees trembled, and I reached for the chair next to me for support.

She either didn't notice or ignored my reaction. "Mrs. Collins? Please direct Miss Hannah to room 4F13."

I turned to Mrs. Collins with the futile hope her actions might give away their plans for me. "Yes, Director." Her eyes did not meet mine.

Mrs. Collins opened the door and held it in expectation. I took a deep breath to steady myself, then moved my stiff legs one at a time. They put up a good fight, but I eventually won out and walked with some ambiance of normalcy.

She shut the door behind us and walked briskly away. I followed slowly, that battle between my mind and legs still waging. The Director had said room 4F13, therefore I was expecting to be lead down the classroom hall. Instead, Mrs. Collins lead me to my room and instructed me to get my books. My fear expanded as some of my earlier imaginings seemed more plausible now.

She stayed outside while I grabbed my bag of books. The temptation to stay in my room was strong, but she was standing in the open doorway staring at me. I watched her face as I stepped into the hallway. Still no answers.

She closed my dorm and led me back to the grand staircase. Some of my strength returned to my legs when I saw her open the classroom hallway double doors. It was looking now more like I would spend four days in a single classroom doing some kind of school work, and since I needed my backpack to do it, it couldn't be that bad. Could it?

Room 4F13 was on the left, and looked like every other classroom I'd seen so far. Less than a dozen students already occupied it. Each were bent over their desks working diligently on something. A few glanced my direction when we entered.

A fat man with thin, grey hair and wobbly cheeks that drew his mouth down so two valleys ran next to it turned his attention from the magazine on his desk to us, his new visitors.

"Mr. Hill," announced Mrs. Collins. "Miss Hannah will be spending the next four days with you."

Mr. Hill grunted and flicked his fingers out to one of the many empty seats before me.

I grabbed one near the back and dropped my bag onto the floor. As soon as Mrs. Collins left, Mr. Hill rose from his desk, grabbed what appeared to be a random book from his sparsely supplied shelf, and tossed it on my desk in front of me. "Start copying," he ordered. He then walked back to his desk and sat down.

I stared at him, unsure what to do. He returned to his magazine and ignored me.

"Psst," the boy next to me hissed.

I stared at him. He looked familiar.

He drew a circle with his finger and mouthed, "Open it up."

I recognized him now. He was Cisco, the dead-at-fifteen year old boy from my Portals class. What was he doing here?

I opened my book. It was on home improvement. The chapter was titled, "How to Fix Shelves." I stared at Cisco, more comfortable now I knew someone in the class. OK, not *know* know, but we had sat in the same class together for a good while now. That's a step up from the rest of the students in here.

"Start copying," he whispered.

I glanced back at the book:

I groaned. "Seriously?" I mouthed towards Cisco.

Mr. Hill cleared his throat. I peeked up at him. He was staring at the two of us with disdain. Cisco went back to work. I scanned the rest of the students' desks. They each had their head bowed low over their own book and were copying its contents onto paper. I glanced at Mr. Hill again, whose raised eyebrows were waiting for me to get started. Well, it's better than demons in the Maze, I thought, and rummaged through my backpack for a spiral notebook and pencil.

I really hoped when she said, "four days" she meant four regular school days and not four literal days. Mr. Prickett was right that first feeding. I felt the hunger by the end of every school day now. It wasn't a bad feeling, just a little "that might be nice" feeling. I mean, I could go four days without feeding, but I'm pretty sure by then it would be an "I must eat now or you will die" feeling. Also, I had work to do. Lin had said he would help me learn who my family was, who I was, but he wanted me to find out why the ghosts were too afraid to visit him in return. And although I didn't think he would hold out on me if I didn't get the information for him, I didn't want to chance it. Besides, I wanted to make him happy. Remembering about Lin made my face glow. I glanced to see if anyone had noticed. I don't think they did.

I copied a few lines and concentrated on how to find the information Lin was looking for. My go-to so far had been the library, but I didn't see it working in this case. As I copied sentences about picking the right fastener for affixing the shelf to the wall, I realized I was going to have to ask people questions.

I peeked through my eyelashes at Mr. Hill. He was picking his nose and flicking what he found off to the side while reading his magazine. The other students continued their copying, the sounds of their pencils scratching their papers the only noise in the room. Did they know the reason no one would visit Lin anymore? Could they tell me about Ronnie?

I returned to my copying. If I had to ask questions, I had to make friends. That thought made me cringe. I let my pencil scribble out another paragraph about proper leveling techniques until the cringe subsided.

Who could I make friends with? Wouldn't it seem kind of weird that the new girl who never talks to anybody suddenly starts striking up conversations?

"Hey!"

My head jerked up in response. Who said that?

"Psst," Cisco hissed.

I glanced at Mr. Hill. He was still engrossed with his magazine. "What?" I whispered back at Cisco.

"What's your name?"

Now's your chance, I told myself. Someone trying to be friends with you. You can do this. "Hannah," I told him.

"I'm Cisco."

"I know," I said. "We have Portals together."

My answer took him by surprise. "Oh yeah." He grinned. "So what'd you do to get in here?"

I chewed my lip. Did I really want to tell him that? "You first," I said.

His smile became a mischievous grin. "I broke into a friend's room."

My eyes widened. "You what?"

He shrugged. "I was playing a joke on him, but the Director didn't think it was funny." He smiled expectantly at me. "Your turn."

I swallowed. "I-I used the school portal without permission."

"Whoa." He drew the word out for at least two seconds. "Why? Were you visiting your family?"

Mr. Hill turned a page noisily. I copied a couple more sentences before answering, "I don't have a family."

"What?" he asked over his pencil, keeping his head low. "Are you an orphan?"

Ugh! This was the stuff I hated. I didn't like talking about my unknown past. It only resulted in endless questions I couldn't answer, surprised expressions others miserably failed to hide, and mocking. I closed my eyes and gritted my teeth. Mr. Hill shuffled in his seat, giving me the excuse I needed not to answer.

"Not now," I hissed back. "We'll get into trouble."

I hurried to scribble the next few words, "using a 3/4 inch wood screw".

"When?" Cisco whispered. He was persistent. Persistently annoying.

I exhaled slowly through my nose. "Whenever we get out of here." I still wasn't clear on when that was.

He nodded and returned to writing.

CROQUET

When the day ended, to my immense relief, Mr. Hill released us with the rest of the classes. "Put your books back on their shelves and your papers on the corner of my desk," commanded Mr. Hill without viewing to see if any of us were doing as instructed. Everyone complied though. Afterwards, we exited into the hallway and became normal kids again, like Mr. Hall had some magic spell over us that was broken by the door frame of his classroom.

"Hey! Wait up!" Cisco called out as he ran to catch up to me.

Oh yeah. Even though I had been dreading this exact moment, I had oddly forgotten about it. I stopped until he was next to me, then continued walking again.

"So are you?" he asked.

"Am I what?" I asked.

"An orphan."

Seriously? This was his opening question for me? "Oh. I don't know," I responded. Wait for it…

"I'm sorry."

Wait. What? I stopped dead in my tracks, causing a couple of ghosts to run into me from behind. "Sorry!" I called out to them.

I had been anticipating Cisco to reply in the usual way of, "What do you mean, you don't know?" or "How can you not know?" not for him to apologize.

"Um, thanks," I said.

"So what'd you do?" he asked.

"What do you mean?"

"To get detention?"

"Is that what that's called?" I asked.

He smiled, displaying a literally glowing set of perfectly white teeth. "Yes. Sitting in Mr. Hill's class all day copying his books is called detention, and you have to have done something wrong to get put in it."

We started walking again. "I told you what I did. I used the school portal."

"Yes, but why?"

We stood at the top of the staircase. I couldn't help but notice he didn't hover even though I know I'd seen him hover in Portals before. He was being nice to me, like, not the fake I'm-going-to-stab-you-in-the-back-when-you-turn-around nice but the real nice, the kind you don't recognize unless you look for it.

"I ran into a Medium when I took my Portals' exam," I told him. "I had read they can help you find out stuff about your Life, so I tried to find him again."

"And did you?" He seemed sincerely interested.

"Yes." I smiled from the memory. "I did, and he agreed to help me out."

"That's great!" His grin grew.

We stood silently as his grin faded away. I didn't know what to say next. This whole friendship thing was new and scary to me. Do I go ahead and tell him everything now or find some obscure topic to talk about, like the weather we don't have?

Since that latter part boggled me to the point of patting my fist against my hip in angst, I decided to let it all out. What was the harm at this point? The worst that could happen is he runs away laughing at me, the word gets out what I'm looking for, and someone somewhere answers the question. Right? Either that or I go from "the girl who shall remain invisible" to "Let's all point and laugh at the moron."

Time to dive in. "There's something he wants me to do for him in return."

"What's that?" His brow dipped in confusion.

I glanced around me, suddenly aware of all the ears close by. "Not here," I said.

Catching on, he said, "Meet me after supper by the croquet field. No one ever goes there."

I agreed and took off for my room. After stowing my books away and then feeding (chicken, someone's attempt at homemade bread, and hot dogs — sadly no fudge brownies), I hung around the croquet field, that place with the little wire arches and colored balls I had noticed my second day here. A short time later, Cisco showed up. He left behind a few chortling guys, who kept giving me funny glances.

"Hannah!" Cisco called out to me.

"This is the right place, right?" I asked.

"Have you never played croquet?" he asked.

"I'd never heard of it until I died and came here."

"Ah." His smile was never ending, like a little kid who always has some internal joke to dwell upon. "Well, you take one of these." He reached for one of the mallets in the stand. "And then you wack your ball through the arches until you hit the stick on the end."

I hadn't noticed the stick before, but there it was, a tiny pole poking out of the ground by the last arch on either side.

He hit one of the balls to demonstrate. It went through the nearest arch and hit another ball before rolling to a stop.

"So your Medium wants something from you." It was a statement, not a question. He nodded his head towards the remaining mallets, indicating I should take one.

As I did, I thought about the best place to start in my story. "Lin, that's his name, said ghosts don't visit him like they used to."

I struck a ball. It bounced off the side of the arch I was aiming for. "He said they used to come several times a week, but he hasn't seen any in a long time."

Cisco drove his ball through another arch, then stared expectantly at me.

"He wants to know why," I added.

Cisco still didn't respond.

"So … um … that's what I'm trying to figure out," I said. "Do you know why?"

His face remained serious. He was no longer the jovial kid with a joke on his mind. "I have heard something," he said.

He peeked over both our shoulders for any eavesdroppers before dishing out, "I heard Darva telling her friends something about disappearing ghosts."

"Wait. Darva? Black hair all over her arms, likes to be mean, in our Portals class Darva?"

"That's the one," he said with disdain.

"Why would you trust anything she says?" I sure wouldn't.

"The Bishops are big around here. If anyone in the Void knows something, they do."

Darva Bishop. Funny, you would've thought I would have gone to the trouble to learn the last name of a thorn in my side that big, but I hadn't.

"Anyway," he continued, "she said everyone in the Void is scared right now because ghosts are going missing, and we're not talking oldies either."

"What do you mean, oldies?"

He spun his head around again, checking for uninvited ears. "They're the really old ghosts close to dying."

I knew we eventually died … again, but I didn't understand how or why or anything else about it. I allowed my face to show my confusion.

He explained, "When the time comes, we don't … *die* die. We sorta … disappear in pieces. Eventually. I mean, it takes a really long time, like hundreds of years, or more. I don't really know. It depends on the ghost. But oldies are on their way out."

My eyebrows rose in utter disbelief. "So bits and pieces of us fall off until there's nothing left?" I wanted to scream my question, but it came out as a strained whisper.

"Basically, yeah." This was old news to him, something he came to terms with long ago. Disturbing.

I stood silent for a minute, unable to process the horrible thing I had just learned. He went back to playing croquet, making it look like nothing interesting was going on between the two of us.

"Ok," I said when I got my wits back. "What else can you tell me?"

"Not much." He shrugged, hitting another perfect shot through two arches and into the stick at the end. "Just that ghosts started going missing, so the others got scared and quit wandering around and stuff." He stood with his mallet over his shoulder.

I bit my lip. So the ghosts were disappearing. But why? How? Were we in danger from it? "I need to know more," I told him. "I need to know what's causing them to disappear."

His face became motionless as he thought about what I said. Then a grin spread its way across his cheeks. "What we need, is a field trip."

"A what?"

"A field trip! We'll leave the Academy and ask the ghosts around the Void," he practically screamed with excitement.

I shook my head fiercely. "No way! I'm already in detention for using a portal. I am *not* going to get in even more trouble for breaking another school rule, and I'm pretty sure it's an even bigger rule than the portal one. Besides, it's dangerous out there! I haven't had Defensive Actions yet. I can't even tell the difference between a wraith and a demon. I can't protect myself."

"Ah." He waved his hand at me, still grinning from ear to ear. "Don't worry about that. That's not the hard part. The hard part is getting through the Veil."

"That's not the hard part?" I asked in disbelief.

He shook his head. "No, we can always run back here. That's what the Veil's for, to protect us. We won't go far," he assured me.

I thought about this for a moment. He got his information from Darva, a link to an outside source. Everyone said her family was one of the most powerful and knowledgeable out there. "What else did Darva say?"

He shook his head. "Nothing. That was it."

If she didn't know more about it… I sighed. He was right. We would have to leave the Veil, or buddy up to Darva. I pondered my choices for a fraction of a second before quickly deciding to take my chances with the demons of the Void. "OK, so how do we get through?" I asked.

He smiled big and put his mallet up. "You ever notice that necklace round the Director's neck?"

I tried to remember what she wore. Yes, the first time I saw her. She had a disc on the end of a gold chain. "Yes," I said.

"That's a special medallion that allows you to travel through the Veil. There's several of them, but only certain people own one. The Director's one of them."

I could see where this was going and backed my head away in response. "I'm not stealing the Director's necklace, Cisco."

He shrugged. "It doesn't have to be the Director's."

My jaw fell. He was serious. He expected me to steal a necklace off one of the Academy's faculty. "And how am I supposed to do this?"

His fingers rubbed his smiling, arrogant chin. "If you want to find out what's going on, you'll find a way."

I felt my eyes squint in anger. "You little—"

"Hey," he said, his arms outstretched as he backed away from me. "I've done my part. There's nothing in this for me." He used his spread palms to tap his chest. "I'm just doing you a favor."

My jaw couldn't decide whether to fall to the floor in horror or grind against itself in outrage as he pivoted around and returned to his friends by the Academy's steps. I threw my mallet to the ground, breaking it in two as I did.

THE RETURN
OF MARYANN

There had to be another way to get the information I needed then stealing the Director's necklace, I thought as I walked back to my room, still fuming over Cisco's arrogance. And there was no way I believed he was doing this selflessly for me. Unfortunately, that didn't matter. I needed him, of that he and I both knew.

I went to my couch and sat down. I had gotten so used to being alone, I didn't bother checking when I entered anymore.

"Hey, roomie."

The hookah on the table proved what her sedated words already had. MaryAnn was back, and high as the Veil on wisp.

"Where have you been?" Not the friendliest words, I know, but I didn't care anymore.

"Out," she answered.

"Out? That's it? Just out?"

A bizarre grin had seized her face, like she was laughing, but there was no noise. Her clothes, although it had been so long I couldn't be positive, were the same ones I last saw her in. Her hair lay in tattered clumps across the arm of the couch, and her glow carried a dull tint, like something had diminished it somehow. How could anyone, after seeing this, after seeing someone destroy themselves with wisp, want to try it?

I grabbed the hookah and held it over my head. She didn't move. Her eyes remained unfocused, staring off to a place which only existed in what was left of her mind. My fingers dug into the hookah's s sides, itching to throw it onto the floor, smashing it into unrecognizable pieces. My arms tensed and untensed, brought the hookah before and behind my head in their repeated indecision. I wanted to watch it shatter, watch it never hurt another person again, but I couldn't.

She may not be aware now, but when she came to, when she found out what I had done… With my fingers still pressed so tightly against it I feared it might crack, I brought the hookah carefully back down to the table and backed away. I had seen her wrath and didn't want to experience it. I was still new enough, and her experienced enough, she could hurt me in ways I didn't know about. Maybe it was time to tell someone.

I glared at the hookah, but then I noticed something. It was empty. That gave me an idea. I went to her drawers against the front wall. She had to have a stash somewhere. While she would massacre me for demolishing her wisping machine, I might be able to convince her she had smoked the rest of it and forgot about it or something. Maybe. I hoped anyway. The fleeting thought of blaming Twila did enter my mind, but I pushed it away with disgust. I was desperate, but I wouldn't do that.

I yanked open the top drawer and ravaged through her clothes: several pairs of pants, some socks, and a few folded shirts. The next drawer contained her school books and another pair of shoes. The last held odd trinkets. One of those trinkets was a set of wet clothes: a T-shirt with a logo and a pair of shorts. I picked them up, and when I did, they dripped water everywhere. I dropped them back in the drawer, where they had soaked into it enough to wet the wood, but not enough to pool. How long had they been in there? I wondered. The only thing that made sense is they were from today, but why would she cram them in the drawer instead of hanging them up to dry? And when did we have water? I didn't remember any mention of it in any of my classes. No, wait. In my Beginning Rules class, the teacher mentioned something about there being no water in the Land of the Dead. This made even less sense now.

MaryAnn halfway mumbled, "I can't find any. I can't do it. I ca—."

I abandoned the wet things and ruffled through the other items: pencils, paper, folded up notes. The items were small and had scattered all over the inside of the drawer. I reached behind them, all the way to the back, my fingers probing for anything I might have missed. As I did, my fingers ran across something hard, metallic. Like a small chain of sorts. I grabbed hold and pulled it out.

My legs pushed me into a standing position, and my mouth fell open without my control. Dangling from my fingers was a gold chain, and on the end of that chain, was one of the very medallions Cisco and I had just spoken about.

What was MaryAnn doing with one of these? I glanced at her hookah again, empty. And I had found nothing in her drawers to fill it with. Of course! I smacked my forehead with my palm. She had to get the wisp somehow, and this was it. Taking it from her would kill two birds, my need for information and her need to quit the wisp.

If I took it now, she would know it was me. She saw me here tonight. But would she remember? I tried to recall what had happened in the past. It seemed so long ago. There were several times she retained no memory of what happened when she was high. Those times became more frequent as time went on. No, I don't believe she'll realize I'm the one who took her pendant. I crammed the necklace into my pants' pocket and slid the bottom drawer shut.

Before I finished standing, someone knocked on the door. I stood motionless a minute, afraid, waiting for them to go away. Who could it possibly be? A teacher? I glanced back at MaryAnn and the hookah — I was doomed.

Could it be another student? The only safe one right now would be Cisco, maybe. But if he already knew where my room was, that felt a little creepy.

"MaryAnn, are you in there?" It was Twila's voice.

I stopped myself from jolting to the door and letting her in. I didn't know the current status of their relationship, but I could only assume it wasn't good. Still, not answering could arouse suspicion.

After attempting to remove all guilt from my face, I cracked open the door and peeked outside. Remorse filled Twila's worried face. "Is she back?"

I nodded, knowing now where MaryAnn had been all this time. Not with Twila, not in class, not under the protection of the Veil. Out in the Void. Alone.

Twila's expression told me I didn't have to explain what state my roommate was in. She shifted on her feet a few seconds before asking, "Can I come in?"

I nodded and opened the door just enough for her to squeeze through, then shut it again.

Twila hesitated as she approached the couch. MaryAnn lay unmoved from her previous position, her dull eyes fixated on a corner in the ceiling, and that terrifying grin on her face. Twila stared at her a long moment. "I told her to quit. I knew this would happen."

This whole situation made me very uncomfortable. I had so many questions, like where does the wisp come from and why was there a pile of dripping wet clothes in MaryAnn's drawer, but this not only seemed the inappropriate time for such inquiries, questions such as those divulged too much of my recent actions.

This did however seem the appropriate time for leaving, for which I was greatly relieved. So, without making another sound, I slid out the door.

As soon as the door shut behind me, I entered another world. A world with prying, dangerous eyes that saw all my secrets just from my standing there. I kept my gaze down and tried to look normal as I hurriedly marched to the staircase. I refused to acknowledge the eyes I imagined focused on me, searching for the disc I now carried. I had to get out of here. I ran down the steps and out the entryway door. The front of the Academy always attracted fewer ghosts.

No one was on this section of the Academy's porch. I utilized the moment to process my situation and figure out what to do next. In my pocket was a teacher's medallion. Well, there was no guarantee it was a teacher's, but I was willing to bet half my essence it wasn't MaryAnn's. I couldn't keep it on me; it was too dangerous. I had nowhere to hide it, not really.

What was I getting myself into? I had lost my mind! That's what it was. I had sucked in enough secondhand wisp that I was as looped out as MaryAnn stayed. What was I thinking? That now I held the medallion I could just run into the Void, get the information I needed, and voila! mission accomplished?

A couple of students neared this side of the Academy's porch. I loped down the steps and onto the black floor of the Veil-protected Void at the front of the Academy. Ahead of me lay the Maze. I hadn't been this close to it since Lydia found me, and I had no desire to get any closer. The Clock stood to my right. With a spin I hoped came across as planned and natural on the ball of my right foot, I headed towards it. I should be alone there. There I could think.

No one stopped me. No one followed. My plan had worked. I was alone. Now what? If I was going to accomplish anything, I seriously needed to think this thing through.

Snuggled up in my pocket lay the key to the outside world. Answers to my questions. I gazed out passed the Veil, into the black black Void. I knew what lived out there. Specters, ghouls, banshees, everything the Veil protected us from. I didn't want to venture it alone.

Cisco had said that part was easy, but I didn't trust Cisco anymore, not after the stunt he pulled on the croquet field. For all I knew, he would take the medallion and abandon me in the Void without a way back. I would be lost and alone, a fun snack for a passing wraith.

But could I do this without him? Could I journey the Void without a guide and make it back in one piece? Would I ask the right people? The right questions? No, I needed someone, and that someone had to be Cisco. He was my only option. It was clear he was using me, but I needed to use him to.

My fingers gripped the medallion through my pocket. My decision had been made.

FIGHT

The last place I remembered seeing Cisco was with his friends behind the Academy. The vents had just closed, so there was plenty of time to go on our "field trip" as he called it before classes began again. Maybe I would even get back in time to return MaryAnn's medallion before she noticed.

I began my search. Cisco and his friends weren't on the back porch where I had left them, nor were they by the croquet field. The volleyball, basketball, and bowling areas all came up empty. I searched everywhere but the football field, because Darva was there, and I was hoping not to go near her. When everywhere else came up empty, I searched again. Twice. Finally I succumbed to searching the football field.

Darva appeared consumed by her friends' attentions on the sidelines, so I crept in between two students in a crowd several yards down from her and scanned the field. I knew it was pointless; neither Cisco nor any of his friends seemed the type to play the sport, but now I had made the decision, I had to follow through with it.

The participating ghosts stood down on one end of the field, lining up for a play. I stretched my head over the sideline and cocked it so I could check each of the players' faces. Several were turned the opposite direction. I would have to wait for them to look this way before I could see their features.

One of them shouted, causing the rest of the players to go into motion. They came my way. As my eyes quickly examined each face, someone pushed me from behind. I landed front first onto the artificial turf, smack dab in front of a dozen running football players.

I felt the breeze of one as they hovered over me. The second one wasn't as lucky. His toe landed in my side, causing me to scream out in pain and him to career over my back and into the turf next to me.

When the players stopped moving, and I could push myself up, the shouting started.

"What is *wrong* with you?"

"You caused us to lose the play!"

Most of the voices were unrecognizable to me. They were the players', big burly teenage boys who thought I was either too clumsy to be near the playing field or that I had purposefully thrown myself in front of them to cause them to lose.

Neither was true, or course. I had been pushed, and I had a good idea by whom.

The shouting behind me started then. The watchers, the audience, the other students who either agreed with the players' assessment of my fall or were in on Darva's plan. Who, by the way, was standing directly in the center of them with a very convincing expression of anger, like she also believed I had done it on purpose.

Her voice was one of the loudest. "You stupid retard!"

I don't know what came over me at that moment. Oh, I do now, obviously, but at the time, I had no idea. I didn't even realize I was doing it until it happened.

My fists started colliding with her face. And then they weren't. See, unlike me, Darva had experience with fighting. She knew what she was doing. I did not. She quickly turned passable, in other words, my fists were no longer hitting her, they were going through her. Their leftover force caused me to twirl around on the spot where I waited, confused and panic-stricken. Terror filled my body as I realized what I just did.

Her tense body turned to face me. Her livid expression held something behind it, something that said, "I'm going to enjoy this." A burn that started in the pit of my stomach spread to the tips of my fingers, pausing ever so slightly to pulse in my throat. Its electric sparkle resonated there. Fear.

The other ghosts had formed a circle around us and were shouting, "Fight! Fight! Fight! Fight!"

I tried to run, but the crowd pushed me back in, laughing, chanting, teasing. Darva paced in front of me, no longer passable. She was entirely solid now, and while the thought of punching her again did cross my mind, I knew she would just change back, and I would fall flat on my face. Besides, the power of surprise was no longer mine, and I was clueless in what to do.

The first blow was the worst. No idea what to expect, no idea how to stop it. The second, third, fourth, the rest that I didn't count, just hurt. The fear had left, replaced by the desire to stop the pain. I brought my arms up in front of my face and cowered into a ball.

Her fingers laced through my hair and yanked my head back, exposing my face, my neck, my body to her torture. My hands instinctively came up to block my face again. Her fists pounded into them, bending my fingers backwards, hurting my nose, my cheeks beneath them.

I stood up. My hair was still in her grip, preventing my head from rising with the rest of my body. My arms reached instinctively for her hands, and my fingers tugged in a futile attempt to pull them away.

Our audience cheered her on while taunting me further. I couldn't imagine anything more humiliating. With my fingernails digging into her hands, my face lay open for her fist to continue pummeling.

She didn't stop there. She hit my neck, the side of my head, my chest, my legs. She kicked my ribs and hips. I heard myself cry out in pain.

I don't know why she stopped. Maybe she got tired. Maybe someone told her to. It wasn't because she felt sorry for me, that much I did know. As much as I had wanted to run, the moment my hair went slack, I curled up into a ball and cried instead.

"Get up, retard."

"Yeah, you stupid retard."

"Re-tard! Re-tard! Re-tard!" The chanting wasn't as boisterous as it had been during the fight, but it told me things were worse for me now than ever. Now everyone hated me, wanted to tease me. Everyone was a Darva.

"That'll teach you not to jump people better'n you, you ugly dork!"

I had to get out of here. They would never stop with me there. Every place she had kicked or hit me now glowed with an electrical throb that matched its pain. I pushed myself up. The burning was so extreme I couldn't stop myself from crying out. I hobbled away with my arm wrapped around my stomach to help quell some of the ache. The jeering called after me.

MaryAnn's absence had spoiled me. My room had become a solace. Presently that solace was shattered by a high roommate on her couch. I knew if I ran to the Clock I would never return. I would hide beneath its face and gaze out into the Void, much like MaryAnn did with the ceiling of our room. And the library, although quiet and safe from people like Darva and her friends, wouldn't want me pulsating and crying. The rest of the Academy was off limits as far as I was concerned. *Any* place with other ghosts was off limits as far as I was concerned.

I pushed my arm tighter against my ribs. The pain had intensified. As I tried to ignore the stares and laughter while stumbling up the Academy steps, I realized returning to my room was my only option.

HUNGRY

MaryAnn still lay motionless, but Twila was gone. I leaned against the closed door behind me and exhaled with the relief of solitude, or as solitary as you can get with a wisped-out roommate on the couch.

I walked to the mirror, my eyes refusing to focus on my reflection. I didn't want to see the damage Darva had done to me, but as the minutes passed, my vision sharpened without my consent.

My entire face pulsed with electrical flashes. Giant bright spots appeared around my mouth, cheeks, and eyes. I raised my shirt to examine where she kicked my side. A large, tender circle glowed over my ribs, brighter than the surrounding area. Every few seconds, a crooked burst of lightning would flicker across it. Whenever it did, the pain was so intense I yelped. I couldn't go back. I could never show my face in public again.

I walked over to my drawers and pulled out a fresh set of clothes. The ones I had on felt dirty, shameful, like they'd caused the beating. I shoved my old ones as far back as possible into my bottom drawer, the one I never used, and quickly placed some empty notebooks and such in front of them so I wouldn't have to look at them ever again. I brushed my hair so it lay neatly down in straight curtains and checked the mirror once more.

The pulsing of my face had lessened, or maybe it was my imagination. I couldn't tell. The familiar clinching of my throat started as tears formed, but immediately swallowed it back. I refused to cry anymore! I punched the air. Again and again. Pretending it was Darva, anyone who wanted to threaten me. I would start a fight with anyone right now just to prove I wasn't the coward I had just shown myself to be.

"Twila?" MaryAnn was coming to.

It was time for me to leave.

Classes wouldn't start for several hours still, something I finally didn't resent, thanks to my present condition. The down time would allow me to stay hidden from prying eyes a while longer.

I left my room with all intentions of hiding in the library when I decided even that wasn't isolated enough. No, I knew a better place, a place no student would be in until well after the Clock struck, a place they wouldn't close and kick me out of. Detention.

The classroom hallway was expectantly empty, as was room 4F13. I chose the same chair as last time and sat with a sigh of relief. No other classes, no Darva, no students.

I sat there until my ears ached from the silence, and my mind begged for stimulation. I tried to push away the memory of what just happened, but with nothing left to do, my thoughts returned to the harrowing experience like a moth to a flame destined for suicide.

Why did I do it? Why did I react the way I did? She had called me names before, names identical to that. Why did I lose all control and throw myself onto her, especially when I *so* had no idea what I was doing?

Maybe my mind stalled because it pitied me, or maybe it needed the time until now for itself, but for whatever reason, it waited until this moment to throw me into a tirade of memories all at once.

"Retard," a girl with books by her side giggled at me.

"Stupid retard," a boy told his friend as they walked past me in the school hallway.

"You're retarded." An older woman with an unsmiling face.

"She can't help it. She's retarded." I heard the voice but never saw the face.

Dozens of voices, all of them talking about me, to me, some malicious, some with pity, none caring how they affected me, and I did nothing. In the hallway at school, I sat and did nothing. At the table of a large family function, I did nothing. In the water while someone held me up, I did nothing. Why did I always do nothing? Why did I never speak? Why were people holding me? Why were people making fun of me? Why did it bother me so much?

I needed to know more. I needed to talk to Lin. Now.

I jumped from my desk and made for the door. Nope. I stopped and twirled back for my seat. It was too close to class time. But if I hurried, I could cycle through a few of the locales now so it would be faster later. I aimed for the door again. No. I turned back to my desk. Mrs. Collins undoubtedly had other classes who would use the portal and therefore lose my spot. I felt like a Yo-Yo on a string, being jerked back and forth between two spots with no control of my actions.

I sat at my desk and drummed my fingers across it.

But I did have control, I thought. I had decided to stay in here. I had decided not to go to my Portals classroom. I had decided to jump Darva (stupid decision there), but again, why? The memories and thoughts ruminated and percolated inside my head until I thought it would burst. When the Clock rang its single bong signaling classes would soon start, I didn't know which emotion was stronger, relief or fear. Relief of no more dwelling on the memories, fear of my classmates soon joining me.

I wished I had a mirror. I could still feel the electrical jolts zapping across my face, experience the throbbing pain between them. Without a mirror, I could only assume how bad they appeared.

I decided to grab a book and start my copying now. That way I might look completely natural behind my hair curtain, hunkered over my book, copying like the good little detention girl.

How to Care for Your Turtle, well if I've never seen excitement, this was it. There were other options: *Cooking with Rice, Growing Dandelions, The Complete History of the United States,* etc., but the turtle book seemed the most interesting of them all. Just shoot me.

I did as I planned. I sat at my desk, hunched over my book of thrills, made sure my hair curtain was in place, and started copying. The thought of the other students knowing or somehow hearing about my plight with Darva did enter my mind. I tried to remember who all was there when it happened, who all would know, then realized the gossip tree would inform everyone soon enough.

The other students entered. No one spoke to me. There were no hidden snickers or whispers. It seemed they either didn't know or didn't care about me or my earlier beating. I didn't chance it by looking up to see. My flashing face would make even the most apathetic student take notice.

When everyone had chosen a seat and busied themselves copying, I peeked around the room for Cisco. He wasn't there. I frowned, wondering where he could have gone to. Without him, detention felt longer than yesterday, which was odd since I had been looking forward to the lack of conversation detention brought. It also made me nervous. I had spent half the night looking for him, ready to start our adventure into the Void, but now it was like he had disappeared completely.

A couple of chapters into my writing, right as I was getting to "Grooming Your Turtle, a Beginner's Guide", a funny thing happened. My chest felt empty.

Up until that point in my Death, I never paid much attention to my lung area. Like I said, I didn't need to breathe. I could, but I didn't *have* to. I never experienced a hunger for air, a need to inhale. But now I did. I gasped, almost uncontrollably. The closest students gave me a weird stare, but I otherwise went unnoticed.

I felt another gasp coming and squeezed my fists together until my nails dug into my palms. I managed to reduce it to a slow, silent inhale. No one noticed this time. This pattern continued for several agonizing minutes. Was this going to become a permanent problem? Was this some stage of Death I hadn't learned about yet? That moment of ghostly adolescence where we suddenly had to breathe? I looked down. My glow had diminished. I was becoming dull, lackluster. Was I to lose that as well? I would lose my glow and be required to breathe all in the same day? Was I, I felt silly for even thinking it, becoming Live? None of this made any sense! No one around me, the other ghosts in detention, Mr. Hill, no one else was having these problems.

Then the violent desire for breath became a pain. My lungs, no longer forcing the atmosphere of the Void to enter them, ached. At first it was just a slight discomfort, as if to let me know they were there. Then it became a debilitating cramp. I had to stop my copying due to what felt like my lungs twisting themselves into intricate knots.

I almost screamed as I clutched my chest in agony. And then it went away. Then it came back. Then it went away again. The pain came and went with random frequency and length. Fear once again hovered over me. What was going on? My leg started shaking from anxiety. There was no way I could just get up and leave. It's not like there was a school nurse, not that I knew of anyway, and considering how helpful everyone had so not been until now, I doubted it would have benefited me.

My fingers wrapped around the top of my hair curtain and pulled. The slight twinge at its roots helped take my mind off my cramping chest. My fist clinched my pencil, which now hovered unmoving over my paper. I peered up at Mr. Hill, wondering if he had noticed I'd stopped the mandatory copying. He hadn't, or at least he wasn't saying anything if he did which, given what I'd gathered so far of his personality, meant he hadn't. Then again, maybe he thought he didn't have to worry about me since I was already seated and busy when he entered the room this morning.

I sat like that, taking deliberate breaths through clinched teeth while my mind raced through one absurd thought after the next, until I found my fingers relaxing. My pencil once again lying loosely between them. The cramping had subsided. A very relieved breath left my body. I quickly repositioned myself in what I hoped made it look like nothing happened and that I was perfectly normal.

It took a few paragraphs to realize it, but my face had stopped throbbing too. I reached up to touch it. Before, I could almost feel the bolts enter my fingertips as they flashed across my damaged cheeks. Now, everything felt normal. My face was no longer sensitive to the pressure of my fingers.

I looked down again at my glow. It was even less than before. I was nearly as dull as my desk now.

Mr. Hill cleared his throat. I glanced up to find him staring at me. Ignoring my Dead body's odd behavior for now, I set back to my copying, all the while making sure my hair curtain was still in place even though I wasn't positive I needed it anymore.

Every now and then a twinge of pain grabbed hold of my chest, reminding me something about my body was unhappy. I was able to copy my exciting turtle words without incident for several hours. But near the end of the day, the cramping returned. It grew to its full strength until a dull throb beneath my ribcage filled every moment of my existence. I gritted my teeth and forced slow breaths to combat the torture. I glanced down at my book. "What to Feed Your Turtle", the title of the next chapter. That's when it hit me. The feeding.

Once the image of feeding at the Vent again came into being, nothing else existed. No detention. No Darva. No Lin. No Life. All I cared about was consuming essence. The cramping increased tenfold as I did. I was hungry.

I had felt the desire to feed before, but nothing like this. This was *real* hunger. My fists renewed their clinched states as I tried not to grunt aloud from the pain I was now enduring. You would think when you figured out what your body was trying to tell you all along it would ease up a bit. Nope. It was like it had earned a free pass to abuse and torment me. Come on, everyone! Now that she's grasped the concept, let's really make her pay! Not a good way to make me want to understand your problems in the future, body. Really.

The Clock sounded. Two bongs. Time for supper.

I jumped up from my desk, slung my still unzipped backpack over my shoulder, threw my assignment on Mr. Hill's desk, shoved the stupid turtle book back onto the shelf, and slammed the door open with the palm of my hand. The hallway was so thick with students my mind entered school mode instead of hungry mode for a second. I realized my open backpack was dangling from my shoulder and probably should be attended to. While maintaining my position in the flow of students, I slung the pack around to the front of my body and zipped it up. Nothing appeared to be missing. Guilt jabbed at me. I had let my hunger keep me from thinking, from being responsible. If I *had* lost anything, it would have been my fault.

My dorm room was empty when I got there. I threw my bag on the couch and took advantage of being alone to check my face in the mirror. My glow was almost as dull as the walls of my room. A small circular area around my nose and right cheek was slightly brighter than the rest of my face, but it wasn't very noticeable.

The voices outside rose in volume. The pain in my chest grew with it. I was ravenous.

I sprinted to the edge of the Vent. The rest of the student body didn't linger far behind. The backs of the Overseers shrank from view, and a few threads of rising essence signaled the beginning of the billow soon to come. A smile spread across my face. The face of a hunter. A monster. Like the first time, only stronger, my body took control. I stood at the edge of the Vent, next to the sparse population of early arrivals, and sucked. Two, three, four times I inhaled. Five, six, I couldn't get enough. The first time I had done this I continued to feed past what I needed to because I enjoyed it so much, because it was new. This time I fed because I *needed* it. As I did, I sensed my glow return.

My fingers throbbed as feeling returned to them, feeling I didn't realize had left. My toes felt too big for their shoes, like the essence I fed them with was somehow making them swell.

When I finished, when I was full, I sucked in one more breath. Not just because I wanted to, like the first time, but because I was afraid not to. I had put it all together then. My body needed the extra energy to heal its injuries, and in doing so, deprived itself of its normal daily nourishments. My insatiable overfeeding was making up for those lost nourishments, so, just in case, I overdid it on purpose.

Most of the other students had finished and were floating away. While trying to make my actions go unnoticed, I visually searched the area for any indication of my nemesis. The last thing I wanted to deal with right now was another confrontation with her. Satisfied Darva wasn't anywhere nearby, or at least if she did me didn't care to make that fact known, I walked back to the Academy. It was time for some answers.

FINDING CISCO

I walked back to the Academy from the Vent slow and meticulous. Not only had the overfeeding caused me to feel heavier, to walk slower, but I needed to find Cisco, and this area between the Vent and the Academy was the only place I knew to look. Unfortunately, my search proved futile once again. I saw neither him nor his friends near any of the sporting areas.

I climbed the side porch steps and entered the Academy doors. While the thought of searching the library did occur to me, I seriously doubted Cisco or any of his friends would take advantage of its resources or solitude. They seemed more of the extroverted type to me. Not to mention non-studious.

I strolled down the Academy's hallways, throughout the girls' and boys' areas. Especially the boys' areas, as it was one of the more likely places I would find them. This was the perfect time too since most of the student body remained outside still. Nada. I didn't bother with the classroom hallways, for the same reason I didn't bother with the library.

I came across several rooms I hadn't paid attention to before. Most of them were locked, but two in particular struck my fancy. One contained predominantly girls doing a variety of crafts: knitting, painting, basket weaving. Something about the room made me feel like I was forgetting something, but I couldn't remember what. With no time to dwell on it, I kept in pursuit of Cisco.

The second room I titled the Factory. Principally boys this time used what I could only assume came from the Vent to make furniture and things. There were two large piles near the front of the room. From my quick inspection, they appeared to be the incoming and the outgoing piles: things from the Vent to be used and/or sorted, and those items labeled as unusable here. I couldn't tell if the students here were being punished, or liked the work and did it for pleasure.

Not really caring at the moment what the correct answer was, I shrugged and resumed my search. On my way to the boys' end of the dorm halls, I crossed the game room, and I wanted to slap myself for not thinking of it earlier. The door opened with no fanfare. Everyone inside was too loud and busy setting up their entertainment methods for the evening to notice my entrance.

I stood in the corner, out of everyone's way, crossed my arms over my chest in determination, and scanned the room with squinted eyes. A group of ghosts fighting over cards with little critters drawn on them. A couple silently engrossed in a chess match. Two couples playing darts in the back. Several tables of students with board games or cards. Ah, there he was, sitting at one of the most hidden tables in the back, surrounded by his friends and playing a game I didn't recognize (not that I had a lot of practice) on an ordinary pack of playing cards.

I walked to him casually so as not to draw any attention. He caught sight of me before I got too close. My expression must have given me away, for he excused himself and rose to meet me halfway. I stayed where I was, not wanting to have our conversation too close to any ears.

"I have it," I said.

His eyes bulged in disbelief. "So soon?" he whispered.

I didn't answer. There didn't seem to be a need to.

"Ok." He nodded, then turned back to his table of friends. I caught a few words of what he told them. "Had to go", "be back later", that sort of thing. When their eyes turned my way, I about-faced and headed for the door. I didn't want to explain what I, what we, were about to do to anyone, especially not to his friends. I don't know what it was about them, but they gave me the same feeling Cisco did, that they wouldn't be completely honest with me. Maybe I was being too hard on Cisco. It's not like I had a lot of experience with people, at least not that I remembered. So it was entirely possible I was overreacting. Still, better safe than sorry, I reasoned.

Cisco caught up with me in the hallway.

"Were you going to wait for me or just keep walking?" he asked.

"I saw you were coming. Besides, I don't like crowds."

"Good to know," he said.

We walked down the grand staircase in silence. At the bottom, he pushed open the front door and held it for me. "Ladies first," he said, holding his arm out in a welcoming gesture and smiling broadly.

I smiled weakly back and did as he commanded. Once off the front porch, and therefore away from prying ears, we spoke, though at near whispers.

"Let me see it." He wasn't demanding, just curious.

I pulled it from my pocket and allowed him to hold it. He flipped it over in his hands several times, admiring it from all angles. "Whoa." He drew the word out again. "I've never seen one up close before."

I gently pulled it away and draped it around my neck, hiding it beneath my shirt. We resumed our walk. "Do you know where to go once we're there?"

"Not really." He shrugged.

Was I wrong this whole time? Was he really just wanting to go on an adventure in the Void, a "field trip" as he called it? I gave him complete access to the medallion, and he didn't run away with it. If he'd immediately answered with where to go, what to do, I would have been more suspicious. But he was walking so jauntily, so carefree, like he was just out for a bit of fun. I pushed my negative thoughts to the back of my mind as we neared the edge of the Veil.

I purposefully didn't walk towards the Clock, instead aiming for the opposite direction. The Clock was my special place, my sanctuary, and even if Cisco did prove to be innocent, I wasn't ready to share it. Not with anyone.

I knew we had reached the Veil's edge because what should have been clear pitch was now a dull, almost brown. If you fanned away most of the fog and looked close enough, you could see a curved, bluish white line that appeared to be blazing a groove into the floor. The bottom of the Veil.

Being this close to it without the cover of the Clock made me nervous. It had to be obvious two students this near the Veil's edge yet next to nothing were up to something they shouldn't be. I kept casting nervous glances all around me, making us appear even more guilty I'm sure.

"OK. Now what?" I asked.

With great satisfaction I saw that he too acted nervous, though not nearly as conspicuous. He just bounced his weight back and forth between his feet like an excited little kid.

"You've never done this before, have you?" I asked.

"What? Of course I have," he said.

No. He hadn't. His face said otherwise. It all made sense now. He *was* using me, but not in a terrible, horrible way. He used me to get the medallion because he had either tried before and couldn't or was too afraid to. He was curious. That was all.

"No, you haven't," I said. "You don't know what you're doing!"

"Yes, I do!" He seemed angry, but almost truthful this time. He must know a little something. "Here." He wrapped the medallion's chain around both our necks.

His face was too close for my comfort, but I let him take control. With our faces so close they often touched, he started walking towards the Void. I had no choice but to follow alongside him.

THE VOID

I closed my eyes as we walked through the wall of the Veil. It resembled entering face first into a horizontal tub of still, lukewarm water. For the brief seconds we were inside it, I felt suffocated. The moment its last touch left the back of my body, and I knew myself to be free of it, I opened my eyes and inhaled. I don't know why. I didn't need to. It wasn't like when I was hungry or anything. I guess I was just relieved to no longer feel so constricted.

Cisco reached up to remove the chain from around his neck, for which I was very grateful. The whole time we were together, my stomach kept tying into knots. It reminded me of when I was with Lin, only different. Yeah, I know, that really explained things for you. Sorry about that, but it's the best I could do.

The fog was identical here as everywhere else. I don't know what I had been expecting. Everything about the Void appeared the same as inside the Veil. Save the Academy and its students. A big black nothing with pinpricks of light in the distance. We both stood in awe of what lie before us. No sounds between us.

Then the voices started.

"Donald! Donald Geoglin, are you there?" The little boy's question reverberated over me from above.

I looked up to find it. A tiny star of blueish white marred the otherwise pitch ceiling of the Void. It quivered and shimmered until, like the voice, it disappeared.

"Cassandra Vera. We are searching for a Cassandra Vera." Another voice rained down from the top of the Void. This time an old woman's. A star did not accompany it.

"Come on," said Cisco, a touch of alarm in his voice. He grabbed my hand. "Let's go."

Something told me to follow him. I'm glad I did.

As we walked, voices continued to cascade from above like a loud drizzle with the ability to go straight through your body and touch your soul. "Peter Cox", "Benjamin Brue", "Victoria Sommers", "If anyone can hear me. If anyone's there", "Joshua Sanders". The voices, the names, they ran together in a stream of echoes until one became indistinguishable from the next.

I turned to Cisco, my face in a state of panicked confusion. "What *is* that?"

"The Callers," he said. His face was full of concentration. "Ignore them."

I couldn't. I stared at the ceiling as he pulled me along, white-blue stars pockmarking it like tiny fireworks, each corresponding to a single voice. Some were larger than others. One had a small black hole in the middle of it. As the woman's voice got louder, became more demanding, the hole grew.

Cisco jerked on my hand, forcing my attention ahead. "The Callers call into the Void for the ghosts they're trying to reach."

"What are they? Live Ones?"

"Yes," he said. "Psychics, Mediums, Necromancers, Spiritualists, Witches, they go by many names. Some are innocent. Most are not."

I immediately thought of Lin. "So, if a Medium wanted to talk to me, all they'd have to do is call out?"

He peered through the corner of his eye at me. "Maybe. I don't know all the details. I just know we should keep moving."

This was a different Cisco, a serious, alert Cisco. That same something that told me to follow him earlier was telling me he was holding something back. I decided not to question it. "Why can't we hear it at the Academy?"

"The Veil," he said. "Duh."

I twisted my mouth. He was right. It should have been obvious.

We walked silently together. He dropped my hand after a while, apparently confident I wasn't going to run off.

"How do you know all this?" I asked.

"All what?"

"All this stuff about the Void, like what the voices are and stuff."

He shrugged. "My friends told me."

My eyebrows rose in astonishment. "Your friends have been out *here*?" I practically shrieked.

"Shhhh," he hissed. "Sorta. They visit their families and stuff." His face drew in anger.

"Wait." I stopped walking and faced him. He would explain this to me. "What do you mean, they visit their families?"

He sighed and stepped back to where I was. "You know. They talk to Dead family members."

"No, I don't know!" I was too angry to care how much of myself I revealed to him. "I don't know anything about being Dead!"

If he noticed I was angry, he must not have cared. "Dead family members are allowed to visit students of the Academy," he explained. "How do you think Darva finds out everything she does?"

My jaw fell. I couldn't breathe. Painful sparks traveled up my back and into my throat. "Families can visit you? At the Academy?" My voice was only a whisper.

Why had none of my family visited me? I had to have some family that was already Dead, right? And why had I not noticed this before? Why had no one yet mentioned family visitation day or whatever name they gave it to me?

"They have to know you're Dead first." He broke off, like he didn't want to tell me what he already had. "They have to care." His face glowed, and he turned away from me.

"What do you mean?"

He walked out into the emptiness of the Void. There was nothing close by. The spots of greyish white continued to glow in the far distance. The voices persisted eerily overhead. I stared after him.

"The Dead don't always learn when their family members die. Some do, like the Bishops, because they're powerful families who see and hear everything. But my family doesn't even live near here, so…" He shrugged.

I vaguely remembered someone mentioning something about the location of your death determining where you showed up in the Maze, but the specifics still confused me.

"Where is your family then?" That seemed the most tactful way to put it.

"Most of them died in Mexico, I guess. I think I had an Uncle Julio who died near Michigan, but that's still too far away for him to be here."

His answer made me feel a little better. My hurt dissipated, making me able to blink away the forthcoming tears. It was entirely possible my already Dead family died nowhere near where I was now. It was possible they were traveling here now to see me! Highly unlikely, but possible. I could live with that. For now.

We walked towards the light again. The grey-white glowing globs got closer and more defined.

"So why are you ashamed of that? What's wrong with dying away from your family?"

He groaned. "Look at me!" He had stopped and turned towards me, his face full of irritation.

So I looked at him. I didn't get it. What was I supposed to be seeing that I wasn't? I shook my head and opened my mouth, but nothing came out of it.

He flung his arms up with a defeated "Ugh!" and continued on our previous course without me.

I held back a moment to let him calm down. When I caught back up, he answered my unasked question. "Hispanic families are tight knit. All my other friends would never stop teasing me about being alone out here."

"Oh." It came out soft and innocent, but inside boiled more questions than I could count, none of which seemed appropriate to ask at the time.

The glowing globs were now close enough to draw our attention away from this awkward conversation. The voices had quietened too, almost as if the nearing city dampened their energy.

We slowed in response, neither one brave enough to go any closer. In front of us lay a hodgepodge of buildings, ghosts, furniture, cars, everything imaginable. It was nothing like the organized structures of the Academy the Gatherers were responsible for. This looked as if stuff fell from the sky like bombs and was just left where it all landed, undetonated.

Mr. Prickett hadn't explained it too well that first day … or night, or whatever it was, but I soon learned the role of the Gatherers. As I had seen then, they collected everything material the Vent deposited and carried it back to the Academy's closets. One of those closets was the one I was first taken to, the one with the endless racks of clothes in it along with all the school supplies like paper, pencils, and my backpack.

The other one, we students rarely got to use. It had all the big ticket items, like furniture and light globes. Anything there took a bunch of rations to save up for. The only reason I got to see inside it is because I nearly ran into a long couch being held midway through the door by two boys who had saved their rations for six months each. Its entrance lay under the boys' dormitory hallway. It was the only door in that area. From what tiny glimpse I snatched over their couch, the storeroom stretched from one end of that hallway to the other and went as far back as the clothing closet did.

Not everything made it into those closets. I stayed around one day after feeding to watch. I was curious, and most of the other ghosts had already figured everything out, so I was alone. After collecting the smaller objects, the Gatherers came back for the bigger ones. They wasted nothing, no matter how dilapidated it appeared. When the area around the Vent was completely cleared, they returned from the Academy with whatever we didn't use, our waste. Car tires, toilet paper, things no ghost that I could ever imagine would want. They threw the waste out through the Veil where a mass of glowing, hazy ghosts flocked to it like starving piranhas. I couldn't hear them, or course, but from my side of the Veil, it appeared some ghosts yelled at others, and maybe even fights broke out. I never waited around to watch again.

It was that memory which permeated my mind as we stood before the populated Void and caused my legs to affix themselves to the floor in what I'm sure they wanted to be a permanent position. I stared down at them to make sure they were still there (they had gone numb) and noticed the black fog climbing to my shins, exactly how it had been in the Maze and on the grounds of the Academy. Yet now, because of that memory I'm sure, that fog felt like snakes slithering their way up to my neck. It caused an electrical pulse of fear to flash up my legs and reside in my chest. A tiny flare in the corner of my vision told me the same thing was happening to Cisco. Whether he wanted to admit it or not, he was just as afraid as I was.

We both gazed forward again. I felt my hand reach out for his. He didn't pull away.

"Ready?" he asked.

I nodded, but it was a lie.

THE ENTRYWAY

The fog swirled up the abandoned cars, the sides of the buildings, the legs and hems of the ghosts who hovered before us. Among the scattering of houses sat a crude wooden structure, its poles woven together by long strips of bark. Leather draped over the front entrance. A little girl whose head barely cleared the fog peeked around it. Near it was a compact square house with white painted siding and shutterless windows. Blinds prevented any passersby from seeing inside. It appeared abandoned, but I knew someone had to live there. Several feet away and at a different angle than the other two, sat a home with a porch that rivaled the Academy's. Behind it was a shanty of sorts. There was no logical order to the dwellings before us, not even the empty spaces used for walking. Each home faced different directions as though someone shook them in their palm like dice and tossed them into the Void.

Off in the distance, I could see a myriad of homes slightly farther apart than the ones near us. Their medley of construction materials made it obvious they had been constructed here in the Land of the Dead, as opposed to being built by the Living and then brought here through the Vents. They ranged from unbelievably exquisite with arched windows and balconies to nothing more than bits of wood and cardboard held together with string. It made me realize how lucky I was to live in the Academy, and fear the day I had to leave.

Save the one or two random glances, most of the ghosts seemed oblivious to our presence as our feet dragged us into their midst. They wore the oddest mixture of clothing: a man in a decorated leather shirt and pants with colored beads strung in necklaces, a woman in a plain dress and apron and a scarf wrapped around her hair, a couple in matching outfits with the most ridiculous poofy sleeves, a sprinkling of normal modern-day people in jeans and shirts or that type of thing. Several ghosts lay strewn against the walls of the local dwellings. Upon closer inspection I recognized they were strung out on wisp. My upper lip curled back in response.

"Now what?" I asked Cisco.

He scanned every detail in front of us. I felt his hand grip harder. He was at least as scared as I was, but he was masking it much better. His gaze fixated on something. "Let's try over there." He pointed to a building on the right behind a stripped, once red car.

"Why there?" I asked.

"See those people coming in and out?" He used his jaw to point them out. "That's a business or something. It'll be like stopping at a gas station to ask for directions."

I pretended to understand what he meant by that.

He was smiling down at me. It was the jovial, confident smile he wore under the Veil. It made me confident. "Unless you had a smart phone. You probably used a phone, right?"

"Uh … yeah, sure." From his tone, I didn't think he had a phone, whatever that was. Me telling him I did made me appear less stupid than admitting my lack of knowledge with the gas station analogy. Again, whatever that was. And since he didn't have a phone, at least that's what I was banking on, I wouldn't have to know what I was talking about on that subject either. Win-win.

The building he had pointed out was the busiest one around. Patrons of every age and appearance entered and exited it with such speed and confidence, brief flickers of anxiety flashed across my face. Several containers with those same swimming, pale blue tufts the Academy used for light were strategically placed around the top to spell out, "ENTRYWAY". The sign made the building seem taller than its neighbors, and most certainly brighter. Any ghost traveling near sight of this place couldn't help from noticing it.

I was in an unknown world all over again, like my first day in the Academy. My stomach clinched from fear. Apparently my fingers did the same.

"Ah!" Cisco cried out, and he reached for my wrist to pull my hand away from his.

"Sorry!" I said. I hadn't realized we were still holding hands. I had to hold something though. Anything would do, but there wasn't much around, unless you counted the trash sprinkling the otherwise unhindered walking areas. I settled for clinching my own fists instead.

Cisco approached the building, leaving me behind.

"Hey!" I whispered through clinched teeth. "What about me?" My feet remained cemented to the floor.

His eyes widened, and he waved his hand as if to say, "Come on!"

But I couldn't.

His expression became impatient. When I still didn't join him, he stomped back, grabbed my hand, and dragged me alongside him without a word. I was too stunned to do anything but try not to trip.

Cisco led us into the fast-paced line of hovering patrons like a smoothly run machine. It drove us up the stairs and near the doorway where a burly ghost with a cowboy hat stood. He surveyed each potential patron before allowing them inside. I cowered next to Cisco, using my hair for a curtain as usual.

Cisco shook my hand. "Look up at the bouncer when we pass by." he whispered to me.

I assumed the bouncer was the burly man. I didn't have time to ask. I forced my eyes up, meeting the bouncer's gaze with them. His scrutiny made my legs shake. I gripped Cisco's hand hard. He winced in response, but I couldn't ease up, not with that man's judging eyes boring inside me.

The bouncer nodded at Cisco who smiled back his confident, airy smile. I looked away and pushed myself closer to him. "You can let go now," he said painfully through his teeth.

"Sorry." I released his hand.

He shook out his fingers and stretched them.

Once inside the building, the incoming crowd pushed us to the side where both our mouths gaped in amazement at what was before us.

The room we entered took up most of the first floor. A small number of glowing globes and mason jars hanging from the ceiling, added to the radiance of the present ghosts, prevented it from being as dark as the Void. I slowly rotated my head from one corner of the room to the other, which despite the constant bumping from the shuffling crowd, allowed me to take in the details.

A five-piece band wailed in the corner, their singer trying to scream over the voices of the crowd without the aid of a microphone. Their sounds just reached the other side of the room where an alluringly dressed ghost with exquisite features hovered above a group of mainly boorish men. Her beads clacked and swayed in time with the music as she twisted through the air in complex somersaults while cheering men swiped at her feet in what seemed like a game of sorts. The dark-skinned girl with ice blue eyes and streaks in her otherwise dark brown hair was giggling, taunting them as if to encourage them to try harder.

I could feel fear overpowering my amazement and turned to Cisco to see his reaction. His eyes were fixated on the dancing girl, his mouth hanging open. No fear.

"Hey!" I smacked him upside the head with my loose hand.

"What!" He screamed angrily at me while rubbing the back of his head where I had hit him.

I gestured to the rest of the area with an open palm as if to say, "Hello! Directions from the gas station?"

His face still bore an irritated expression as he continued to rub the back of his head, but he now focused his attention on the rest of the room.

Unmatching tables of wood, metal, plastic, and sometimes all three combined into one filled what wasn't taken up by the dancing girl or the band. Both on the floor and suspended from the ceiling, they allowed customers to either hover or sit next to them, whichever they chose. Their chairs were just as random, as if arbitrarily harvested and pieced together from the different deposits around a Vent, which they undoubtedly were. Hookahs sat on about half of the occupied tables. Their contents, though not as bright as what I had last seen MaryAnn use, were being sucked out by surrounding patrons. And although a few users hovered near the ceiling in a wasted state, the majority treated the wisp indifferently, as though it either didn't affect them the same way, or they were purposefully trying not to let it dominate their thoughts and actions.

Someone bumped us from behind, causing us to fall into the current of patrons. We allowed the current to carry us to the table area where we hurried to the opposite wall in an attempt to stay out of everyone's focus. Only a few people stared at us as we walked by.

From this angle, I saw other areas I hadn't been able to before. One held a set of stairs made of irregular pieces of wood and metal. It led to an opening in the second floor which remained tightly closed. Another was the furthest corner away from us. Two additional walls came out to form a small room. By its single, plain, brown door stood a man whose appearance alone was enough to keep me away.

Adjacent to the little room sat a desk with a no nonsense male attendant. An open space allowed guests to interact with him but not get behind the desk without effort. I watched as each ghost in line gave him an item. He would then examine it carefully before either returning it or taking it out of sight in the back and then handing the ghost a ticket of sorts in exchange. I was too far away to identify it. The ghosts that received the ticket would then use it to acquire a hookah or leave with it. One or two went to stand in a line near the bouncer by the corner room.

We remained leaning against the wall for a long while, observing everything happening before us. Cisco's face was calculating, but it still showed signs of astonishment. I couldn't help but grin a little. Here he's tried to look like he knew what he was doing, like he was so cool, and he was just as out of place as I was.

I crossed my arms in front of my chest. With all the people in the room, I felt more ignored and out-of-sight than had there only been a few. The crowd was comforting somehow. I continued to watch the surrounding people, more relaxed this time, until I sensed there was nothing left to gain from it.

"So what now, oh wise one?" I asked Cisco, all future pretense lost in the stark reality we now faced.

He pursed his lips and glanced at me sideways through sardonically squinted eyes. Pushing himself away from our wall, he strolled casually into the midst of the tables. I had to admit, he was a natural.

In case you haven't noticed by now, this was not my type of environment. The "lost in the crowd" feeling might have been comforting from the sidelines, but walking around and interacting with said crowd was very much on my never-to-do list. So I stayed where I was and let Cisco do the legwork. He could ask the right questions, and I could—

"I said it was good enough!" A tall, thick man at the exchange counter was holding a small, cylindrical device in the palm of his hand and pressing it at the attendant's face.

"We don't take motors." I could hear the anger building in the back of the attendant's gravelly voice.

"I got this from the Vent! It's fully intact!" The man continued to shake the motor in front of the attendant's nose, whose massive crossed arms and pockmarked face were both tense from restraint.

"How long have you been in the Void?" the attendant shouted, his true feelings almost breaking through the thinning surface. "Long enough to know we *don't … take … motors.*" He separated each word to get the point across, his face beginning to glow ominously near the end.

The man's face matched the attendant's in its glow, and his arms bulged out.

My back tingled with tiny sparks of unease. I didn't like where this was going. I just knew the man was about to throw the motor, and then things would only get nastier.

The attendant, almost laughing, said, "Motors take electricity, nimrod! There ain't no electricity in the Void!"

Other patrons laughed with the attendant. The man's face glowed brighter, but he still hadn't thrown the motor.

I quickly scanned the crowd for my traveling partner. He was conversing with some tall, once hazel-skinned guy with a wide mustache and a low, slick once-black ponytail. They hadn't noticed the shouting.

The man with the motor slammed it down on the desk and thrust his face into the attendant's. "You know, we're getting pretty sick and tired of this ... es-*ta*-blish-ment controlling our lives. *I* say it gets me a visit, and I'm not leaving until I get one!"

The laughing stopped. Backs stiffened. Ghosts backed away, but not in fear, more like to give the arguing men room. The pony tail man and Cisco glanced in their direction then returned to their previous conversation. The attendant stared straight back at the disgruntled customer, his anger completely under control. He radiated confidence. He had done this before. "I said, we don't ... take ... motors." His voice was almost a growl now, and barely audible over the music in the background.

The customer screamed in rage and threw the motor at the attendant's face. It bounced off, leaving a terrible white shine which quickly blossomed over the entire left side of his face until even his eye was covered in the painful glow I was intimately familiar with. Acidic sparks pulsated along the glow's edges on the attendant's forehead, his mouth, threatening to make the bruise bigger. The attendant's lip curled back into a snarl. He opened his mouth, threw his arms back, and let out a wail that caused the man and several adjacent ghosts to fall backwards. I covered my ears. It reminded me of the time the Clock had bonged so close to me it hurt.

The bouncer by the door flew over the heads of the patrons to the hole in the ceiling, knocked rhythmically on the cover I hadn't noticed before, and then shot back to his post by the door, all the while never once taking his eyes off it. Other ghosts joined into the fight now. The bouncer by the little room licked his palm, cracked open the door he so vehemently protected, and slipped inside. But I didn't get the feeling it was out of fear. More like protocol.

Before I could acknowledge what just happened, three more bouncers, each bigger and scarier looking than the one now inside the little room, swooped out of the hole in the ceiling.

I backed away with my jaw open. The fear of current events quickly dominated my initial fear of the crowd. "Cisco!" I searched where I had last seen him. He and the pony-tailed man had abandoned their conversation and were focusing on the commotion now taking center stage of the room. Cisco's head whipped around, taking in the details of the situation. The dancing girl stopped her performance, much to the anger of her previously cheering crowd.

She floated as gracefully as a mermaid over their heads and to the covered hole in the ceiling where she too knocked in pattern. When it opened, she flitted through, worry and anxiety twisting her formerly beautiful face.

Her audience demanded her return. When they didn't get it, they rioted, throwing anything they could get their hands on: chairs, tables, the containers of glowing wisps. The rest of the bar joined in, little fights breaking out everywhere, above me, in front of me, next to me. One of the light vessels shattered against the wall over my head. I ducked and covered my head with my arms to protect myself from the shards of glass. The first sight I saw when I rose back up was the light tufts dissipating into the atmosphere of the room. I saw another jar fly across the room, nearly hitting the band members cowering in the corner.

With every broken vessel, the room became that much darker. I tried to melt into the wall behind me, pressing myself against it in the hopes I would remain unnoticed through it all. I wished I was better at invisibility.

Something else hit the wall next to me, a chair I think. Splintered bits grazed the edge of my glow. I was unharmed, but it was enough. The tears came full force. My body shook from the sobs, and I didn't try to stop them. I knew I needed to run, to get out of the building, but I didn't know how. Enough of the light vessels had been broken so the room's only source of illumination came from the mass of battling patrons. I whipped my head back and forth, wildly searching for another way out besides the front door. You know, my goal at the end of a path through the twisting, banging, shouting bodies of rabid ghosts.

Someone grabbed my hand and jerked. "Time to go!" It was Cisco's voice.

"Where?" I screamed, ducking out of the way of two ghosts entwined in conflict.

He didn't answer. He just ran.

A wail came at me from the right. I'm sure they meant it for the girl in the tank top and not me, but I caught the brunt of it. My body vibrated in its wake as the wail's force threw me down and to the side. If Cisco hadn't slowed and tightened his grip, I would have been lost down there, somewhere on the bar's floor, trampled, probably not found until morning. He reached back, grabbed my wrist with his other hand, and jerked me off the floor and into the air behind him. Releasing his second hand, he hovered quickly towards the exit.

He pulled so strongly I floated behind him like a long line of tissue paper in the wind. I reached my other hand up to grasp his, strengthening the bond, my tears flying off my face. As Cisco weaved through the soaring objects, the flailing fists and bodies, the wails so strong they caused visible waves in the air, my body did the same. I let it without protest. He wasn't faking confidence this time. He knew what he was doing, and I allowed him complete control.

We exited the Entryway and sped down the stairs. The crowd previously clamoring to get in was now nowhere to be seen. I remained tethered to Cisco's arm, gliding behind him like his personal pet kite until we were clear of the populated area and close to the homes I had seen earlier in the distance.

NAOMI

"You're going the wrong way!" I shouted as I continued to flap in Cisco's wake. "The Academy's back there!"

He didn't stop. "Don't care right now!" The Entryway lay far behind us, its violent situation no longer a threat.

I tried to reach the ground, using my arms to pull my feet down to it. If I got some traction, maybe I could break away and head back through the Veil. It was no use. Until he slowed down, I was at his mercy. "Could you at least slow down?" I screamed.

He did. I guess he too finally realized we were away from the fighting. When my feet hit the floor of the Void, I immediately tried to break free from his grip. He let go without a fight. I turned and ran for the Academy.

It took a moment for him to notice, but when he did, he reeled around and screamed, "What are you doing?"

"The Academy is this way!" I shouted back.

"Yeah, and so is a huge angry mob!"

His words sunk in, a little. I gradually slowed my pace from a sprint to a walk. He was right. We couldn't go back. Yet.

I didn't like this, stuck in the Void. I needed to get back to the Academy. Our field trip so far was a disaster, and I didn't want to add the cherry on top by being late for my last day of detention. Panic was coming. Not as bad as when it found me in the Maze, but it was there, whispering against sanity's door with the fluttering breeze of moth wings.

"Hey! Hannah!"

The familiar sound of Cisco's voice grounded me. "Yeah," I answered, my back still to him so he couldn't see the hysteria lingering on my face.

"You coming?"

"Y-yeah," I stammered. I shook out my arms, took a deep, unnecessary breath, and blew it slowly through rounded lips.

Cisco returned to scanning the mishmash of houses as I made my way to him.

"What are you looking for?" I asked.

"I think I have some family here."

I didn't believe this! Why did he drag me to the bar if he already knew where to go? Wait. I stopped myself. He said the bar was a place to ask for directions. "Is that what the guy with the ponytail told you?"

He nodded. "He said a Delgado lived over here."

What was a Delgado? "Is that … someone in your family?"

He shrugged. "Maybe. It's my first apellido, my first last name."

First last name? "Um, how many last names do you have?"

He concentrated on a house midway into the distance. "Two."

Mr. Consolver had mentioned something about my last name. Did everyone have two? Does that mean I needed to find two for me now? Erg! I wanted to scream! Why did everything have to be so complicated?

"I need to get closer." He started walking to the center of the cluster of buildings.

"What about my answer for Lin? Did you find out why everyone's so scared?"

He slapped his hand over my mouth. "Shhh! Not now!" he whispered. "I found out something. Not enough, but something. I'll explain it to you later."

I bit his finger.

"Ah!" He jerked his hand away.

"You will explain it to me *right now*!" I kept my voice as low as his.

He glanced around us. "It's not safe yet, chica. Back in the Veil. I promise."

I didn't like trusting his promises, but I nodded. Besides, he *had* just saved my life back there. He could have left me behind.

"I'm sorry I bit you," I said, feeling guilty for reacting so badly to him.

He grinned. "No problema. My sister bites harder." He laughed, then continued his trek to the houses.

I followed.

The desolation made my back prickle. I kept pivoting my head around to see who was following me. No one. Which made it that much creepier.

We passed a similar assortment as what surrounded the Entryway, only not as tightly crammed together. Houses of every shape, size, color, and material stood before us. Most were constructed from short, split wood, ex-firewood, stacked together for walls with makeshift roofs placed atop. I suppose it was rare an entire house burned in the Living world and therefore landed near the Vent for the Dead to use. I wondered how one would go about transporting said house. It's not like you could just leave it there, in the way of all the other deposits. Did several ghosts band together to carry it? And who got it in the end? Was the Void rationed in the same way as the Academy? Considering the brawl we recently left over a single bad barter, I highly doubted it.

When we got to the heart of the buildings, Cisco slowed to nearly a stop. He stared at a house just ahead and to our right. It had a painted wooden porch off its front door. Cisco's eyes squinted in thought.

"I think that might be it." He walked towards it without waiting for me.

I followed along.

He stepped up onto the porch, his feet skimming the top layer of the fog which danced across the porch floor. "If I do this—" He threw one arm out two times with two of his fingers pointing straight in the direction of the Academy. "It means run."

I drew back and nodded. "Do you think it's a trap?"

He shrugged. "Not really. Better safe than sorry though."

"I don't get it," I said. "Why is this dangerous but talking to that guy in the Entryway wasn't?"

Pity relaxed his previously serious face. "Street-smarts, chica." He tapped his temple with his finger. "I can't see what's behind this door."

"Can't we just look through a window?" I asked.

He opened his mouth as if to say something, then bit his lips and sighed. "Just, just look for the signal. OK?"

I nodded, feeling even dumber than before for not knowing what any of that meant.

I reached for the pendant through my shirt for comfort. If anything went wrong, I could always make a run for it. That knowledge kept me safe. But what about Cisco? If he was in danger somehow, could I leave him here and save myself?

He knocked on the door. I gripped the pendant tighter. I couldn't see his face to know how nervous he was or wasn't. The rest of his body seemed calm. I hoped his face did too.

Several suspenseful moments later, the door opened. A plump woman with glowing skin as dark as the dancing girl's answered, "Yes?" Her hair hung in long braids pulled back into a messy knot at the top. Her mouth and eyes were tight with suspicion.

Cisco's eyes widened, and he took a half step back. She was not what he expected. "Um…" He acted ready to pounce, like maybe it was all a trap.

I waited for his signal.

"I heard you were a Delgado?" he asked the lady. His voice tremble with nerves I hoped I alone noticed.

The woman's eyes drew tighter. "Why you asking?"

Cisco raised one hand with spread fingers to his chest, much like he had with me on the sporting grounds. "I'm … I'm a Delgado."

Although I didn't believe it possible, her eyes squinted even further, until barely more than paper-thin slits separated her lids.

Her lids suddenly flung open, allowing her wide eyes to bulge outward. She stood upright, took a deep breath in, and lunged for Cisco, wrapping her arms around him in a hug that shot tiny electrical bolts up to his head and down to his feet. He gave me the signal, a desperate expression on his previously well masked face.

I giggled. I know, I should have been ready to leave or jump in to save him after he had just saved me, but I just started laughing. She had a smile on her face that matched her hug.

When he saw me laughing his panicked expression turned angry. I laughed harder.

Still hugging him, the Delgado woman leaned back with Cisco still in her arms. His feet dangled beneath him, their kicks not affecting the woman in the least bit. When she put him down, he staggered backwards until his hands reached one of the porch posts. He grabbed hold of it for support.

"And who's this pretty thing?" The woman headed my way.

I stopped laughing.

When her massive arms reached around my body, I felt trapped and wonderful all at the same time. Her hug crushed me painfully. Yet, her body emanated love. Pure love.

I had experienced this before. A memory. Arms. Mom's arms. Dad's arms. Arms around me. Hair on my face. Mom's scent. It brought back that sensation I had been trying so hard to remember. The cake memory. The feeling of comfort. Safety.

I wrapped my arms around the Delgado woman and squeezed back. I drew in the scent of her hair. The memory of my mother's scent flashed before me. They smelled the same. I felt a sob start and quickly held my breath to squelch it.

She released me, keeping one arm around my shoulders. "Well, come on in to your auntie Naomi's house! I'd offer you some tea, but I don't have none!" Her hearty laugh at her own joke was treasure for the ears.

Cisco still appeared skittish, but I allowed her to lead me inside.

SAVAGERY

The inside of Naomi's house reminded me of the homes outside; nothing matched. A black velvet sofa filled up one wall. A dark brown rocking chair sat in a corner aimed at the window. Slightly melted plastic flowers sat in an otherwise empty pot on a green table next to a well-used red vinyl recliner. Small, decorative quilts and knitted items of beautifully arranged colors adorned her walls. She fell back into her chair and picked up a set of knitting needles from the basket next to it.

Her needles clicked together as she spoke. "So, tell me all abou' errybody! When'd you die by the way?"

Cisco and I glanced at each other, trying to convey our thoughts without words. We agreed the woman seemed harmless enough. I lowered myself onto the black couch. It felt soft. I couldn't help but rub my hands across it. Cisco sat next to me, crossing his leg in front of himself and draping his arm across the sofa's back.

"I've been Dead over six months now. You?"

"Now now, it's not nice to ask a woman her age you know." She kept her face serious for two seconds before bursting into raucous laughter again. I didn't get what was so funny, and from Cisco's painted expression, neither did he.

She continued as if we had laughed right along with her. "Oh, that's a good one."

I copied Cisco's false smile. Hopefully it passed as genuine.

"I been Dead goin' on … twenty years now I guess. More or less. Ain't found nobody from my family yet, and they ain't worth traveling them streets for either."

She lowered her knitting and leaned forward, serious. "How'd you get here by the way? Where you from?"

Cisco hesitated before answering, "The Academy."

Her eyes widened a moment before she sat back and continued her knitting. "Didn't know they let kids outta there without a chaperone. Where's yours?" Her tone was softer now, not as vigorous.

Cisco propped his elbows on his knees and announced like he would our choice for supper, "We snuck out."

She eyed him cautiously over her knitting. "Best be careful out there. Lotta people goin' missin'."

"Yeah, what's up with that?" He lounged back again, allowing his arm to touch the tops of my shoulders. I felt uncomfortable but didn't act like it. There was enough tension in the room.

"Ah, you can thank the wispers for that," Naomi explained.

I stiffened. Cisco's arm twitched in response.

Naomi continued unaware, "Worse than any meth head ever was! They'll do anything for it." She wrapped the yarn around her needle several times before her next stitch. "You know what it's made of, don't you?"

I shook my head, terrified what the answer may be. Cisco retracted his arm to his lap and twiddled his thumbs uncomfortably.

"Us," she said.

I stopped moving. No, not froze. My muscles didn't lock up, or, whatever it is us ghosts use to move about. They quit working. My eyes saw nothing. My ears heard nothing. If I had still needed to breathe I would've suffocated and died.

I concentrated hard on reacquiring control of my body. Their voices slowly came back into focus.

"—now it's errybody."

"Where are they concentrated?" Cisco asked.

They didn't act like they noticed my moment of paralysis. And I tried to act like it didn't happen.

"You're safest in the cities where there's more people. Round here's not too bad, but I wouldn't go near the outskirts, out where the Ancients used to live."

"The Ancients?" I asked.

"Oldies," Cisco answered.

"Oldies!" Naomi laughed. "I like that name! Ha ha! He's right though," she said. "That's where it started."

One glance at Cisco staring at his shoes told me he knew about this. My eyes squinted in suspicion of what else he knew.

"So, the old ghosts are the most dangerous," I clarified to Naomi.

"Oh, no, no!" she chuckled. "The Ancients are *in* the most danger. Wispers used to follow them around, sucking in their discarded pieces with anything they could, old straws, skinny pipes, rolled up newspaper."

I felt my jaw plunge but couldn't find a way to lift it back up.

"Now the wispers are sucking in new ghosts." Her eyes flashed up at me and Cisco. Sadness and worry hid in their depths. "The newer the better." She repeated the same stitch five times in a row before dropping her knitting with a sigh. "Don't you need to be gettin' back?"

Cisco shrugged. "We've got until the Clock strikes again. Plenty of time." His award-winning smile won her over.

"Ok, but don't you let time sneak up on you. I'd hate for you to get into trouble. Or worse," she mumbled under her breath. Naomi made herself more comfortable while I peeked at Cisco's face to see his response.

His face held his famous, unphased grin. "So all the disappearances, they're ghosts being wisped away?"

She hesitated for several seconds, starting a stitch, putting it down, starting it again. "Well, you *are* Dead, and you look over thirteen, so you've prol'ly seen worse than what I'm 'bout to tell you in your horror films or in whatever killed you." She lay her knitting in her lap, pressed her lips together, and sighed in frustration. "They all work for this ghost named Ronnie."

My ears perked to attention.

"Ronnie Brown. He came here a few years ago, got mad 'bout somethin', and formed his own gang of sorts. He gets 'em all hopped up on their dope, then when they want more, he makes 'em do stuff for 'im." She paused a minute, wondering whether to divulge the next part or not. "Like get 'im a ghost to … use." She went back to her knitting, unable to talk anymore about it.

Horrifying. Absolutely horrifying. If those two men from the Maze had caught me… I now lived in a dimension where people consumed other people for pleasure. My own *roommate* consumed … oh my gosh! My room had bits of … *dead people* in it, and MaryAnn was… Would she have smoked me too if they had turned me into wisp? "I think I'm going to be sick."

The pit of my stomach, the part that filled up when we fed, lurched and screamed at me to run outside. I didn't understand why until I got there. My body bent itself over as thick, smoky bits of partially consumed essence shot out of my mouth, curled around my lips, and floated up to the top of the Void. It left a nasty, burned flavor in my mouth.

I felt better then, still freaked out and grossed out, but no longer on the verge of puking my guts up, or whatever it's called when you shoot used essence out of your mouth at high velocity.

"Sorry," I said as I came back inside and shut the door behind me, my eyes still watery from what had happened.

"Don't apologize to me, hun," Naomi said. "I'd worry if it *didn't* make you sick."

"So is that why everyone's afraid to travel?" I asked.

"Most of it," she answered. "Safest place to be right now's with the Living. It's the gettin' there that's dangerous."

"What do you mean?"

"Well, take tonight. Cisco was just tellin' me about the brawl you two ran from. Tension's high. Everyone's on edge."

"Yeah, what was with that? Why were they fighting over a motor?"

Naomi chuckled. "Brian's not goin' to take jus' anything for a trip! Whoever owns the portal, owns the town."

The portal? For once, Cisco acted as surprised as I was. "There's a portal in the Entryway?" he asked.

"Course! What'd you think was goin' on?"

He shrugged. "I didn't, I mean…"

"Ghosts take something of value in exchange for a trip through the portal."

"Like what?" I asked.

She turned her palms up in a shrug. "Anything really. A jar of essence from the Vent, a rare piece of furniture or art. Oh! He's real fond of cats, so anything with cats usually gets you in."

"So the only way ghosts can visit their Live families is to buy their way in?"

She nodded, but not sadly, more like "that's just the way it is". "Well, unless they can make their own portal."

"Wait, what?" We both asked in unison.

"What do you mean, make their own?" I asked.

"Some ghosts can travel to the Living on their own. I call 'em portal poppers." She chuckled at her joke. "Nah, they're called shifters. I just like my name better. They're them you heard ghost stories 'bout when you's alive, like Bloody Mary."

Bloody Mary, now where had I heard that name before? I gasped. Darva! "One of Darva's ancestors is a por— is a shifter?"

"Who's Darva?" Naomi asked.

"One of the Bishops," explained Cisco.

"Oh yes, the Bishops have all kinds of gifted. I wouldn't be surprised if they didn't have several shifters."

"So wait." This was a lot to take in, and I wanted to confirm my understanding. "The way people talk about Darva's family, it's like they're really old. But if ghosts die when we get old…"

Naomi shook her head hard. "It's not age, honey. It's memory."

"Memory?"

"When a ghost give up. When they ain't got no more family or friends. If they was a legend, and that legend got forgot. *That's* what kills us off. Now I know what you're thinkin'. Auntie Naomi done give up on her family. I live alone, but I'm *happy* that way. For now anyways. I'm just waitin' on my husband, Carlos. And until I know he ain't comin', I ain't givin' up. So don't you give up. You find something to hold onto, and you keep holdin' onto it."

I needed to sit there, let my eyes drift to whatever corner of the room held less work for them, the less new to take in. I needed to be alone. I needed my library, my Clock, my solace.

"Course that's not all can kill a ghost," she added. "That's just the natural way."

The way she said "natural" made my glow shimmer, like there were a bunch of unnatural ways I didn't want to know about.

Cisco glanced my direction. "Thank you so much, Naomi." He stood cordially. I followed along beside him with a forced smile.

"Time to go already?" She put her knitting down and stood to join us. "I would ask you to come back, but it's too dangerous, ya hear?" Her tone was serious. Deadly serious. "Just in case though, I'll see if I can find any more of us Delgados out there for you."

"Thank you." Cisco grabbed her hand with pure sincerity. "My other name's Valdez, by the way."

She smiled and nodded, making her way toward the door. "I'll keep an ear out."

We stood on her porch, each wanting to say more but unsure how. I wanted her to hug me again. It was like she could read minds, well mine anyway. She wrapped her arms around us both and squeezed until I saw Cisco's eyes glow brighter from the strain. I smiled and sniffed in her hair. It smelled so good. Home.

"Go by the center of town, the Entryway, and keep to the populated areas. Don't dawdle!" She shooed us off her porch.

I was torn between wanting my time alone and wanting to stay with her. It was a new and complicated feeling. We turned and started our journey back.

With his hands in his pockets, he kept his head down and acted like I didn't exist. It must have been disappointing to him not to learn more about his family. I decided to give him some Cisco time.

We trotted in silence. The only noises were the Mediums' calls sounding into the Void. I paused a second. Did I just hear "Hannah"? Was it Lin's voice?

"What's wrong?" Cisco stopped and turned back to check on me. Good to know he was paying attention and that if a mad wisper had snagged me and run off to Ronnie he would have at least noticed. Hopefully before it was too late.

"I thought I heard—" There it was again. I was sure of it!

He stared above us and lowered his brow in concentration. I strained for over a minute, but I didn't hear it anymore.

"Nothing," I said. "Let's get back before the Clock sounds."

REVELATIONS

We kept our heads low. Even though Naomi said to stick to the crowded areas, I instinctively kept to the outskirts. After calling me back to his side at least four times, Cisco gave up, grabbed my hand, and refused to let go. I gritted my teeth, feeling like a little child the whole time.

We reached the Academy, the voices of the Callers all but non-existent now. The new day must be near.

Cisco reached for the chain of my necklace and wrapped it around his throat. Even after all we'd been through, being this close to him, our cheeks bumping into each other as we walked, felt awkward. Uncomfortable.

When we got to the other side, he pulled the necklace off his neck, allowing me some space.

"Thanks," I muttered. "For back there and all." If I had tried that on my own, I would be wisp fuel.

He spread his hands out in truly annoying Cisco charm and said, "Sure. No problem. Hey! I better go. See ya 'round." His hand gave a sloppy salute before he floated off for the Academy.

I walked slowly. Finally alone. I had a lot to think about. I wouldn't get the time I needed, however. The Clock sounded before I could take two steps.

With a gasp of terror, I sprinted for my room. "No no no no no!" I could *not* be late for detention!

No time to take off the pendant. I grabbed my bag and ran. "Excuse me! Sorry!" I screamed at what I assumed were students I bumped into.

By the time I arrvied at room 4F13, I knew it was too late. The door was shut. Detention had already started.

My head bowed to my chest. I opened the door, grabbed the first book my fingers touched from the shelf, and plopped into the first seat I came to, not my usual one.

I pulled out my paper and pencil from my backpack, opened the book randomly, and started copying.

"Bub screamed to the tongue one day, 'Hey, what are you doing?' But that day, Martha popped out with a squeal of excitement.

Lizzie called after her, 'Oh Martha! Wait for me!!'

Bub yelled, 'No Martha! No!'"

I stopped copying. What in the Dead's black Void was I reading? The front cover read, "Bub the Tooth, a Book for Children Afraid to Lose Teeth." This can't be a legitimate piece of literature, I thought. I continued my copying, too embarrassed to get up in front of everyone and switch my book out so soon after arriving.

The fact I had picked probably the smallest, and therefore shortest, book on the shelf allowed me to take my work slow and think, something I desperately needed to do. I had absorbed a lot of information in the last eight or so hours. As my brain processed it, my body reacted to it.

My roommate was smoking dead people. My freaking roommate was freaking smoking freaking dead people! I rested my forehead in my palm, my hair falling through my fingers. Breathe, I told myself. Slowly. Deeply. Breathe.

I peeked from under my hand. Either the other students didn't give what I did much notice, or they didn't care about my weirdness factor. It didn't seem Mr. Hill noticed my tardiness either. Yay! One point for me! Maybe today wouldn't suck as bad as I thought.

I resumed my reflection on recent events. I couldn't return to my room. Ever. There was no way.

No, I had to go back to return the medallion.

No, wait. That was what she used to get the stuff. I would be doing her a favor by *not* giving her back the medallion. I would be doing *everyone* a favor by not giving her back her medallion.

I scribbled some more words on my paper. The classroom door opened before I could argue with myself again. A girl I thought I recognized floated over to Mr. Hill with a paper in her hand. I nearly gasped. It was Robin! The girl who was so nice to me after Darva acted so mean. The girl who had invited me to hang with her and her friends and I never went. How could I have forgotten about her? Yeah, well, getting into fights, sneaking off into the Void, trying to discover my Live self, dealing with a cannibalistic roommate. These things take a toll on you, Hannah. Lighten up.

When she placed the paper for Mr. Hill to read, he flung his fingers in my direction, indicating she should hand the paper directly to me. Great. Now what? Had MaryAnn turned me in for stealing (technically borrowing) her necklace? Had someone seen us outside the Veil? That had to be it. Someone had seen us go through the Veil.

Robin's eyes recognized me at once, but they weren't prepared for what they saw. For the first time since being put in detention, I felt shame. I had not lived up to her expectations.

My face glowed hot with embarrassment, and I cast my eyes downward, unable to hold her gaze any further.

"This is for you," she said, kind, but overly so.

I took the paper. It was a note from Ms. Papenfuss.

Please return to the library at your earliest convenience to return your books to their shelves.

Violetta Papenfuss.

Ugh. The books! All those books on portals and Mediums and amnesia… I had never put the extra ones up. More shame climbed my neck and brightened my already glaring face. I was glad Robin had already left by the time I raised my face from the note. I hadn't meant to snub her. Like I said, I had forgotten about her.

Feeling terrible for disappointing a girl I barely knew, I shoved the note in my pocket and went back to copying before Mr. Hill yelled at me. Wasn't trying to return to a Medium with information I had to steal — ahem — borrow, enough for one person's agenda? Did I also have to have library duties and making new friends added to the pile? I would visit the library and put up my books, and I would visit Robin and apologize for not taking up her invitation. But *after* trying to see Lin again.

Lin. The thought of going back to him, of proudly telling him what I had found out, of possibly learning about my family and Life made it difficult to do my work. I couldn't help but smile. I found myself daydreaming about our next meeting. I considered every detail at least twice. Me telling him about visiting the Void and meeting Naomi. Him giving me a list of names of Dead family members I could visit. Oddly though, whenever I relived the details of last night's journey, my mind skipped the images of Cisco.

I didn't understand why. Well, maybe I did. Cisco wasn't exactly the poster child of morals in this school. I might also be ashamed to admit I took my roommate's necklace and used it to sneak out of the Veil with someone I met in detention, although technically we met in Portals first.

No, I didn't mind informing him I did all those things. I might have even been a little proud of it. It was Cisco I didn't want to tell him about. Every time I pictured it, narrating the adventure in my head, and I got to the parts where I mentioned Cisco, my mind jerked to a stop and yelled, "No!". But why? Why would I—

I gasped. Loud enough my neighboring students turned to see what was wrong. I felt the electrical charge of chagrin fire across my face for the third? fourth? time today. In this room alone. I hurriedly scribbled some more words onto my paper and ignored their stares. They returned to their copying.

I had gasped because I realized something. The reason I didn't want to mention Cisco to Lin was… I *liked* Lin.

FLEE

I closed the terrible book on baby teeth and grabbed a fresh one, this time paying more attention to the title, *How to Care for Kittens*. Not ideal, but better than its predecessor. I was in the middle of the chapter on which type of cat litter is best — flushable, newspaper, scoopable, etc. — when the Clock sounded. Feeding time.

I was hungry, hungry enough to stave skipping dinner for a trip to my Portals classroom. But not hungry enough not to at least peek inside. Just once, I told myself. Just one locale. The teachers will all be eating; it's the perfect time.

While everyone else jumped to put away their books and join their friends at the Vent, I took my time. The further I lagged, the easier it would be to go unnoticed as I sneaked into the classroom that got me put into detention.

The other students rushed past me in the hallway. I acted like I had forgotten something. I dropped my pencil at least three times. I thought about acting lost but didn't want to chance anyone trying to help me find my way. Eventually I was alone. I opened a few classroom doors to make sure. Yup, even the teachers were gone.

Ah, Portals. I hadn't been to my regular classes in three days now. It felt weird entering one. The inside was dark and empty save the globes of shining wisp hanging from the ceiling. My stomach gave a lurch when I saw them. Was globe wisp the same as ghost wisp? Surely not. Surely the teachers and Director of the Academy weren't siphoning off oldie essence just to light their classrooms. As my shaking fingers wrapped around the door's handle, I made a mental note to check on that tonight in the library.

My mind continued to conjure terrible thoughts however. Like, what if one of the globes broke, setting its wispies loose to dance in the Academy's atmosphere so any of its students could get a cannibalistic high from them? "You're letting your imagination get the better of you," I told myself. "Stop overreacting."

With a shudder of disgust, I pushed myself away from the door and walked to Mrs. Collin's desk. Once I pushed it out of the way, I reached for the switch next to the chalkboard.

It wasn't there.

What? I groped the wall with my hands, searching for anything they would have replaced the switch with. It was as smooth as if it had been freshly formed, which considering what MaryAnn had told me about the hallways on my first day, was entirely possible. I spun around, facing her desk. Maybe the switch was under it somewhere. I probed the underside with my fingers but came up short.

It was then I noticed the ticker. Well, that's what I called it anyway. A small, blue dome affixed to the top of Mrs. Collin's desk. It held a tiny globe of light tufts, and as it ticked, the tufts swirled in time with it. Glowing brighter every time it passed by so it resembled a flashing light.

A memory.

My mother behind me, holding me with her arms, shouting at my father, "Hurry! I can't let go of her long enough to enter it in!"

A tiny red light on the bottom of a tan box with numbers. Flashing. Flashing.

My father running to in front of me. His face never towards mine, only his back. His hands on the numbers, punching, mumbling. "There," he said.

The blinking stopped.

An alarm, I remembered as I returned to the present. They were disabling an alarm. It alerted the police if someone was breaking into our house.

This ticker on Mrs. Collins' desk… It was…

I sprinted out of the room and down the hall towards the entrance. In the far distance, I spotted the tiny glow of several ghosts walking together towards me. No, floating towards me. Quickly. Very quickly.

I ducked into the first classroom I came to, praying they hadn't noticed my glow.

Before me stood a tall glass cylinder filled with the brightest ghost I had yet to see. Its glow was yellower than I was used to, and upon closer inspection, it didn't look human.

"What kind of a class is this?" I whispered to myself.

I could hear the teachers in the hallway. "Someone was here alright," a woman's voice said.

I peeked out the classroom window.

"I observed someone down this way as we approached," said a man's voice.

"Well," I recognized Mrs. Collins speaking. "Let's check the classrooms. They're bound to be close by."

I swallowed. It was a dry, painful swallow that went all the way to my ears.

"Not here." A male staff member peeked in one of the classroom windows.

"Here either." A female member did the same with a different classroom.

If my glow gave me away from the other end of the hall, it certainly would from the door's window. I glanced behind me. The yellow glowing thing in the middle of the room might work to mask my light. I crouched on the floor behind it, clutching my bag between my legs.

I couldn't hear anymore voices, but I could feel them peering, boring their gaze into the wooden base I leaned against. "Please be enough. Please be enough. Please be enough," I whispered to myself. I strained my ears to hear them. I held my breath lest they detect it. Silence. Deafening, terrifying silence. Were they gone? Were they inside with me? Waiting for me to sheepishly stand from behind my hiding spot so as to make my shame worse?

I counted. 100. 300. 2000. I chanced craning my head around the podium to see what, or who, might be staring back at me.

No one.

Quietly, slowly, I rose to a crouch, then I stood. Half behind the glowing creature, half beside it. I crept to the door's window. On the way, I caught some wording on the chalkboard. "Specters, how to detect, avoid, and destroy them." I stared at the creature within the cylinder. Its head lobbed to one side. Its mouth hung open, displaying two rows of tall spikes for teeth. The palms of its hands held a single opening each. I allowed myself a closer look and realized, with great horror, the openings were additional mouths. Another shiver ran down my body, all the way to my feet. I stared up into its face and stepped away from it.

Its eyes opened, causing me to fall backward onto a row of desks. The entirety of its eyes was solid black. Its body twitched left, then right. It floated up then down, like a trapped mermaid in water. I scrambled to the door. The creature spun around and stared at me with its soulless, black eyes. It could not escape, that I knew, but it frightened me anyway. I swiftly righted myself and made for the door. I left the fallen desks where they lie.

Without turning my back on the spectre, I cracked the classroom door and allowed one eye to stare through the skinny crevice it made. The teachers were gone. I didn't trust them though. The specimen behind the glass continued to freak me out, but I forced myself to wait for ten deep, slow breaths until I was sure the hallway was empty. Then I opened the door, took one more glance over my shoulder to make sure the creepy black-eyed monster wasn't following me, and tiptoed down the hallway. All the while keeping close to one side lest I should have to slip into another classroom last minute.

Since the teachers were looking for someone who sneaked into the Portals classroom, and I had just completed detention for doing said act three days ago, I decided that being seen with my backpack would be a little too obvious for my liking. Kind of like a giant neon billboard that said, "Hey! Sneaky girl over here!" So I went to drop it off in my room first thing. If I had known what I was in for however, I would've taken my chances with being noticed or left my bag in the hallway or something, anything other than what I saw.

DESPERATE

I opened the door to my room in a rush, hoping to toss my bag and hide for a few before starting on my growing to-do list. But the door wouldn't open fully.

I glanced down to see what blocked it. A sofa cushion. I scanned the rest of the abnormally dark room. The sofas lay torn apart, the rest of their cushions scattered across the floor, in the corners. Our drawers and their contents filled up what empty space was left. One of them sat at an odd angle, broken from whatever force had put it there.

Writhing shadows danced atop the debris, attracting my attention to their cause. MaryAnn. Hovering on the ceiling, using her feet as leverage while she attempted to pull our light globe off its base. Before I could react, the globe broke away with a crack. MaryAnn somersaulted in the air, then landed on her feet on the floor.

She hunched over her treasured claim. Her hair hung in tangled strands, dangling around her face and hands like a closet door hiding a naughty child. I took a step in, my fingers still grasping the edge of our blocked door. My jaw fell in disbelief. Her body shook uncontrollably with desperation as her hand groped her back pocket until it produced a small straw. She then used the straw to suck the light tufts from the globe in deep, exaggerated breaths.

Her chest expanded to its fullest with each huff. When the globe was empty, she threw it against the back wall where it shattered. A tiny squeal escaped my throat when she did, catching her attention.

She turned her head to face me, and my mouth fell open further with fresh horror. Her eyes. Her once soft, full of expression eyes now drooped, their lids swollen and glowing. The skin on her face, drawn in from pain, quickly spread with rage when she recognized who I was.

"Where's my pendant?" she screamed, desperate, harsh. Her voice cracked in a thousand places.

"I-I-" A burn, born in my chest, radiated to the tips of my fingers, my toes. It was terror, taking control of my body, taking control of me. I knew what she wanted, the necklace I had taken from her and now wore around my neck. She needed it to get back to Ronnie. To get her beloved wisp. Her black, fury-filled eyes told me if I didn't give her the pendant, she would do the same to me as she had the light globe.

With a primal snarl, she flew at me, her arms outstretched. I had no time to react. Her hands found my throat. And squeezed. I didn't need the breath. In retrospect it wasn't that big a deal to be strangled as a ghost, but my instincts told me differently. They told me to panic.

I pried at her fingers with my own.

"You took my pendant! What did you do with it?" Her face, scrunched and contorted from her thirst for wisp and the anger, was all I saw as her hands yanked me back and forth by the neck.

I tried to answer. Her grip was too tight. I had the air with which to speak, but I couldn't force it through. I mouthed the words instead. "It's on … my neck… It's on…"

I don't know what made her so strong, or me so weak, but she threw me to the floor. My hand reached for my now stinging neck.

"If I can't get to my wisp, I'll just have to make my own."

I wondered if she would retreat to the globe, but then I saw the straw in her hand. She jumped on top of me before I could think to react. I pushed against her, but again, I was too weak. It was like she was filled with extra weight to go with her extra strength.

She pressed my head to the side, stretching my neck at the bend, forcing my cheek against the floor. From the corner of my vision, I saw the straw come down, felt its tip against my skin.

"No!" I screamed, my throat raw from where she had squeezed it shut.

I tried to tell her the necklace was there, that I would hand it to her, for her to just take it, but her palm pressed my face so tightly, my mouth couldn't form the words right. In her state of mind, she might not have understood them anyway.

She sucked. Hard. I felt my neck pull away. It wasn't painful, just a pinch. She stopped, gasping for air. "Why … isn't … it…"

She tried once more. Again, I felt the pinch. I pushed against her, struggled to touch the necklace. If I could just get one finger around it, I could pull it off, divert her attention to what she really wanted.

The pinching stopped. The pressure her hand held against the side of my face lessened. I rotated my head as much as possible to find her eyes now gleaming with joy.

Her nails scratched the side of my neck as her fingers grasped the pendant's chain. She pulled it from around my head. Harshly. My hair caught in its folds and ripped from my scalp with a million sharp pains. I cried out, but she didn't hear me.

With her hands now busied with their prize, I turned my gaze cautiously to the door. Could I make my escape?

Her fingers fumbled with the pendant, turning it over and over while her eyes searched for something in particular on its back. The diversion allowed me to crawl out from under her.

She sat between me and the door now. A single finger stroked some writing on the back of the pendant. A smile formed before it quickly vanished. Before she ran out of the room as silently as if she had never been there, I managed to catch what her fingers had traced. An engraving. "MA/Twi". MaryAnn and Twila.

TWILA AND MARYANN'S STORY

The moment my brain registered MaryAnn had left, that I was safe, I started sobbing. I crawled quickly to the door and slammed it shut so no one could spot the mess. Could spot me. I let the sobs come. I lay on the floor, my arms wrapped around my legs, and didn't try to stop a single one of them.

I don't know how long it took to regain control of myself, but when I did, I sat up and wiped the tears from my face. I then rubbed my palms dry on my jeans. Part of me felt like I deserved what she did to me for taking her pendant without asking. Oh, I had justified it to myself over and over in various ways, but stealing is stealing. I denied the guilt and pushed it away.

If my passed experience with MaryAnn was any indication of her present behavior, I wouldn't see her for a long time, maybe forever. I stood up and surveyed the damage. I considered this room more mine than hers, and I didn't want it to look like this. I wanted no memory of her attack. Of the guilt.

I picked up the bigger things and put them away, the cushions, the clothes. I hung the mirror back up. My face was fine. There was a slight glow to my cheeks where they had touched her hand and the floor, but it was symmetrical enough not to draw any attention. My neck was a different story.

Distinct, glowing echoes of MaryAnn's fingers wound around it. Tiny bolts pulsated along the shapes, up my chin, and down to my chest. That, I would have to hide.

Someone knocked on the door. I could pretend I wasn't here, that I was in the library already or doing normal ghostly things.

They knocked again. "Hello? It's me. Twila."

I swallowed, and almost cried out from the pain it caused to my damaged throat.

"Hannah? Are you there?"

My brows dipped in puzzlement as to why she asked for me instead of MaryAnn.

I cautiously walked to the door and turned the knob. I refused to open it more than a sliver. She was alone. She glanced up at me, worried. Her stance showed she was giving me my space.

Her eyes darted up and down the hallway, making sure no one would overhear her words. "I watched MaryAnn run out of the Academy and towards the Void," she whispered. "What happened?"

I opened the door, keeping behind it so my body wasn't visible to the students in the hallway. There were still some items strewn across the floor. Twila's eyes took them all in as I closed the door behind her.

When her eyes landed on me, she gasped. "What happened?"

I motioned for her to sit down. She complied, and I faced her from the other couch. I briefly, and carefully, told her about the "event". It wasn't as upsetting to do as I thought.

Unlike with Darva, I fought back this time, and also unlike with Darva, I considered MaryAnn slightly justified. I felt better when I'd finished. Twila acted sad, but unsurprised.

"You don't know what the wisp does to you," she said, her elbows on her knees, her fingers fiddling with an imaginary object.

"At first, it's wonderful." A slight smile of remembrance passed across her face. "You forget all your troubles. Everything that hurts goes away." She stared at the corner of the room, never focusing on me.

"Instead of pain, instead of fear, you feel good. Happy." The corners of her mouth turned up further, but a deep sadness loomed over them.

"When you're on the wisp … nothing bad can ever happen." She turned her head to stare directly into my eyes. "But then…" She glanced down at my injured neck. "You come down. And the down is so much worse than the real. Real life, once scary and overwhelming, becomes nonexistent. And not in the good way it did on the wisp. It doesn't exist because you now live in a dark cloud of sadness where you can no longer feel. Anything. And you will do anything, *anything*, to experience happiness again."

I thought about how scared I had been in the Maze, how scared I was to walk the hallways when I first arrived. If I had been able remove all that fear and replace it with happiness, would I have? The memories of my mother, my father, their love for me, their arms around me. If I could relive their love like it was real… If I had tried wisp that first night, before I had seen what it did to MaryAnn, would I be addicted to it too? Would I be like her? Ready to suck the very soul of my roommate just to feel loved again?

"That's why I quit," said Twila, snapping me from my thoughts. "I saw what MaryAnn was becoming. It changed her. It changed me to, but…" She ran her fingers through her straight, dark waterfall of hair. "When I saw what it was doing to her. When I found myself thinking of nothing but the wisp. Nothing but the wisp. Nothing but the wisp." Her eyes closed tightly, and she took a deep breath, like she was trying to force the memories out of her mind.

When she calmed, she opened them again. "I knew it was time to quit. I didn't want it controlling me like that. Besides," she sighed. "MaryAnn was getting more and more selfish with it all the time. Even though I helped her get it."

My eyes widened. Today's events had broadened the differences between Twila's and MaryAnn's personalities to me. MaryAnn had become desperate, dependent, angry. While Twila was sweet, kind, and courageous. I couldn't imagine the two together anymore, not that they ever appeared to fit well. So the idea of Twila traversing the Void with MaryAnn to seek out wisp was inconceivable to me.

Twila saw my thoughts in my expression. She rose from the couch and strolled to the corner of the room where MaryAnn's drawers stood. In front of them lay her sopping, wet clothes, the ones I had found when first hiding her hookah. My stomach lurched at the memory.

She picked up the clothes. Her hair hid her face. "Did she ever tell you how she died?"

I shook my head. Her eyes didn't leave the clothes, so I whispered, "No."

"She drowned."

Her fingers reverently stroked the clothes resting in her other hand.

"Her parents favored her sister. The older sibling she had idolized as a child."

She placed the still wet clothing on top of the drawers and straightened them into a perfect stack.

"Her sister always got everything. Money. Love. Adoration. Praise. They always treated MaryAnn as the failure. She was never good enough. She was the better one though." She paused, needlessly tidying the stack as she thought.

"The family went on a trip together. Her mother, her father, her sister, her sister's little girl. They were near a large creek in Virginia, some silly camping trip her parents had wanted to take in the States with them, when her little niece fell in. She was only two.

"While her sister stood screaming on a log, MaryAnn jumped in. She wasn't a good swimmer. She saved the child, but she'd inhaled too much water.

"Her parents grabbed the child from her arms, gave it to her sister, and comforted the young mother for nearly losing her. MaryAnn tried calling for help. She doesn't remember if they heard her or not, but they didn't come for her."

I stared silently at her, trying not to gawk. Her face held that peaceful smile she always wore that made you wonder if she realized all the awful stuff around her. After that story, it was clear she did. I guess she just chose not to acknowledge it.

She stopped stroking the clothes and faced me. "So you see, Hannah, I can't blame her for what she does."

For getting high on wisp? No, not really. She was trying to find the happiness she never knew in Life. But, I could blame her if…

"Did you, um, did you know where the wisp came from?" I asked. I didn't want to ask the question. But I had to.

Her smile was sardonic. "You mean did I know we were smoking other ghosts? Yes."

I felt my jaw loosen and fought to keep it shut.

"MaryAnn and I… We died in similar ways. Bad ways," she corrected. "My parents were nothing like hers, but how I died was… She had already been here awhile when that happened, and, I guess she saw some of herself in me. By then, she was already wisping.

"We started hanging out, and she introduced me to it." Her head lowered, like she was ashamed. Her gaze kept to the floor. "She was my only friend at the time and…"

I let her take her time to finish.

After several moments she took a breath and said, "Whenever we needed more, she would go out in the Void and get it. One day she asked me to come along. That's when I learned what wisp was." She sucked in her lips and chewed them for a long, silent moment. "She scratched our initials into the back of the pendant and told me I was part of the family now. I went with her a few times after that, but never again." She shook her head.

I sat silent. What could I possibly say to that? Sorry? There was nothing, nothing I could do or say to make this better for anyone.

Her fingers gripped the edge of the sofa cushions. I noticed a tear in one of them, probably from the earlier chaos. She glanced over at me, reading my expression.

"Be careful with her," she warned.

"A bit late for that." I smiled.

She shook her head. "No, that's not what I mean. Today she just wanted the pendant. Next time, she'll want something more."

I felt my forehead crumple. "What do you mean?"

She huffed out a disbelieving laugh. "They don't just *give* you the wisp! You have to pay for it!"

The crumple deepened.

"Ronnie,"—I straightened my back with the mention of his name—"he asks for things. Services, items, it depends on what mood he's in. Sometimes,"—she stared at the floor again—"he asks for people."

She glanced up to watch my reaction. I tried to position my face into the correct one. I knew exactly what she meant by that: ghosts to turn into wisp, people to murder.

"Did um, did MaryAnn ever…"

Twila's wide, fearful eyes glistened as they stared into mine. She whispered so faintly I barely made it out, "I don't know."

HOVERING

Twila left shortly after that. She never asked me any questions, and I didn't push her to explain anything else.

I finished cleaning up, saving my backpack for last. A note was peeking from its front pocket. Its corner tore when I pulled it out. It was the one from Ms. Papenfuss. I sighed heavily and straightened the note's corner as best I could before neatly folding and returning it to my backpack's pocket.

I checked my reflection in the mirror. My neck had already started to heal, but it wasn't normal looking enough to wander about without attracting unwanted attention yet. I tried to cover it with my hair, which only made it to my shoulders. It might hide the sides, if I held my head right, but would do nothing for the front.

I searched both our wardrobes and sets of drawers for a shirt with a high collar or something. In MaryAnn's wardrobe, I found a hoodie with a high enough neck to cast a shadow over my injuries. If I tucked my head in just right … perfect!

I knew it was way past time to eat, but I felt compelled to stroll by the Vent before checking in with Ms. Papenfuss. I don't know, maybe a tiny hope lingered in the back of my head telling me a latent strip of essence a la strawberry milkshake was waiting for me. I was beyond hungry, and all the healing I was doing was only going to make it worse. My pace quickened, and I found myself, now that I was thinking about food again, actually hoping, not just wondering if I was hoping.

The usual after dinner groups of students filled the Academy hallways. Laughter wafted from the game room as I walked under the entryway stairs. I walked through the regular cliques that dotted the sporting areas between the Academy and the Vent, the students thinning as I approached the Vent until I was alone.

I stood in the center of the Vent, where the essence would have normally risen through, and looked up. Not even the hovering ghosts from outside the Veil lingered overhead now. I stared down at the floor beneath my feet and kicked at the black fog with my shoes. The onyx floor beneath it remained solid. If I had not known this was where the Vent opened every day like literal clockwork, I would have never known it from the rest of the floor of the Void.

I looked back at the Academy. The remnants of a line of its staff twisted around the back corner of the building. The Gatherers.

My insides sank down, angry with me for choosing to miss my feeding. Although technically if I had tried to eat, MaryAnn would have stopped me when I went to drop my bag off in my room. I tried telling my insides that and pressed against them with my arm, but they stubbornly refused to listen. I gritted my teeth. A full night and day would have to pass before I would be able to squelch the pain.

I returned to the Academy. About halfway there, the last Gatherer disappeared behind the side corner. I stopped. While I assumed all that stuff ended up in the closet or factory, I wanted to know exactly what happened to it. I mean, why not?

It's not like it was forbidden to watch or anything. That I knew of.

The other students ignored me as I passed. I placed my hand on the outside corner of the porch and peeked around it. The back of the last Gatherer was just disappearing through a door. I ran to see where the door led.

There were enough students on this side of the porch, I didn't feel out of place. I climbed the steps and peeked inside. Gatherers were placing their items into organized piles: piles of clothing, piles of furniture, piles of small usable items, and a large pile of stuff I had yet to see in the Land of the Dead. One rectangular item on the top of that pile stood out, a microwave. I stared at it, wondering why I hadn't seen it or any of the other items in that pile before.

A memory hit. I was in the kitchen. My kitchen. I remembered it from the memory I had gotten while visiting Lin. The green numbers on the front of the microwave flashed 12:00. 12:00. 12:00. 12:00.

"Power must've gone out." Mom's voice.

"It's OK. I'll set it." Dad.

An unknown man's voice jerked me to the present. "Can I help you?" One of the Gatherers was staring down at me. It must've been his voice I heard. His face wore an amused smile.

"S-Sorry," I sputtered, and sped down the porch to the side entrance. He hadn't acted like I was in trouble, but I felt that way all the same.

I heard him shut the door behind me.

Electricity, I realized as I slowed to a walk inside the Academy's lower hallway. Microwaves, lights, stoves, they all ran on electricity. That was why I hadn't seen any. They were useless here, like the motor from the Entryway. I wondered what they did with them.

I entered the library and walked straight up to the desk. Ms. Papenfuss stared down at me. I handed her the note. "I'm sorry, Ms. Papenfuss. I got busy and forgot about the books."

She pressed her lips together in an unforgiving manner. "I suppose you expect me to float up the ones from the higher shelves."

I gritted my teeth and smiled a pathetic smile. I hadn't thought about that. "I'm sorry, unless you have a ladder, or something."

Her hand dropped to her desk, and she peered over her chained spectacles at me. "Miss Hannah, do you honestly believe we have ladders that go all the way to the top of this library?"

I glanced upward. The shelves had to reach four stories. "No."

She glared at me another two seconds before readjusting her glasses to their normal position and focusing her attention on a paper in her other hand. Our conversation was over.

I dragged my feet to my corner of the library. It appeared untouched since I was last here. I had so many questions. I was itching to look up my topics, to sit in my corner and contemplate recent events, but I had to put away these— Geez! How many books did I collect? I distinctly remembered putting each one up as I finished with it. I guess I didn't finish as many as I thought I had. Stacks of books teetered across three tables. This was going to take forever, I groaned silently.

I shuffled through each one. My research had been thorough, which meant my books were various in subject and therefore shelving location. After checking the numbers on the spine, I either put the book away, or placed it in one of the many exceedingly neat piles I was creating for Ms. Papenfuss.

I bit my lip. She wasn't going to be happy with how many I was leaving for her.

Hours later, I pushed the last book into its empty spot between two other books on portals and stood back with my fists on my hips. There. All done.

Boy, it's quiet in here tonight. I glanced around to see how many students were left. None. Ms. Papenfuss was though, and her body made the distinct bounce of someone tapping their foot on the floor.

"I'm done!" I called out. I walked up to her podium to make sure she heard me. "All the books I couldn't put away I placed in piles for you on the table over there." I pointed to them for her.

She eyed the piles then focused on me again, her lips in their perpetual purse, her glasses against the bridge of her nose. "Thank you, Miss Hannah." She tapped a newly affixed sign to the front of her podium which read, "Students may only remove three books at a time from the shelves."

"No more than three at a time from now on, Miss Hannah," she said.

Demon spawn! I felt terrible! The library literally had to make a new rule just because of something I did. I hoped the other students never found out I was the one responsible for it. I let out a heavy breath and nodded I understood, then left with my head hung low.

If the library was closed, then classes would start soon. I went to my room to get ready for them. I opened the door and stepped inside. The only light for the entire room came from my personal glow, our light tufts having been consumed by MaryAnn. The darkness added an extra layer of creepy to the already eerie atmosphere. I felt too alone, a tiny speck of dust in a large vacuum of space. The walls closed in on me, my mind's way of making the too wide room smaller. I was able to force myself far enough in to drop my backpack, but that was my limit. I fumbled for the doorknob behind me and backed into the hallway. I pulled the door shut and took another step back, separating myself from the now uncomfortable solitude.

I had to get away from where I was, standing in the middle of the hallway, awkwardly staring at a closed door. If there was anybody left who didn't think I was crazy, all they had to do was look now to see what all the hubbub was about.

I turned and started walking. Anywhere. I had no clue what direction I was going, nor did I care. I just wanted away.

As I aimlessly wandered the hallways while trying to give the impression I had a destination in mind, I passed a room filled with girlish laughter. I stopped to listen. Something about it sounded familiar.

I peeked inside. There, in the center of the room laughing with her friends, was Robin. The invitation! I slapped my forehead with my hand. This was twice I had forgotten it! I started to approach her and apologize for not coming sooner, but then I realized the last time she saw me was in detention, and I had detention again tomorrow. Would she still want me to sit with her now I was classified a troublemaker?

I stood in the doorway, deliberating my options. Option one? Go inside and potentially cause a terrible scene with Robin and her friends because she would like to rescind her previous, thoughtless invitation. Option two? Blindly roam the Academy and its hallways until the Clock sounded. Option three? Go back to my room and wait. Alone. In the dark. With the walls that grew tighter around me with every second that passed.

I studied Robin and her friends from the doorway. They seemed nice, approachable. Robin said nothing to me when she recognized me in detention. Then again, she may have thought (hoped?) I had forgotten the invitation. I turned to leave.

No! I stomped my foot in defiance against my cowardice. I refused to spend my Death running away from everything that made me uncomfortable. I would do this.

I looked down. My hands were shaking. I clinched my fingers into fists to stop their trembling. I closed my eyes and took a deep breath. When I reopened them, I turned back around to face the craft room and weaved purposefully between the tables towards her. A few curious onlookers glanced my direction. Their expressions made me realize I was probably walking a little more purposefully than I should, like aggressively purposeful. I relaxed my stance and slowed my pace. My shy nature reappeared, helping me come across as less hostile. The change in their stares told me it worked.

Surprise filled Robin's eyes when she saw me. This was it. This was when she stood up and denounced me as detention girl, the shame of her regretted invitations. I wanted to run away, to never see her or anyone in this room ever again, but I didn't. I forced myself to stay. "Hi, Robin." My voice cracked as I pushed down the tears that wanted so desperately to join the party.

"Oh, hi!" She smiled welcomingly, but I could tell her emotions were conflicted.

"I-I'm sorry I didn't come when you first invited me. I was still new and … didn't know … um…"

Her face softened with compassion. "It's OK, Hannah. We've all been new once." She glanced around at her friends who giggled and nodded in agreeance.

"Oh!" She stood, her knitting dangling from one hand. "Would you like to join us?"

I wrung my fingers to keep them from noticing their trembling. What was it about a circle of smiling girls that had me more scared than a bar full of strangers?

The other girls in her circle wore friendly expressions, most not as friendly as hers but none full of animosity or anything else to drive normal people away. Note the word "normal".

"Um, sure." My voice continued to shake, and I blinked several times to clear my too wet eyes.

"Here," the girl closest to me said, standing as she did. She handed me her chair.

I glanced around the circle. All eyes were on me, expectant. I took the chair, feeling rude the whole time for doing it. The other girls smiled in response. The one girl walked a few yards over and got an extra chair to sit in. Everyone scooted their seats back to make the circle wider. I followed along.

Robin introduced everyone, "This is Natalie, Jocelyn, Brooke, Melissa, Kathy, and Tiffany." They all looked up at me and smiled cordially.

I forced a smile back at each of them. My hands were still shaking, though not as bad.

"So, where are you from?" asked the girl named Natalie. Her hair hung in blonde spirals that bounced whenever her head moved, which was quite often since she turned out to be the bubbly sort.

Great. I thought I was finished with the "I don't remember my Life" explanations. I felt my face brighten. "I don't know," I said, glancing around at the even more curious than earlier eyes.

Natalie didn't know how to respond to that one.

Robin, in a true attempt to be nice by changing the subject, asked, "Did you and Darva ever get along?"

Why thank you, Robin. I had forgotten all about that hateful beast, but thanks for bringing back the sweet, sweet memories.

Some of the others smirked in response to Robin's question. A few snorted and mumbled under their breath something about who would *want* to get along with Darva. It sounded like they were on my side.

"Actually, um, no." I shook my head. "We never did."

She pursed her lips into a sympathetic grimace.

"It only got worse. Actually."

The others went back to their crafts, their faces portraying thoughts of "Duh, what did you expect, Robin?"

Robin's eyes shifted back to the work in her lap. A tiny blue blush glowed from her cheeks. Was she sorry she asked that question?

No one was speaking now, and the quiet made me anxious. "How about you?"

She looked up at me.

"Did Darva do anything to you after you helped me? Like you thought she would?"

All shame left her face. She dropped her knitting to her knees, enthusiastic with the conversation again. "No, she didn't! But we don't have any classes together, so that's probably why." She shrugged.

Jocelyn rose six inches above her chair and stretched. Her straight, bleached hair with at least a full inch of black roots draped down her back as she did. She did not return to her seat.

"How do you do that?" I asked.

"What?" She looked up from the grey kitten she was cross-stitching.

"Hover."

"Oh." She shrugged. "It's easy. You just focus all your energy at the top of your body."

I tilted my head.

Brooke put down her project and scooted to the edge of her seat. Her hands waved about emphatically as she spoke. "Close your eyes. Be real still, and think about whatever part of your body is the closest to the ceiling." She demonstrated, looking like she had entered a type of meditative state.

Her body rose several inches. She opened her eyes and leaned forward, propping her elbow on her knee. "Now, you try."

Seriously? Just like that?

"Um … OK."

I gripped the sides of my chair and closed my eyes. The top of my head pushed upward towards the ceiling, and I concentrated on that part of my body alone. As I did, I felt it move further and further away from me, almost like my head was leaving my body. Was that possible? Visions of failed hovering attempts, ghosts walking around with their heads on balloon strings, filled my mind, and I giggled.

My bottom hit the chair with a distinct *plop*.

I gasped. "I did it! I hovered!"

"Good job!" Tiffany told me.

A couple of the others murmured and nodded in agreement. Brooke was the most enthusiastic, clapping hardily like I was the student who made her proud, which technically I guess I was.

I smiled, an honest to goodness feel-the-happy smile. Melissa, the girl to my right, patted me on the back.

"Time to go, y'all," Jocelyn announced.

I heard the chairs scraping against the floors behind us as the other groups started to leave.

As the girls in my group put away their projects, I stood and walked over to Brooke. "Thanks," I said.

She looked up at me, her arm still in her knitting caddy, and smiled. "You're welcome."

"Oh!" she called after me, catching me as I turned for the door. "You're not supposed to hover on school grounds without a license. Not that anyone ever notices, but just in case."

"Thanks." I already knew that, but it was nice of her to remind me.

REAPER

The Clock sounded when I reached the hallway. I rushed through the flow of students to my room, feeling more confident than usual. I had made friends, and they seemed to like me. I told myself I would have to visit them again.

The fresh noise of the other students made it easier to go into my room and fetch my bag, but the ominous darkness inside it tugged at my happy mood. I left quickly.

As I made my way to what I truly hoped was my last day of detention, I wondered if I should mention to what classified as maintenance around here that I needed a new light globe. I decided asking would raise too many questions and dropped the thought.

I chose my book carefully this time, trying to pick one I wouldn't mind spending the day copying, and settled into my routine. The shuffling of the other students died down. Classes had started.

A note slid onto the corner of my desk. I raised my head to see who it was from. Mr. Hill. He was already walking back to his desk.

It was a small, unfolded slip of paper:

I grimaced. I guess he had noticed my tardiness yesterday after all. One more day of detention wasn't *that* bad, I realized. I mean, I had broken the rules. Technically. If you really wanted to think about it that way. And a single day of detention was much less than whatever they would have given me for setting off that alarm in Portals.

The moment Mr. Hill's bottom filled his seat, he droned, "Have it signed by Director Richards."

Like now, or…? He didn't meet my gaze. I decided to err on the side of caution and visit her *after* today's detention, not during.

I wadded the paper in my fist, then realized my error and flattened it as best I could between my book and desk before neatly folding it and placing it between two pages of my Rules book in my bag. I returned to my copying.

The whole time of detention my insides screamed in hungry protest. I went straight to the Vent afterwards and gorged myself on apple pie and hotdogs. Then I headed for the library. I wanted to research the light tufts. Maybe I could get light back in my room without calling the school's attention to it.

I entered the library without glancing once at the podium. I didn't want to see Ms. Papenfuss's reaction to my reentry the very next day.

The piles I had left for her were gone. Guess she got around to them in my absence. I plopped my bag on my usual desk and went to the card catalog. "Wisp," I whispered aloud, then immediately bit my lips together. This was one research project I couldn't have others knowing about. Questions would be asked, explanations would be made, then everyone would want to know why I didn't turn MaryAnn in earlier.

Acquiring Light by U.C. Lambent. That one showed promise. Its call numbers put it on the second set of shelves up, something I couldn't reach without help. Unless…

I stared at the book's location and chewed my lip. There were no other students in the library, and Ms. Papenfuss was giving me a wary stare. I smiled back, hoping to break the tension. It didn't work.

I walked to where the book I wanted was located and poked around the bottom shelf. It held mostly books about plumbing. Not something I remembered in Life, and after fake reading a couple of the books there, not something I would ever need in the Land of the Dead.

Three books later, which I purposefully placed each back in its spot before removing the next one, Ms. Papenfuss's attention was finally drawn away from me. Other students were coming in, chatting with each other, joining their reading and study groups. None of them would care if I owned a hovering license or not, even if by some weird coincidence they happened to know.

I closed my eyes and breathed deep, even breaths. Every breath traveled to my head. I was a balloon. I felt my toes dip downward and opened my eyes. I gasped, lost my concentration, and fell back to the floor. I stumbled to the side and quickly checked to see if Ms. Papenfuss or anyone else had noticed anything. She was busy helping a new student. I watched her take a boy to the card catalog and knew I had several long minutes to do my thing.

I shook out my hands, took a deep breath and held it, pushing it into my scalp, tipping my head up, up to the ceiling

I needed to move towards. My toes fell. I knew I was rising. I smiled, afraid to open my eyes lest I fall again.

My toes were free. I was no longer in contact with the floor at all now. I had to open my eyes. I had to see where I was. I braced myself, willing my body not to react when my vision returned. They fluttered open. The books in front of me were moving down, slowly, like an underpowered elevator. When I was sure I wouldn't overreact, I peeked further out. I was only a foot or so up. I had at least three more to go before I could reach my book. I didn't dare turn around to check if I was still safe from Ms. Papenfuss. I couldn't handle that much movement, not yet. I concentrated on my current goal instead of allowing myself to dwell on getting caught.

I reached out and touched one of the books, scanning its numbers as I did. No, another level or two up. My hands held the shelves in front of me like climbing stones on a rock face, guiding me upward. There. The right area at least. I stopped pushing up in my mind. My body started to fall. While using my hands to pull myself back up, I concentrated up, up, up, in little pulses. Fall a little, rise, fall a little, rise. This seemed far more difficult than it appeared when others did it. The book I wanted was to my right. I pulled myself to it while concentrating on moving in that direction and maintaining my altitude. When I got it from the shelf, I thought about how I would descend.

Oops, hadn't been taught that part. It was too far to just drop, and if I concentrated on down like I did up, could you imagine the speed? The Dead did still have gravity, you know.

I held to the shelf, just in case, and let myself fall; much like I had fallen earlier when I stopped thinking "up". It worked. I floated lazily down, my free hand using the edges of the shelves like ladder rungs while my other one clutched my prize to my chest.

I allowed myself three seconds (yes, I actually counted) to enjoy being on the ground again before peeking to see if I had made it unnoticed by the eyes that mattered. Ms. Papenfuss was still instructing the new student. A wave of relief made me lightheaded.

I went back to my desk and flipped through the table of contents.

Chapter 7, Capturing light wisp. page 137

Bingo! I turned to page 137 and skimmed until I found it.

Unlike the essence of spirits, light tufts, or light filaments as became the term after the Living invented the electric light bulb, is most often captured from noble metals and ignited gases such as hydrogen and acetylene. It differs from the main essence of the Vents in both color and texture. While feeding essence is flavorful with blue tents, light filaments are yellow and frail in comparison, and great care must be taken when attempting to capture and utilize the filaments so as not to destroy them in the process. While inhaling a single light filament by accident during feeding will most likely not damage the feeding individual, persistent use will damage the internal structure of the individual until they become incapacitated. Healing is slow, but possible. Most ghosts, however, will immediately realize they are feeding on something caustic as coughing and spluttering disallows them to continue inhaling the burning essence.

I was about to shut the book when I noticed a drawing on the adjoining page. I let my fingertips graze the penciled patterns across the paper. This was the original drawing. It made sense. Cameras and photographs weren't exactly commonplace around here. Modern cameras, of course, required electricity, which means they were useless, and older cameras required chemicals, flammable chemicals which probably only made it up here in the form of light filaments, just as the book said.

I read the caption beneath the drawing. "Just as the Reaper uses filaments to traverse the Void and the Maze, so do ghosts use them to light their homes." The girl in the drawing carried a familiar lantern, and bore a face I recognized well. Lydia.

RETURN

What was a Reaper? Was it bad? Lydia, although creepy and possibly rude, wasn't evil. At least I didn't think so. She saved me from the Maze and brought me here. Prevented me from being turned into wisp. I shuttered at the thought. She'd rescued most if not all the students currently here. Two or three a week from what I'd heard, though it varied. So maybe a Reaper was a good thing.

Still, I wanted to understand what one was exactly. I returned to the card catalog and searched for "Reaper". Not as many as there were with "Medium" but certainly more than with "wisp" or "one-way sailing boats".

This one looked promising. *Distinguishing Between Myth and Fact of the Reaper* by Geraldine P. Manes. I glanced around for its location. Higher than the last one but far enough in the back so as to hide my hovering from Ms. Papenfuss more easily.

I memorized the call number, shut the drawer back and headed to the book's shelf without succumbing to the temptation to peek over my shoulder as I did. Ms. Papenfuss was a misty figure in the distance from where I stood now. A couple of students sat at nearby tables, but they paid me no notice.

I closed my eyes, took a deep breath, and concentrated. When I felt my feet leave the floor, I opened my eyes and allowed my hands to guide me to my destined location. I felt more relaxed this time, free, out from under judgmental gazes.

When I reached the book, I slid it from the shelf and concentrated on not lowering too quickly.

"Miss Hannah!"

The ground met my feet with a jarring impact. My ankle twisted, and I fell sideways. "Ah!" I reached for my ankle, already larger than the other one and brighter in color.

My prize lay several feet in front of me, open with pages down so as to bend them. I quickly abandoned my injury and grabbed the book before Ms. Papenfuss had more reason to yell at me. I doubted it mattered at this point though.

"Your license, please." She held out her hand expectantly.

I knew what she wanted, that hovering license I was told probably wouldn't matter. I realized I shouldn't have tried to get the book on my own, but it was the desire to avoid a scenario identical to this that made me do it in the first place. I should have known better.

"I don't have one," I said, my voice as soft and meek as a small child's.

Her expression said she knew that already.

I got to my feet, hopping off my hurt ankle the second I put pressure on it.

She eyed my limp with the hint of satisfaction. "*That* is why we require proper training and licensure in this school!"

Yeah. Yeah.

I sucked in my lips and stared at the floor to hide my sarcasm.

"I shall report you to Mrs. Richards. I trust you won't be attempting any more wrongdoings while I'm gone?"

I nodded, not really knowing if my answer were truthful or not. But if I were smart, which I just proved myself to not be, I would do as she commanded. "Yes, ma'am." I kept my eyes locked down.

With one foot still higher than the other, I watched her walk away and out the library doors. Great. It appears Mr. Hill and I are going to grow quite close before this is over. I limped back to my desk, wondering if I would be allowed to check out a book of my choice to take back and copy. One more day of please-shoot-me instructional books, and I might take up the wisp myself.

Never. Joke. Like that. Again. Hannah. I told myself. Wisp was *not* a joking matter.

I couldn't help but notice, the moment I sat down and placed my new book before me, the leather cover of the reaper book had an engraving of that all too familiar lantern. Lydia's lantern.

The pages were old with torn edges and handwritten words on them. I flipped through them as gently as possible, more afraid of damaging them then of what Ms. Papenfuss would do if I did. There were several illustrations. One of the Academy, one of the Maze, one of Lydia, but the one that brought pause was a labeled blueprint of Lydia's lantern.

Each part had a line connecting it to a larger, more detailed drawing of it. The lantern was filled with light filament, that I knew. I even gathered it had more light filament then what our normal light globes did. What I didn't know, is it had its own pendant.

A round disc, identical in appearance to the one I took from MaryAnn and wore around my neck, was hidden in the upper portion of Lydia's light. Which allowed her to leave the Veil so she could enter the Maze. Which—

I gasped.

The Entryway.

I practically slammed the book shut and placed it on Ms. Papenfuss's podium as I hobbled my way out. I would definitely try using Cisco on the school portal first, but if that didn't work, I had another option. I could trade my way into the Entryway portal to see Lin. Because one way or another, I was going to see him.

It was like an obsession. Every moment's thought centered on getting back to Lin. But was I more interested in learning about my Life or visiting him? I paused with that curiosity, but my ankle throbbed more intensely so I started limping forward again.

I found Cisco next to the side porch with his friends. I caught his eye and motioned him over. He made his excuses and joined me, to much catcalling and jeers of his peers. From what I could tell, they thought I was his girlfriend.

I felt my face tingle with a radiating blush. Their opinions mattered more to me than they should have. I *wasn't* his girlfriend. Wasn't that knowledge enough? Why did it bother me so much they thought that I was?

"Chica!" Cisco called out, his arms stretched as wide as his grin.

I wanted to shout out, "What did you tell them?". I wanted to accuse him of making more out of our friendship than there was. But thankfully I had my wits about me and held my tongue. I needed him right now, and lashing out wasn't going to help.

"What's going on?" he asked, still in a loud, friendly tone with his arms stretched out.

I backed away, unsure what he was about to do. His body slammed into me; his arms wrapped around mine. My eyes bulged as he squeezed. It wasn't too tight, just surprising.

His friends stared more intently than before, and their jeers got louder. I pushed against his chest. This made me uncomfortable.

He pulled away. I peeked once more at the laughing boys on the porch. They only threw sporadic glances now. The drama was over.

I smiled quickly and took another step back, wincing from the pain in my ankle as I did. He was too busy blowing a peace sign to his buddies to notice.

"I need a favor. Please." I searched his eyes, trying to predict his reactions to my words. I wasn't sure why he was acting the way he was towards me, but I knew I didn't want him to hug me again. "I tried to go back to Lin, to tell him what I found out, but the portal switch is hidden."

One of his eyebrows dipped slightly. "The one in our Portals class?"

I nodded.

That wide grin came back. "Another adventure, baby. Let's go!"

He grabbed my hand, interlacing our fingers, and faced the Academy. The close contact made my stomach twist uneasily. I tried to pull my fingers away, but when I nearly fell over taking my first step, I wound up squeezing even harder to keep my balance.

"You alright?" he asked, noticing my limp.

"Fine." I bit my lip and put full force on my wounded ankle. I didn't like him holding my hand, and if I wasn't limping, I didn't have to.

The pain shot up my leg and into my hip, but I kept walking normally. If I thought I could have hovered in a straight line without hurting myself even more, or getting called out by a teacher again, I would have.

I tried to walk my normal pace. I didn't want to give him any excuses for touching me again, but my body refused to cooperate. He walked slowly next to me, his hand brushing mine from time to time in a friendly gesture, letting me know he was there if I needed him. Although it hindered my balance greatly, I crossed my arms tightly across my chest so I didn't have to graze his fingers.

"We have another problem," I told him, remembering the newly installed alarm.

"What do you mean?"

"Ms. Collins has installed an alarm."

"Oh I know all about that!" He waved the danger away with his hand.

"How could you—"

"It was there when I got back from detention. I've had three days to crack it. It's not difficult. You'll see."

I gawked at him skeptically. "How could you *possibly* have cracked it that quickly?"

He grinned his arrogant, mischievous smile. As annoying as he was when he did it, I was starting to like that smile.

"Bow to the master, baby."

When we reached the classroom, Cisco flew to the alarm. I tried to reach him in time to watch what he did to it. The bottom of the device, in a row of round, wooden buttons, were the numbers 0-9. He pressed six of them in a special order. I caught the last two he pushed, eight, zero.

"What was that?" I asked.

"Her birthday."

"Her what?"

"The day she was born, her passcode to shut off the alarm. I watched her enter it my second day back from detention. She types in her passcode every morning to turn it off, then again at night to turn it on."

"How does it work without electricity?"

He shrugged. "I don't understand all that yet. It has something to do with light wisp. Stuff's pretty valuable round here."

I analyzed the alarm from where I stood. The buttons he had pressed were back in their original positions. The light filament was dead now, unmoving, dark.

I reached out to touch the tiny globe that contained it. My fingertips grazed the cold glass. Lifeless. Like the wooden desks of the classrooms. "How does it work?" I whispered to myself.

Meanwhile, Cisco had started searching the room for the portal's switch. He rubbed his hands along the wall, under Mrs. Collin's desk. He kicked at the baseboards and floorboards with his feet.

"I don't know, chica." He stared at the place the portal normally appeared on the blackboard.

"Hasn't she said anything in class about it?" I asked.

He shook his head. "The only thing different is the alarm, and I just noticed it because I saw her messing with it that morning."

Something about what he said seemed off. Then I realized what it was. "Cisco," I said.

"Hmmm?" He turned his head to face me.

"If you saw her enter the code to turn off the alarm, that means you were here before class started. Which means you were early."

His face glowed brighter.

"Why were you early for class, Cisco?" I teased.

He turned away from me and stared at the opposing wall.

"Cisco was early for claaa-aass. Cisco was early for claaa-ass," I sang.

"I didn't want to go back to detention, OK?" he yelled.

I giggled. "Don't worry," I said between chuckles. "I won't tell anyone."

He glared at me, but I kept laughing.

Then I gasped. "Oh crap!

"What?" he asked, whipping his head around in alarm.

I suddenly remembered the stupid detention note I was supposed to get signed by Mrs. Richards. "I gotta go!"

I turned and ran for the door only to cry out in pain from my ankle and fall over, onto a desk, slamming it into the desk in front of it and seriously damaging my left wrist and the right side of my rib cage.

Cisco stood frozen with an expression of disbelieving astonishment. "What is *wrong* with you?"

I tried to push myself up. That's when I noticed the damage to my left wrist. It was swollen like my ankle and glowing almost pure white. When I stood, my hand automatically shifted to my injured ribcage. I whimpered from the new pain.

"Are you alright?" Cisco asked, his amusement now concern. He grabbed my elbow and helped me out of the dangerous area of predatory school desks.

"Yeah yeah," I said. Good thing I had fed so much during dinner. I would need the energy for all this new healing I was about to do. Maybe I should gorge myself more often, I wondered. I seem to get injured a lot, and the extra essence might come in handy.

"Can you stand here without falling over?"

He sounded serious, but I still rolled my eyes and pursed my lips at him in frustration. "I'm fine," I forced through gritted teeth.

I think he swallowed a chuckle.

I stood, leaning up against the safety of the sturdy, unpushoverable wall, while he straightened up the desks for me. "Thank you," I said.

"No biggie." He shrugged. He took me by the arm and helped me to the door. I wasn't going to stop him this time. "What were you in such a hurry for?" he asked.

I sighed. This was embarrassing. "I got another day of detention."

He laughed, but quickly cleared his throat.

"I was late yesterday morning, OK?"

"OK." He was still smiling. Big.

I waited for him outside while he went back in to reset the alarm. He then wrapped his arm around my waist and half carried me to the grand staircase.

I let him touch me without complaint. I couldn't think of a place that didn't hurt, and his kind aide made the journey easier.

When we reached the top of the stairs, I tried to straighten up. Every student there was staring at me with curious, judgmental eyes. I ground my teeth together, fighting the tears that stung at the corners of my eyes, the bridge of my nose. I gripped the railway for support as we descended the grand staircase, all the while gazing anywhere but at the gawking, giggling, whispering onlookers and trying not to cry.

We reached Mrs. Richard's office. "I'm OK now," I said, still clutching my right side with my injured, glowing arm which burned with every frigid spark that pulsated through it.

"You sure?" He eyed me skeptically.

"Not really," I admitted. "But I don't want Mrs. Richards to think I hurt myself worse than I did from—" I suddenly remembered I hadn't explained the hovering incident to him and pathetically tried to cover my tracks. "That, that I'm hurt, because she might think I was up to something I shouldn't be and punish me even further." Of course, I was up to things I shouldn't be, several things, but that was beside the point.

He didn't buy my story. "Uh-huh."

"Can I please just face my punishment alone?" I asked.

He held up his hands in surrender. "Whatever you want, chica. I'll catch you later." He raised his eyebrows and kissed two fingers before holding them up in a peace sign to me.

My jaw fell. I couldn't help but think that kiss was meant more for me then his fingers.

When Cisco was out of sight, and I had taken several deep breaths to steady myself, I knocked on Mrs. Richards' door.

"Come in."

I turned the knob with my good hand and quickly pulled my sleeve over my left, hiding the glow of injury.

Mrs. Richards sat behind her desk, going over some paper work. Another glimmer caught my attention before she looked up. Lydia. She had just finished hanging something over a hook on the wall.

"Yes. Miss Hannah," acknowledged Mrs. Richards. "Mr. Hill told me I would see you tonight."

Lydia's arms were still covering whatever she was putting away when I was forced to focus all my attention on the Academy's Director. I nodded sheepishly and pulled the note from my pocket. It was folded and creased, one might say crumpled. I tried to straighten it out as best I could before handing it over.

Mrs. Richards' stern stare made me want to crawl under her desk and hide. I could feel my hand shake as I held the note in front of me, waiting for her to take it. My submissive behavior seemed to reduce her anger.

She took the note from me and sighed, her expression grim. While she had her head down signing the note, I chanced a peek at Lydia who was standing next to the wall with that scrutinizing gaze of hers that still creeped me out, even without the freakiness of the Maze surrounding me.

"Ms. Papenfuss has also spoken to me about your behavior."

I know. I was waiting for you to get to that part. I tried to look remorseful. It wasn't like I had to fake it, but it wouldn't hurt to play it up a bit, maybe get some sympathy. "I just… I had already upset her with my research—with my books." I corrected myself. "So I didn't want to bother her anymore by asking for help. She said there were no ladders… I'm s-sorry. I wasn't trying to break any rules. I was trying to … not bother her any more than I already had."

"What were you researching, Miss Hannah?"

Dang it! She caught it anyway. "Just … stuff I haven't learned yet. I don't understand a lot of my Death yet, and I still don't remember my Life, not all of it anyway, so I try to read what I can. So I can understand more."

Her mouth twisted around as she thought. I self-consciously tugged at my sleeves to cover my blazing injuries and reminded myself to walk normally out of here no matter how much it hurt.

"You will learn all you need to in your classes, Miss Hannah."

I nodded.

"You do not need to try to go faster than your peers."

I nodded again.

"Do not let me see you in here again."

"Y-Yes, ma'am." I took the signed paper from her hand. She went back to whatever she was doing before I arrived.

As I turned to leave, I glanced one last time at the wall where Lydia had been standing. I don't know why. I guess it had become a challenge at this point, something I felt like I needed to do whether I did or not.

Hanging motionless from the hook, glowing the same way it did in the Maze, was Lydia's infamous lantern.

THE PLAN

Well, now I knew where the lantern was, aka, my ticket to Lin. What was I *thinking*? Was I seriously contemplating stealing—ahem—borrowing Lydia's lantern, leaving the safety of the Veil, again, venturing to the Entryway alone, and then trying to get past the bouncer into a portal?

Yes, yes I was.

Maybe the book was still on her podium, I thought. If I was … wow … actually going to do this, I needed to study that diagram again. I couldn't wander around with her lantern on me. That would be over obvious, and she would notice it was gone. But if I took out the disc and left the lantern, I would be OK.

Surprisingly, getting the book back from the library was the easy part. I didn't even have to hover for it again. It still sat on Ms. Papenfuss' podium, as if waiting for our rendezvous. I wanted to spend time with this book, more than just the afterhours I normally spent in the library.

I waited patiently for the librarian to return, no need to rock the boat already in shaky waters. She checked me out without incident, and I walked back to my room as innocently as possible.

It felt like my first day all over again, every eye upon me. Only they weren't actually watching me this time. It was my paranoia working in overdrive.

I sat on the couch and studied the diagram until I was positive I could open the lantern and take the disc within seconds, because I was sure that was all I would have. Seconds. Then reality hit. The lantern was in Mrs. Richards' office. You know, that room she was always in or kept locked. My head fell back against the sofa's arm in despair. How was I possibly going to pull this off?

The Clock bonged. Time for class.

It wasn't like someone's life was depending on me getting back to Lin at a certain time, but the idea of adding an entire day to our time apart constricted my chest painfully. It made me feel like I needed to gasp for breath, even though there was no air in the Void, any part of it.

I threw on a change of clothes, not really paying attention to what they were, and grabbed my bag for yet another glorious day of monotonous paradise, otherwise known as detention.

Even though us Dead people didn't have to rest, there were still times when allowing your mind to quit thinking helped. Think of it as a study break. This was one of those times. Maybe detention was all I needed, a time of complete monotony to allow my thoughts to mingle on their own for a while.

The journey through the hallways seemed boring now, just another day for me. I passed Darva, who scowled and probably made some hateful remark about me being in detention or stupid or something, but I didn't care. My thoughts were elsewhere. None of that mattered anymore. Weird. Nice, but weird.

I opened the door, set my signed note on Mr. Hill's desk, grabbed a book, and took a seat. I sat my backpack in the floor and removed the necessary paper and pencils from it. No pens in the Void. Very little ink. But pencils could be sharpened and rough ones even made if resources became scarce enough.

I had thought of bringing my library book, but I didn't want to do anything that would make me a potential suspect when Lydia's disc went missing. The fact I checked it out of the library was bad enough. I was banking on no one noticing that part. Naive, I know.

I opened *An Intimate Study of the Complete History of the Revolutionary War* and set to copying, not noticing when the classroom door opened for more students to taper in. I was just realizing I had chosen from the shelf what was quite possibly the book most prone to cause clinical depression when someone sat next to me. I didn't bother to look up. It's not like we could talk in there anyway.

"Hey!"

My head jerked to the sound of the boy's voice, and my eyes widened when my suspicions were confirmed. "Cisco! What are you doing here?"

An amused grin spread across his familiar face. "Seriously? This is a surprise for you?"

I chuckled. "No. You're right. It shouldn't be."

Mr. Hill closed the door and went to his desk. "Quieten down," he commanded. The shuffling of papers intensified for a brief moment before the room settled into its usual silent mode.

I wanted to ask Cisco what he was doing here, but I didn't dare chance getting a *fifth* day in detention. I wrote a note instead.

I glanced up to see if Mr. Hill was watching. He had his face buried in a new comic book. I passed the paper to Cisco. He took a moment to read it, chuckled silently, then wrote back. I tried to copy some more boring history as he did.

He handed it back to me. I snorted.

I smiled and put the note under my book.
The sounds of my pencil scratching my paper soon lulled my mind into a numbed state. Even so, some of what I was writing made it into my head. "The siege of Boston, March 1776, a time when Washington planned an interesting diversion." When I felt an appropriate amount of time had passed, I wrote him another note.

He turned to me slowly after reading the note, his brows high into his hair. I nodded in affirmation.

Now I'm REALLY cuRIouS.

I can tell you all about it later, but can you pick the lock or something?

I heard a tiny snort escape him. He covered it with a cough.

Does youR Room HAVE A kEy?

Oh yeah. I felt stupid now.

No. But isn't there some way to, steal her snot or something so I can get in?

He rolled his eyes.

ARE you sERIous?

Yes! I need to get into her office!

You couLD ALwAys GET INTo TRouBLE AGAIN.

It was my turn to roll my eyes. "Be serious!" I hissed through clinched teeth.

"I am!" he whispered across to me.

"The last thing I want to do is get into trouble again," I whispered back.

Mr. Hill cleared his throat and readjusted his comic, crinkling it in the process. Cisco and I dug our noses into our work, abandoning the conversation.

I had a hard time concentrating on my tedious detention work. Gee, go figure. But this time it wasn't just because it was the most boring work known to man. It was because my mind kept ruminating over how to get safe access to Lydia's lantern.

Cisco was right. I could be late or do something to be taken down and have Mrs. Richards give me detention again, but I wasn't Cisco. And the thought of getting into trouble again tied my stomach into knots. The good thing about detention though is you don't *have* to think. I didn't actually have to read and understand the words my fingers were scrawling out in zombie-like fashion. So it didn't take long to devise a solution to my problem.

I glanced up at Mr. Hill, who was heavily engrossed in his comic, took out a new sheet of paper, and wrote my plan on it. Cisco's brows rose when I handed it to him. He nodded as he read it, jutting out his bottom lip in impressed agreeance.

"You in?" I chanced to whisper.

He wadded up the paper and threw it in his bag. "Duh!" he mouthed.

I couldn't help but smile.

GETTING THE DISC

I tried to think of what time it was when I had seen Lydia hang up her lantern. It was late, I remembered that. There was always the chance Mrs. Richards wouldn't be there, but I doubted it. I gathered from her little room on the side, and the fact I've never seen her anywhere else except the Vent during feeding time, that she lived in her office.

"Three hours after feeding," I told Cisco as we were leaving.

"See you then," he agreed.

Most people would think I would want to break into her office while she wasn't there. But I intended to waltz right in and talk to her. I had either become very brave, or very stupid, and considering the company I was keeping, aka, Cisco, I was afraid to know the answer to that choice.

I put away my things, fed, and paced around my room for over an hour. It was nightmarish! Anxiety crawled through my veins, down my arms, my legs. It felt like mites had suddenly taken refuge on my ghostly glow.

While we didn't have electricity, we did have old-fashioned pendulum clocks here and there, though they were rare. The closest one to me I knew of stood against the wall when you first entered the Academy. I must've run to check it at least twenty times.

When time was close, I practiced what I was going to say and studied the diagram one last time. I then changed my clothes into something dexterous and with pockets baggy enough to hide something. I went for a pair of ripped jeans and a hoodie with a pouch in the front. My injuries had completely healed by this point, and I felt full from the recent feed. I took a deep breath, and walked to the Director's office. I checked the grandfather clock by the front door. Cisco would be here in five minutes. I had spent longer than I meant to practicing. I was out of time.

I held my breath and knocked on the door. I was so scared, the tears were coming naturally for me. I encouraged them to flow.

"Come in," I heard her call from the other side. At least she was there.

I opened the door and stepped inside, closing it behind me for privacy. My first course of action was to ensure we were alone. We were. My second course was to check for the lantern. It hung on its peg, just as I had seen it last night. So far, so good.

Mrs. Richards was standing next to her office window, staring out into the Void. Her face seemed contemplative, sad, reminiscent.

I took another step forward, hoping the sound of my shoe hitting the floor would grab her attention.

"Yes?" She did not take her eyes away from the window.

I opened my mouth and shut it several times before letting out the breath I had been holding and beginning my almost half-truth lie. "I'm scared," I said. That was very much the truth. I was terrified. "Mr. Consolver can't help me anymore because I can't remember anything else."

She sighed once, then turned to face me. Her face appeared sunken in, and her attire slightly neglected. "What do you mean, you're scared?"

Her appearance took me by surprise. I wanted to ask what was wrong instead of cry. But I knew I couldn't. "Mr. Consolver said he can't help me until I get more memories, but I haven't had any. I don't want to fade away like the Ancients."

Her face returned to normal, like a switch had been flicked. She was no longer the forlorned soul searching for happiness, she now wore the serious face of the Director of the Academy. My fear easily returned. "Take a seat."

I complied, putting my hands into my pouch as I did.

"Who has been telling you about the Ancients?"

"Er…" Great, was this something I wasn't supposed to know about? "I don't remember. I just … picked it up here and there." That was pretty much the truth. At that moment, my mind had drawn a blank, and technically speaking, I had picked up facts about the Ancients fading away here and there.

Whether she believed me or not, she never said. "How old do you think I am?"

"Uh…" My fingers tied themselves into knots inside my pouch. I had no idea what answer she was looking for.

"I died in 1691. That makes me over 300 years Dead. Does it look like I'm fading?"

I shook my head. I didn't try to stop my fear or my tears from coming. They were both working for me this time. I did wipe away a few stragglers that were tickling my cheeks.

"The truth is, no one knows what causes a ghost to fade away." Her eyes focused on something over my head. I turned to see what it was but found nothing. Her face carried that longing look again.

"So, if I never remember my Life, if my family forgets me, I'm still OK? I'll still be a ghost and everything?"

She shook her head and redirected her attention to me. "What?" Her expression became stern again. "No. No, there is no reason to worry."

This was not going as planned. I sniffed, wiped away the remainder of my tears, and coughed loudly, hoping Cisco was already in place. "What's the longest you've ever heard of a ghost existing?"

"Well," she began.

Knock. Knock.

Yes!

"Come in," Mrs. Richards called, her right hand massaging her drawn forehead.

Cisco came in, smiling big and full of finesse as he spoke. "I'm sorry to interrupt you, Mrs. Richards, but there's a fight down the boys' hallway."

I felt my eyes widen as my head whipped around to face him. I had asked him to create a distraction, not start a fight! I almost mouthed the words, "What did you do?" but caught myself.

I turned back to Mrs. Richards, who sighed and said, "Excuse me. I'll be right back."

I nodded.

The second the door shut, I jumped to my feet and grabbed the lantern. Lever to the left, press in the latch. The cylindrical section between the container of light filament and the handle snapped open. I tilted the lantern forward, catching the disc in my hand. I quickly buried the disc in my hoodie's pouch before snapping the opened pieces of the lantern shut and hanging it back up. I then sat back in my seat and waited.

When the door opened, Mrs. Richards burst inside with a single boy held by each of her hands. Shame no one squealed when Darva was beating the crap out of me.

I jumped out of the way as she roughly dropped each of the boys into a seat. She towered over their snickering bodies as she verbally assaulted them, completely forgetting I was even in the room.

I inched behind them and opened the door. "Thank you, Mrs. Richards. I'm leaving now," I said.

Her tirade against the offenders continued without interruption. I shut the door and battled the path of post-fight gossiping students to my room.

The moment I got inside, I leaned up against the door and panted. I couldn't stop. My breaths came faster and shallower. I pushed myself away from the door and lay face down on the couch, burying my face into my arms.

THE SEARCH

What had I just done? I was dead, no, not Dead, dead. As in, someone was going to find out and do to me whatever the Dead equivalent of killing was, because no matter what Mrs. Richards said, I know we die. It was the only thing that made sense. The wisp had to come from somewhere. I believed the stories of the Ancients, and being forgotten was as good a reason as any to fade away in my book. And since I had just stolen Lydia's Veil-crossing disc from the freakin' Director's office, I was dead.

I lay on that couch, afraid to move, afraid to be seen outside my room until the Clock bonged for the next day to start. I sat up and turned the disc over in my pouch. I couldn't keep it there, too easily dropped. I didn't want to hide it in my room. They would search the school the moment it was found missing. I would have to wear it. There would be some kind of warning before they started searching our personal bodies. Right? I hoped.

I pulled the string from the hood of my shirt and tied the pendant around my neck. It hung unnoticeable beneath the thick hoodie's front. Satisfied, I grabbed my backpack and headed for class.

Going to detention for five days does something to you. It makes regular class far more interesting then you could have possibly imagined. I took notes. I sat on the edge of my seat. I ignored the stares and whispers behind my back. I didn't care anymore. Their whispers were nothing compared to what I had been through over the past few days.

When the Clock bonged for dinner, I put the strap of my bag over my shoulder and exited my last class for the day with a smile. This day felt good. I felt good. I wish it felt like this every day.

"What's going on?"

"Move out of the way!"

"I can't! The door won't open."

The flow of students in the hallway was backed up halfway to my classroom door, disallowing me or most anyone else from seeing the cause. Students hovered over the crowd, shouting observations down below. No one knew the cause, just that our normal flow had become a trickle. I eventually made it out of the classroom hallway and into mine. It was packed with angry students, and I wasn't going to take the time to battle through the mob just to drop off my backpack. I headed straight for the Vent with my bag still on my shoulder, hoping it was still open at this time.

Every exit from the Academy was bottlenecked. I was getting irritated. I allowed the current of students to push me to the front door.

Two staff members waited for us there, Mr. Prickett, and someone I didn't recognize. When it was my turn, the unfamiliar staff member held his hand out to me and said, "Your backpack, please."

My brows dipped in confusion. "What?" I asked while being shuffled from behind by the understandably angry students. "I don't understand."

"Your backpack, please," he said slowly and with more authority.

I handed it to him. The search for Lydia's disc had begun. I tried to look innocent. My breaths started coming in shallow gasps. I held my throat closed to keep from hyperventilating. He opened each pocket, placing the items on a table which had been set up on the porch as he searched it. I kept waiting for him to notice my guilty face. He never did. When he finished, he handed the now empty sack back to me and called, "Next!"

I hurriedly picked up my belongings and piled them into my bag before they could get lost in the shuffle. I glanced behind me. The rest of the students looked confused. Keep it together, Hannah. No one suspects you.

I walked quickly to the Vent. I couldn't stop my hand from going to where the pendant hung against my chest. My fingers found it, grabbed its shape beneath my shirt. I pulled my hand away, hoping no one had noticed, then reached up to scratch the back of my neck in a ridiculous attempt to pass off what I had just done as an innocent maneuver.

I tried to act natural as I finished my walk to the Vent. My pack bounced against my back as I did. I met Cisco on the way and avoided eye contact. The idea of being seen with him terrified me, made me feel guilty.

"Did it work?" he asked amidst the throng of hungry students.

"Yes," I whispered.

"What?" he asked.

"Yes!" I said. I picked up my pace, purposefully leaving him behind, and kept my head down the rest of the way.

Supper was sparse. Most of the essence had disappeared into the Void by the time we got to consume any of it. I got enough to last me until the next day. Others weren't so lucky.

I watched the last of the essence leave as I was halfway back to the Academy. Everyone would be irritable until the next feeding.

When I reach my room, I understood the reason for the angry congestion of students I had seen earlier in my hallway. My room had been searched. Clothes and books lay strewn all over the floor. Thankfully I had gone to the trouble of disassembling MaryAnn's hookah and hiding the parts in different areas after she had last used it. Unless someone really knew what they were seeing, it would just look like random items: a vase here, some rubber tubing there, a brass item that could almost pass for a candlestick.

I put up my bag and got to work tidying up. I placed the library book on my desk. The sooner I turned that back in, the better. Just looking at it made me shudder with the idea someone would put the pieces together and know it was me who stole the disc.

After my room was livable again, I took the book back to the library and dropped it into the return bin. There. I didn't even have to make contact with the librarian.

PREPARATIONS

I went back to my room. I had work to do. Passage outside the Veil was one thing, using the Entryway's portal was another. They weren't going to let me use it for free, that much was clear. I sat on my couch and stared at my pitiful possessions. I didn't know what was valuable and what wasn't. I was pretty sure clothes weren't worth much, and I didn't want to make trip after trip with various items, making an inquiry with each one to see if they would accept it or not. I needed something good the first time, something rare, something they wouldn't easily get outside the Veil.

MaryAnn's instruments sat in the corner. They might be worth something, but I couldn't just take them. I hadn't used any of my rations since I bought my backpack. Maybe I could get something with them.

I took my ration book and headed for the Factory. I opened the door and went in. It wasn't as full as usual. The others were probably still cleaning up their rooms or fuming about the search. I searched for small, yet valuable items. A difficult combination.

Sofas and chairs were lined in neat rows against one wall. Too big. Jewelry sat on velvet cushions behind a locked case. I glanced at their prices. It would take months of rations to afford even the cheapest piece.

A few students were searching through the piles of fresh stock in the back. I walked closer.

Each pile was over four feet tall and divided into their various materials such as wood or metal. The metal pile contained useless electronics and wiring the Factory workers would craft into something useful. A single car door leaned against it, its window gone.

"What happened to the window?" I asked the closest boy. I was so nervous my voice shook.

He considered my presence for a moment before answering, "Glass is hard to pass through the Curtain. It's one of our most valuable commodities."

I smiled. I knew what I needed now.

"Are you thinking about becoming a Factory worker?" he asked me skeptically.

"Maybe." No, not really, but if I played along I might get some useful information. "What are the perks?" I asked.

"You get half off anything made here after thirty days," his friend chimed, joining our conversation.

Thirty days? I didn't want to wait thirty days. "Um, do you have any glass here?"

"Yeah," his friend said, eying me with suspicion.

My hands squeezed tightly together in the pouch of my shirt.

"It's over there." He pointed to the corner of the factory.

"Thanks," I said and trotted to the glass section.

There were several options: jars, vases, globes, aquariums. I thought about each one in particular to how the Entryway could use it. There weren't any fish, or water, and the aquarium was too big anyway so that one was out. However, I picked up a jar and turned it over in my hands. That bar fight busted a bunch of their light globes. They would probably be looking for more. This might be just the ticket.

One thousand rations. I only got twenty-five a week. It would take literal months to save that up. I placed the jar carefully back on its shelf and left. I would have to find another way to do this.

As I walked back to my room, I tried to think of where else I could get a glass jar or globe to trade. My room had one, shattered into a million pieces where MaryAnn had thrown it against the wall. I could ask Cisco where to find one, but I had relied on him enough. He would've probably gotten it by means I didn't approve of anyway. Like stealing.

I halted, my right foot hanging in the air, unsure of whether to take the next step or not.

Stealing. No, I didn't approve of stealing, but I wasn't taking it from some*body*. Not really. It was more like getting there first. I may not have enough rations for glass, but I did for clothes. Hiding clothes. Clothes with big pockets and a bulky fit.

Most of the students wore whatever suited their personality. And since there was no weather here in the Land of the Dead, it didn't matter if their personality was a sundress, a T-shirt, or a sweater. Mine was going to be sweaters for a while. And hoodies. Hoodies with big pockets and thick material.

Mr. Haught met me soon after I entered the closet and asked to see my rations book. I showed it to him.

"And what do we plan to purchase today?" he asked.

I wasn't doing anything dishonest here in the closet, so I don't know why I was so nervous. I kept stumbling over my words, and I couldn't look him in the eye when I spoke. "Just some shirts. Um, you know, hoodies and things."

In retrospect, he always did eye everybody like they were about to take off with the entire contents of the Academy's closet without paying for it, but this time it felt like he knew exactly what I was up to and he didn't like it. I swallowed. The lump in my throat refused to go down. I tried to swallow again, but it got stuck somewhere, disallowing me from breathing.

"Three sections down on your left, madam."

I nodded. Talking was impossible.

As soon as I was out of his earshot, I cleared the blockage in my throat.

The closet had so many clothes, it made choosing anything challenging. I found several that fit my requirements and went into the nearest fitting room to try them on.

I mimicked a glass globe by sticking my fists into the pockets, under the sweaters. I checked their prices. I could afford three. I tried them again, stuffing their bulky areas with other clothes along with my fists to make doubly sure until I narrowed it down to the three of my choice.

I exited the fitting room. I put away the clothes I didn't want as neatly as I could and found the attendant.

"Mr. Haught?" I asked.

He turned, annoyance flashing across his features. Oops. Since my arrival I had learned Mr. Haught had been a salesmen in one of the old department stores of 1930. He preferred "Sir" to calling him by name.

"Sir?" I corrected.

His frown straightened. That was as close as I would get to a smile. "Are you ready to leave, madam?" he asked.

"Yes, sir," I said.

He checked out my choices and used his hole punch to mark my used rations. I had five left. If I really wanted, I could find me a fancy pair of underwear or socks. Not today.

I thanked him and went back to my room. Every eye stared at me on the way. Did they know what I was planning? It felt that way.

When I got back to my room and hung up my clothes, I told myself how silly I was being. No one could possibly know what my plan was. I just bought some new clothes. That's all. Students do it every day. No one had been watching me on my walk back. I had imagined it all. Paranoia was going to do me in if I didn't stop it.

I changed into one of my new shirts, a bulky sweater of pale blue, and waited impatiently for the Clock to announce classes. Classes were a chore to get through. My leg kept bouncing up and down. I couldn't concentrate, and Mr. Prickett told me if I didn't sit still he was going to tie me to my seat.

"Sorry," I said for what felt like the dozenth time. I *couldn't* stay still. I knew that after class came dinner, and after dinner came the Gatherers, and *that's* when my newest plan went into motion.

THE DAY OF THE DEAD

The Clock bonged. The thing I had been waiting for was finally here.

But I couldn't do it. My arms were frozen around the book on my desk. I needed to put it away. I needed to put up my stuff and go to dinner with the rest of the students, but my body refused to cooperate. All the other students had left. I was alone in the classroom with Mr. Prickett.

"Miss Hannah? Are you alright?"

My arms burned with the adrenaline of fear, fear of him finding out, fear of him asking the right question that I answer the wrong way. That fear set me into motion. I dropped my book in my bag, zipped it up, and threw it over my shoulder. "Yeah, I'm fine." I was already halfway to the door.

After ditching my backpack, I approached the Vent with caution. I had to hang out until the end without looking suspicious. I sucked in a few bits of essence. Mmmm, someone had a cookout. The threads of smoke thinned. Feeding time would end soon. I inhaled a deep breath of essence, filling my body with its nourishment, and waited.

The other ghosts were leaving. I saw the Gatherers exit the Academy. This was it. It was now or never. My body weight shifted from side to side. I shook my palms out at my sides.

I saw something. Something shiny within the tufts of smoke. I ran into the final remnants of the essence. From inside, I could grab what I needed, hide it, and run out before anyone noticed. Maybe. I hoped.

I found the shiny thing by tripping over it. It was a toaster. Useless. I nursed my stubbed toe while hopping on one foot. "Blasted!" My toe quickly healed. I glanced over my shoulder. The Gatherers were closer now. The ribbons of smoke were faint. The fog was coming back in. I had precious seconds left.

I continued my search. I found a bed next, a grill, a pile of wood, a barn. I drove my hands through my hair. Where was the freakin' glass?! The Gatherers were too close now. I had to go. I ducked out the side of what puny wisps of essence remained and marched back to the Academy, my head down. I couldn't chance peeking to see if anyone noticed.

It was stupid of me to think it would happen on the first day. Glass was their rarest commodity, they had said. I had to give it time.

The next day brought similar results. Piles of books told me a fire had broken out in the Land of the Living. The books nearly filled the entire area, making it difficult to search for my precious exchange item without tripping all over the place. The next day's supper delivered the most amazing meal I had had my entire deathly existence. Pizza.

Students shoved each other out of the way to feed on its garlicky goodness. Fights broke out. A pizza shop had burnt to the ground. Iron pans, steel mixing bowls, plastic utensils. The Gatherers were called early. Noble gases and metals came with this feeding. The Gatherers brought empty glass containers to fill with the light filaments. There would be no searching tonight.

The rest of my evenings were rather dull, but that was the way it was. One day excitement, the next nothing. The moments of excitement gave us all something to talk about until the next, not that I joined in on the conversations, but they were sometimes interesting to listen to.

"Did you get the pepperoni?"

"I tasted Hawaiian! I remember my brother's birthday party when—"

"I wish we could bake here! I know a lot of great recipes, and those pans they just got—"

But when the one day of nothing turned into several, and then several more, I wondered if it would be quicker to work the thirty days at the factory. Of course, even with the globes half off it would take forever to buy one, and I heard the Gatherers used all their stock for the light filament from the pizza shop, so there was probably nothing to buy anyway.

Speaking of light filaments, seeing them gather the new ones tempted me again to ask for a replacement globe. I was still afraid to though. What if they wanted to know what happened? Oh, who am I kidding? They would *demand* to know what had happened. What was I to tell them? The truth? That wouldn't go over well. My room would be searched, again. They would find the hookah parts and this time recognize them for what they were. I would probably be punished for not saying something sooner, they would think it was me and I was lying to protect myself. I shuttered at all the consequential thoughts running through my head. No. I wasn't telling them the truth.

I lie then. I could tell them a lie. "Yeah, the globe just fell one day"—shrug—"I don't know what happened."

Nope. No lies either. Darkness it was.

The glow of my body did give me all the light I *needed* in my room, but the loneliness soon became unbearable. I craved companionship. Me, the girl who wanted nothing more than to be left alone, isolated from the scary people who surrounded her, now required the company of others to replace the company she once had of a wisphead. Ironic, I know.

I lay on my couch. My homework was done. I had fed and searched for my coveted glass. There was nothing left to research, and if I read one more book, my eyes were going to rebel and leave my body.

I thought about visiting Cisco. We had started sitting near each other in Portals class. That turned out to be a big mistake. It reinforced his feeling our friendship was more than it was. He kept passing me notes to meet him places after class, but I always came up with an excuse. Hanging out with him for no reason was just asking for trouble.

I had given up using the Academy portal over a week ago. Armed with the alarm's code, I had visited it several times, but I never found where they had moved the switch to. We hadn't used the portal in class since the test either, and Ms. Collins wasn't giving away its location by her actions. She didn't even glance to a dark corner of the room.

Robin popped into my head. I had met with her and her knitting friends a couple of times since that first visit, and they had always been kind. I still struggled with the thought of making friends, but I was trying. Maybe I should make another attempt at it tonight, I thought. I was complaining about being lonely. I rose from the couch and headed for the craft room.

The girls were in their usual spot. Robin saw me first. "Hi, Hannah." She acted genuinely happy to see me there.

"Hi." I waved to everyone. They waved and smiled back. "Um, do you mind if I join you?"

"Oh, not at all."

"Of course."

"Here, I'll just grab another chair."

Their enthusiasm was daunting. I took a step back. They viewed it as an attempt to get out of the way so they could add in my chair. My shaking hands went unnoticed.

I took my seat between Melissa and Kathy. Melissa had a half-completed sweater in her lap, Kathy an emblemed pillowcase.

"Where have you been? I haven't seen you in a while." Robin continued her knitting as she spoke.

Oh, just trying to steal from the school so I can leave the school illegally with the disc I stole from Lydia which caused that room search a while back, that's all. "Oh, nothing much." I shrugged. "Just class and stuff." I rubbed my palms on my pants. "You?"

"*I* am getting ready for graduation."

"Graduation?" I asked.

The girls were used to my ignorance by now and kindly explained my questions, sometimes before I asked them. Jocelyn, hovering cross-legged without a seat while doing her needlepoint, did it this time. "That's when we've finished all our classes and can leave the Academy."

Oh, I formed with my lips. Nothing came out.

Kathy added, "We can take the tests anytime, but Mrs. Richards likes to have a group graduation ceremony."

Robin, probably sensing I still didn't understand fully, explained further, "Since we come during random times of the year and learn at our own paces, we finish at different times too. I've passed all my tests, so now I'm just waiting for the ceremony."

"What do you do instead of classes and stuff?" I asked.

"I've been helping out a couple of the teachers as a teacher's aide. I've worked a little in the office. I hang out here," she added with a smile. "They said they could use me here when I graduate, but I haven't decided if I want to stay or not."

The idea of leaving the Academy did not frighten me like it used to. I had left once before and I was planning to again. But permanently? The Academy had become my home. It was all I knew. I was fed. I was safe.

The circle grew silent as everyone concentrated on their individual projects. My fingers tied themselves into knots. I needed something to keep them busy. Maybe that was why everyone here was knitting or crafting in some way. To keep their hands busy. To give them something to do when it wasn't time to talk, to give them an excuse *not* to talk.

I glanced around at everyone's projects. Each of them seemed equally difficult. I watched Kathy's fingers, gliding her metal hook in and out of the loops of yarn in an unseen pattern. Three loops, two, one, push through, wrap around. I watched Melissa. Her fingers danced a rhythmic push-wrap-pull, push-wrap-pull.

"What are you doing?" I asked her.

She stopped to answer me. "I'm knitting. Do you know how to knit?"

I shook my head.

She reached down into a cloth bag held by wooden legs which sat on the floor. "I think I've got some spare yarn and needles in here." She rummaged around for several seconds. "Ah *ha*! Here you go."

She handed me two identical needles and a small ball of yarn. She pulled the end of the yarn from the ball, handed it to me, and put the needles in my hands. "Hold them like this."

She placed my fingers just so around each needle and wrapped the yarn around those on my left hand.

I held both hands very still, out in front of me, daring not to move them. It felt like I had two aliens attached to my arms, and if I moved, they would bite.

"Put this finger this way, and this one that way." Step by step, she taught me to knit.

It was the most basic stitch, but enough to keep my hands busy, and enough to give my brain a place to go instead of worrying about every movement I made or word I said.

Their conversation continued without me. I found I could listen to the parts I wanted to and ignore the rest. Their chatter became a soothing background noise and gave me the company I needed, while the knitting kept me from feeling forced to be a part of it.

"So where is everyone going for the Day of the Dead?" Kathy asked.

I stopped my knitting to listen.

"I think I'll visit my Aunt Pearl," answered Tandy. "She lives in Ireland now."

My brows dipped into a confused V.

Melissa said, "My brother and his wife should have had their baby by now. They live in Idaho."

The V deepened until a ditch formed between them.

Jocelyn laughed sinisterly. "I don't really have anywhere I want to go. I'll just visit my gravesite and scare people."

A couple of the other girls laughed with her.

"Wait," I said, unable to take the confusion any longer. "What are you talking about?"

Their eyes widened. Jocelyn lowered her hover.

"The Day of the Dead," said Robin. Her voice was soft, like when you break bad news to a child.

"It's the one day of the year we can visit any place in the Living." Melissa's voice was equally gentle.

I shook my head. "I still don't understand. I thought we could only visit with a portal."

They smiled understandingly.

"Any time of the year, we can use a portal to visit the area of the Living which corresponds to the area we are up here," explained Brooke.

"Yeah, once you pass Portals, you can use your rations to visit anytime," said Natalie. "But it's really expensive, so students rarely use it."

"Right," said Kathy. "And you can only visit areas of the Living that are close by with a portal."

Natalie put down the cat she was cross-stitching. Her blonde curls bounced, and her hands waved all over the place as she explained, "OK, like, let's say you die in Japan, or something. So when you die, you go to the part of the Void that's over Japan. And when you want to visit the Living, you can only visit that part of the Living world that's near Japan."

"We're over Maryland," said Brooke. "That means a portal can only take us to Maryland, Delaware—"

"East West Virginia." Natalie giggled.

The others chuckled at her joke. I didn't get it. What they said sounded vaguely familiar, but I couldn't place it. "What if I were to walk across the Void, go to another part of it, could I visit someplace else?" I asked. "Like, could I travel over Japan and visit it?"

"Yes," answered Melissa. "But you don't need to do that on the Day of the Dead. That's the cool part about it!"

Brooke added, "You have to know where you're going on that day though. You can't just say, 'I want to visit Jacob Tanner' and go there. It isn't a magic genie lamp."

"Oooo, Jacob *Tanner*." Kathy fanned her face with her hand dramatically.

"Is he not the *sexiest* man *alive*?" chimed in Robin.

"Oh!" said Natalie, hands flapping with excitement. "If you don't know where you want to go, you can appear at your bones, no matter where they are. You don't even have to know where they're buried."

"Right," said Kathy. "Just think 'gravesite', and you'll go there.

"Even if they're far away?" I asked.

Natalie nodded. "Yes."

"We have to be outside the Veil for it to work though," added Tandy.

A few nodded in agreement.

"Yes."

"I forgot about that."

"How does that work?" I swallowed. The pendant weighed heavily on my chest. I stopped myself from glancing down to ensure my shirt was still over it.

Robin answered, "Every year, we all hold hands and leave as one giant group while Lydia stands in the Veil, holding it open for us."

"We all take a day off from class and everything!" added Natalie.

"Lydia," I said. "She holds the Veil open for you?"

"Yeah," answered Jocelyn. "Why?"

Because I have her disc, that's why. "Can't, someone else do it? Don't other teachers have d— the ability to hold open the Veil?"

The other girls glanced furtively at me.

"I think Mrs. Richards does," answered Robin. "Why?"

I shrugged and returned to my knitting, trying to appear innocent. "Just wondering."

"Some of the other teachers used to," Brooke quietly said. "But not anymore."

The other girls paused their needlework to stare at her.

"What happened?" asked Natalie, her light blue eyes wide with interest.

"One got stolen," Brooke quietly explained, like it was a secret that shouldn't be shared outside the circle we were now in. The other girls leaned in slightly.

Brooke continued without looking up from her embroidery. "A student named Robert, or Lonnie, or … Ronnie! That was it! Ronnie."

My back stiffened. I forced my gaze back to my unmoving fingers so no one could read the shock in it.

"Ever since then, there's only just been the two, The Director's and Lydia's."

Kathy held her needle in mid-stitch, over the edge of her pillowcase. "I think I heard something about that. Didn't he get expelled or something?"

"So, the Director can use hers then," I interrupted. My questions were more important at the moment.

Kathy flashed her irritated eyes at me.

"No," answered Brooke. "She always spends the day in some colony somewhere."

I was afraid to ask my next question. "And when *is* the Day of the Dead?"

"Soon," Brooke said. "When the Clock strikes midnight."

TURNING POINT

"Excuse me," I said. All the glow had drained from my face with the realization of what this information meant. "I forgot about something." I placed my knitting back into Melissa's bag.

"Did we upset you?" asked Robin.

"No! No. I just … forgot to check on something. Thank you for teaching me to knit," I said to Melissa. "And thank you for explaining the Day of the Dead," I said to everyone else.

Tandy flapped her hand at me. "You would've learned about it in Portals before it got here anyway."

"But you're welcome," said Brooke.

I smiled in return. "Thank you."

I tried not to run. Tried not to trip over the other ghosts, tables, and chairs as I hurried out of the craft room and out the Academy's doors.

My feet hit the black fog of the Void's floor with audible smacks. I pivoted around to face the Clock and skidded to a stop. 11:48. It had said 9:25 when I first arrived. I did the calculations in my head. Once. Twice. Three times.

Six days. I had six days.

I walked several zombie-like steps toward the Clock. I fell back against its leg and allowed my body to slide all the way to the floor. The fog rose to my chest, swirling beneath my chin like a black ocean current. I lowered my chin to my knees and wrapped my arms around my shins. I pulled the disc from its hiding spot and held it up to stare blankly at it. There was no promise of MaryAnn's return. Quite the opposite really. Once I returned this disc to its rightful owner, the chances of me acquiring another one were slim to none. My time was limited.

Lin had to know everything there was to learn about my family by now. If only I could get to him!

My head dropped to my hands where my fingers wove through my hair and threatened to pull it out by its roots. If I didn't get to Lin in time, it would be another year before I could see my family again, unless they just happened to be hanging around my gravesite on the exact same day I could visit it. My luck said otherwise.

I didn't want to wait another year. I felt so close now. If I could just get to Lin within the next six days… My nose burned. My vision blurred. Forget memories. I could *visit* my still-alive mom and dad. See them in real life!

I wiped my happy, hopeful tears away. But if I didn't get to him in time, and I held onto this disc past that day, the other students could miss out on visiting their families. Their brothers, their sisters. Their Jacob Tanners, I thought with a wry laugh.

I sat there in the fog, listening to the Clock as though it somehow had the answers. My focus became fuzzy, and my mind wandered. Memories of the day passed through it. Irrelevant subjects: dogs, cats, rain, cars. I wondered why electricity didn't work here, why we didn't have animals or weather. The Clock bonged.

Five days.

I rose slowly to go inside.

I knew if I was late I would get detention, but I couldn't force myself to walk any faster. I went to my room, picked up my things, and made it to the first class just in time. Mrs. Collins glared at me. I ignored her and took my seat.

Times like this I wish I could dream. From my understanding, dreaming was the mind's way of sorting things out, of putting together pieces you wouldn't while conscious, of letting go of all the things that are bothering you. I couldn't keep my mind off my current situation. A thousand questions marched through my head, and zero answers stopped them.

"Miss Hannah!" Mrs. Collins snapped at me.

I must have missed a question she had asked. I raised my chin from where it had been resting on my crossed arms. My thoughts were too severe for me to act as sheepishly as I should have. "Yes, ma'am?"

She glowered at me, her brows high in expectation.

"I'm sorry. I wasn't listening." I immediately regretted my blatant honesty.

Whether she had just remembered the taste of lemons or was about to blow a gasket, I wasn't sure. Her lips were pressed so tightly together, they were almost invisible. Her nostrils flared with every angry breath she took.

I sat up straight, trying to appear the attentive student. "Um … what was it you said?" I allowed my voice to sound timid and weak, not that it was a difficult task.

It took her a moment to calm down enough to speak. "Miss Hannah! I would have thought *five days* of detention would have been enough for you to learn re*spect* for the Academy's rules!" Spittle flew from her mouth as she spoke.

I opened my mouth to apologize again.

"Do you need a *sixth*?"

I shook my head vehemently.

"Then maybe you can answer this simple question. Who was the first ghost to develop the long range portal, and why is it not used today?"

My jaw fell open. I had no idea. I don't think I heard a single word that lesson. Of course with all the detention she'd just mentioned I'd been in, it's a wonder I'd learned anything in any of my classes.

I heard the faint, familiar chime of the grandfather clock this side of the hallway. This class was over. The other students began packing up their things. Voices grew in volume outside our door until, had I known the answer, it would have been impossible for me to answer Mrs. Collins as she wished.

"Read chapter 45 on the dangers of visiting the Living too often by tomorrow," she shouted over the noise.

A collected groan issued in return.

I threw my bag over my shoulder and headed for the hallway. A firm hand grabbed my arm before I could reach the door. Mrs. Collins.

"I want a three page essay on the long range portal by tomorrow. That's chapter 44, in case you weren't paying attention."

I tried to swallow but couldn't. "Yes, ma'am."

She let go.

Well today was gonna suck.

In Ethereal Dynamics, Ms. Peach went over all the different licensures the Academy releases and how to qualify, along with announcing a test over each of them tomorrow. I wanted to be mad at her, but she was so sweet I couldn't be.

Mr. Dinwiddie had each of us turn invisible for the class while trying to pick up an item from his desk. Benjamin turned almost completely clear, then tried to grab a notebook and fell through the desk and floor into the closet below. Mr.

Haught knocked on the door several minutes later, returning a now visible, abashed Benjamin.

My performance went rather well. My outline was nearly imperceptible as I walked across the front of the room two times with a book in my hand. Mr. Dinwiddie clapped his hands and shouted, "Well done!" to me.

History was as boring as ever, and Ms. Ohlson of Beginning Rules continued on her rant about stealing, something she had been going on since the day after the search.

When the Clock announced supper, I couldn't leave class fast enough.

I cracked my door just enough to throw my bag in and marched to the Vent. I didn't feed as enthusiastically as I usually did. My heart wasn't in it. I wanted to go back to my room, curl up in a ball, and disappear. I didn't want to make the choices I was going to have to make.

When the items started to materialize, I had to force myself to look through them. I wasn't going to find anything. I had realized that long ago. This whole idea was stupid.

A tiny, upside-down reflection of myself caught my attention. I went closer and bent over to get a better look. My eyes widened as my torso shot up with a gasp. Glass! I couldn't believe it.

Quickly, I glanced around to see if anyone was looking. I saw the Gatherers. One was close, close enough he could catch me if he faced this way. His back was turned. No one else was watching. I grabbed the jar. My hands fumbled until they almost dropped it trying to fit it in my hoodie's front pocket.

It wouldn't go. I started to panic. I had to suck in my lips and bite hard to keep from cursing aloud. The Gatherer turned. He was facing me now. I froze, surveying his face. His eyes were cast down. I shoved the clear cookie jar under my shirt and ran.

I had to hold it as it jostled back and forth with my stride. Several students gawked at me. I didn't stop. Let them think what they wanted. No one had seen this jar but me, and I didn't plan to hold onto it long.

The idea of going straight to the Entryway had crossed my mind, but I needed a better way to carry my treasure. My hand slid on the knob to my room. The door wouldn't open. I tried again, leaning against the wall to prevent the jar from falling out. Nothing. Shuffling the jar's weight into my free hand, I used the other to grip the knob tightly. I grunted as I tried to turn it. The door still wouldn't open.

Heat filled my body. Sweat broke out in my pits, my back. Sweat. Duh. I spit on my hand. The door opened effortlessly.

I slammed it behind me and snatched my backpack, unceremoniously dumping its contents onto the floor. Using a nearby piece of clothing, I wrapped the jar and zipped it up in the bag. The bag felt oddly light when I slung its strap over my shoulder. The jar bounced with every step. I was glad I had thought to wrap it.

At first, my pace was quick. I wanted out of sight, out of mind. But I soon noticed the other eyes, the stares. My frantic face must've set off their "this isn't normal" alarms. I slowed to a walk and tried to act guiltless. For all they knew I was meeting with a study partner on the front porch. I had never seen any study groups on the front porch before, but that's what I told myself to prevent an inner explosion. I exited off the Academy steps and walked towards the Void.

The Veil seemed further away than usual, like it had purposefully moved to annoy me. When I was far enough away from the Academy that I should be alone, I peeked over each shoulder as innocently as possible, and, feeling confident no one was following me or rubbernecking to keep me in their view, I put my head down and walked as briskly as my legs would allow to the Entryway.

JOURNEY

I stopped when I reached the Veil. I didn't want to enter the Void unprepared. I pulled the pendant out of my shirt. It wasn't that it had to be visible to work, it just made me feel better to see it when I went through.

My fingers readjusted around the strap of my bag over and over, my body bounced on my toes. Another cool wave came over me, a flush of anxiety-filled terror. Every possible way this could go wrong and then some flooded my mind. I wished I wasn't alone.

No, I didn't. I wanted to be alone. Every time I told someone I knew nothing about my past, it felt like an invasion of my privacy, like it was something too intimate to share. Being alone while learning about my Life allowed me the option of picking and choosing which parts of it to share. If any.

It was time.

I stepped through the Veil. The blackness of the Void welcomed me. I dropped the pendant back into my shirt and hitched my backpack higher up my shoulder. No one was around. Not a single glow polluted the dark, save the distant grey of the Entryway square, showing me the direction to travel. It was still early. People would be near the Vent or returning home from it, not patrolling the outskirts of the Veil.

The darkness grew as I walked, a giant amoeba surrounding its prey. I quickened my pace. It didn't help. The silence had turned into the loudest noise I could remember, pushing in on my eardrums like invaders. I couldn't breathe if I had wanted to. There was nothing where I was. Nothing.

Then the voices came. The Callers. They grew in anticipation. A chorus of out-of-tune voices screaming overhead. The silence was worse, but this chaos made my head hurt. So many names overlapping, I had a hard time distinguishing a single one from the many. My pace quickened again. I was running now.

With every step the jar hit my back, over and over until I knew a bruise would form, but I didn't care. I wanted to be out of the voice-filled darkness.

I reached the square. There were more ghosts out now than last time. Had the Void become safer? Had the disappearances stopped? Had Ronnie gotten all he needed?

A line was forming on the steps to the Entryway. I took my place in it. Others crammed in behind me, pushing against my bag. What if they knew what was in it? What if they wanted it for themselves? I pulled it around to the front. I had come this far with my treasure, I wasn't going to lose it to a thief. A thief besides myself, I thought with shame.

The line moved quickly enough. I was halfway up the steps when one of the bouncers came trotting up to the door, a large jar full of what appeared to be essence in his hands. He was led straight in.

The first thing I did when I entered was survey their lighting system. I wanted to know how much they had cleaned up, in other words, how valuable my glass jar was. As I did, I noticed the bouncer I had seen earlier climbing the stairs to the normally closed off upper chamber. He passed the essence-filled jar to a pair of hands, then took his position. I guess whoever resided up there was never seen in public, even for feeding.

Most of the damage had been cleared out, but not repaired. The desired items must be hard to come by even for the Queen bee of this area of the Void.

I stayed against the wall as much as possible. I was largely ignored, but my aversion to crowds was still strong. Isolation becomes too much, yet I can't handle crowds. I could see this factor of my Death was going to be annoying.

I grimaced at my realization and continued to the bouncer by the portal door. No one was in line yet. I checked the trading attendant next to him. No patrons there either. I approached the counter.

"Yes?" the pockmarked attendant asked. His hands rested on the counter. His eyes pierced past mine, seeing deep into my innermost thoughts.

I clutched the bag to my chest. "I, uh…"

He cocked his head to the side, dipping one puzzled brow.

I bit my bottom lip. "I want to use the portal."

He nodded. "OK. Is that what you have to trade?" He bent his head towards my bag.

"Y-yes."

His brows raised, adding kindness to his face. His hands reached out to me. Underneath the thick arms and gloved palms, I saw a tenderness.

I handed over my bag. He opened it up, curiously eying me the whole time. When he pulled the shirt from around the jar, his eyes widened, and he whistled a long tune of approval.

"OK," he said, and jerked his head to the portal's entrance. "You can go."

I looked to the bouncer. They exchanged glances, acknowledging my payment. I took back my bag, stuffed the shirt inside and zipped it up.

The bouncer opened the door for me. "You've got one hour."

I nodded.

He shut the door behind me.

The portal filled the entire room with a swirling, blue light. I had no idea what to do. The portal in class was random but eventually fell to where I wanted to go. How was I supposed to find Lin here? I thought a minute. Melissa had told me I had to know *where* I was going on the Day of the Dead. I couldn't just say the name. Maybe it was the same for a portal.

My time was limited. I had to try something. "Tao Lin," I said in a clear, commanding voice. The portal did not change.

Where was Lin? Where was Lin? Oh, I was so *stupid!* I paced in circles, hitting my forehead with my fist. How could I have not thought this part through?

I concentrated on the time I went to see him. He had told me his name, but was there more to go on? I closed my eyes and relived the evening moment by moment.

I'd arrived in the kitchen. I fell. I climbed the steps. He was asleep in his underwear. I grinned at that memory. He asked me to turn around so he could get dressed. I grinned larger and blushed.

My eyes flew open and I gasped. The street sign!

"Tao Lin of Cecil Street!"

The lights of the portal pulsed. Brighter and brighter until I raised my arm to shield my eyes. The inside burst outward with a tiny explosion, casting white rays into the darkest corners of the room.

When the portal subsided, the silhouette of Lin's shadowed kitchen appeared. I lowered my arm. Happiness spread from my chest to my arms, my legs, my face. I was going to see him. Now. Fear welded my legs to the floor. What if he didn't find anything out? What if he didn't want to see me? What if his family had moved and I had spent all this time and effort only to arrive in some stranger's house? What if what if what if?

I was being a coward. I told myself to consider everything I had done to get this far, and how far I had gotten. To give up now would be unforgivable.

I took one shallow breath, held it, and jumped through.

LIFE

The portal remained open behind me. The kitchen appeared different this time. Orange rays of setting sunlight cascaded over the tables, the chairs. The microwave flashed 7:03. I didn't remember the sun. I held my arm out into its rays. My jaw gaped at my body's reaction to them.

I had disappeared. I jerked my arm back to see if it was an optical or physical reaction. My arm glowed the exact same blue it had before touching the rays. I extended my fingers into the sun's light again. They disappeared again. I flexed them. I could feel them, could almost see movement in the sunlight, but that was it. I was no longer visible.

I stepped my whole body into the rays and gazed at the orange and yellows, the reds and purples. It was a beautiful sight. I felt no—

I gasped as the first memory in weeks filled my eyes.

Sand. Hot, bright sun. Blue waves. I wore a hat with a floppy brim. My mother bent over, lathering something on my face. I had to close my eyes to keep it from getting it into them, preventing me from seeing her face.

"Here, honey. This'll keep you from getting too hot by that mean ol' sun."

My eyes still shut, I heard Dad's voice to my right. "You want to go into the water, sweetheart? Huh? Do ya? Do ya?"

His finger tickled my side with each "Do ya?". I giggled, contorting my body in response.

The memory left.

I opened my eyes. Frigid tears stung at the corners. I was so close that time. I swallowed, willing the swelling in my throat to lessen. I was here now, I told myself. Lin would tell me who they were. I smiled, the tears sliding down my cheeks no longer sad ones.

I stayed in the sunlight, wishing I could feel the warmth I felt in my memory. I could still smell the ocean, still taste the salt when it splashed in my mouth.

A howling sound sliding from high pitches to low ones broke my reverie. It came from upstairs. It was a horrible, screaming sound I couldn't place. I remained fixed in my position, silent. I didn't know what it was. Perhaps there was some ritual, some method of traveling to the Land of the Living I hadn't performed, hadn't yet learned, and whatever was making that terrible noise, was here for me as a result.

I inched my way to the portal, ready to jump back in if need be. I heard Lin scream, his voice ragged, raspy. I made out a few of his words. "Gonna make you burn, gonna make you sting." I strafed closer to the portal. He was clearly in battle with whatever demon had hold of him.

The howling screamed in response. This time it sounded rhythmic. His raspy voice joined the demon's. It became a melody to me, a dance of notes between the two.

I was being a coward again. If Lin was in trouble, I couldn't leave him to face it alone.

I dropped my bag and climbed the steps. One, two, I kept my pace slow, cautious. Lin screamed again, "Eyes that shine burning red."

The volume increased as I neared his room. I hesitated, my hand on the doorjamb. I swallowed, breathed in once, smelling the air around me, and stepped inside.

Lin was jumping, twisting left and right across his room. He held something in his hand, and appeared to be strangling it. I felt my eyes widen and my brows rise as I took in what was occurring before me.

He turned to face me. My eyes widened in response. It was a guitar. He was playing his guitar and singing to it. I felt. So. Stupid.

He continued to sing and play his guitar, fiercely nodding his head up and down as he did. His back was to me now. He still didn't realize I was there.

His faded jeans were ripped on the thighs, allowing his dark skin to shin through. His shoulder blades stretched his already tight white T-shirt across his back. My shame had been replaced with another feeling. My face blushed so hard, it was its own electric storm. I didn't want him to see me. I didn't want him to stop what he was doing.

He turned. Then, mid-jump, he stopped strumming and singing in the same half-second. He had seen me.

He landed off balance, catching himself with his other foot, shaking his black hair out of his face. "Hey," he breathed. The longer he stared at me, the redder his face grew.

"Hey." I smiled, the sparks on my cheeks fading quickly.

He pulled the strap off over his head and placed the guitar on its stand.

"What was that you were doing?" I asked.

"Oh, that?" His face turned red again. "That was 'Black Dog'."

I had no idea what that meant. My face must have indicated so.

"By Led Zeppelin?"

I shook my head. "No," I giggled, surprising myself as I did.

He waved the conversation away with his hand. "It doesn't matter." He had caught his breath by then and sat on his bed. "Where've you been?"

I shrugged. "It's a long story."

He patted the bed beside him. "I've got all night. My parents are gone to the opera."

I shook my head. "Can't. Remember?" The last thing I wanted to do was fall through the bed and get stuck on the floor or something.

"Oh yeah."

"Besides, I only have an hour."

His bottom lip jutted out, and a tiny ditch formed between his eyebrows. "You're timed?"

I nodded. "Well, not exactly." I explained to him about the Entryway, which led to explaining about how I got there, which meant admitting I had practically stolen glass from the Academy.

When I got to that part, an awe-filled grin spread across his face. "You stole? Just to see me?"

I felt my face glow cold and bright. "I *had* promised you I would tell you about the disappearances, and I wanted to know what you found out about my family."

His face fell. My glow disappeared, and I felt my features fall too. "You didn't find out anything, did you?" I said.

"Oh, no, I did." He got up and did something with his computer. "Tell you what. You tell me about the disappearances first, and then you can have the rest of your hour to learn about your Life."

Something seemed off. I couldn't tell what it was. Still, informing him about the disappearances wouldn't take long at all, and I liked the idea of having the majority of my time to learn about my Life.

I smiled. "OK."

It felt awkward standing in the middle of the room talking, so I dropped to the floor, crossing my legs as I did. "Well," I began.

I told him about Ronnie and wisping. He sat in front of me, his legs crossed like mine, his elbows on his knees. When I got to the part about the Ancients and how wisping got started and what ghosts were actually inhaling when they did it, his face twisted in disgusted horror.

"Are you serious?" he asked.

I nodded and continued my story. By the time I was done, we both had our elbows on our knees, leaning into each other. It felt comfortable, like all the time we had been apart hadn't existed. Even though I had just told him the most horrific story he's probably ever heard, I was happy. Being with Lin felt normal, like I belonged there.

"Wow," he said. We sat silent for several moments, letting him process everything. When he had finished, he looked up at me with a smile that didn't reach his eyes and said, "Well, it's your turn I guess."

He rose from the floor and went to his computer. "Your parents' names are Leslie and Abraham Matthews." He sat in his swiveling black chair. "Which makes you Hannah Matthews."

I rose too, but didn't follow him to his lit computer screen. "Hannah Matthews. Hannah Matthews," I mouthed to myself. Leslie. My mother's name was Leslie. My father's name was Abraham. I could feel my ears lift from the smile forming on my face.

I stood next to him. He cleared his throat nervously. "Once I learned who you were, it was easy to find out more."

He cleared his throat again. "Your, uh, parents took your Death pretty hard."

He clicked his mouse. Little squares, each labeled, "AbrahamLeslie" formed a column in the center of his screen. He scrolled the squares up, allowing me to read each one.

AbrahamLeslie:
It's been two months since our precious Hannah died. I don't know what to do anymore.

AbrahamLeslie:
If I could just hear her voice one last time, tell her good-bye, tell her I love her. If I just knew she wasn't suffering anymore.

AbrahamLeslie:
I don't know how we're going to survive this world without her. I don't know how to move on.

Each post got more depressing as they progressed. Hundreds of their friends had commented on them, telling them how much they love them, how I was safe and happy now. But my parents had lost faith. They weren't sure where I was.

"They loved you very much," Lin almost whispered.

I felt my nose and throat start to swell. "Yeah." I sniffed. "They did."

"Would you like to see some pictures?" His face wore a hopeful grin.

"Yes, please." I had formed fists so tight, my knuckles glowed brighter than the rest of my hand.

He clicked his mouse. Dozens of pictures came up. I chewed my thumb in anticipation.

I saw my parents in them. Their skin was dark, darker than mine, darker than Lin's. My father's hair was cut very neat and very short against his head. My mother's was thick; its tight, black curls reached to her chin. Not all the pictures had them in it but every single one had me.

Me, in a wheelchair.

Me, with a walker.

Me, as a baby, lying on a white bed with tubes coming out of me.

One side of my face always hung flaccid. My mouth never shut completely. My arms and legs were disproportionate to the rest of my body. My fingers were deformed and lacked the dexterity they have now.

"Your parents adopted you as a baby. You were born this way." His eyes flickered in my direction before staring intently at the screen and away from me. "It's probably why you can't remember any part of your Life now."

My breath held in my throat, and I fell back to the floor, landing on my bottom. Every memory of Life, all seventeen years of it, came back at once.

My mother singing to me. Me trying to form words with my mouth, but even when I couldn't get them right, she understood them. My father feeding me, because I couldn't do it myself. Miss Denise, my high school attendant, chastising some of the regular girls for calling me names: Stupid, Retard, Idiot.

My mother changing my diaper. My father bathing me. Me trying to tell them how I felt, what I wanted, them not understanding.

"There's a whole page devoted to you," Lin practically whispered. "People donated money for your treatments when you needed them. They all loved you very much."

I heard his words, but I didn't comprehend them. I huffed little breaths, each one harder than the first. Tears fell from my face and splashed against my arms. Darva had been right. I felt stupid all the time because I *was* stupid. "Retarded," just as Darva had said. I was so messed up, my own parents had put me up for adoption.

"I … was … disabled," I said.

He stood up and faced me, his arms outstretched. I stood and stepped away from him. I couldn't handle him seeing me like this.

The sobs overpowered me. "I-I … have to … go." I turned and ran. I felt his searing hand pass through me.

"Hannah! Wait!"

I couldn't face him. I couldn't answer him. I had to get away, had to be alone. I ran down the stairs, to the portal. I grabbed my bag at its foot and jumped through to the Entryway, Lin screaming at me to stop the whole way.

The bouncer on the other end lurched out of the way when I returned. I have no idea what he said to me, if anything. I hit the door open and pushed my way through the crowd that had formed. A few of them pushed back or yelled at me. I ignored them.

Once I reached the outside, I sprinted to the Academy, only wiping my eyes when I couldn't see through them. The moment I reached the Veil and knew I was alone, I let the grief overtake me. The fog engulfed me as I lay on the Void's floor, blubbering like the idiot I now knew I was.

I wrapped my arms around my knees. My torso convulsed with every sob. The crying didn't hurt. It felt like a release, like every pain, every crushed desire, every hurt was coming out of me at one time.

The floor of the Void felt cool against my cheek. My tears had collected beneath it, giving it a slimy sensation. I had cried until there was nothing left. Now I lay there, wishing I wasn't. Wishing I didn't exist.

I had wanted to remember my Life so badly, and now the memories I had stolen for, had lied for, tortured me with their presence. Every name I was called, every time I was told I couldn't do something everyone else could. Each one wrapped another chain around my heart and squeezed. Some of the chains had burrs. They pierced my heart until it bled.

I don't know how long I lay there. The world was absent for me. I heard nothing. I saw nothing. I felt nothing.

INSIDE

The Clock struck once.

The Clock struck two bongs.

My first sensation when I came to was the atmosphere of the Void, like it was the first time. Then came the hunger. I had lain in the same position for a long time. I had not fed. I saw the blurred image of the Academy before me. I lay on the outside edge of the Veil, safe from their eyes.

The Clock struck one bong, time for class. I ignored it.

I saw the students floating around the Academy. Did they notice I wasn't there? Did they care?

My stomach screamed in hungry protest, forcing me to face the harsh reality I was trying so hard to avoid.

I pushed away the painful memories. If I was to feed my hunger, if I was to ever get up again, I had to.

The other students were in class now. How many days had passed? If it weren't for the hunger I felt, I would not have believed more than an hour had gone by. Could I enter the Academy now? Go to second period like nothing was wrong?

I stood, readying myself to do just that, to face my demons. I stared longingly into the Void behind me. It looked as I felt. Empty. Black. It welcomed me. I stepped into it.

How could I have been so afraid of this the first time? It felt nice to walk through this. Alone. Unbothered. Not on display for everyone to watch and stare at and mock. I remembered Cisco and our "field trip" as he had called it. I remembered Naomi.

I saw a faint glow in the darkness ahead. Naomi's neighborhood. I had been walking towards her without knowing it. Her house was a welcomed beacon in the darkness of the Void, and my thoughts.

I knocked on her door and stepped back so as to give her some room. A few seconds later, I heard her open it from the other side.

"Hello there, youngun! What'chu doing here?"

"Hi, Naomi." Then I collapsed into her arms and cried.

She patted my back and rubbed it with her hands. "Oh, baby, what happened?"

Her surrounding arms felt so familiar somehow, not from when we met, but something else. I couldn't place it yet, but it felt so good, so comforting. I wanted to tell her. I wanted to tell her everything. Her body surrounded me with love and understanding. But I couldn't. The sobs wouldn't let me.

"Come on inside, girl. Tell Auntie Nay Nay all about it."

I continued to cry as she half drug me to the couch Cisco and I had sat on last time. She sat next to me, her hand rubbing my arm. My breath felt like it was climbing ladders when I inhaled, hitching on every step. After several minutes, my sobbing slowed to a controllable pace.

"I … found out … about … my Life." I had to force the words out between the whimpers.

Naomi's eyes tightened, and her mouth turned down with concern. "Now, it couldn't have been that bad."

I nodded. "Yes … it could."

I felt her hand rub my arm again.

"Do you want to tell me?" Her voice was soft, different than her normal one. It held nothing but compassion.

I nodded again. "I don't know if I can though."

The corners of her mouth went deeper. She paused a moment, thinking I suppose. "Would it help if I turned the other way?"

Without turning my head, I glanced at her out of the corner of my eye. "Maybe."

"OK." She removed her arm and turned on the couch so her back was to me. There was no way she could see me now.

"I, um." I cleared my throat. "I was born…" I took a deep breath and closed my eyes. I can do this, I told myself. "I was born … disabled." I felt no reaction from her, so I continued, "My parents didn't want me, so I was adopted by another family."

I waited. She said nothing. I absentmindedly rubbed my palms up and down my thighs several times, waiting even longer.

She turned halfway. "Is that it?"

I started to nod but realized she wouldn't be able to see it. "Y-Yes."

She turned the rest of the way to face me. "That's it?" She almost sounded mad. "You had a disability and were adopted?" Her expression was no longer filled with care and concern. It held confusion, disbelief even.

"Girl, what's the matter with you? That ain't nothing to cry over!"

I turned my wet face to her. "I was born so disfigured, my own parents didn't *want* me!"

Her lips pursed, dismissing my statement. "Poppycock! Ain't no woman out there that don't want her children. Well, actually, there's a few, but they're rare and you're better off without 'em. What makes you think your parents didn't want you?"

"I was adopted."

She waited for me to say more. When I didn't, she turned her palms out expectantly. "And? Maybe your momma died! Maybe your daddy didn't even know abou' chu! Maybe your real momma and daddy couldn't afford to take care of you. For all you know, there are two Live 'ens right now crying their eyes out because they'll never see their baby girl again."

I stared sheepishly at my hands in my lap. "There are, actually," I mumbled.

Naomi pulled her head back and lowered her brows. "What do you mean, 'there are'?"

"My parents, my adoptive parents, they're crying everyday seems like. They can't go on without me. They keep saying how they'll never get over it, how they were thinking about adopting again but don't think they can now. How there's nothing left for them in Life anymore. They feel like they no longer have a purpose. They've lost the will to live."

"You look at me now." She held my arms in her hands and gently stared into my eyes. "Your parents loved you very, very much. Your Death has caused them a pain…" Her lower lip started to tremble. "You can't imagine the torment they're goin' through. They *wanted* you! Without your birth momma to give you to them, they wouldn't had no child at all! They *dying* withou' chu with 'em! All they want is to put their arms around you one more time, to tell you they love you one more time, to…"

She kept talking, but I was no longer listening. I remembered why Naomi's arms had felt so familiar to me now. My mother, my father, they had held me like that a lot. When I was happy, when I was sad. The memories I had neglected when the sad ones cascaded down on me, the happy ones, were poking through my shield. My parents singing to me. Kissing me. Telling me they loved me. Reading me a story in bed. Telling me how proud they were when I did something, even for the fortieth time.

I smiled and allowed the rest of my memories to flow out of their cage.

My school teacher, the classmates I was with all the time, they did the same as my parents had. They encouraged me. They loved me. They made me smile. The few people like Darva who were mean to me were just that, few. So very few I could still remember each of their names and faces, but the others, the kids in my swimming class, the friends I made in Special Olympics, they were all nice.

I felt so stupid, so ridiculous. So selfish. I had let the words of one girl pronounce the bad memories and push away the good. I had been a coward.

"I'm sorry." I cut Naomi off from whatever she was still trying to get across to me. "I've been…"

Her fingers stroked my hair, pushing it behind my ear. "Normal, baby. You've been normal. And you're normal *now*."

I raised my confused gaze to meet her kind face.

"You're *healed*. All the Dead are. All of us had something wrong with us, but no more. No matter what was wrong with you then, it healed the moment you passed through that Curtain." She cradled my face in her hand. "It's probably why you couldn't remember who you were for so long. Your brain didn't work right when you were alive, but now it does."

I smiled with the single chuckle that left me. I still felt the stiff remains of my tears on my cheeks. I rubbed my face clear and stared into her eyes. "Thank you, Naomi. I feel silly now."

"Well, you should!" She teased more than scolded. "Don'chu let me catch you talking like that again. You hear?"

I nodded. "Yes, ma'am."

"Now, how's everything else going? How's that cute boyfriend of yours?"

Her statement took me off guard. "Cisco?" I asked. "He's not my boyfriend."

"Coulda fooled me." She got off the couch and went to her usual chair to knit.

"No, Lin's my…" I felt my face glow so cold it burned. What did I almost say? That Lin was my boyfriend? I wanted to run out of the room, just like I had with Lin.

Oh, Lin! I let my face fall into my hands. How could I not have seen it? He was being nice by letting me go last. He had tried to stop me from leaving. His face held compassion and worry when he spoke to me, not ridicule. He wasn't ashamed of my past. It didn't matter to him at all. The realization made me feel even worse.

I tilted my head up and peeked through my fingers. Naomi had a smug smile on her face, like she knew all along what she was doing. I appreciate her insight now, of course, but at the time, it was very irritating.

"I've got to go," I said, and jumped up to leave.

She resumed her knitting as though once again, she expected my reaction. "Come back anytime. And say hi to Cisco for me!" she shouted just before the door slammed shut behind me.

I ran back to the Academy, not out of fear, not out of shame, not because I was going to be late, but because I had my self-respect back. I could see Lin again. I *had* to see Lin again. I had to apologize for running out on him.

My smile grew. My pace increased. My hair flew back with the breeze I created by running. It felt almost as good as my first feeding, no, better. I couldn't wait to scavenge the Vent.

CISCO

Classes were well underway when I entered the Veil of the Academy. Again, I thought of using my invisibility only to realize it would look worse if caught. So I ran around to the side entrance to get to my room. A few students loitered about, probably waiting graduates like Robin. I tried to act like I belonged where I was.

I made it to my room without incident and used the rest of the day to write that essay on chapter 44 for Portals. Thankfully I hadn't forgotten. I would be in enough trouble as it was for skipping however many days I was gone.

When the two bongs announced supper, I checked myself in the mirror before I went. Good gosh! How long had I been wearing these same clothes? My hoodie was twisted sideways and so wrinkled it looked like I had used it to stuff the over-baggy jeans I had on. I changed into the complete opposite, tight jean shorts and a white tank top. There, much better. I grabbed my empty, save for the shirt, backpack and left for the Vent.

As promised, I searched the closing Vent for something, anything to trade for passage to the Entryway. The attendant's reaction to my last gift had told me I didn't have to have glass every time. Something of lesser value would work just as well.

It didn't matter because I found nothing.

My elation became heartbreak. There would be other chances, I told myself. Other nights of essence I could glean my treasure from. My backpack, as empty as my hope was now inside, bounced against my back as I walked back to the Academy.

"Where've you been, chica?" It was Cisco. He was hanging with his friends next to the porch steps.

"Oh hey, Cisco." I smiled. It was hard not to when he was already wearing such a large grin.

He came closer to me. I could feel his cool, radiating glow. "Why weren't you in class today?"

I didn't back away. After the last several days, it felt nice, reassuring, for someone to not have a problem being this close to me. "I went to see Naomi."

He flinched back, a mixture of hurt and surprise. "Why?"

I felt bad. I hadn't thought how that would make him feel. "She said to tell you hi!" I said as enthusiastically as I could, hoping to make him feel a little better.

"Did she say anything about my family?"

My face fell. I had forgotten about him and his family when I went to visit her. "No." I was too self-absorbed to ask. I'm sorry. "She didn't mention anything about that. She just said to tell you hi. I guess she hadn't found out anything." That much was true.

He acted disappointed but less angry. "Why did you go?"

I glanced over his shoulder at his friends, and over mine at the students bumping into me as they went up the stairs behind me. "Is there somewhere we can talk? Privately?"

His grin didn't have his usual edge. It was soft, unguarded. "Sure," he said. "Wherever you want."

My answer was, of course, the Clock.

I wasn't sure I was ready to share this information with anyone yet. Technically I didn't have to share what I found out, just that I had found out. The rest, I could keep to myself.

We were about halfway there. He glanced behind us and asked, "We're far enough away you can talk if you want to." He sounded kind, reassuring. Like he was leaving this all up to me and would take "No, I screwed up. I'm not ready for this," as an answer. How could I *not* tell him now?

I looked behind us too, secretly hoping he was wrong. He wasn't.

I took a big breath and pushed my hair out of the way. "Well," I started. "A couple of d—"

The sound of girls' giggling cut me off, making me halt midstep. Cisco saw my pause and stopped just a step ahead of me. "What's wrong?" he asked.

The giggling sounded again. "Don't you hear that?" I asked.

He squinted his eyes and stared at the Clock. Three glowing figures, that I could see, were standing between the legs of the Clock. "Yeah," he said. "I hear it."

"Let's go someplace else," I said, and started walking back to the Academy.

I bit my lip and concentrated. Locations scrolled across my mind like images from an old piece of film. The craft room, the game room, the factory, all too crowded. The library, too quiet. There was really only one place I could think of, my room, but it was still missing its light. Then I realized he had a room too. Maybe we could use it.

"Can we go to your room?" I asked.

His upper lip curled in distaste. "Eh, my roommate's got a new girlfriend. They're usually, uh, busy…"

I didn't ask him to elaborate.

"What about yours?" he asked.

I grimaced. It did seem to be my only option. "I don't really have a roommate, but I don't have any light, either."

"What happened?"

By then we were too close to the rest of the students for me to feel comfortable announcing MaryAnn had been a wisper and as a result demolished our only light source. "Uh, I'll explain when we get there."

His brow raised and lowered with first curiosity then confusion.

"My roommate … got mad one day."

His curiosity grew.

"Like I said, I'll explain later."

We wove through the throng of students in the hallways to my room. When I opened the door, several nearby girls gaped at us. A couple of them called out to me.

"Woo! Go, girl!"

"Should I knock first?"

I felt the icy cold of embarrassment chill my face and knew it must be glowing white at this point. I didn't want to know how Cisco was reacting to their taunts.

I threw my bag in the corner and sat on the nearest couch. He shut the door and sat on the other end, facing me. Our own glows were the only two lights in the room. My face still radiated brighter than normal. It looked like his was too from where I sat, staring at the dark floor.

"Was it bad?" he asked.

I jerked my head up to meet his gaze. "What? Was what bad?"

"Your Life?"

"Oh." I shied away again. "Y-Yes. No. I don't know." I sighed and shifted my focus to the ceiling.

I saw the empty base for the light globe. A distraction.

"My roommate was a wisper. She was jonesing real bad one night when she tore the globe off our ceiling and sucked the light essence out of it." I nodded where the globe used to hang from.

Cisco's face was scrunched into an expression of pure disgust.

"She's gone now," I said. "I haven't seen her in awhile." I honestly didn't know how long it had been at that point.

"I heard there's a kid in our hallway that does the stuff," he said. "I smoked weed when I was alive, but this stuff,"—he shook his head—"I won't go near this stuff."

A school presentation during my Life came to mind. "Just Say No!" it was called. Everyone was required to attend. I smiled wryly. It was silly for my class to attend. Some of us couldn't feed ourselves. How did they expect us to smoke something, or use a needle? I shuddered at the thought.

"Thinking about your Life again?" Cisco asked.

"Oh," I said. "No. Well, actually, but not like you think." I took the deepest breath I could and blew it through my mouth, puffing out my cheeks in the process. It was time. I couldn't put it off any longer.

"I was born…" My eyes prickled. My nose burned. There's nothing to be ashamed of, Hannah. Get ahold of yourself! I squeezed my eyes shut and dragged the image of Naomi wagging her finger at me, scolding me for acting this way.

It worked. I was able to force the impulse to cry down with a swallow. "I was born disabled. That's why I couldn't remember anything."

I couldn't bring myself to watch his reaction. I kept my eyes on the opposite wall. "My parents adopted me. I don't know who my real parents are."

He didn't say anything.

The silence felt right at first, but then it grew awkward. I kept waiting for him to say something, but he never did. When I couldn't take it anymore, I glanced up at his face. It held a similar expression to Naomi's. Like he couldn't understand what the big deal was.

"I'm sorry if I'm overreacting. When all my memories came back—" Tears formed in my eyes. I stared at the ceiling again, hoping they would go back where they came from or that the angle wouldn't allow him to see them.

He reached for my hand. His fingers wrapped around it. His thumb stroked the back of it.

I met his gaze. The eyes I was peering into weren't the ones I was used to. His were always cool, collected, guarded. This was the real Cisco I was looking at. Vulnerable, kind.

His face came closer. He reached his free hand up to touch my cheek.

None of what he was doing felt right, but after he had been so kind to me, after he had just shown me his true self, I couldn't push him away. I couldn't hurt him.

His lips were soft, the same temperature mine were, not like when Lin's hand went through my leg. His fingers had felt like fire. Pain.

Without slowing his kiss, Cisco pulled his body closer to me. His breathing quickened. He pressed against my lips, parting them.

"No!" I pushed against his chest.

He pulled away. His face was stunned, hurt, and I immediately regretted my actions.

"Sorry. I didn't mean to—"

The fake grin I was used to seeing spread across his face as he rose from the couch. "No problem, chica. I should've asked first, yo?"

"Cisco, I—" He made for the door. I tried to stop him. "Cisco!"

"Hey, I said no problem. Look, I've got stuff to do so, see ya 'round, K?"

The door shut. I had hurt him. He had trusted me, he had been so kind and understanding with me, and I had hurt him. I fell backwards onto the couch's cushions. I was officially the world's biggest screwup.

As I lay there, staring at the ceiling, trying to let my mind go blank, to rest, my fingers reached for my lips. Cisco's kiss had felt wrong, but it had felt good. I wanted to feel it again, lips on mine, hands pulling me closer.

Lin's face passed through my thoughts. Lin jumping and screaming to his guitar. Lin lying in bed, bare chested. I imagined his lips against mine instead of Cisco's. Him holding my hand, saying my name. Tiny sparks exploded throughout my body.

Memories invaded my visions. His hand reaching out to grab me, the slice of his fiery fingers burning through the back of my thigh as I fled the room. I had run out on him, ashamed, terrified of how he then thought of me. The sparks became a dull chill.

He hadn't thought badly of me. He had tried to stop me. He had shown me all the good things about my Life. The page set up in my name for money. Hundreds of people who had loved me, wanted me to live, wanted my parents to be happy. Not a single hurtful word had left his lips.

I had to go back.

UNEXPECTED VALUE

I spent my night on the couch, thinking. The problem with going back to Lin was, I didn't have anything else to trade, and not enough time to wait for another precious commodity to come through the Vent. As if the countdown until the Day of the Dead weren't enough, my remorse for my actions was tearing a hole in my stomach.

The Clock rang. It was time for class.

"Dang it!" I muttered to myself.

I removed the wadded shirt from my backpack and replaced it with my books and finished essay before leaving for class.

Mrs. Collins was not happy with me. I turned in my essay, something that seemed to upset and satisfy her at the same time. I received several more days of detention for my absence from all my classes, but I didn't care. Detention wasn't so bad, and I couldn't do anything during class time anyway.

I glanced at Cisco when Mrs. Collins led me from the room to detention. He didn't look up at me.

The rest of the day was impossible to get through. I couldn't stop fidgeting as I copied from Doll Collecting Through the Ages. More than once the girl in front of me turned around to glare at me for making her chair shake. I murmured an apology and tried to stay still as long as possible. Which was less than a minute. Mr. Hill kept peering up at me and clearing his throat. I ignored him. I had enough on my mind. Several times I caught myself doodling portals instead of copying from my book. When supper time came, I tossed my book on the shelf, slammed my papers on the corner of his desk, and sprinted to the Vent. I was drawing attention to myself, being careless, but I didn't care anymore.

I inhaled my first breath. It was a cool, vaporous stream of meat and potatoes. It filled my chest, my shoulders, my hips. I sucked in another breath. Bread, nothing but bread. A few nearby ghosts mentioned something about it too. A bread factory must've burned a bunch of loaves or something. I fed until my entire body was satiated.

I lingered in the thickest streams until the items began appearing. I wove through them, my bag on my back. Wooden planks, a few factory parts, a chair—probably worth a good trade but too big to carry out of here, some sheets. I stopped. The sheets, they might work. I bent over to pick them up. The essence was still thick. The fog hadn't moved back in yet. Another hand grazed mine. I looked up and gasped. It belonged to a Gatherer.

"Oh! Sorry," I said. "I was just wondering what that was."

"They're sheets," she said. "Bed sheets. They belong to the Academy." She eyed my backpack suspiciously. "If you would like to purchase them with your rations, I would be happy to hold them for you." She didn't sound happy. She sounded irritated.

I stared at her, my mouth open. She continued to watch my backpack like paraphernalia was going to drop out its bottom any minute.

"Oh!" I said. "I haven't been—" I had actually. I reached for my bag. "This is just … my books." I unzipped it, showing her the insides.

She craned her neck to peer inside. I opened it wider for her. When she could no longer justify her behavior, she backed away, suspicion still a heavy residence on her face.

I waited.

She continued to stare at me.

I smiled sheepishly.

She was waiting for me to leave. I realized that now.

I zipped up my bag and backed away. "I'm sorry. I didn't…"

She didn't respond.

With one strap of my bag over my shoulder, I walked briskly back to the Academy and straight to my room.

I threw the backpack on the floor. It skidded past the rug and into the far wall.

I was resentful, frustrated, lost. I paced the room longways. If I had been a living person, my feet would have sent angry stomping noises torpedoing into the hallway.

I could never glean from the Vent again. This wasn't the first time a Gatherer had noticed my odd behavior. They would suspect me now, be watching. I had no idea what the punishment was for such an offense, but the way that Gatherer glared at me, it had to be more than just a couple of days in detention.

Even if I found something to get me to Lin this time, it would be my last. For a very long time at least. It would take forever to save up enough rations to buy my ticket to see him again. My eyes started to burn just thinking about it. The idea of only seeing Lin once or twice a year was unacceptable.

I fell to the couch with an agonizing growl. It was the couch I didn't normally use, my couch, the one I hadn't touched since MaryAnn ripped the globe from the ceiling. I jumped back up and rubbed my bottom with my hand. I had sat on something, hard. I lifted the cushion.

Part of MaryAnn's hookah stared back at me, affronted. Ironically, I had forgotten all about her wisp paraphernalia.

I pulled it out and placed it on the table. I thought about throwing it, shattering it against the wall as she had our light source. It was the bane of the Void, as far as I was concerned, and needed to be destroyed.

I returned to my couch, my chin in my hands, my elbows on my knees. Seeing her mouthpiece there, on the table, reminded me of something. Ah, the wispers in the Entryway. There had been so many. I wondered if it eventually affected them as it had her.

I sat up.

The Entryway.

I pushed myself off the couch and darted to MaryAnn's drawers. I yanked out every item of clothing I came to until I found it. The bowl of the hookah.

I held it in my hand. Its beautiful blue glass was cut into a diamond pattern, making it shimmer next to my glow. I threw her drawer back into place, leaving her clothes where they lay. I placed the bowl carefully on the table next to the mouthpiece I had sat on.

The only pieces left were the hoses, and I had left them together. I reached one hand into the mouth of her guitar. The strings protested a twangy tune as I foraged for the hoses. When I found them, I had to twist my wrist around to keep from tangling them. I held them up next to each other. They were in the same condition as when I had put them in there.

I brought them to the table and tried to remember how to reconnect all the pieces. It took me a long time, but I eventually made it whole again. I wrapped the hookah in a baggy sweater and placed it in my backpack, much as I had the glass jar before. Don't worry, Lin. I'm coming.

RETURN TO THE ENTRYWAY

I swung the bag over one shoulder and kept my eyes down as I exited my dorm room and made my way to the front exit of the Academy. Few people used the front door, making it easier to avoid suspicious stares. Once outside, I gazed over at the Clock. Its hands read nearly midnight. The Day of the Dead was almost here. A warm elation spread from my chest to the edges of my body. It made me smile. I would know where my parents lived in time to visit them. "Thank you," I whispered to the Clock. I knew it couldn't hear me, but it didn't matter.

I clutched the pendant under my shirt for security, pivoted on the ball of my foot, and walked straight to the Entryway.

The shouts of the Callers were rampant this time. Must be because the Day of the Dead was so near. Several ghosts were in the distance, close enough for me to see, but far enough away not to notice my magic trick with the Veil.

As I approached them, I noticed their heads were turned up, listening to the echoing voices of the Void. Some were disappointed, others busy concentrating. A woman on the right of my future path unexpectedly gasped. She clasped her gaping, smiling face with her hands. A Caller had just called her name. I stopped to watch.

It took her a moment to compose herself. When she did, she dropped her hands and said, "I am Katrina Bastianich."

The diameter of the faint blue burst of the Caller grew until it was as wide as a portal. The woman stared up at it, transfixed with delight, and floated up, allowing it to swallow her.

I stood still a moment, processing what I just saw. I had completely forgotten about the ability to be called by a Medium. Maybe I didn't need the Entryway afterall. The echoes of the other Callers crescendoed. I resumed my journey.

There was a line of several patrons out from the steps to the Entryway. I joined it at the end, careful to keep a firm grasp on my backpack. I kept casting furtive glances at the strangers near me, checking for suspicious actions or faces. When I reached the top of the steps, the front bouncers looked me over, saw my bag, and nodded me through. I waited in line to trade in my hookah.

The attendant acted impressed again. It made me feel cheated. Oh well, I thought, if my idea about Lin calling me was right, I wouldn't have to do this anymore.

I remembered being alloted one hour for my turn. There were five people in front of me. That meant five hours, plus my one… I would be bored and anxious, but I would have plenty of time to do what I needed before morning.

The wait seemed to go on forever, but I didn't dare leave the line. Two patrons in, a ghost from the crowd cut in front of another one in front of me.

"Thanks for saving my line, man," the cutting ghost said.

"No, problem," the one who let him in answered.

The bouncer approached them. "Hey! No cuts!"

"I didn't! He saved my spot for me!"

The other ghost backed him up.

The bouncer grabbed the cutting ghost by the collar and yanked him from the line. "I said, no cuts!"

He threw him on the last word. I stepped back but made sure to keep my place.

The ghost fell onto a group of tables but became ethereal at the last moment, going through them instead of crushing them. He uprighted himself. A fierce snarl twisted his face in fury. He threw himself onto the bouncer.

Did a fight happen here every night? No wonder they were always in search of certain items!

The men were nearly equal in size and ability. The rest of the crowd jumped out of their way as they broke chairs and rolled around on the floor. Just as they took their fight into the air, the rest of the Entryway's bouncers jumped in, pulling them apart. The offending patron was thrown out of the building. Order was quickly restored.

The rest of my wait seemed to take twice as long as it should have after that.

When my turn came, the attendant gave the bouncer the nod of approval, and I went in.

"One hour," he reminded me.

I nodded. I didn't need the reminder.

I approached the portal. Its swirling blue tried to hypnotize me, prevent me from concentrating on what I was about to do. I let it succeed, but only for a moment. It calmed me.

I called out Lin's name and location. The portal locked onto him. I took a breath, held it, closed my eyes, and stepped through.

APOLOGY

Lin's kitchen was the black I expected it to be. I glanced at the microwave clock. 1:23. Lin would be asleep. I bit my lip remorsefully. Barging in on him half naked in bed wasn't the best introduction for an apology. Still, a tiny spark warmed my chest and made my blush from the memory of our similar first meeting.

I dropped my bag at the portal's edge and climbed the stairs. He was asleep, his right arm reaching to the opposite corner his left leg was, my glow reflecting off the golden skin of his back so I could see the way his muscles curved around his shoulder blades. His face was buried in his pillow so deeply, I worried he got enough oxygen.

His back rose and fell with a heavy sigh. I smiled. I wanted to touch him, stroke his hair. Seeing him like this caused me to forget all about my reason for coming here, my shame. I had to remind myself I had a time limit.

I tried to wake him by clearing my throat. Nothing. I cleared it louder.

A muffled sound came from the hallway. I froze, silent. I had forgotten about his parents. I crept towards the door and peeked around the corner. I didn't hear or see anything else. I went to stand by Lin again, this time trying to think of a silent way to accomplish my task.

I thought about poking him, but I knew my touch was hot on his skin and didn't want to burn him. I bent over and blew on his back instead. He wriggled a little. His arm reached around to scratch at it. I started to chuckle but bit my lips together to keep any sound from escaping.

I blew again, harder, and on his neck.

He mumbled something into his pillow and raised his head.

I couldn't help it this time and laughed.

"What the—?" He pushed himself up and turned to face me. His squinting eyes blinked several times as they focused on me. "Oh, hey," he said groggily.

"Shhh," I told him.

He sat the rest of the way up, causing his sheet to move. I quickly faced the wall to give him his privacy.

"What's wrong?" I heard him ask from behind me.

"I'm letting you get dressed," I whispered.

I heard a chuckle and heavy movement. He must have been fetching some clothes. I could feel my face glow hot with embarrassment.

"Why are you whispering?" he asked.

"I don't want to wake your parents."

He stopped moving a second. "They can't hear you."

Oh yeah. Oops.

"I um, I came to apologize," I said, now the fear of being overheard was gone.

I continued to hear the shuffling of sheets and clothes behind me.

"For walking — running out on you the other day." I paused, waiting for a response. The only thing I heard were legs going into jeans followed by a zipper. "I'm sorry."

More shuffling. This time it sounded like sheets again. I waited. Maybe I was too late. Maybe I had made him angry with my actions.

"I don't, um, I don't know what else to say." My voice shook, and I could feel the oncoming birth of tears. "I'm kind of new at this—"

"Hey."

I felt the biting cold of his fingers around my forearm. I gasped and jerked away, but not before he had me turned around to face him again.

I stared up into his eyes, instantly regretting my jerking away. I rubbed my arm the same time he rubbed his fingers. "I'm sorry. I— You startled me."

His brows dipped in concern. "Why are you sorry?" he asked.

"For jerking away just then. It's just—"

He shook his head at me. His hands reached for me again but he caught himself before we touched. "I shouldn't have touched you like that." He ran his hand through his sleep strewn hair. "I keep forgetting what happens when I do."

He suddenly turned his attention to the hallway. I could hear the remnants of restless sleeping. He walked over and quietly shut the door and locked it.

My arm still tingled where he had grabbed it. I rubbed it again. It was then I realized something interesting. He had touched me. Not passed through me like before, but actually touched me.

I was still rubbing it when he returned.

He misread my actions. "I'm sorry. I didn't mean to—"

"No!" I nearly shouted. I made sure to lower my voice when I spoke again. "You touched me." I smiled when I said it.

Two little ditches formed between his eyebrows. "I know. I said I'm s—"

I interrupted his apology, shaking my head. "That's not what I mean. The last time I was here, I couldn't touch anything: you, the chair." I remembered the horrible embarrassment my clumsiness had caused me then, and flushed in response. "But this time, your fingers didn't go through my arm. They … stayed on my skin like they should."

He looked down at his hands, at my arm, back to his hands. "Why?" he asked.

"I don't know."

"Did you learn something new in your Academy?"

I shook my head. "No." I just wanted it this time.

My mouth fell open with the realization of what I almost said. I snapped it shut. It did not go unnoticed. I immediately tried to act normal.

"What?" he asked.

Oh, nothing. I just want you to touch me bad enough that it worked. Nothing embarrassing there, so I'll just keep that to myself, thank you. "Nothing," I lied.

He sat on his bed. I wanted to join him, but I didn't want to know if I would fall through or not. If my idea was correct, and he was able to touch me because I *wanted* it bad enough, and I fell through the bed, then that meant I wanted him more than anything else in the Land of the Living. And even though I wouldn't admit my discovery to him, finding that out in his presence would mortify me to a second Death.

I backed away and quickly tried to put myself back on track, by saying what I should have said the last time we were together. "Thank you."

His head tilted to one side. "For?"

"For researching my family and everything."

"You're welcome," he said.

I could practically see the eggshells we were walking on.

"Did you find anything else out about them?" Yay, Hannah! Way to make the conversation more awkward. I mean, you did just apologize for running out on him the last time he helped, so why not ask for more favors?

"What would you like to know?" He jumped up from the bed and went to his computer.

I couldn't help but wonder if he really wanted to help me or was just an overly nice guy. "Are you sure I'm not bothering you?" I asked.

"Yes, Hannah," he said. "I'm very sure." He wiggled the mouse to get the computer going. "I *want* to do this for you. I—" He swallowed whatever else he was about to say.

I was too embarrassed to ask him to finish. "Can you find out their address?"

He shifted awkwardly in his chair and stared at the monitor. I thought I saw a red tint on his face.

A few clicks of his mouse and tapping of keys later, he said, "They live on 2729 Rockcrest Rd, in West Virginia."

I repeated the address over and over until I was sure I had it memorized. "Is there a way to know where they'll be on the Day of the Dead?"

"The Day of the Dead?" he asked.

I explained what happened in the Land of the Dead on that day and what it meant to the ghosts.

"Oh, wow. That's really cool. I had no idea about that. I mean, I knew the day held some mythos around it, but I hadn't gotten around to studying any of them yet. When is it?"

I didn't want to answer his question. It made the truth more finite, that my time here was limited. But I had to. "In two days. I would like to visit them, if I could, but I would have to know where they're going to be in— on that day."

He puckered his lips in concentration and nodded. "Let's see." He turned back to his monitor. "Oh," he said a few seconds later. His eyes darted to me then turned back to the screen. He hesitated.

My stomach knotted. I didn't like it when he hesitated before telling me something. It usually meant something bad.

He rose from his chair and stood out of the way. "Here," he said.

I peeked at his expression. It wasn't quite as distressed as when he had told me about my Life. The knots in my stomach loosened slightly.

I whispered the words as I read them. "On the first of next month, we will be placing our Dear Hannah's headstone. We ask this to be a private affair. Thank you, everyone, for your thoughts and prayers during this time."

"The first of next month," I said. "When is that?"

He smiled, amused. "That's the Day of the Dead, the day after tomorrow."

A little flame lit between my shoulders. Happiness. My family was going to be at the one place I could get to no matter what on the one day I could go there. My gravesite.

"I get to see my family again." A giddy smile spread across my face.

Lin's face lit up in return.

"Will you be there with me?" I asked.

He paused before answering, "It's … not that I don't want to, Hannah. It's just really far away. I don't know if I can get there or not."

His rejection hurt. "Do you like me visiting you?" I asked.

He blushed. "Yeah. Why?"

I recalled the woman from the Void I saw earlier and wondered if he had ever tried to do that for me. I knew he could. He had told me so himself. "The first time we met, well, the second time really, I remember you saying you called for other ghosts. Have you ever called for me?"

He stood up. "Hannah, I called for you the moment I found out your full name."

I stared up into his eyes, unable to breathe. "You did?"

"Yes," he said, coming closer to me. "I did."

Was he one of the Callers of the Void? Did I hear him and not realize it? "I saw a woman do it tonight. Enter a Caller's portal. I've learned how to hover, sorta. I think I could do it if you tried again."

"Of course, Hannah." He smiled.

Him saying my name like that did funny things to my stomach. "Will you do it tomorrow?" The tears started again, and I don't think I had the power to stop them.

He cocked his head, curious with my behavior. "Sure. Is something wrong?"

Yes, everything was wrong, but telling you would make it real, and I can't handle that.

"What's that?" he asked.

"What?"

He was pointing to my chest. "That thing you're holding."

My pendant. The thing I have to give back in two days. The one and only ticket to ever see you again.

"Hannah!" Lin reached his hand up to my face.

I shook my head and wiped my tears for him. "Lin," I tried to say, but my crying made it come out strangled. I sniffed and swallowed. "Lin, I can't do this anymore."

He acted hurt. "I don't understand."

"I have to give this back," I sobbed.

"Give what back?" He was confused.

I didn't want to explain everything. Repeating it just made it worse. But if I didn't, I would regret it and I knew it. He deserved an answer. "The other ghosts, they need this disc to visit their families. I can't keep it."

He didn't want to believe what I was telling him. I could see him trying to find a solution, a way to make it work. "But you'll graduate from the Academy and live in the Void, right?"

I shook my head. "A long time from now," I said. More tears flowed. Happy because he wanted me as much as I wanted him, sad because I knew this had to end. It wasn't fair to make him wait, to make myself wait. It would be too painful.

He reached his hand out again to wipe my cheeks but stopped himself, allowing his hand to hover close to my face. I stepped closer to it, closer to him. If I had been with anyone else in the world, Living or Dead, I would not have wanted them to see me crying like this. But with Lin, it was the exact opposite. The more I hurt, the closer I wanted him to be.

He didn't retreat from my approach. His hand was a blazing inch from me now. I had stopped crying, stopped breathing. I lifted my hand to his face, hesitating millimeters from his skin. Sparks fired from my palm against his cheek, causing him to wince, but he didn't move. I pushed my hand further, against his skin. It felt like holding fire. A soft, warm fire that swelled my chest with the most wonderful feeling. I felt him shiver against my palm.

The fire soon became tolerable. Like that second sip of cocoa after the first, too hot one. I smiled and exhaled. His face relaxed until he was no longer wincing. His shivering eased. He opened his eyes. My smile grew.

"Can I?" he asked, his hands next to my neck.

I hadn't breathed in so long, I had forgotten I needed air to speak. "Yes," I less than whispered.

His hands came down on my shoulders, searing hot. I gasped from the pain but gritted my teeth, knowing it would soon fade.

We stood, my hand on his face, his hands on my shoulders, for an eternity of seconds. Soon the blaze was a pleasant warmth, and I wanted more of it. More of him. I wanted to realize my earlier fantasy, for him to kiss me like Cisco had.

I stared into his eyes as I brought his face closer to mine. He responded by drawing me in.

Then we both stopped.

Our faces stood a single inch from each other. Sparks formed on the surface of my glowing skin, traveling across it like living spiders. His face reddened wherever one touched it, but he didn't flinch.

I gazed at his full lips, his thick nose, his deep, brown eyes. Our eyes met. I realized he was silently asking me if it was OK to keep going. I let my eyes tell him it was.

His lips got closer but still out of reach. The heat from them scorched my own. I closed my eyes and waited, not knowing if he was ensuring he wasn't hurting me or my lips were too cold for his, but I was almost to the point of not caring anymore. Having him hover this close to me was torture.

The scorch intensified. Our lips were touching, unmoving, but touching. When the blaze cooled, they moved. I whimpered.

My reaction kindled a fury in him. His lips turned demanding. His breath came heavy and hard, blistering steam against my face. With my hand still on his cheek, I rubbed my thumb against his skin. Tiny lightning bolts danced wherever it touched. He let out a moan in response.

He pulled away. I felt cold when he did. I wanted the heat to return. I had to stop my fingers from grabbing him. He was breathing heavily. I was still quite literally breathless.

"Wow," he said. "That was…"

"Yeah," I said, finally taking a breath to do so. "It was."

We backed away from each other. The clock on his nightstand happen to catch my eye as we did. 2:24

I gasped.

"What's wrong?" he asked.

"I'm out of time."

His face fell. "Oh."

My throat tightened. My eyes and nose burned. I swallowed away the pain, refusing to let it mar our time together. "We still have tomorrow," I said. "Will you call me then?"

"Of course I will, all night if I have to." His face drew closer. He was going to kiss me again. The desire to let him lit a fire in my chest which prevented me from moving, breathing, doing anything other than stand there and stare at him. But the anxiety of knowing what would happen if I didn't sprint for the portal right then snuffed that fire with a thousand waterfalls.

"I have to go," I said. While I still can.

I turned on my heel and ran for the portal. He did nothing to stop me, and I didn't want him to. I grabbed my bag at the last second and jumped back into the Entryway. The bouncer was waiting for me inside the room.

"You're late."

I sniffed. "Don't worry. It won't happen again."

I ignored the bouncer's response and left the portal room door open when I went through it.

CAUGHT

Every other step back to the Academy brought with it a different feeling. Joy from the memory of my time with Lin. Pain from the knowledge we only had one more night together. Agony over the decision I had to make.

Should I visit him again? Would that be wise? Knowing it was our last time, knowing how much pain it would cause the both of us, maybe I should just turn the disc in now and be done with it.

I had already decided not to attempt to see him again after tomorrow, that's why I didn't mention the possible use of my rations for the school portal to him. Between that and the Day of the Dead, that would only give us a scant two or three times a year to visit. I would derive no pleasure from torturing myself, or him, with such a ridiculous schedule.

Yet. Lin said he would call for me tomorrow. Could I really let him stand there all night like he said he would and never show up? Could I let him think I didn't want to be with him anymore?

No, I was not strong enough for that. And not just for his sake. I knew at the end of the next day's classes, I would have forgotten the pain and would do almost anything to see him again, even if for one night. Even for a last night.

I would visit the Void after feeding tomorrow. Then, before the new day began, in plenty of time for the others to use it on the Day of the Dead, I would return the disc.

I reached the Veil. It was dark on the other side. Students were getting ready for class probably. They should be starting soon. I closed my eyes and stepped through it, longing for it to wash away my current anguish. It did not.

I opened my eyes and sighed. I readjusted my backpack and walked towards my room.

"Hello, Hannah," a familiar voice said behind me.

I stopped moving. All the essence drained from my face. I didn't have to turn around to know who it was.

"Hello, Lydia," I said.

Her now visible body floated to in front of mine.

"I need it back, Hannah," she said.

My biggest fear confirmed.

"Need what back?" I knew what she wanted, but there was always a chance I was wrong. A small, invisible chance, but a chance.

A hint of a smile twitched the corners of her mouth. "The disc for my lantern." She held her light source up for display, enhancing her point.

I reached for the pendant, my fingers curling around it like it was child. "I'm not done with it yet."

Her eyes jerked back to mine. Malice shined from their depths, making me take a step back. "It is not yours to use, Hannah."

"I know." My voice was hardly a whisper, but I knew she heard it. She heard everything, knew everything, of that I now realized. "Please," I whispered still. "Please. I just need it for one more day, just one more day," I begged.

She held out her hand. "You have had it long enough. It is time."

"How did you know?"

Her eyes widened in surprise. "Do you think your actions went unnoticed? Do you think the Gatherers said nothing? How many times have you left and returned, and yet you feel your behavior was invisible to us?"

I blinked, and stared up at her face. "Why didn't you say anything?" I meant, why hadn't she turned me in, but she understood.

Her expression turned stoic, guarded. "I could see your pain, but enough time has passed. You will heal. The others deserve their turn."

This wasn't happening. I had just gathered enough strength to tell Lin goodbye, and now she was taking it away from me?

Her eyes bored into mine. I considered running away, into the Void. I could throw the pendant back through the Veil and live with Naomi. Maybe, hopefully. But Lydia would not let this go. She would follow me. And I knew from experience how easily she could catch me.

I pulled the string from around my neck and held it out for her. "Please," I begged. "Please, just one more night. I promise I'll return it. I was going to anyway." I was out of tears to cry.

She took the pendant and untied the disc. "I will say nothing, Hannah. Not now."

Her piercing gaze told me she would hold this over me if she had to. I spoke no more.

HOSTAGE

The Clock sounded. Lydia was gone. Whether because I had stood there long enough for her to enter the school, or because she turned invisible again, I knew not.

The Academy grew bigger, closer. I looked down. My feet were taking me there without my command.

I would never see Lin again, never tell him goodbye. He would call for me, and I would never answer. How long would he call for me? How long would he search before he gave up?

I heard the flutter of the students rushing to class, their friends calling out to them and giggling, the class doors shutting. I entered detention.

I was the last one to enter. Every student stared at me. I realized then I was still crying tearless sobs. My eyes must have been swollen and white. I sat in a desk at the back. I thought Mr. Hill called my name, but I didn't answer. A book appeared on my desk. I looked up to see Mr. Hill walk back to his desk and eye me concernedly. I began my copying.

It was a fictional book about a family living in early America. It made me think of my own family and how I would get to see them very very soon. Somehow that elation had been diminished.

Detention ended. I had only copied a couple of pages. My heart and mind were elsewhere.

I skipped feeding and sat alone in my room instead. Was Lin already calling for me? Would someone else go in my place? Anxiety crawled across my skin until I roared in frustration. I jumped up from the couch and began pacing my room like the proverbial caged lion.

Someone knocked on my door. I stopped pacing. Was it time to enter the Void?

They knocked again, quick, desperate sounds. I opened the door.

"Hannah?" Twila stood before me, her expression frantic and desperate.

"Twila?"

She shoved passed me and into the middle of the room. I shut the door behind her.

"Twila? What's wrong?"

"He's got her!" she screamed at me.

"Who's he?" I asked.

"Ronnie! You've got to help me get her back!"

The mention of Ronnie's name caused an unwelcome shiver to travel down my spine. "Ronnie? Has MaryAnn?"

She nodded.

"I don't understand."

Twila was so agitated, it was hard for me to make out the words. "When she never returned, I tried to find her, but I couldn't leave the Veil. Then I saw it." She grabbed my arms with her desperate fingers.

"Saw what?" I asked, trying to pull away. I was beginning to wonder if she was having a bad reaction to some fresh wisp.

"The pendant! *Our* pendant! On a new boy here in the Academy."

"How do you…?" I didn't understand what was going on.

She reached into her shirt and pulled out a necklace with a disc on the end, just like Lydia's, just like the one MaryAnn had fought to take back from me. She turned the disc over. Scratched into the back were their initials. "Ma/Twi" It was their pendant.

"How did you…?"

"I told you! I found it on the new boy," she snapped, impatient with my ignorance.

"But why would he have MaryAnn's pendant?"

"He got it from Ronnie!" she screamed at me, furious. "When I saw him wearing it, I made him tell me where he got it. When he said Ronnie, I ripped it off his neck. He tried to stop me, but I threatened to turn him into Mrs. Richards if he did. He's young. He's new. He doesn't realize…"

Did my eyes deceive me, or did she feel sorry for the boy she just told me she'd attacked.

"My threat must've scared him more than Ronnie's because he backed off. I used the pendant to search for MaryAnn."

Her frenzied eyes implored mine. "I followed the path we always took. To get the wisp? From Ronnie? But our dealer wasn't there. I had to go all the way in, into Ronnie's den. There…" Her expression was unfathomable. "He has so many. On the Day of the Dead, tomorrow, he's going to turn them all into wisp."

I couldn't process everything she was telling me. I didn't understand. I went around to the front of the couch and sat down. I motioned for her to join me. She paced the room instead.

"I don't understand. I thought you knew that's how wisp was made. I thought you knew it was from the essence of others."

She turned away, unable to face me. "I did. We all did. But knowing it and seeing it…"

Are two different things, yes. "But why is he waiting until tomorrow? Why not do it now?"

"We can visit anywhere on the Day of the Dead for several reasons. One is that the Curtain is its thinnest then. The other is we are our strongest. If Ronnie takes their essence tomorrow, when they are at their strongest, he will get the most intense, purest wisp he can."

This was horrible news. I mean, I knew Ronnie was a murderer, but like earlier, knowing it and having an eyewitness tell you about it in detail are two different things. "Why are you asking me to help? Shouldn't you tell the staff here or … something?" I knew better than to say "the authorities of the Void". Ronnie and his goons were the authorities of the Void.

She looked at me disbelievingly. "And what should I tell them, Hannah?" she snapped. "That I'm a wisper trying to save another wisper's life? Do you think they'll try and help me? Tomorrow's a big day for the Academy. Do you think they'll leave all the other students unattended so they can save one?"

"But what about the others? What about—"

"They don't *care*, Hannah!" she screamed at me.

Whether they did or not, it was clear she believed the latter.

"Why do you need me? Why didn't you just do it while you were there?"

Desperation washed her anger away. "I can't do it. I tried. They're all in locked cages. You have to be one of Ronnie's guards to set them free."

I let out a short laugh. "And you expect *me* to be able to do what *you* can't?"

"You're smart, Hannah, smarter than I am."

I glanced back up at her and shook my head. "I'm not—"

"Hannah! *Please!*"

I felt my head continue to move slowly back and forth. There was no way. I didn't know what she expected me to do. I wasn't some warrior police officer that could go in and rescue her girlfriend.

She placed the disc in my hand and wrapped my fingers around it. She held my one hand with both of hers, her desperate eyes staring up, imploring mine. The pendant's chain dangled from between my fingers, onto cushions of the couch below. That was when it hit me.

"Give me the pendant," I said.

Her brows dipped in the center. "I just did."

"No," I said. "Give it to me forever."

"What are you going to do with it?" she demanded.

"I have friends in the Land of the Living I wish to see. This will let me."

Malice formed a tiny spark in the farmost corner of her left eye.

"I won't use it for wisp, Twila. I promise."

"You must also promise to keep it from MaryAnn. I *never. Want. To see her on wisp. Again.*" Tears rolled down her face as she spat the angry words through clinched teeth.

I nodded. "Agreed."

We stared silently at each other for several seconds.

"Thank you," she said, and wrapped her arms around me.

I hugged her back. I held the disc up behind her so I could see it. My ticket to see Lin as often as I wanted. My promise to break MaryAnn free of Ronnie's prison.

What had I just agreed to?

BESEECHING

When Twila left my room, I sat on my couch with my eyes fixated on the door, rubbing the disc with my thumb, letting its chain slither across my fingers like it was alive. I eventually stood and placed the necklace around my neck, making sure to tuck it away from sight. I left my room.

I took nothing with me. No weapons (I had none anyway), nothing to trade, no map or directions to guide me. Twila had told me how to get there. She had also told me what I would need, so to speak. Cisco. If anyone could help me with this, it would be him, and I believed I needed all the help I could get.

I found Cisco hanging with his friends in their usual spot by the stairs. I kept my distance. The last time we spoke, he kissed me and I shoved him away. Then I went to the Void without him and made out with Lin. Oh yeah, and my sole purpose in doing this was to keep the pendant so I could see Lin again. So basically, I was using Cisco.

I turned back around to leave. I could do this without him. I had the pendant, the directions, the instructions. It was just a few wraith guarding some cages only they could open that set outside freakin' Ronnie's freakin' den. *Sure*, I could *so **not*** do this.

I stopped and ground my teeth together. There was *no way* I could do this alone. Robin and the other girls weren't cut out for this type of things. Twila was way too scared and upset. I *needed* Cisco. No matter how uncomfortable this was going to get, no matter what it did to our friendship, I had to do it. Souls depended on it.

I opened my eyes, clinched my fists, set my jaw, and spun around on the ball of my left foot. One of his friends alerted him to my approach. I was wrapped up in forcing myself to do this, I didn't realize how angry my face must have looked.

"Um, hey, Hannah. What's up?" Cisco asked hesitantly. He was purposefully avoiding my immediate area.

"Oh." I straightened up and compelled my body to relax. "Sorry. I was just, um, never mind."

He and his friends stared like there was something wrong with me, which all things considered, there was. I was in an awkward situation, confused, and totally stressed out.

"Cisco, can we talk in private?"

A layer of hope lay under his skeptical expression. I would have to crush that hope before it grew. Great. This was not getting any easier. "Sure."

He followed me onto the porch. I led him to an abandoned corner. No one was near enough to hear.

I explained the whole situation to him, making sure to do it as platonically as possible. When I finished, he answered, "I don't know, Hannah. It sounds dangerous."

"What?" I couldn't believe my ears. Cisco avoiding danger? "But you were the one carrying me away from the bar fight at the Entryway, the one who taught me how to act with Naomi, the one who skips class and goes on adventures and, and…"

"Skipping class and running from a bar fight are nothing compared to what you're asking." His guard was down.

I made sure to keep my own actions within check. I didn't want to hurt him again. "But Cisco," I pleaded. "These ghosts are going to *die*."

"They're already Dead, Hannah!"

I pressed my lips together and looked away.

"You know what I mean."

"Yes, I do," I retorted. "Why won't you do this? I would do it for you!" I regretted my words the moment I felt them exit my mouth. I saw his hope flicker.

I knew I needed to stop it right then, do something, anything to show him how I really felt, but I didn't. Instead, my traitorous hand reached out and grabbed his. "Please," I begged. "Please. If you don't come with me, I won't be able to do this."

It was working. I could see him considering it, see his desire for me overtake his logical thought. He knew I didn't feel that way for him, but his deep down longing was surfacing anyway. I was a terrible terrible person.

"The Day of the Dead starts at midnight tonight. Can't we wait until it's over?"

"No." I shook my head, releasing his hand as I did. "That's when Ronnie's going to do it, something about getting stronger wisp out of them or something on the Day of the Dead."

Cisco winced when I mentioned how wisp was made.

"Tonight's the only time we can," I explained.

I could see him thinking about it, see the gears of his mind turn. My hand tried to reach for him again. I grabbed its wrist with my other hand. I refused to lead him on anymore than I already had. I felt guilty enough as it was.

Please, Cisco. Please, I thought to myself, biting my lips and trying not to bounce on my toes.

"OK, chica. I'll help. But you *owe* me!"

That I do, Cisco. I so do.

I led Cisco to the edge of the Veil nearest Ronnie's den. "You ready?" I asked.

"Yeah." He nodded.

When he and I entered the Void last time, he had wrapped the necklace's chain around both our necks, but I didn't think that was necessary. When I took Lydia's disc, it made me think. She had never held my hand. She just stood close to me when we exited the Maze, unless, of course, the Veil didn't separate the Academy from the Maze. That, I seriously doubted.

"Wait," Cisco called as I stepped into the Veil.

I stopped and turned. "What?"

"What about me?"

I took a step towards him. "Do you mean this?" I held out the pendant's chain to illustrate my point.

"Yeah." His expression was dumbfounded.

"I don't think we have to both be wearing it. I think we just have to be near it."

He peered sideways at me, skeptical.

I smiled. "If it doesn't work, I'll come back for you."

He didn't move.

I stepped closer. "Do you remember coming here with Lydia?"

His eyes darted to a memory in the corner of his mind. "Not really. Maybe." I don't think he liked that memory, not that I blamed him.

"Did she do anything special when you exited the Maze?"

He hesitated, his eyes wandering for that moment in time. "No, I don't … No."

I raised my eyebrows as if to say, "See?" then turned back around and walked through the Veil.

I could see his blurred blob on the Academy's side of the Veil. I waited. One second. Two. His image moved a bit, like he was losing an inner battle, then got closer.

I watched as he slowly exited the Veil, his body morphing from distorted blob to real life Cisco.

I smiled. "Ready?"

He sounded perturbed when he answered. "Yeah, I'm ready."

My smile vanished. I hadn't meant to upset him. I opened my mouth to apologize, but he interrupted me before I could.

"Let's just go, OK?" He hovered away without so much as glancing my direction.

His rebuff made me feel guilty. I needed to make things right, but now wasn't the time. His actions made it clear he wasn't ready for my atonement. Hopefully that wasn't a permanent condition.

I ran to catch up with him. He was going the wrong direction. I held a hesitant hand over his shoulder, afraid to point out his mistake.

"Whatever you're going to say, say it."

I curled my fingers back into their palm, withdrawing my hand. I said nothing. I couldn't. His cold shoulder had glued my mouth shut.

He stopped.

I barely prevented myself from running into him. "I'm sorry," I whispered.

He huffed a heavy breath out his nose. "No, I'm sorry. I overreacted."

I knew better than to ask the next question, but I couldn't help myself. "What, um, what made you ... so angry?"

"I don't know." He shrugged, but I could tell he did.

Should I apologize again?

We stood there, him staring at his shoes, me fiddling with my fingers, until I couldn't bear it any longer. "It's this way." I told him. If he didn't want to tell me what was wrong, then I wasn't going to push him to.

"What?" he asked, turning his head my direction.

"You're going the wrong way. Ronnie's den is this way."

He mumbled something in Spanish, I didn't want to know what, and followed my lead.

We saw a few ghosts shortly after we left the Academy, but unlike the Entryway, the path to Ronnie's became less crowded the closer we got. The eerie feeling was magnified by the echoes of the Callers from overhead, something I would have thought I would be used to by now. The number of names I heard was easily tenfold the normal amount. With the Day of the Dead but hours away, it was no wonder why. But I saw no ghosts, no spirits jumping through portals to join them. This area was not commonly traveled.

Cisco hovered closer to me. His shoulders were hunched slightly, and he kept glancing over them. I had always thought of him as the brave one. My step faltered in response to his paranoia.

I couldn't stop myself from listening for Lin's voice as we walked. I was thankful when I didn't hear it. I don't think I would've been able to resist visiting him, and Ronnie wasn't going to wait for me to start damning souls.

A faint glow appeared up ahead. We both halted at the same time.

Black dots moved fluidly in front of the glow. I couldn't tell what they were from where we stood, but I knew they couldn't be ghosts.

I swallowed. "OK, Twila said MaryAnn is with the rest of the ghosts on the righthand side of the house."

"What house?" asked Cisco.

"I guess whatever all those guards are patrolling around." I caught myself cowering again, shivering like when I was alive and cold. I ground my teeth together and forced my unwilling body to stand straight.

We walked closer. As we did, a giant mansion came into view. I felt my jaw drop. This monstrosity outshined every other house or building I had seen in the Void so far, including the Entryway. Dark red brick sculpted a curved entrance with several misty areas I assumed were supposed to represent ponds from the Living. The lighting from the inside was subtle, giving it just the right enough accent to look purposefully dark. Not a single window was missing a pane. Full French doors with black trim stood between the rest of the floor-to-ceiling glass panes which formed the front wall of the house.

It was beautiful. It was Ronnie's den.

CHOICE

Cisco gasped. "Wraith!"

"What?" I turned to see what he was talking about. When I did, I nearly fell backwards. Horror filled more than his face. His entire body was stiff and paled to the point of almost clear.

"Cisco?"

He swallowed, his eyes following a pattern in the distance.

I matched his gaze. Two black, flowing figures were quickly approaching from their guard above the den. Against the Void, they were nearly invisible.

Twila's words came to mind. If you run into a guard, just pull out MaryAnn's pendant. They'll know you're OK after that.

Cisco grabbed my arm and started to flee.

"No, not yet!" I held his arm with my free one, forcing him to stay.

He watched me with anxious eyes as I grasped the pendant by its chain and held it up into the air. "What are you doing?" His voice cracked.

"Twila said this would work on the guards."

"You do realize what wraith do, right?" Cisco was frantic at this point. He kept pulling his arm away, but I held firm.

"I have to at least *try*, Cisco. If this doesn't work—"

"If this doesn't work, we're *dead*!" he screamed.

I let him go. I felt him arm drop from my hand, his presence grow smaller as the distance between us grew, but I didn't turn to watch him fly back to the Academy. I remained still with my hand holding the pendant up high. The wraith slowed. Then they stopped.

Black, whirling smoke, like the fog of the Void, made up their bodies. They came closer. Irregular white spots shone through the smoke. As they neared, I saw them to be the tips of their fingers, the thick tail where their bodies ended at the waist, the bit of bone shining through the rotted skin on their faces.

I felt Cisco next to me again. His hand reached for mine. I clasped my fingers through his hard enough to make him grunt in pain. I was terrified, but I wasn't going to let them see it.

Of the two wraith now floating before us, one eye remained. The rest of their sockets stood empty and black. I watched as that one eye moved, its gaze eventually landing on the pendant. The wraith's hand reached out for it, allowing me to identify the white splotches as bone. My body started to shake. I squeezed Cisco's hand harder.

It dropped the pendant, causing it to swing back and forth like a pendulum from my hand. They seemed done with it, so I lowered it to my side. I wasn't ready to unclinch Cisco's fingers with my other hand so I could place the necklace back around my neck yet.

What sparse skin remained on the creatures' necks strained as they turned their heads to face each other. I could tell they were communicating somehow, but I heard nothing.

"Follow." They spoke as one. Their voices sounded like flowing water. Their mouths did not move.

They parted for us to pass through. It was good I hadn't needed to speak again, because I had not breathed since I held the pendant up as my shield. I heard Cisco hyperventilating next to me.

Unable to keep our eyes off the wraith, our heads turned in unison as we walked between them. My left hand held the pendant up again on its own accord, like it was a medallion of protection or something.

They closed in behind us, herding us toward the den like cattle to slaughter. Seconds later, a light, frigid breeze blew on us as one of the wraith flew overhead and entered the den, presumably to announced our presence.

As we approached, a glow grew from the right side of the building until it outshined everything else, including the mansion.

"Cages," Cisco whispered.

I glanced their way and felt my face slacken. Dozens of makeshift enclosures littered the floor of the Void. Each held a single ghost. A wooden box, two feet wide, two feet long, and seven feet tall held a little girl. She had huddled as far into one of the corners as possible with her arms wrapped around her knees. Her head was buried in the hole that formed.

Next to her pen was one made of metal pipes. It had toppled sideways onto the ground where the angry ghost inside it continued to bang against the pipes in a fruitless attempt of escape. All he was managing to do at the moment was slide it a few inches at a time across the floor.

The prisoners eyed us wearily. A few begged for our help, tears falling into the black mist beneath them. We passed by the captives like damned souls, awaiting our trials. Their hands grabbed for us. Their voices pierced my inner being until I nearly crumbled beside them.

A chill ran up my spine. The wraith. They didn't like that I had slowed my pace. I held my hands over my ears and pressed forward. As I did, my promise to Twila surfaced my sea of thoughts. Save MaryAnn. I resumed my pace but scanned the cages out of the corner of my eye in search of her. There, on the outer edge of the cluster of cages, near the back of the mansion, MaryAnn hovered inside her pen.

One foot stumbled in front of the other, causing me to trip. Cisco caught me before I could fall. I memorized her location and followed beside my unwilling traveling companion to the French doors which formed the only visible entrance to the mansion before us. On either side of the doors were thick hedges in stone pots. *That cost him dearly*, I thought to myself, then shuddered when I realized he probably didn't pay for them, and their previous owner was probably wisped by addicts years ago. Thick ivy crawled along the entire outer surface of the building, and delicate pale flowers poked their heads out of a raised bed behind us. It felt I was entering a botanical garden, not a villain's chamber.

The wraith stayed outside, dutiful, submissive to the guard now approaching us, and avoiding all the plant life as if their lives depended on it. Their action made me wonder if those plants served a purpose other than beauty.

The guard was a muscular man with once brown hair that grew thick to his ears until it tufted out at the sides. He opened a single door for us to walk through. The wraith floated away without needing to be ordered. I turned my head to watch them leave, but Cisco quickly pulled me into the den behind him.

The guard eyed us threateningly as I walked and Cisco floated along the ceramic-tiled floor with even more shrubbery lined up in pots along the sides. Retro arcade machines with lifeless screens lined the walls in the back of the room. A small man in jeans, sneakers, and a screen-printed T-shirt approached us. "I don't recognize you. Who sent you here?"

My mind raced for what to say but could think of nothing. Cisco chimed in with his usual charm, "We're new middle-men, here to get some more wisp for a few buyers."

The small man in jeans chuckled. His guards smiled in disbelief.

"I don't *have* middle-men."

Ah, well this is just faaaaantasmaglorius! I dragged my friend who wants to be my lover here by flirting with him in order to save a girl who tried to kill me only to lead us to the very man who wants to wisp us all dry. Ronnie.

Cisco may have charm, but I have the ability to play dumb. OK, maybe I wasn't playing all the time, but I'm still good at faking it when I need to. I widened my eyes in innocence and said, "I don't understand. They said we could get more here and they would buy it from us."

Ronnie took a step forward. "Who said that?" He was no longer smiling.

My fingers clutched the pendant that was still in my hand even tighter. His eyes caught the movement. He roughly snatched it from me. I didn't resist.

He twirled it over in his palm, pausing to read the back. I stiffened with the realization he might know what "MA/Twi" meant. A satisfied grin stretched across his face. He did.

"Now why do you have this?"

Cisco's fingers brushed the edges of mine. I interlaced them to stop the shaking.

Ronnie's eyes bored into mine. Impatient. Angry.

My voice shook as I spoke. "My, um, my roommate gave it to me so I could get her and the others some wisp." It was sorta true. Not that it mattered.

"Did she now." He didn't believe me. That I could tell.

He handed the pendant to the nearest guard and muttered, "Bring her."

Ronnie turned and walked away from us. I wasn't sure whether I should follow him or not, and with two guards standing behind us and all those wraith out there, not to mention the loss of the pendant (aka our way back into the Academy), running wasn't a very valid option either. I squeezed Cisco's hand hoping he would lead me as to what to do next. He squeezed back, just as terrified and ignorant as I.

I heard MaryAnn's screams long before she entered the room. The guard returned with her cage. As small as all the others, it was made of woven barbwire. Even the floor. Due to the movement of being carried into the den, her body came in contact with the barbs, causing her to scream every time she did. As she neared, I noticed tiny glowing places all over her body from the current and many previous encounters with the walls of her cage.

The guard threw the cage roughly onto the floor, causing her to cry out in pain. She quickly hovered in the cage's center so as not to get hurt again. Streams of tears flowed down her face. I covered my gasp with my hand. She looked up at me, startled at first, then angry.

Ronnie knelt beside her and asked in a mockingly caring voice, "Tell me, sweetheart, do you know this couple?"

"No!" she spat. "Why, should I?"

Ronnie chuckled. "Oh, come on now. How else would they have this?" He laced the pendant's chain through his fingers and dangled it in front of her. The recognition in her eyes gave it away.

He placed the pendant into his pocket, allowing the chain to dangle, and said, "As I thought."

Her eyes grew wide, desperate. "What's as ya thought?"

"One of these was to be your payment, weren't they?"

MaryAnn's mouth gaped open and shut like a fish suffocating on land.

"That's OK, better late than never. However, due to them being late, and due to …"—he eyed the shiny welts of damage on her body—"the fact you are no longer in pristine condition, I believe I shall take them *both* … as interest."

I felt Cisco bolt next to me, but he didn't get far. One of the guards caught him. His arms and legs flailed wildly as the guard held him in place.

"Cisco!" I screamed.

Another guard pulled my arms behind me and held them there. I kicked out and attempted to jerk away, but it was useless.

A third guard entered from the back, carrying an empty cage in each hand. He flung them onto the floor. Their doors were already open. The guards holding Cisco and me forced us roughly into our cells. Mine, a tattered lattice work. Clearly they didn't think I needed a stronger cage. They were right. Cisco's was a solid cage of glass. I saw his mouth move, could tell he was cursing the nearby guards, but heard nothing, not a single sound.

"The time is near," said Ronnie. "We might as well get started."

"No! Let me go!" The terrified screams of a little boy echoed through the mansion loud enough for Cisco to stop his silent yelling at the guards.

One guard carried the arms, and one the legs of the child. He screeched and cried, begging for them to stop, to put him back in his cage. He must know what is coming, I thought. I cried silently for him, not even thinking how I … we … would be next.

"You know, you should feel privileged. Very few get to see how wisp is actually collected."

I felt my eyes widen, my stomach lurch. I glanced to MaryAnn. Her eyes connected with mine. I saw no emotion. I don't think she had any left to give. She was broken.

A bald guard with pale skin covered in tattoos wheeled in a device from a bad chemistry lab from the back. A large, glass cylindrical chamber with a metal top stood at one end. Out of the top came a wide hose, connected to an old-fashioned accordion hand pump and finally a metal top where the many empty glass jars on the bottom shelf of the car assumedly attached. They threw the boy into the chamber and shut it tight. Cisco pressed his hands against the wall of his cage.

The boy cried and pleaded while beating the inside of the cylinder, but we heard nothing. Two guards stood on either side of the pump and began pushing its wooden handles up and down like an old railroad handcart.

The boy's body began to rise. His eyes bulged in fear. Wisps of his essence began to ascend away from his body, away from his soul, and into the connecting hose.

On the other end, one of the other guards had already screwed an empty glass jar into the metal top. I watched, disgusted, astonished, as this boy's wisp filled the jar, then another, another… Even though my ears couldn't hear his screams, my mind could. I could feel him gasping for his last breaths, hear the squeaking of his hands against the sides of the chamber as he attempted to not enter the funnel. Then I watched, as his face, and then his head, sucked into the machine like smeared ink. The rest of his body floated headless and limp now. His essence flowing into the hose and jars, one by one, filling them each, until there was nothing of him left.

Ronnie laughed, satisfied, joyous. "Awesome! Ten jars already of the purest, more potent wisp available in the Void!

With all the wisp we get today, we'll be set until next year at least!"

Those working the machine stopped. The boy was gone, divided into over a dozen jars of a fog to be consumed by addicts all over the Void, just so they can fill Ronnie's pockets, fill his lust for power. I looked to Cisco. His face was wet from tears, his mouth hung open in shock. My stomach heaved tiny bits of vapor from my last feeding into my cage.

Ronnie laughed again. "Still think you could be my 'middle men'?"

Well, no, not actually. That was obviously a bluff, but thank you for pointing out how weak I am in your eyes. I mean, not that it matters. I would rather—

"Owens! Taylor! Get the collector ready to start collecting the rest." Ronnie interrupted my thoughts. "You!" He pointed at the guard closest to me. "Take her and the other two outside. We'll collect from them when we do the others."

They carried us to the crowd of cages we passed on our way in and sat us down among them.

"Hannah!" MaryAnn had been placed next to me and Cisco.

I turned my head to her, still in too much shock to ask a coherent question.

"What are ya doing here?!"

Her question infuriated me, overshadowing my anger. "Saving your ass!" I screamed back at her.

She flinched. Shocked. I was rather shocked myself. Guess traumatic events do something to a person. "What did he mean by us two being your payment?" I motioned to Cisco.

She chuckled at some dark joke she kept to herself, her eyes cast down ashamedly to her damaged arms. Her response was slow and penitent. "Ronnie gives out the wisp, gets ya hooked. Once ya are, he threatens to take it away. He starts out with small demands. Clothin', bottled essence, services." She nearly choked on the word, "services". "The clothes he throws away. The essence he uses…" She gritted her teeth angrily and scanned the cages surrounding us as though they held meaning to her anger. "The services…" She closed her eyes and shook her head as if trying to erase a memory.

"Then the demands increase. He wants harder ta get items, items ya have to steal for, people." She stared hard at me then.

"But why me? I've never met Ronnie. I've never done wisp."

She shrugged. "He didn't care who it was, s'long as it was a strong ghost with good essence he could milk the wisp out of. Ya were just someone I knew I could bring in." She stared at me, her expression as unfathomable as her words. "Ya were new, naive. He mentioned Twila but"—she shook her head—"I couldn't do that."

She sighed thoughtfully and fiddled with the bracelet on her left wrist, unable to look me in the eye. "I was about to bring ya in then, that night ya found me suckin' the light essence from our room. I couldn't do it." Her eyes rose to meet mine. "Guess I'm not as bad as I thought I was."

"You tried to suck me!" I countered.

"I was only going ta suck a drag or two, nothing more!" she pleaded with me. "Ya would've never noticed the deference! But what Ronnie was going to do to ya… I guess ya saw that already." She played with her bracelet again, unable to meet my gaze. "I'm sorry, Hannah. I was on the wisp. It makes ya do crazy things."

I stared her down, disgusted.

She did not act surprised. "I don't blame ya. I understand." Her eyes remained fixated on her bracelet. She meant what she was saying and was ashamed for what she did.

I turned to Cisco. Would he have done the same if the wisp had controlled him?

Would I?

I focused on MaryAnn again. "You said you couldn't do it. Why?"

She shrugged. "I know ya want me to tell ya some wonderful story about how much I care about others or how I'm really a good person deep down, but I was out of my mind with desire at the time. I don't remember why I couldn't do it. I just remember that I didn't." She lowered her gaze again and mumbled, "Guess I'm just as big a coward as my sister is."

The monster faded. In its place stood the girl who died saving her sister's child. The girl whose parents never loved her like they should have. The sweet girl who guided me around on my first day and helped me before she became another one of Ronnie's victims. I saw MaryAnn.

"How do we get her out of here?" I asked her.

"We can't," she said. "Only the wraith can open the cages. Their essences are the key."

"Twila said the guards were the ones who opened it!" I shouted.

"The wraith *are* the guards," MaryAnn said.

I pleaded silently with my eyes to Cisco and mouthed the words, "What do we do?"

He mouthed back, "You're asking *me?*"

A cold shiver ran down my spine.

We were all three silent for a moment, me deep in thought, MaryAnn coming to terms with the consequences of her actions, and Cisco quite possibly singing an opera at the top of his lungs but there was no way for us to hear it.

"Wait." I realized something. "You said the wraith's essence can open the cages.

"Yeah. And? The only way ta get their essence is ta cut 'em. They don't cry or sweat or—"

I stared overhead, where at least six wraith could be seen hovering close at any given time. Close enough I could reach out and touch them. "What if we caught one?"

"Are you serious?" MaryAnn screeched.

I focused on her cage. "The barbwire." I tried to reach it through my own cage, but the lattice work was too small. "See if you can break off a piece."

She rolled her eyes and sighed, "What good is that gonna—"

"Just do it!" I shouted.

She gingerly grabbed a piece of the wire and started folding it back and forth.

"No," I said. "A longer piece."

She grabbed another piece, a longer one, and soon had it broken off. I held out my hand for it.

A faint tapping came from Cisco's area. He was beating on his cage. He pointed behind us and mouthed, "They're coming."

One of the wraith neared my cage. I hid my weapon behind me. "Break off more," I whispered to MaryAnn. She complied.

But the ghastly creature didn't grab my cage. It reached for one next to me and MaryAnn. One with a hunched over man with a cane.

I tried reaching my arm through my lattice once again but couldn't. The wraith cried out and turned its decayed head to MaryAnn. She had swiped at it with her barbed weapon like a whip. Its breath rattled with anger, and it reached to undo her cage instead of the little old man's. But her swipe had done the trick.

Upon the barbs of her weapon held bits of wraith. Its skin, a torn piece of its clothing. And slime. Droplets of thick, green, glowing putrid slime which slithered up the twisted wire and tried to join themselves together. Rancid brown spots writhed within the slime, like eyes searching for each other.

She swiped the slime-covered wire at my cage. It opened.

"Here." She grabbed my arm, shoved something into my hand, and closed my fingers around it. "Run!" She screamed.

I ran. Through the cages. Between the prisoners crying and shouting for themselves and me. I felt the breath of a wraith on my neck. I couldn't look back. It would make it too real.

I ran past the cages. The wraith was still behind me. I changed direction and sprinted into the open Void. A second wraith came around, forcing me to change my direction again. Behind me was death. To the right of me was death. To the left of me was Ronnie's den. I ran straight.

The second wraith circled around, or maybe it was a third, I couldn't tell anymore. They forced me against the side of the den. I slammed into it, hoping, like when I had first hovered, a spontaneous reaction would allow me to suddenly be able to go through walls or something. It didn't. The force knocked me back.

I turned around, placing the very solid wall against my back. Three wraith hovered inches from my face. What rotten skin hung from their bony faces was contorted in anger. I tightened my grip on the piece of barbed wire I held and helplessly swiped it at them. I felt it catch their bodies, their clothes. I smelled the rancid essence and knew I had captured some, but I was far away from any of the cages and surrounded.

My body cowed into the wall behind me. Two eyes with no lids bored into mine. Blackened teeth snapped at my face.

FLIGHT

I felt it come out of me, felt my chest not rip open as it made its way up my throat and out of my mouth, but I didn't realize it was me doing it. My eyes were shut. My fear released itself with the wail.

When I opened my eyes, the wraith were far away, tumbling backward through the vast atmosphere of the Void. I remained with my back against the wall, my hand clutching my precious barbed key to the cages, and panting. My fear was still in control of me.

The wraith stopped tumbling. They hovered several yards up from the floor of the Void and stared at me. They were too far away for me to see their faces, to guess what they were thinking.

I ran back to Cisco and MaryAnn, hoping I wasn't too late to save them.

"Cisco? Cisco?" It was foolish of me to call out for him, considering he was in a soundproof cage and all, but I did it anyway.

"Hannah!" Cisco ran out from between two cages. "Are you OK? What happened?"

"Cisco!" I wrapped my arms around him in jubilance. "You're alive! You're *free*! What happened?"

"MaryAnn let me out before they took her away." He held her wire in his hand. "She threw me this when they did."

His words made me remember that MaryAnn had placed something in my hand. I opened it to see. "The pendant! How did she—?"

"It doesn't matter. We have what we need now. Let's go!"

"I can't just leave her here!"

"Are you *insane*? The wraith have her! Look, chica, we gotta get out of here!"

"Not until I save MaryAnn!"

I could tell he was about to abandon me, and I was going to tell him to go, that I understood when a scream sounded from ahead.

"Let go of me ya puss filled sack of—" A single wraith was carrying MaryAnn by the back of her shirt over the cages towards the front of the mansion. They must have started collecting.

"MaryAnn!" I ran to her. The other caged ghosts reached out for me as I went, their fingers snagging on my clothes, their pleas begging me to help. I ran the slime of my barbed whip across their cages as I went. "Run!" I screamed at them. I didn't wait to see if they did or not.

"Use the slime," I told Cisco. I didn't have time to explain. Thankfully he saw what I was doing and caught on.

"MaryAnn!" I was directly under her now. Her feet dangled above my face.

"Hannah! Run!"

I wasn't afraid like before, not for myself. I was afraid for her. I stood in place and pleaded with the wail I knew was somewhere inside of me. "Come on. Come on."

Cisco stopped to see why I stopped running. I ignored him.

I closed my eyes and let the fear grow. Let the shivers run up my spine. I took a deep breath. "I can do this," I whispered. And then I did.

The wail drove both the wraith and MaryAnn back, but as I had hoped, it dropped her in the process.

"What was that?" Cisco screamed at me.

"I … I don't know. It's just something I—"

"You're a *wailer*?"

"I — I guess so. If that's what it's called. I was trapped over there and—"

MaryAnn clambered up from between the cages where she landed and threw her arms around my neck. "Thank you! Now go."

I stopped her. "What about the others?"

The fallen wraith had not fully recovered, but others were coming for us.

"Forget the others, Hannah! We've got to get out of here!" She grabbed mine and Cisco's arms and pulled us away in a sprint.

"No, MaryAnn! Wait! I can't be your sister!"

She stood still so fast our bodies went a few inches into each others' when we bumped together. I gasped at the shock and pushed away.

"You two do your thing. I'm going to go open some cages." Cisco ran back to the hot mess of wraith and cages.

MaryAnn acted oblivious to it. "What did you say?"

"I know these people are no one to us, but I can't leave them to die."

Malice shined in her eyes. Whether it was for me or the memory of her sister I didn't ask. It didn't matter, not to me anyway and certainly not now.

"What do you mean, you can't be my sister? What do you know about my sister?"

I glanced back at the wraith. They were still advancing, but slowly, hesitant, like they were afraid to get too close too fast. "Twila told me how you died."

"She has no *right!* That was *my* Death!"

I took a step back. "Yes, MaryAnn. It was. It was a horrible, treacherous and inexcusable Death." I saw the corners of her eyes soften. I gestured at the cages behind me. "I can't leave them like that. I can't just let them *die*."

As if to illustrate my point, they cried out for us to free them like they had seen me and Cisco free the others.

MaryAnn stared into nothingness. I watched the wraith as she did. They were starting to get close now, close enough I wanted to run again.

Her eyes drifted to the cages, focusing on each one of them individually. Multiple expressions crossed her face as it did. Pity, anger, humiliation, regret. Finally, determination.

"Ya're right," she said, turning her face to me as she did.

Her eyes suddenly flew up, and I felt the cool breeze of what had caught her attention.

I didn't wait for her. We sprinted back towards the den. I felt the bony fingertip of one of the now very angry wraiths scrape my shoulder. I turned and swiped at him with my barbed whip, reloading it for freeing Ronnie's victims.

"Here, use this!" Cisco handed MaryAnn an extra piece of barbed wire. The three of us flailed against them. I watched the whips rip through the wraiths' bodies. They snagged at clothes, tore off fragments of skin. The smell of their rotting bodies intensified every time a whip made contact. I made sure not to breathe and covered my nose and mouth with my hand, nauseated. I couldn't keep my eyes off the swinging barbed metal weapons, the atrocious smell they emanated, the pieces of wraith flesh attached to them.

But our attack wasn't enough. The wraith were winning. I backed up and prepared another wail.

"Look out!" Cisco saw me, grabbed MaryAnn and threw her to the side, out of my aim.

My wail drove the attacking wraith back. Ronnie's men called out to them, commanding them to stop us.

We turned to run, but I didn't get far. My fingers were on fire!

I screamed in pain, dropping my weapon as I did. I held my injured hand by the wrist. Tiny wisps of my essence wafted like smoke from the holes in my fingers. This caught the wraiths' attention. One glared at my hand with its single eye. Its mouth opened hungrily. I panted through gritted teeth to combat the pain, but my arm still shook from it. The wraith came closer. I wailed, throwing it back several yards, but not far enough.

The pain was too much. Tears fell from my face, each lighting the Void's floor for the briefest of moments before fading to black beneath the fog.

Cisco reached into the dense fog where my tears had fallen to grab my weapon.

"No!" I roared, my throat growing sore from all the wailing and screaming I had been doing.

"What?" He stared up at me, confused, startled, slightly angry at me for having stopped him.

I was still holding my hand by the wrist, shaking and seething from the intense pain in its fingers. "Look what it did!" I growled through my gritted teeth. "The wraith's essence must be like acid. Look at my hand!"

Cisco and MaryAnn both stared at my injured fingers. Chunks had been burned out of their palm side. The edges glowed brilliant white. Blue swirls swam over the exposed insides of my fingers. My essence. My very soul, now open for the Dead, for the wraith to see and consume. Vulnerable.

MaryAnn dropped her key in fear.

"No!" I screamed. "We still have to free the others!"

Cisco held his cautiously by the end and pointed the slime-coated half down so it didn't drip onto him. "What do we do now?" his voice cracked in panic.

I nudged my toe forward, hoping to touch one of the keys with my shoe. I felt nothing. With a grimace I released my injured hand and used my good one to feel around the Void floor.

"What are you doing?" Cisco grabbed for my arm before it hit the floor.

"I'm already injured. It only makes sense for me to be the one to search for the keys."

His expression was one of disbelief. I glanced at MaryAnn. She was eying the wraith who remained hovering over us, waiting to make his move and consume me. It was closing in again. I wailed it away from us. This time it joined the others in taking the ghosts for processing.

"Cisco, we don't have time. You have to let me do this."

He thought for a second then threw his hands up in surrender. "Whatever, chica. I was just trying to keep you from burning your other hand. But, if you want to destroy yourself, be my guest."

I ignored his anger. He was obviously upset because I was hurt, not at me.

I knelt down and reached again for one of the keys.

"Wait," said MaryAnn.

I paused.

She bent over my probing hand and blew. The fog spread, not a lot, but enough for the glowing acid slime to guide me. I fanned over one of the glowing spots and made to blow on it myself, but she beat me to it. This time I clearly saw the clean end and grabbed it. I stood and carefully returned it to MaryAnn.

She blew over the remaining makeshift key's glow until I could grasp the clean end with my good hand.

Cisco looked back at the mansion. "Ronnie's men are out now. They're starting the harvest."

I heard the screams of his first victim. "They'll be after us soon. We don't have much time." I ran toward the cages.

"We can't save all of them," MaryAnn urged beside me.

"No," I said. "But we can save some."

The moment we reached the first cage, I slapped it with me key. "We're setting you free now. Run! Run as fast as you can away from the den and never come back!"

MaryAnn and Cisco followed suit.

I heard more than screams now. I heard Ronnie's men. They were barking orders at the wraith, commanding them to capture us. The wraith were still slightly hesitant after being attacked by my wails so many times. "We need to hurry. We don't have much time."

"You're telling *me*?" Cisco asked from several cages away.

The freed victims floated high into the ceiling of the Void, and I wondered if there was a ceiling, or if it rose into infinity. One of the ghosts, a bedraggled middle-aged man with sunken eyes stopped and turned back to stare at Ronnie's den. He had a hungry expression on his face. It reminded me of the time MaryAnn had attacked our light.

He saw me staring at him and flew away.

"Uh oh," said MaryAnn. "We've got company."

At least two dozen guards were streaming from the den like bees from their angry hive. The wraith lead the army, following the orders of the guards behind them.

"Keep working!" I commanded them both, then braced myself for battle. I took a deep breath and let out the strongest wail I could. It surpassed the previous ones but made me dizzy as a result. The foremost wraith tumbled backwards, but the rest continued unaffected. I let out another, and another. Wave after wave of wraith and guards fell to the wayside, only to be replaced by those waiting behind them.

They were getting closer. I backed away.

"MaryAnn? Cisco?" My words were slurred. I could barely stand. I felt faint, and very very hungry. My wounded hand throbbed. My weapon fell from my good one. The closest wraith was thirty feet away. I could see both its eyes. One still had its lids.

I took another breath and let out a pitiful cry. I was spent.

Twenty feet. Ten. I felt my knees buckle, my eyes close.

My shirt jerked from behind, lifting my feet from the ground. I was floating backward. I tried to rotate my head around to see what was going on, but I could only glance through my peripheral vision. Cisco was dragging me behind him as he flew over the mostly empty cages, tapping all he could with his key as we passed. MaryAnn hovered beneath us, smacking what occupied ones she could with her nearly depleted key. I saw a few ghosts escape. Several more cried out in vain for us as we passed. We were helpless. They were to be eliminated, turned into wisp, and there was nothing more we could do.

The wraith were still gaining on us. Half a dozen stared at me with determined eye sockets, their rags fluttering behind them, their deteriorated mouths parted with angry snarls, the tips of their spines twitching like anxious cats, ready to pounce on their prey. My legs banged into the cages' edges as we snaked and zigzagged our way out.

I just had the strength to pull the neck of my shirt away from windpipe so I could breathe and yell, "We're not going to make it!" My voice was faint, but they heard me.

The last cage flew past, its prisoner freed, only to be scooped up by one of the swarm. Whether he was dragged to the den or consumed by the wraith I could not tell. I never saw his glowing body again.

MaryAnn threw down her strand of barbed wire. It disappeared into the fog. Cisco must've thrown his away earlier. The wraith continued their pursuit past the boundary of the den and its cages. Without the cages, our pace increased enough to keep a "safe" distance between us and the wraith. But just.

"How much further?" It was a silly question. It had taken us a long time to get where we were. It would take a long time to get back to the safety of the Veil, but I had to ask. My only sight was the following swarm.

They didn't answer.

I let my body ripple behind Cisco, much like it had when he saved me from the bar fight a lifetime ago. I closed my eyes.

I missed sleep. Before, when I had no memory of it, it wasn't bad. But now, I would give almost anything to lie down and dream, to escape the Void, reality. To rest.

My hand throbbed, causing my face to scrunch up in pain, but I refused to open my eyes. I refused to watch the rotten, murderous mob chasing us.

MaryAnn said I would miss sleep. She had wondered why I wasn't upset when I found out I couldn't anymore. Now I know why. I wanted to see MaryAnn, make sure she was OK. I assumed she was still with us. Cisco would have said something if she had left.

"Almost there," Cisco said.

I opened my eyes. The wraith were still close behind us.

"Take my hand," he told MaryAnn.

I felt the waterfall of the Veil cascade around my body, then I fell to the floor. The wraith hovered outside. The Veil blurred them, so I couldn't see the details, but they were there. Their blurs spread out around the dome. MaryAnn and Cisco hovered close by. The Academy was deserted.

I WISH I COULD SLEEP

"Where is everybody?" asked Cisco.

"The others are out already, visiting their Live Ones," said MaryAnn.

I stood, then fell over. MaryAnn caught me.

"Whoa," said Cisco. "You don't look so good."

I felt nauseous, which considering I didn't have a stomach was a very weird sensation. I couldn't think straight. My vision was blurred. I tried to push myself away from MaryAnn and stand on my own. It didn't work.

"What's wrong with you, chica?" Cisco caught me and held me us.

"I don't know." My words came out slurred. My lips were numb. The pain in my fingers had stopped. I examined them to see if they had healed. The glowing area around them had expanded but there was no other change.

"Leave me at the Vent," I said. "I need to feed."

They shared a worried glance. "There won't be anything there all day."

"I can't walk. You guys go ahead and visit your Live Ones. If you leave me at the Vent, I can feed as soon as it opens. No one will have to help me."

They didn't move.

"What are you waiting on?" I asked. "What's wrong?"

They continued to give each other furtive glances.

"We're not leaving you here while we go visit our families," said Cisco.

"Wha? No." I shook my head feebly. "You have to go!"

MaryAnn grabbed my arm. "Let's take her ta the Vent. We can decide there."

"I'm not leaving her here!" Cisco argued.

She shushed him and mouthed the word, "later".

I dragged my feet while they half carried me. They spoke in conspiratorial whispers, but I heard every word.

"If it weren't the Day of the Dead, she wouldn't be here." It was MaryAnn's voice.

"What do you mean?" asked Cisco.

"I've seen the wraith's essence before. I didn't realize that's what it was at the time. The wraith use their essence ta melt their prey's soul shortly after contact. I think it's what Ronnie uses ta turn his victims into wisp."

Cisco faltered but didn't lose his grip on me. "You mean if that stuff had touched me… And you didn't *say* anything?"

MaryAnn pulled harder on me.

"Why don't you hover so I don't weigh you down so much?" I asked, the tops of my feet dragging the Void's floor.

"We're too tired to hover," said Cisco. "And you never answered my question," he directed at MaryAnn.

"I told ya. I didn't know what it was at first."

"When *did* you realize it?"

"After I started releasin' prisoners? I don't know. I was busy fightin' for my soul!"

Cisco huffed through his nose.

"So why am I still here?" I asked.

"Because it's the Day of the Dead," MaryAnn answered. "Your strongest day of the year."

"Will it eventually kill me?" I wondered.

It took her a moment to answer. "I don't think so." But she didn't sound confident. "I think if we can get some essence in ya, ya'll be OK." She glanced meaningfully at Cisco. I didn't check his expression.

They sat me down near where the Vent opened up. I lay in the fog. "Just leave me here. I'll be fine."

Cisco sighed. "We're not leaving you here. I told you that."

"But your family. Don't you want to see them?"

"I don't," answered MaryAnn. "There's no one I want ta see."

Cisco acted like he didn't believe her, but I did. I wouldn't want to visit a family like that either.

"Fine," I said. "Then you can stay. But Cisco goes."

"I can't leave her if that stuff's going to melt her soul," he hissed through clinched teeth. I don't think I was supposed to hear him.

"I don't think it will," said MaryAnn. "I think she'll be OK." She sat down next to me, in the fog.

"You said he uses it to make wisp, and he's using it today. That means it will eventually change her like all those prisoners."

"No. She barely touched it. While yes, barely touchin' it would normally eventually melt her completely into wisp. Today, it would take more than that. My guess is he's using a lot more than normal ta get the job done."

I flinched at the thought of having more of that poured onto me. I wanted to ask how he did it exactly, but stopped myself. I didn't need images like that in my head.

"I think he uses enough ta kill a couple of wraith too, if that makes ya feel any better."

"No! It does *not* make me feel better!" Cisco roared.

I shushed him. My eyes were closed now. My body was so tired it hurt. I remembered feeling like this once when I was alive. I had had a fever that kept me up for over two days straight. I was so exhausted I started to ache all over my body. That's what it felt like now. Every part of me ached, ached to rest in a way it never could again.

MaryAnn began to hum. As she did, her fingers stroked the hair across my temples. "We'll be OK," she told Cisco between notes.

"Yeah, Cisco," I slurred. "Go find your family."

He stood quiet a moment while she continued to stroke my temple.

"I feel awful leaving you two like this."

"Don't," I told him. "Just go."

MaryAnn didn't respond. She hummed instead.

I closed my eyes and pretended I was sleeping. Horrible images and thoughts filled my mind. I wondered about the ghosts we weren't able to save. I wondered about the man who reminded me so much of the wisp-craving MaryAnn. Would I see her again? Or had she disappeared for good? I clutched the pendant beneath my shirt. I could never let it out of my sight again. It was too dangerous, especially for her.

Cisco was gone by then. I supposed to visit his grave. Maybe his family would be there. Maybe he would find out more about them and fit in with his friends better. I really hoped so.

MaryAnn continued to stroke my hair. "Will you miss it?" I asked her.

"Miss what?" she responded.

"The wisp."

She thought a moment before responding, "Every day for the rest of my Death," she said. "I hated it every time, but I loved it more."

I ran my fingertips across the smooth floor of the Void, not sure if I should continue talking to her about it or not. Curiosity eventually won out.

"What about now? Do you hate it now, or do you love it?"

She sighed. "I hate what it is. I hate what it does. I hate where it comes from. I hate everything about it. But I love the memory."

I hoped that meant she would at least try to stay away from it.

I had asked her enough questions. I struggled to drown out the rest of them by picturing what I used to dream about when I was alive: multi-colored balloons held by Mickey Mouse, the Pink Panther chasing a blue dot across some sheet music. I almost laughed.

We spent the rest of the day like that, me pretending to dream, MaryAnn playing with my hair. Students drifted in from the Void, some elevated from their visits with their family, some saddened. None of them bothered us. I was too deep in the fog for them to notice, making MaryAnn appear to just want to be alone, not uncommon behavior after visiting a Live One.

When the Clock struck, I pushed myself up. Not all of the students were back. Some would give up their dinner to extend their visit. I didn't blame them. I thought about my family then. Was I too late? What if they weren't still at the gravesite, could I come back and try their home?

I repeated the address to myself. Yes, even in my exhaustion-induced delirium I remembered it.

The Vent opened. MaryAnn helped me to stand. I sucked in a weak breath. The second one was stronger. The third stronger than that. I inhaled essence until the Vent shut. I don't know where it all went, leaking out the holes in my fingers I suppose.

I examined them. The holes were still there, their edges still glowed. I didn't know if they would ever heal completely or not.

I had the strength to walk now, but just. There would be no running or hovering. I prayed I had the power to open a portal.

I found Lydia. She was by the Clock standing guard, allowing the students in and out of the Veil. I asked her where I should go, what I should do. She pointed me to a member of staff I wasn't familiar with.

He was a thin, white man with large, brightly colored glasses and a boa. He was very outspoken and seemed to be stressed at the moment. He was also very curious why I was just now choosing to visit the Land of the Living. I hedged his questions, keeping my injured hand in my pocket the whole time. An incident involving a student who tried to bring their pet cat back with them prevented him from pushing the issue.

I went to my assigned location and followed his instructions. To my immense relief, a portal opened for me. Thankfully, I had remembered to ask him whether I could visit two places or not. He said it's possible, but dependent on many variables. He suggested I try their residence first, as they were probably finished with my tombstone. I could try my gravesite later if I had to, he said. That was when the girl with her cat appeared, and he trotted away muttering to himself, "Oh, why do I volunteer for these things?"

I stepped through the portal.

HOME

A white house with a black mailbox stood before me. My house. My parents' house. Where I had lived.

I checked the driveway to see if they were home. Several cars were there, including both of my parents'. I smiled.

I stepped onto the porch and approached the door. It was shut, of course. I walked through it.

Casserole dishes lined the kitchen counters. Two liters and glasses sat next to a large bowl of ice. Hushed voices flowed from the living room. I followed them with great hesitation. I wanted to see my family again, yet the idea frightened me. Would I be able to control myself? How would they react? How would I?

My throat tightened as I rounded the corner. Uncle Jim sat in the corner recliner. Grandma Pauline sat on the couch. A round ball of fuzzy black hair poked up from the chair in front of me. Momma's hair. Momma's head. I had sat in that chair with her, sat in her lap while she held me and sang to me. I would reach up and touch her cheek as she rocked us back and forth.

My throat tightened further. The bridge of my nose burned, and cold tears fell onto the floor where they faded into the carpet. I wanted to feel her arms again, hear her sing to me.

"Leslie." Daddy! He went over to comfort my mother.

I ran around to see what was wrong. My mother was sitting in her chair, our chair, holding Boo-boo, my favorite stuffed bear, in her fidgety hands. She was crying too. I reached for her, put my arms around her. Her body was warm, not searing like Lin's had been. I held onto her.

She shivered and rubbed her arms. I stepped back. I didn't want to make her uncomfortable.

"If I just knew, Abe. If I just knew." My mother stared up at my father. Both their faces were wet.

Grandma Opal brought over a tissue and handed it to Momma. Daddy held Boo-boo for her so she could wipe her face more easily.

I wanted to hug my grandma too. I wanted to hug them all: aunts, uncles, friends, cousins. But I couldn't. Well I could, but it wouldn't do anything but make them cold. They wouldn't know it was me. They wouldn't hug me back.

The doorbell rang. Everyone, including me, whipped our heads around at the same time. I stood out of the way as Daddy passed by to see who it was. I waited by Momma. I didn't want to leave her side.

"Hello?" Daddy's voice sounded confused.

"Mr. Matthews?"

I gasped. That was Lin's voice! I ran to confirm it.

"My name is Tao Lin, and … I have a message—"

"Lin!" I called to him.

"Hannah!" He almost took a step inside the house, but my dad's body blocked the way.

"Tao, you said?" My father's voice sounded harsh now, angry. "This isn't funny. My wife and I are grieving, and if you upset her any further—"

Lin's words came out so fast they almost ran together as he tried to plead with my father to listen. "Mr. Matthews, I'm a Medium. Hannah came to me as a ghost."

Daddy threw the door to shut it. Lin threw his hands up to stop it from closing.

"Mr. Matthews, please!"

"Daddy!" I yelled. "Listen to him!"

"He can't hear you, Hannah."

Daddy turned to see who Lin was talking to, my teddy bear still clutched in his hand. He stared straight through me.

"I'm here, Daddy! I'm *here*!"

My father swung back around to face Lin. His face was livid. His words were dangerously quiet. "If you don't run from here right now, if I ever see you again…"

"You've got to get him to listen, Lin!"

"He can't see you, Hannah! He doesn't know you're here!

"GET OUT OF MY HOUSE!" Dad growled so loudly, Lin took a step back.

Dad reached for the door again, ready to slam it in Lin's face, breaking his nose if possible.

"Boo-boo! Tell him he's got Boo-boo!"

"She says you've got Boo-boo!" Lin yelled.

Daddy stopped mid-swing. "What? What did you say?"

"T-The bear! That's my bear! That's Boo-boo!"

"She says the bear is hers, and its name is Boo-boo." Lin glanced my way again.

Daddy followed his gaze, searching for me, anything that could explain what was going on. He raised the bear from behind the door. Lin couldn't have known it was there without me telling him so.

I reached for my Daddy, allowing our hands to touch. He gasped from the cold.

"That was her." Lin's voice was gentle with my father.

"That was, that was my Hannah?" Daddy gasped.

I nodded, my vision blurring.

"Yes," said Lin. "She's standing right there." He pointed at me.

Daddy took a step forward. I let the tips of his fingers touch me. They felt warm, familiar. I wanted to hold them while they held me, but I knew it was impossible.

"It's me, Daddy." I sniffed. "It's me."

"Abe, what's going on?" Momma entered the kitchen.

"Leslie, Hannah's here." He was speaking to her, but his eyes and hand never left me.

Her hand went to her throat. "What? Abraham? Are you OK?"

"Hi, Ms. Matthews. I'm Tao Lin. I'm a Medium. Hannah came to me looking for you. She wanted to let you know she was OK."

Momma came closer to where Daddy was looking. I grazed her cheek, the same way I had when I was alive, when she had held me and rocked me in the chair. Her hand flew where I had touched her. Her lids brimmed with tears.

"It's me, Momma," I whispered.

"She's trying to tell you it's her," Lin said, stepping into the kitchen.

Momma stared into my eyes. Neither she nor Daddy could see me, that I knew, but I loved it anyway.

"Tell them I'm alright," I told Lin.

"She says she's alright."

"She is?" Momma choked out the words.

"Tell her how I'm not disabled anymore. Tell her I'm sorry it took so long. Tell her—"

"Calm down, Hannah. I'll tell them everything you want me to. But, one at a time," he almost chuckled.

Daddy offered him a coke and a place to sit in the living room. Nearly everyone had gotten up to see what all the commotion was about, so he had his pick of seats. I spent the next several hours consoling my parents, telling them how much I loved them and convincing them to move on. I wanted them to be happy. I wanted them to adopt another child, to give someone the most wonderful life they could, like they did me. I told them it would be selfish to prevent another child from what they had to offer. Lin acted as my translator, telling them everything I asked. I kept the dramatic stuff out of it — MaryAnn, wisp — I didn't want them to worry.

Their clock struck eleven.

I jumped up. "I have to go!"

"Hannah only has so long here. She has to return to the Land of the Dead," Lin told them.

Mom started crying again. "Will I get to see her again?"

I paused. I'd had plenty of time to think about this while I was waiting for the Vent to open. It was possible. I could ask Lin to travel out here, call me through a portal, and translate for me. He would do it, of that I knew. I could come back out in a year's time without him and visit again, but I had decided on neither of those options.

I shook my head no.

He did not question my response. I guess he knew I would explain later. "No," he said, trying not to look my mother in the eye. "This is goodbye."

She began sobbing.

"I want them to move on." I swallowed the sadness. I would not cry over this. I knew this moment was coming. Just like I had decided with Lin before I got the disc, it wasn't fair to anyone to keep doing this to each other. "They can't move on if they're waiting on me all the time." I blinked rapidly and swallowed again. My words still came out wet and garbled. "It will hurt now, but… It's what's right. Tell them I love them. Tell them I love every single one of them. Tell them I'm sorry I can't stay, but, I'll be waiting for them when they come through."

He did as I asked.

I stood and told them goodbye. And then I left.

I stood on the porch and sobbed. My body jerked uncontrollably as the tears flowed freely. I wouldn't see any of them for a very long time. But it was worth it. This way they could have a Life.

By the time Lin made it out, my crying had subsided to just a few hiccups. He exited alone. "Your father has offered to drive me home, and to pay for my fair here."

I smiled, the dried tears on my cheeks cracking as I did. "That's nice of him." I sniffed.

"Oh, Hannah!" He reached out for me.

I collapsed into his arms, the scorching pain encompassing my entire body. I did not pull away.

"You were amazing. Not everyone could've done what you just did," he said through gritted teeth, his body beginning to shake from the cold. "I'm so proud of you."

I pulled away and sniffed. "Thank you for coming here, Lin. I don't think I could have comforted them without you translating. You don't know what this meant to me."

He ran his hand through his hair. "Pretty sure I can guess."

He smiled in such a way I couldn't help but laugh.

"Oh! I'm so sorry about not showing up! I hope you didn't wait long."

"What happened?" he asked.

I briefly told him I got distracted with promises to fill in the details later.

"How are you going to do that?" he asked. "I thought you lost your pendant."

With a devilish grin, I reached into my shirt and pulled out MaryAnn's and Twila's pendant, now mine. His eyes widened as he smiled in return.

"Are you serious?" he asked.

I nodded. He threw his arms around me, picking me up in a giant hug. I screamed out in pain. "Sorry! Sorry!" He quickly put me back down.

We straightened ourselves up, each rubbing where the other touched. "You know," he said, "I wouldn't have minded coming out here for you again, if you wanted to visit them."

Oh, Lin. You are way too good for me. "I know, but they can't get on with their lives if they spend all their time waiting on me."

He nodded like he understood.

"Why did you come here?" I asked. "I thought it was too far for you. Is it because I didn't show up last night?"

He shrugged, his hands shoved deep in the pockets of his ripped jeans. "That was part of it, but not the main reason. It's kinda like you coming here for them. You'll do all sorts of things for the people you love." He stared at his feet and blushed.

I smiled so big I saw the tops of my own cheeks. "I love you too, Lin."

He came closer. His hands were held out for mine. I placed them in his, both of us gritting our teeth from the hot and cold.

His face was inches from me. I could smell his scent. I started to rise up on my toes when the door opened. It was my father.

Even though we both knew he couldn't see me, we backed away from each other. He called Lin over, who silently gestured good-bye to me.

"Call me tomorrow?" I asked with a grin.

"Of course." He smiled, his perfect white teeth gleaming in the darkness.

I turned and headed for the portal, glancing one last time at Lin over my shoulder.

He winked at me as I jumped through.

ABOUT THE AUTHOR

N. A. Cauldron grew up on the outskirts of modern Cupola. As a young child, she enjoyed listening to the tales told of Cupolian's history. This ultimately led to a successful career as a research historian and her recent authorship of historical fiction. She is an avid herbologist, and spends her free time hunting out and collecting rare herbs for her potion making. She is especially fond of the snaggled tooth humpmoss, and has been known to spend weeks at a time on fungal expeditions.

https://nippi1.wixsite.com/nacauldron

If you liked what you read, please leave a review.